Southwest Tennessee Community College
Gill Center Library
3833 Mountain Terrace
Memphis, TN 38127

# PAINTING JULIANA

A NOVEL

# PAINTING JULIANA

MARTHA LOUISE HUNTER

G

**GOLDMINDS**
NASHVILLE, TENNESSEE

Goldminds Publishing, Inc.
1050 Glenbrook Way, Suite 480
Hendersonville, TN 37075

Copyright © Martha Strain Wilkinson, May 2014

ISBN: 9781930584624

Cover art by Martha Strain Wilkinson
Cover design by Martha Strain Wilkinson and Steven A. Anderson
Interior design by Steven A. Anderson

All rights reserved

Library of Congress control number: 2011928604

PUBLISHER'S NOTE

This is a work of fiction. Names, characters, places, and incidents either are a product of the author's imagination or are used fictitiously, and any resemblance to actual persons, living or dead, events, or locales is entirely coincidental.

Printed in the United States of America

Without limiting the rights under the copyright reserved above, no part of this publication may be reproduced, stored in or introduced into a retrieval system, or transmitted, in any form or by any means (electronic, mechanical, photocopying, recording or otherwise), without the prior written permission of both the copyright owner and the above publisher of this book.

www.goldmindspub.com

For Daddy

# PROVENANCE

❖   ❖   ❖

The summer before I started second grade, my mother said our home needed protection from the outside world. Unconcerned that she didn't know how to sew, she said that by the first day of school, every window in our house would be covered with double-lined, black-out drapes. It didn't matter that it was almost August already, it was too late. And it had been for a while.

The Sears Catalog delivered miles of fabric and a shiny Singer sewing machine to our door. Maybe I should've told my mother before she pulled them in off the porch, but she wouldn't have listened. My mother never heard me. Still, I felt bad watching her get the hems even and the seams straight like she said she would, because I knew she was wasting her time. But considering I was getting drapes out of the most adorable fabric in the entire Sears Catalog, violet with little yellow daisies, plus a matching quilt for my bed and a frilly dust ruffle, too, I didn't feel quite as bad.

Hanging the upstairs first and working her way down, deadline in sight with no question she'd make it, my mother began lugging the drapes up the aluminum ladder in my room, while I got the lucky job of holding it still. More interested in watching the gross mole on her leg than what she was doing, I didn't realize she'd tacked the front panels together until bedtime when she shut my door and switched out the light.

Lying under the covers scared silly, I stared into the dark oblivion knowing that with the drapes how she wanted them, my mother expected them to stay that way: Closed. I also knew there was no way I'd ever get them open without her catching on.

Sure there is, I told myself in the morning—it's called being sneaky. So, little fingers trembling, I loosened the thread, parted the panels just a smidge, and then stood back to see how I'd done. Rats. I tried again, and the daisies were even more crooked.

When my mother still hadn't said anything at dinner, I knew she would when she tucked me in, but her hand reached for the lamp and all she said was, "sleep tight." I held my breath as she walked to the door. Shutting behind her, a bright sliver of moonlight cut between the panels.

And, I wasn't taking my eyes off it. Not for a second.

Even blinking, the room would go black. Just for an instant, I knew that, but it would. But I can't *not* blink, I thought, or else my eyeballs will dry out, then they'll fall out and I'll end up wearing creepy glass ones instead. I considered holding my lids open with toothpicks, but since we'd used the last ones at dinner eating Little Smokies, those yummy miniature hotdog things, my only option was watching the light with one eyeball at a time.

Left eye.

Right eye.

While straining to hear the train blowing outside the window.

Left eye. Right eye. The sound of tires rushing on pavement.

Left eye. Or a siren.

Right eye. Anything but thunder.

I wasn't afraid of the dark. Left eye.

I was afraid of sleep.

Right eye.

And, I could only fight it off for so long.

Left eye.

Right eye.

Left eye. And right eye.

Both...

Lights out.

Completely.

Inescapably.

Asleep.

But, not through the night.

I jerked up in bed, gasping for air as if I'd been stuck on the bottom of the ocean. Scrambling to the top of the mattress, my eyes searched the darkness, but I didn't know my lonely room. Shoulders flat against the headboard, thin, cotton nighty clinging to the skin on my back, I hugged my knees to my chest and began rocking myself like a baby. I couldn't help it; I was just a little girl.

The sliver of moonlight fell across the foot of my bed. Just able to make out a fuzzy pattern on the quilt, I began squinting through the shadows. When the daisies came into focus, I suddenly knew where I was, and where I'd been. Swallowing hot tears, I roughly whispered, "I hate you, stupid dream. You're a bully."

I threw back the covers and began groping the drawer of my wobbly nightstand. Finding my little red notebook, I scootched to the bottom of the mattress and dangled my tiny feet over the edge. Wiping my stinging cheeks, I spread the little red notebook across my lap and stared down at the wrinkled pages.

They were covered in tiny, penciled hash marks, one for each time I'd had the dream. There was just the one, always just the same, always just as real. What had I done to make the dream hate me so much? Or, maybe it liked me, and that's why it kept coming back. Twice in one night sometimes.

Keeping the dream log was the perfect post-dream, no-sleep strategy for an obsessive little masochist like me; tallying the hash marks over and over in my head kept me not only too distracted, but also too freaked out to ever fall asleep again. But, an eight-year-old with black circles under her eyes? My nickname at school was Freak Girl. It was pathetic, really. And it was a lot to handle alone.

You'd think I might've told my mother, but she was paranoid enough already, which left my big brother, Richard. Hardly a pillar of compassion, all he said was, "How come you get to have a cool dream like that?" Well, he could have it. I'd wrap it in a bow for Christmas if I thought it'd work. And it's not like I was exactly broadcasting the news all over the playground, either. People might jump to conclusions, like thinking I had a dream for an imaginary playmate, or something. But, dreams aren't real, the kiddie-psychiatrist would pat my hand and say. Well, it sure seemed like it to me.

I needed a new strategy. A fall-asleep strategy this time, because I had to come up with something. A heavy-duty, fail-safe mantra—that's what I needed, because convincing myself the dream wasn't real would take some serious brainwashing. So, here's what I came up with: While running my pudgy finger down the rows of hash marks, I'd repeat, "I woke up, I'm alive, the dream's not real. I woke up, I'm alive, the dream's not real," while sucking a piece of hair in my mouth. For it to work, that last part was essential. After I'd done it enough times to convince myself, an enormously time-consuming process, I could finally scribble that night's hash mark in the little red notebook, snap it closed and shut my eyes. Yes, I'm aware it sounds totally stupid, but for an eight-year-old, it was the best I could do.

This one particular night, however, I didn't have time for the whole long routine. I had to get to sleep fast because school started the next morning and there's no way I was coming back as Freak Girl again. As I fished through the bedside drawer for my number-two pencil, I smugly told myself that falling asleep all by myself would be easy-breezy for a big second grader, but as I lowered the pencil, my eyes lingered on the page. You know, I won't actually *be* a second grader until tomorrow, I told myself, so I might should tally the pages a few times just to be safe. I mean, coming back twice in one night—if the dream's not real, how does it do *that*?

Oh, quit being a goofy-goose, I thought. You woke up, remember?

The line was already too sardined for another hash mark. As I began searching the drawer for my crummy plastic ruler, I had a weird thought: What if it makes the dream feel welcome when I draw it a new line to fill up? I counted the last one. A new line is like inviting *that* many dreams to come back? What'd they say in that grody vampire movie Richard made me watch on TV? Vampires can't enter your domicile unless you ask them in? This was pretty much the same thing.

So, I made the hash mark, all right, digging my pencil up and down so many times that it left a gray, gaping gash. Then, I wedged the little red notebook behind an Archie comic book in the drawer and slammed it shut. Closing the notebook away was the only way I knew to stop the dream from coming back.

But, it's never stopped haunting me.

The dream keeps playing through my mind.


I'm on the back of a speeding motorcycle wearing groovy high-water corduroys and a skimpy orange halter top. Wind whistles in my ears as towering street lamps blur past, and my bare shoulders are roasting in the sun. It's live action, not one of those distant dreams like you're watching yourself in a movie. It's hot, it's loud, it's smelly, and I'm seriously on the back of that bike.

The MoPac expressway is slick and shiny-oily like asphalt gets on an Austin summer day. It's rush hour and all four lanes are packed. The right ones are for the pokey people, but we're to the left with the rest of the manic drivers who'd never dream of signaling to change lanes.

Other dads drive Buicks to work, but mine drives a vintage Indian motorcycle. That's his leather jacket I'm holding onto.

Gripping the throttle, he gives it the gas. Behind him on the smooth, vinyl seat, arms strapped tightly around his waist, I lean with him into every twist and turn of the pavement. We blow past glass office buildings, overgrown neighborhoods and a couple of ball fields. The hulking, yellow and black MoPac train surges down the railway beside us. Rusted boxcars trail behind, spray-painted with sloppy neon graffiti. I try counting them, but we're going too fast.

Dad's face is reflected in the side mirror. It's one he'd never wear at home, only here in the dream. Invincible. Zestful, I guess. I didn't mention he has glasses—little round, wire-rimmed ones, like John Lennon, and his curly, blonde hair is long—not down to his shoulders, like he was trying to be some hippie or something, he just never had time for the barber. When my mother would offer to cut it for him, the expression on his face said he'd rather she not.

He takes the next exit and we fall in behind a dented El Camino with a ratty sofa in the back. The El Camino suddenly brakes for a green light, and Dad has to downshift fast. Touching down his left foot on the pavement, he revs the engine a couple of times.

Noticing tall, black, crazy-stretched shadows on the worn pavement beside us, I realize it's Dad and me, as if we were ABC gum flattened by a steamroller. I wave my arms to the side and my shadow flaps its wings like a cuckoo bird. When Dad's shadow doesn't seem to think it's funny, I give it rabbit ears by making a peace sign behind his head.

He lets out the clutch and makes the next couple of lights no problem. My curls trail behind us on the pavement like a long, black scarf.

Passing a corner phone booth, our tires bump over a single, red tennis shoe in the road. Outside the U-Totem, cars are stacked at the pumps. A round, yellow sign has a black X in the middle.

I peer around Dad's shoulder. Red blinking signal just ahead.
He speeds up.
Another sign.
Do Not Stop On Tracks.
I look down them.
The train has the face of a mean, black robot.
I tighten my arms around Dad's waist.
Honk-Honk.
Striped gates begin crossing, and he punches it.
Red flashing lights.
Ding! Ding! Ding! Ding!
Closer, closer, the angry train blows its horn. Longer this time.
Daddy, why won't you stop?
Gates narrowly missing our heads, he rips across the tracks.

5

My rump bounces high on the seat.
Mad whoosh of wind against my back.
Chuck-chuck-chuck-chuck-chuck-chuck.
Looking over my shoulder, all I see is smeared color.
Yellow. Black. Mostly red.
Am I supposed to think that was fun? Did he?

A packed school bus stops at the next signal, brakes hissing. Dad pulls close behind the bumper and I see a skinny little girl standing in the back with tight blonde curls who looks just like me. Making eye contact, the little girl tilts her head like she knows it, too. When the bus turns right on red, she rests her forehead against the rear window and watches me through the glass.

As Dad and I wait for the light to turn, the sound of the cycle's rumbling engine fills up the air between us. I don't understand his silence, but I'm used to it. If I stopped coming down to breakfast one morning, would he ever speak my name again?

Really fast, I bury my head in his back and hug him tight.

I don't look up again until I feel us turning.

Seems like we're on the outskirts of town on a long, straight highway; wildflowers hem the edges as our tires hug the white stripe that splits down the middle. Nice and easy, Dad's not speeding for a change. Wood-frame farmhouses on both sides of the road have sagging, metal roofs that reflect the sun, and archery targets in an open field are really coils of golden hay. Soon, there's no more billboards and we leave the traffic behind.

I begin counting everything—I can't help it—fence posts, telephone poles and a dozen silver mailboxes in a row. Next, I become fascinated with the highway through the windshield. Tapering in the distance, it's a long, black arrow shooting toward the horizon, skinnier and skinnier the closer it gets; then it vanishes, the asphalt becomes the violet sky, and I don't know how. Sun at our backs, brilliant orange fills the rearview mirror, and the only clouds in the sky are thin as stretched cotton.

A speeding fire truck barrels toward us, lights flashing and siren blaring, the first vehicle we've seen for miles. Turning to watch it whiz by, I spot a pile of burning trash I hadn't seen moments before, and a lonely scarecrow in a field of corn. Only violet around the edges, clouds are taking over the sky. The marquee of an abandoned drive-in theatre says there's a double feature playing: *A Lion in Winter* and *Wait Until Dark*.

There's an unsettling chill like the onset of a fever, and leaves on the oak trees begin to flutter. Steering one-handed, Dad flips up the collar on his worn, leather jacket. I study his reflection in the rearview mirror. His blue eyes glance behind us and his gaze lingers. Glowing behind filmy clouds, the sun seems more like the moon.

A herd of cattle scatters. Thick, hot air begins to churn and twigs skitter across the pavement. I peer warily over my shoulder. Behind us in the distance, clouds are balling together, moving in sped-up time. In moments, they're dense and bloated, completely blocking out the sun.

My eyes dart to the mirror. Dad's face will tell me everything's okay. Sweat beaded on his forehead, he scans the sides of the road, as if he's looking for a turnoff. There's not one. I always thought my dad knew what he was doing, but I get the sinking feeling we're lost.

He suddenly launches down the pavement wide open throttle, like the road's on fire. Nnneeaoowww! I clamp my knees around his thighs just to hang on.

When I check the mirror again, Dad's looking in it, too—staring behind us as if he recognizes something back there. Way back there. I squint, trying to make out what he's seeing. The hulking, gray clouds seem textured with tiny holes in them, like the wire mesh on an old screen door. Thin, pinkish straws of light begin leaking through, and his eyes freeze. The gray suddenly becomes an intense, rainbow spectrum of color that glistens like wet paint.

A fierce south wind kicks up. Poor, rangy cedar scrubs claw their way across the dry landscape and dust stings the tender skin on my back. Fixing his gaze on the horizon, Dad thrusts out his chest and races on. A gasping, gravely roar from behind joins the sound of the cycle's rumbling engine. Feeling scared, and just so little, I hug him tight, wishing his arms were hugging me instead. I think the storm is chasing us.

With a booming crack of thunder, lighting rips across the sky. Dad's back stiffens against my chest and I look over my shoulder. Rain is trickling down the clouds like blood and their surface is becoming rough and gritty, as if their holes are scabbing over to keep the glistening light from shining through.

Dad immediately downshifts and the cycle pitches forward violently. Quickly looking over his shoulder while pivoting his torso, he leans his weight to the left.

He's going back for it.

A wicked gust slams the cycle from behind and a mangled tin roof rakes across the pavement beside us. As Dad wrestles the handlebars, the barbed-wire fences squeeze in tightly on both sides, and the highway is suddenly only one lane, with no way to turn around.

A cool puff of air hits my face. With a hypnotic pull too strong to resist, my eyes are drawn down the black, tapering highway to the horizon. A tiny, white cloud hovers over the vanishing point, as if it's exactly where it's supposed to be. Before I can blink, it inflates spontaneously, just like a hot air balloon pumped with helium, and I'm staring at a massive funnel cloud, luminous white and outlined in brilliant gold. Irresistible and mesmerizing, the cloud seems to beckon me ahead.

Dad's shoulders buckle and the handlebars begin to shimmy. My eyes dart to the rearview mirror. The clouds have only a dim flicker of color left, and they're rippling eerily, as if bulging, meaty muscles are writhing on the other side. As the movement becomes more frenzied, I realize what I'm seeing is the fourth dimension of the wind, and that the storm has morphed into a horrifying, hybrid monster of clouds, wind and rain.

"Hurry, Daddy!" I scream. "Race like you did with the train!" But it's like he doesn't hear me.

With the deafening rumble of a space shuttle at takeoff, the funnel cloud detonates like a mushroom cloud, and wind white as smoke spirals from crown and spreads through the air, like a disease. Faster and faster, twisting in one spot, it seems as if the funnel cloud is waiting for us.

We're trapped. Boxed in.

That's what the storm is chasing us into.

Feeling a sonic tremor building from behind, I twist around on the seat, only to see sturdy oaks yanked from the ground by their roots and spit into the sky like shingles. Power poles split, their tangled wires spark, and cedar bushes burst into flames.

A savage, feral roar heaves from Dad's gut.

"Damn you," he bellows. "Not yet!"

Towering thunderheads rear up tall, with crests curling over like whitecaps. Peaks too heavy to hold, the storm breaks over like crashing waves, accelerating full-steam.

Dad hits the brakes. Back of the cycle almost flipping over the front, he flattens his torso over the engine and I go after him.

I choke my arms around his neck as the vicious storm rakes over my naked back; the pain like every layer of skin is ripped over my head in one piece. Using my body as his shield, my cries drown out the rolling thunder, but I won't let go.

Steam spills from the engine and rises around us, and the brakes and the tailpipes sizzle. Raising my head, I gape in awe as the storm floods the tree tops along the barbed wire fences. Limbs, rubble and fence posts wash through the pastures as the storm rolls out like the tide.

Wup-wup-wup-wup. A powerful rotating sound.

I look up.

Astounded, I tilt back my head so far, my neck aches.

Skyscraper-tall, glossy and lined in gold, the funnel cloud is a mighty, whirling mass of air.

Dad plants a boot on the asphalt and kick-starts the engine. As he swings the cycle around in the opposite direction, the storm sucks back into the trees with a rough, ragged gasp.

Remission. A stealth awning in the branches.

As we peel away, I lean my cheek against his drenched leather jacket and tighten my grip around his waist to ride it out with him.

But, what choice did I have, really? Typical of all the men in my life, of course my dad was driving. And, true to form, he acted like I wasn't even there. For all the times I had the dream, I've never been sure if he even realized I was behind him. And, there's another thing—what's he looking at behind the clouds?

I used to think a tornado was the same as a funnel cloud. Not true at all. They're both violently-rotating columns of air, but a funnel cloud doesn't become a tornado unless it touches down. Maybe you didn't know what makes tornados dark is all the debris they suck off the ground. Okay, call me weird, but I looked it up in the middle school library.

Sure, I probably give the dream too much energy, but I'm not the first person interested in figuring out their dreams. Crystal gazing, maybe. All I know is that my dad *always* tricks the storm. And, for the record, I never opened my bedside drawer again.

If only I could shake the silly, little girl's worries still stuck in my head—like, what happens if I stay in the dream and never come back? And are there new parts of the dream I haven't seen yet?

It's probably not a bad idea to sleep with one eye open.

Because it's scary up front.

## CHAPTER ONE

❖ ❖ ❖

The chatty bellman tells me that staying at the thirty-six-story Bellagio Hotel, with its jet-propulsion fountain and ten-acre, man-made lake is just like being in Italy. He transfers the suitcases from the luggage cart and begins laying them on the folding stand.

A clear, Lucite writing desk in the corner is equipped with a fax and internet connections. The bellman sets Oliver's laptop in the middle. Pulling out the matching chair, he takes the leather-bound room service menu from the center drawer. Leave your selections on the door by midnight and your Bloody Mary will be delivered by six. Or, Screwdriver, he says with a saucy smile, if that's your pleasure.

I'm just not going to believe the dramatic black bathroom. Super-sexy, he tells me and theatrically flips on the lights. It's black, all right. From the wallpaper and marble vanities to the gleaming toilet, all the way to the floor. Even the sunken whirlpool tub is black. Looking up, I notice the coffered ceiling. Black, of course. He's right. I didn't believe it.

As I scribble my name on the ticket, he switches on the flat-screen television. I pretend I'm listening when he shows me how to use the remote. The hotel's video promo touts the Cirque du Soleil production running downstairs. It's called "O," he says. Like the Big O. He winks. I stare back at him, expressionless.

He directs me to the floor-to-ceiling windows. Punishing sunlight blares through the glass. Our suite on the twenty-first floor overlooks the glittering Las Vegas strip. A towering billboard of the Backstreet Boys stands ten stories high. Carrot Top's name is in lights at the MGM Grand. Joan Rivers and Sinbad are both playing at the Stardust. In case I missed it, he makes sure to point out the historic Eiffel Tower just across the street. Plus, the Sphinx is right around the corner.

Someone shoot me.

I tip the bellman generously. Ushering him out, he can't help getting in a last word as the door's closing. Something or other about the nightly turn-down service, complete with a cheesy red rose on your pillow. I hook the Do Not Disturb over the knob.

Overnight case in hand, alone at last, it's back to the black, super-sexy bathroom. Lining up my toiletries on the vanity, I check out the hotel freebies. Lotion, body wash, shampoo and conditioner by Crabtree & Evelyn. The miniature sewing kit and awesome shoe-polishing cloth. Peering through the glass walls of the party-sized steam shower, I switch on the tub. Taking a bath is the only thing I know to do to relax. As it's filling with water, I read the label on the bubble bath and pour it under the faucet. Black Narcissus.

Hair wrapped in a turban, I lower myself into the water, deciding against the jets because I couldn't stand getting my magazine wet. It's the latest *Oprah*. Got it at the airport. "A Whole New You" is emblazoned on the cover. Using the matches from the back of the super-sexy black toilet, I light the red candle and breathe in the lovely scent. Ah, aromatherapy.

This could work.

I lean my neck against the soft, terrycloth bath pillow and settle in with *Oprah*. First off, I tear out the annoying subscription postcards, sniff the perfume samples, flip through the designer collections and ignore the latest advice from that smarty-pants, Dr. Phil.

There's a tap on the room door.

"Housekeeping," says a high-pitched voice. "Clean your room?"

Seriously? We just checked in.

I start reading again. They'll go away.

"Hellooo. Housekeeping!"

Good God. Did they *not* see the Do Not Disturb sign?

A card-key jiggles.

I freeze.

My eyes dart to the chrome knob on the bathroom door.

Shit. Not locked.

A muted click. The sound of wood dragging across carpet.

My heart jackhammers.

The tub's only half full, bubbles barely up to my navel. I look left and right for a towel. I'd have to stand up to pull one off the high rack.

11

There's a sharp rap on the bathroom door. "Anybody home?"

"Someone's in here," I yell. "Don't come in!"

I drop *Oprah* on the furry, black bathmat, sink low and spread the tiny washcloth across my chest.

There's a rush of cold air as the door flies open.

"Gotcha!"

"Oliver," I breathe. "Don't you ever do that to me again."

The faucet's still running. Washcloth held to my chest, I lean up and pour more bubbles in bath.

He looks down at me in the water. His cheeks are flushed. He started drinking on the plane. Single malt scotch. On the rocks.

"Come on, babe. Lighten up." He laughs. Gives me his megapixel smile.

For a little getaway, I was thinking more like Napa. Even Bourbon Street would've been better than Sin City, but Oliver was set on coming here, yet even a three-hour flight, crossing four states and landing in another time zone can't disguise the fact that the Trial Lawyers Association is here this weekend. I read it on a placard downstairs in the lobby.

Oliver drops to the fringed stool and begins untying his shoes. Polished, oxblood wing-tips. He stands to slip off his suit pants, then folds them neatly and arranges them between the sinks. He runs his hand over the crease. Straight as a knife. I study his perfect face in the mirror. Turning his head from side to side, he does the same.

"I guess you're presenting at the conference again this year?" I say softly.

"I'm giving the keynote at the luncheon tomorrow. Golf after that," he says briskly. "Sunday's the panels and I'm on three."

"Hmmm-m," I say. "Where are your clubs?"

He sips the little green bottle of hotel mouthwash and spits it in the sink. "Had them shipped to the course directly."

"Great idea," I say.

He slowly steps out of his boxers. Leaning down, he drops his hand in the water and begins tickling my thigh with his thick fingers. "Mmm-m. Looks like you've got something naughty in mind," he says. "I like that."

I look up at him. "I thought you said you'd be warming up the craps tables downstairs while I brought up the bags."

He grabs his toothbrush from his dop kit, looks at it, then hurls it in the sink. "Fantastic," he yells. "Typical."

Hopping on one leg, he tries threading his left foot into his boxers. Giving up, he drops them on the floor, squeezes his eyes shut and begins stroking his moustache, his old courtroom technique for soothing himself. I've told him he'd look tons younger if he shaved the damn thing off, but he never will because someone said it makes him look like Tom Selleck. Which, I have to admit it does.

"Oliver, listen," I stammer. "We'll come back up here later. Let's just do that, okay?"

He scowls at me in the mirror. "Seeing you covered in hot suds turned on my hot, animal lust." His eyes fly open. "So sue me!"

Still covering myself, I lean forward and begin switching off the faucet. He reaches down and takes my wash cloth, balls it up and casually pitches it on the vanity.

"You look better like that."

There's a loofa on the edge of the tub. I soak it in the water for a minute, then rub it over my feet.

Taking his sweet time, he tucks a fresh, pink dress shirt into his slacks, zips the fly and fastens his belt. Without even looking, he lines up his gold cufflinks with the holes in his French cuffs, pushes the posts through and opens the swivel bars.

He checks his Rolex. "The tables are getting cold."

"Can't we just meet downstairs in a bit?" I say. "I still have to shave my legs and things."

"And things?" His eyes brighten. "Bet there's one of those bikini waxers downstairs. Get yourself one of those Brazilians."

"While I'm down there, why don't I book you a massage?"

"Deep tissue," he says. "And not with some prissy masseuse. I want to feel it."

"I'll make sure and get the roughest one they have," I say.

Damn sure will.

He peels a few crisp bills from his wallet and slides them under the candle. Red, melted, wax sloshes onto the marble. He steps out of the room, then sticks his head back around the corner. He points at me. "And, get all dolled up. You know how I like showing you off."

I look up at him and smile. "Sure thing," I say sweetly.

I wait for the sound of the door closing to crank the faucet back on, reach over the edge and rescue *Oprah*, then lean back in the bubbles.

Fifteen minutes later, I've finished all the good articles and the water's perfect: Warm, simmered, and now finally boiling, I wing the magazine at the wall.

Drying off, I avoid my soft body in the mirror. I unhook the hotel's plush robe from the back of the door and slip it on. Tightening the sash, I march to the mini-bar. Inside is a tall, yellow bottle of Lemoncello liqueur. I watch my fingers reach for it.

I stare at it hard. No, I tell myself. You promised.

Throw some cold water on your face. Isn't that what you're supposed to do at a time like this? Screw that. I don't wear waterproof mascara. I freshen my eyeliner and dot fresh concealer under my eyes. I powder my forehead and nose. My chin. Roll the red lipstick from the tube. I swap the robe for my black skirt and ruby scoop-necked blouse. Bending down, I slip on my matching stilettos.

Crossing the room to retrieve my dressy purse from my suitcase, I'm unconsciously pulled to the flickering lights out the window. Like watching a car wreck, even if you wanted to, you can't take your eyes off the swanky, sinful, sequined Las Vegas. Bally's neon, skyscraping hot air balloon illuminates the desert for miles. Airbrushed Siegfried and Roy stare hypnotically from the marquee of the Mirage Hotel. As my eyes stop on the historic Arc de Triomphe, I snap out of it and draw the drapes.

I fluff my curls. Put on my ruby dangle earrings and check my look in the mirror one last time. Spraying perfume on my wrists, I eye the diagram of the fire exits posted on the door.

I'll get a Brazilian only if he takes me to Rio.

Let's do this.

◆ ◆ ◆

The windowless casino is bright as poolside at noon. Twenty-four-seven.

Forging through sweet cigar smoke, I snake between the gaming tables in search of my husband. The craps pit is elbow to elbow. Ante up. The gamblers place their bets and the shooter rolls. Dice tumble down the green felt and land on double sevens. A shiny marble skips around the roulette wheel and parks on black. Some people celebrate. Others don't. Like a bulb to a moth, the brilliance draws them in. The rush keeps them there.

A shiny, yellow Corvette pirouettes on a revolving, elevated platform. A pouty-lipped Marilyn writhes provocatively on the hood in a billowing, white dress. A hayseed cowboy in a Stetson and Wranglers sticks two fingers between his teeth and whistles. Marilyn rewards him, dangling a shapely thigh over the fender.

Checking for Oliver behind the exclusive, red velvet rope of the baccarat tables, there's only sharp Asian tycoons in dark suits and sunglasses and a bee-hived granny holding court in the middle, showing them how it's done. Her tie-dye T-shirt reads, It's Vegas, Baby. I check the golden martini gusher in the middle of the floor. An orange, neon sign blinks rhythmically, Buffet

All Day. You Don't Pay. Underneath, a bachelorette party bellies up to the bar. The bride's flashing tiara has Bridezilla written on top. She's plastered, screaming at one of her bridesmaids. Obnoxious, college guys holler, "Chug, chug, chug, chug!"

When they cart me out of here in a strait jacket, I'll claim environmental insanity.

Ready to pack it in, I finally eyeball Oliver sitting at a crowded blackjack table. Tie Bets Pay is scripted in gold lettering on the green felt. With a soggy, chewed-down cigar between his teeth, plumes of smoke circle above his head. He flags down the cocktail waitress and she's there in a jiff. Spandex unitard, plunging neckline and fuzzy wrist bands, she must be a Solid Gold Dancer. She gives him the same enchanted wide-eyed expression he routinely gets from women encountering him for the first time. He's fifty-three, hairline and muscle tone not what they once were, but his magnetic sex appeal isn't going anywhere. I used to find the attention amusing. Now, it's just irritating.

Oliver likes it just fine.

A bearded, tuxedoed dealer distributes stiff cards. Oliver peeks at his, waves his hand directly over them, and then flips them over. Victorious, he pitches his head back and howls, drains his cocktail and slams it on the table. Men on both sides clap him on the back and a couple of blondes throw their arms around his neck. The rode hard, put-up-wet variety. Lots of spray-tan and cleavage.

As the dealer sets everyone up again, I turn from the blackjack table and peer over the stretch of flashing slot machines. *Money Storm*, *Pharaoh's Fortune* and *Stakes Are High*. The one-armed bandits. I'm too chicken to try anything else.

I take a seat in front of *Pharaoh's Fortune*. Looks like I'm falling on this grenade all by myself.

The next chair comes open and the bee-hived granny snags it and loads in a fistful of gold tokens. Next thing you know, tack, tack, tack, tack, and the machine spits out so many they spill onto the floor.

Oliver sidles up beside me and eyes my machine. "How much are you up?" he says.

I yank the brass lever down. "I'm not keeping count."

"Lost it all, didn't you?"

I check the token cup in my lap. "Most of it, yeah."

Another Solid Gold Dancer gathers glasses and crumpled napkins from the machines, Brandee, her name badge says. Oliver catches her eye. Same enchanted, wide-eyed expression.

"What are you having, my sweet bride?" he asks me.

"I better not get started too early."

He tells Brandee, "She'll have a margarita."

She raises a long, chipped nail and says, "You got it, sugar."

As she glides toward the bar, graceful as an ice skater, my eyes trail after her. "Oliver, why did you do that?" I say.

He puffs his cigar. "What are you talking about?"

I wrinkle my brows at him. "I think you know."

"Babe, you need to quit being such a crab apple."

I pull the lever down. It chugs and the cherries spin.

When Brandee hustles back with my drink, Oliver watches me take a few sips. "You look beautiful tonight," he says. "And, I really am glad we're here together."

I smile at him. "Me, too."

He peels off five twenties from his thick money clip. "Come catch up with me at the high-rollers table when you lose all that," he says. "Shouldn't take long."

I watch him until he's swallowed up by the crowd, then empty my margarita into the glass one chair over.

Bee-hive Granny still one-arm-bandits like crazy. I sit back and study her skills. Learn a thing or two. Before the hour's up, I take my two hundred-plus tokens to the money booth, swap them out for chips, and head to the high-rollers table.

Oliver's there. So are the two rode-hard blondes. Taking a few steps back, I watch the bustier of the two lean close and whisper in my husband's ear. He gives her a foxy grin. The nine of spades showing, he lifts the edge of his bottom card and motions the dealer for the next one. A one-eyed jack. The dealer takes away all of Oliver's chips and he glowers.

I've never played blackjack before, but, really, how hard can it be? Standing at the edge of a few tables, I watch the best players, and I watch the worst ones, too. Hit, stand and bust. Don't be a weenie. Don't get cocky. A little skill. Mostly luck.

A seat comes open at the far end of Oliver's table and I take it. Settling in, I cross my legs and arrange my purse on the chair back.

Aware of Oliver cursing and slapping the other end of the table, I keep winning hand after hand. A crowd is beginning to form, including Bee-hive Granny. When the blondes take notice, Oliver looks down the table and leaves his smoking cigar in the ashtray.

The dealer swaps my four greens for another black.

Oliver rests his wrists on my shoulders and murmurs in my ear. "Good job there, Rain Man."

It's been a long time since he thought I was good at anything.

Wayne Newton croons from the sound system.

"Danke Schoen," indeed.

Brandee plays deaf when Oliver says to bring me another drink.

Six purple chips, nine blacks and six greens sit in front of me. The dealer looks over his shoulder for a replacement. None coming, he slides another black chip towards me. I push it into the betting circle and stack a purple on top.

He looks up at Oliver. "You might want to take lessons from this one, partner," he chuckles. "She could wipe up the floor with you."

Stroking my neck with his fingers, Oliver tips his cocktail as the dealer swaps my blacks for an orange and sets me up again. Ace showing.

I check my hole card. Looking good. It's the queen of hearts and the house loses again.

The table cheers loudly. The blondes do the end zone dance.

Oliver reaches his hand under my bicep and grabs my breast.

I slap it away. "Cut it out!"

The dealer holds off with the cards.

Oliver laughs. "Watch out, babe, don't get your bowels in an uproar."

If I weren't such a lady, I'd nail my stiletto through the top of his foot.

With a shaky smile, I look around the table. People are staring. The embarrassed ones look away. The blondes put their heads together and whisper. The bustier one sticks out her lower lip at him and wags her finger.

Betting two purples and a black, I hear Oliver at my shoulder swirling ice in his glass.

"Hit me," I tell the dealer.

Yes, sir. Blackjack. Twenty-one.

Oliver does it again. This time with both hands.

That's it.

"I'm going to the room!"

"I'm not taking any of your shit tonight, Juliana, and I mean it." He says it through his teeth.

I spring to my feet and look around me, trying to get my bearings. Make eye contact with no one. From my periphery, I see Oliver raking my mound of chips in front of him.

I weave through the maze of craps, baccarat and poker. The jangling slots. I can't find the stupid elevators. Beginning to panic, I retrace my steps through the crowd the best I can until I find the damn things. I push the button several times, but the doors don't open any sooner. Finally, a rowdy crew in matching Caesar's caps piles out. Squeezing past them, I punch the button for the twenty-first floor.

I rush down the ridiculously-long hallway to our room. Cursing my four-inch heels, shoulder bag bouncing on my hip, I dodge dirty plates and drunks stacked outside the doors, narrowly missing the housekeeping cart. My chatty bellman emerges from a swinging door. Drawing a silver ice bucket to his chest, he flattens himself against the wall. I tear past.

Finally inside the room, I yank off my stilettos and fire them against the wall: one, two. Out of breath, shaking, I fall on the bed. Hot tears drip onto the Egyptian cotton, five-hundred-thread-count pillowcase. A thorn from the red, wilted, turndown rose scratches my cheek.

I've never cried more violently in my life.

Too soon, there's a knock at the door. I jerk my head off the pillow.

"Open up!" Oliver's voice is choppy. Angry.

I bolt to my feet.

"Juliana!" He knocks louder.

My eyes search the room. I drag the rinky-dink Lucite chair and wedge it under the knob.

The handle jiggles. He's fumbling with the card key.

The dreaded click, and the door's unlocked. He pushes it, but it doesn't budge.

Bam-bam-bam!

"Are you shitting me?" he yells. "I suggest you open this door!"

He rams it with his shoulder several times.

The door flies open and the chair topples backward.

Red-faced, he steps around it, laughing.

"Nice try," he smirks. "How about I show you how to do that over?"

He threads the metal catch through the door latch and secures it, then with both hands on the knob, he yanks the door toward him as hard as he can. It only opens an inch.

He pivots his head toward me. "See that? It's just like magic." He says it in a light, bubbly voice. Pupils dilated, lit up like a crazy man's.

Backing up, I swallow hard. Not realizing it' so close, I stumble onto the bed. He picks up the overturned chair, carries it across the room one-handed and slams it behind the desk. A couple of hotel pens roll across the carpet.

The look in his eyes does scare me. Oliver may be a lot of things, but he'd never hurt me. Not like that. Still, I skittle to the top of the headboard.

"What's your problem?" he yells. "Throwing your little bitch-fit downstairs? Grow up."

"I'm sorry, Oliver."

"You ought to be!" he yells. "You will not make a fool out of me again. Make no mistake."

"It's just, I don't understand why you would treat me that way."

He spins around to face me. "What way?"

"Like a piece of trash," I say, my voice almost a whisper. "That's not the way to treat a lady. Certainly not how to treat your wife."

"Well, excuse me. I didn't realize I was married to a Sunday school teacher," he says. "We're in Vegas for the weekend. One measly weekend."

I lift my chin. "That happens to coincide with your conference."

His green eyes flash. "You knew who I was when you married me."

He's always right.

I lower my forehead to my knuckles and take a deep breath. Feeling the foot of the bed drop down, I look up. Oliver's bent at the waist, wrestling with his cufflinks. He put them on blind earlier; now he can't pull the posts through the cuff holes.

"Here," I say, reaching for them, but he shrugs me off.

Finally popping them out, he tosses them next to the crystal lamp on the nightstand, then takes something from his pocket and gently sets it next to me on the bed. It's a red velvet jewelry box with a matching silk ribbon.

He suddenly begins to chuckle. "For your information, the whole table laughed their asses off when you stomped away in a snit. The dealer even gave me a cigar." He reaches into his breast pocket and produces a fresh Cohiba. Sliding it under his nose, he sniffs deeply. "Matter of fact, he told me to come up here and fuck your lights out."

My cheeks burn.

At the mini-bar, he uses the corkscrew on the chilled chardonnay and pours a couple of glasses. Balancing them between his fingers, he reclines beside me on the bedspread.

"I told the dealer I might just do that." He takes a long sip of one of the glasses, then holds the other out to me. "That is, if you're game, of course."

I slide my tongue over my teeth and look at him blankly for several moments. "Tempting as that sounds," I say, "I'm not near drunk enough."

His jaw twitches.

Head down, I gingerly inch off the bed, make my way to the bathroom and shut the door behind me.

Trembling like I'm cold, I brace both hands on the vanity. Whose face is that in the mirror? Lipstick feathered, mascara smeared, I barely recognize it. My blonde curls wild and tangled, it's like a windstorm followed me here.

19

Listening, I take a Q-tip from the crystal jar and absently swipe it under my lashes. It's silent. No sound, but I feel Oliver's looming funk. Before his feet blot out the light under the door, I know he's on the other side.

He raps softly. "Why would you want me when you hate me so much?"

His voice cracks. It's never done that.

I rest my cheek on the door and watch my blue eyes in the mirror. Everything somehow seems slowed down, inching at warped speed. My gaze drifts to the red candle on the lip of the tub. Its drooping edges curl under and there's a hole melted in the side. Hot liquid wax bleeds down onto the black marble until it circles the base, clotted, thick and hardened.

The door vibrates against my ear as he bangs it with his fists.

"I'm talking to you!" he screams. "Answer me!"

Strangely calm, I turn the knob and push open the door. He's standing there, red face pinched and twisted, winded, like he's run up a flight of stairs. Heavy, he falls into my arms and his shoulders shake. I hold him until they don't anymore.

Taking his hand, I guide him to the bed. There's still the warm spot from where we were before. I pull back the covers and hold them open like a tent, as he slides between them. Rolling on his side, he draws his arms and legs to his chest and tightly balls his fists. His eyes are glazed and open wide, just staring at the maple nightstand. Slowly, tenderly, I graze his perfect profile from his forehead to the base of his chin. I trace the curve of his eyebrows with my fingernails, continuing the line across his graying temple, down to where his sideburn ends on his cheek. I follow the edge of his ear and softly stroke his lobe. Soon, his breathing calms and I imagine he'll close his eyes and fall sleep, but he still stares at nightstand. I lay my palm flat against his cheek and keep it there as I study his auburn hair against the pillow. Finally, his lids drop, and I lightly touch them before switching off the light.

Now the room has a pale glow. Like a faintly burning flame inside a hurricane lamp. I look to the windows. The drapes are drawn back. I'd swear they're swelling from a breeze, but it's not possible. Windows don't open this high up for a reason.

"Juliana?" He sounds like a child.

I tuck the blanket around him. "Yes, Oliver."

"You have no idea what it feels like, afraid someone doesn't love you."

Turning back to the window, I reach for the sweating wine glass on the bedside table. "Don't say that, Oliver," I whisper. "It's not true."

## CHAPTER TWO

❖ ❖ ❖

Just now, I'm in a comfortable air conditioned office. The ambience is attractive, without trying too hard, intended to be non-threatening, I assume, since having to come here is atrocious enough already. The brass floor lamp has a linen shade. Tastefully-framed botanical prints. The throw pillow on the Chippendale chair is a nice touch. This love seat I'm sitting on, while a tad lumpy, I have to say the upholstery is lovely. There's a crystal candy dish on the chenille ottoman brimming with classic pink, yellow and white valentine candy hearts.

*My Guy.... So Fine.... True Love.... Ask Me....* And, in the middle...*Say Yes.*

It's Wednesday, the first time Oliver and I will see each other since he loaded me in a taxi for the airport on Sunday. As the plane made its ascent, I watched the noxious neon nirvana shrink smaller and smaller, until it was like a flattened bottle cap, then out of sight at last. Home in Austin by sunset, I gathered Lindsey and Adam from the Magruders', whipped up their favorite spaghetti and helped them with their homework, feeling pretty darn confident I'd never be carted off to Vegas for a romantic getaway again.

Lindsey and Adam are our fourteen-year-old twins and the Magruders are our best friends. Mary Ellen and I are closer than sisters and Mike and Oliver have the forty-lawyer Morrissey & Magruder firm downtown. He said that's where he's coming from right now; the red-eye flight touched down only hours ago. Originally booked in adjoining seats on the way home, Oliver opted to stay behind for a few days and network. After the only true fight in our fifteen years, I agreed it was probably best.

When breakfast arrived the morning after, I scarcely remembered having hooked the room service menu over the knob. I poured his steaming coffee and set it next to the toilet along with the unfolded newspaper, like I do every morning.

He hadn't moved all night, still coiled in the same position. When I gently shook his shoulder, he jerked violently. Switching on the lamp, I was horrified to see his shoulder was burning red, down to his bicep. Pressing his lips together, he creaked toward the bathroom while massaging and rotating it several times. Fighting my impulse to help him wasn't hard; I had as much small talk for him as he certainly had for me, which was a big fat zero.

When he finally emerged from the bathroom, I was under the Egyptian cotton sheets playing possum. I listened to the wire hangers scrape against the steel rod, papers shuffling, and the double locks of his briefcase clicking open and closed again. His slick soles on the carpet approached the bed, and then they stopped. Breathing in his strong Polo aftershave, I imagined him looming over me with a pillow. Cracking my lids, I peeked through my lashes. He was just staring down at me. Fine wrinkles around his eyes, green irises vibrating slightly, he was focused on me in a way I'd never seen. My face, my hair, my neck, my ears. Transfixed. As if he was memorizing me.

His cufflinks were on the nightstand where he'd tossed them the night before. Jingling them in his palm, he headed downstairs to the conference. I rolled over and nabbed the red velvet jewelry box. Opening it, my eyes widened. It was a heavy cuff bracelet, 18 karat gold, about three inches wide with a blood-red, ruby-encrusted horseshoe. He always gives me rubies.

Speaking the words aloud, I said, "Thanks, Oliver. You shouldn't have, but I'm glad you did." Then, I slipped it on my wrist, lifted the dome on his untouched breakfast, doused the limp, greasy hash browns in ketchup and washed them down with cold, black coffee.

Most of the day, I was on the phone with Mary Ellen. It's what friends do, right? Boundaries, Juliana. Boundaries. Oliver's almost ten years older than you, but he's not your dad. It's time you pulled in the reins, she said, and she was right. I didn't see him until he caught up with me in the waffle line Sunday morning, having wandered over from the casino, I assume. He lowered his wraparound sunglasses and pushed Eggs Florentine around his plate. A little ticklish at first, it turned into the most heart-felt conversation. He begged me to say what I was really thinking, because he really wanted to know. To my surprise and his credit, we made an agreement about how things would be from now on. Talk about progress.

When he called Monday, he was happy to tell me that not only had he and Mike picked up a new case over the weekend, but he'd made this appointment with Dr. Phillips himself. That's Dr. *Marsha* Phillips, actually, Ph.D. I hear she has clients lined up around the block. Couples in crisis. But, she won't for long if she doesn't get her little butt in here. She's about fifty. Poufy gray hair, perfectly arched brows. I know from the chilled waters on the coffee table. Her picture's on the label. Cool, I know.

Mary Ellen says Dr. Phillips is the only marriage counselor men will tolerate, even if she doesn't take insurance, which totally means she's one of those women haters. That, or she's smart enough to have the husbands go along with the wives' solution, after convincing them it was theirs to begin with, because that's the only way it would ever work. Manipulating the male ego is the way to get what you want from a man. Every woman knows that. But, for me, it's the execution that's never especially panned out.

How will I make this woman understand how we got here? In the space of one emergency consult session? It will be like dismantling a time capsule. Most importantly, how can I get her on my side?

3:18, Oliver rushes in. Three minutes late, and it's about time. Without acknowledging the petite little blonde lady waiting for him to sit down, me, he loosens his tie and unbuttons his navy suit jacket. His glistening forehead better mean he sprinted across the parking lot to get here.

He collapses beside me on the lumpy love seat. Exhaling loudly, he grandly eases back against the cushions. Trying my best to ignore his flirty grin, I can't help giving him a small sideways glance. His pink silk tie matches the handkerchief peeking from his breast pocket. He says pink's his signature color, because only a real man can pull it off. At least that's what his mother told him. It's the color she wears, too.

Here she comes now. Dr. Marsha Phillips. She strides into the room with confidence, no nonsense in her double-breasted tweed suit. I'd guess she's Oliver's height, five-ten or six feet, depending on who you believe—his doctor or his driver's license.

Dr. Phillips settles into her striped, high-back wing chair, sets her can of SlimFast next to a vase of red tulips, and makes only brief eye contact with me before looking at Oliver. If she has the enchanted, wide-eyed Oliver experience, I'm walking out.

He dimples and she gives him a pastel smile.

Good girl.

Come to think of it, she's kind of pretty, really, with her delicate bone structure. She's better looking since she got rid of her teasing comb. She should consider getting a new picture. Definitely.

"Mr. and Mrs. Morrissey, before getting started, I'll tell you what I tell all my new couples." Her serious voice matches her demeanor. "Years of problems aren't fixed in one session. Secondly, while I prefer that you not censor your comments in here, kindly refrain from scratching each other's eyes out."

Oliver whispers in my ear, "You cool with that?"

I discreetly elbow him.

"And, there's something else I like to throw in from the For What It's Worth Department. No matter how much time you've spent together, no matter what you've shared." She pauses to look at Oliver, and then me. "You can't make somebody love you."

Taking a small sip of her SlimFast, she watches Oliver straighten his lapels and cross his legs. "So, why did you make this appointment, Mr. Morrissey?"

"Well, you know the expression—happy wife, happy life?" he says.

"Can't say that I do."

"Well, I thought it was better to kill the infection early before having to chop the whole leg off."

I don't expect it when she bears down on me, "Tell me, Mrs. Morrissey," she says quickly. "What qualities made you want to spend the rest of your life with this man?"

Is this a trick question? She seems to be scrutinizing my body language. I swallow hard.

Finished waiting, she says, "All righty, then. Start with why you're here."

I smile nervously.

Oliver strokes my arm. "Relax, babe," he says gently. "Take your time. It's okay."

I nod. "We talked through our problems, Dr. Phillips," I say tentatively. "We made a deal and need your help ironing-out the details."

"What changes did your husband agree to make in this deal of yours?"

I rub my new ruby bracelet. "Well, there were several of them. Most of them have to do with his being so self-involved."

"Which are?"

"Treating me like I don't matter," I say slowly. "Oftentimes I can't be myself around him. He can be very intimidating."

She addresses Oliver. "How do you feel about that?"

He holds up his hand like a traffic cop. "Let her get it all out," he says. "I may not have heard everything, and I think I should."

She leans forward in her chair. "Mr. Morrissey, I asked how you feel about what your wife just said."

He looks at me lovingly. His eyes are so green. "It breaks my heart," he says. "That's not the kind of husband I want to be."

I lean into him. "You're sweet, Oliver. Thank you."

Nodding sagely, Dr. Phillips hums and closes her eyes like she's responsible for a therapeutic breakthrough.

"Mrs. Morrissey, your husband being self-involved, as you put it, does that equally apply to his interactions with the children?"

Taking my arm, Oliver lowers his voice. "Let's just focus on us in here, babe."

"That's absurd," Dr. Phillips says. "A marriage doesn't exist in a vacuum when children are involved."

He takes a handful of valentine hearts and tosses them in his mouth.

"Well, all right, Dr. Phillips," I say. "Our son's thing is guitar, but Oliver hammers him into becoming a scratch golfer because *he* is. And our daughter, with his emphasis on her making the elite dance team, how can that happen when he insults her performances?"

"Ok, that's not fair," he says.

He thumbs past the platinum cards in his wallet, and holds out the baby pictures that I put in there. Dr. Phillips slides on her black readers and glances over at them pleasantly.

"It feels like I'm raising them alone sometimes," I say softly.

"You know my schedule, Juliana."

I look at his golf-sunburn.

"Someone has to make a living. My wife loves being supported in style, and it's time consuming." He flips his hand in my direction. "Look at her, Dr. Phillips."

She does. I consider tucking my pink pedicured toes in their Manolo Blahnik sandals under the sofa. Ridiculous. Also physically impossible, I tuck my curls behind my ears instead.

"Perhaps we should explore the possibility of family therapy." She poises her gold pen above her clipboard and looks up. "The children's names are...?"

Oliver takes my hand. "Lindsey and Adam," he says. "They're eighth graders at Hill Country Middle School."

I watch Dr. Phillips write their names in loopy cursive.

"Okay, Mrs. Morrissey. Forget about the deal. Forget about Lindsey and Adam for a minute." She steeples her fingers under her chin and looks at me thoughtfully. "Why are you really here?"

"I want to get it back again, whatever it is we've lost."

My quick answer surprises me. Tells me it's how I truly feel.

I check Oliver's expression. He's giving me that look from the hotel room. The one when he was watching me in bed. He squeezes his eyes shut, then quickly laces our fingers together and kisses my knuckles.

25

"When we leave here today, babe," he says, "things will be completely different between us."

Dr. Phillips breaks in. "If we could back up a moment, Mr. Morrissey, do I sense that you feel taken advantage of? Maybe your wife feels similarly, for staying home to raise the kids."

Oliver crosses his legs at the knee.

"In the interest of compromise, Mrs. Morrissey, could you show more interest in your husband?"

Is that supposed to be funny?

"And, Mr. Morrissey. Could you think of changes that would please your wife to see in you?"

Oliver plucks a bottled water from the ice bucket and begins peeling off her face.

She raises her eyebrows. "Just a thought." Her voice trails off at the end.

There's a knock on the door. She ignores it.

I don't expect it when Oliver pulls me to him and gives me a lingering kiss. I mean a deep, searching, lingering kiss.

Flustered, I look at Dr. Phillips. Stifling a laugh, she licks her finger and flips through her calendar.

"Okay, lovebirds," she says. "Let's get another appointment on the books."

"That won't be necessary, Doctor," Oliver says.

I tilt my head. "Oliver?"

He wipes my pink lipstick off his mouth. "You see, my wife's quite the little actress. We already made a deal," he says. "When we got married. With very favorable terms for her."

Dr. Phillips closes her calendar and stares over her glasses at him as he rises from the couch and smoothes the pleats on his trousers.

There's another knock. Louder this time.

He sneers down at me. "Understand which side your bread's buttered on, cupcake."

His keys jingle in his pocket as he walks to the door. He pushes it open. A large man is standing there. Dark brown shirt. Matching tie. Brown pants. Boots. Cowboy hat.

And a gold badge.

Entering, the man looks directly at Dr. Phillips.

Deep folds like parentheses hold her nervous smile in place.

He's arresting her?

He suddenly crosses the carpet in my direction. My heart jumps.

"Mrs. Morrissey?" Voice gruff and serious.

I don't have *that* many parking tickets.

He's standing over me now. "Juliana Morrissey?"

Looking up, I see my reflection in his mirrored aviators. "Yes?"

The man's hat is pulled down low on his forehead. Badge says he's the constable. He holds out a thick, brown envelope. My name's typed on the front.

Oliver's moustache hangs down the sides of his mouth like holsters. "Open your hands," he says. "Take it."

I always do what he tells me.

The constable places the envelope in my palms. Dark hair grows on his knuckles. He says, "You have been served."

Heel-toe, he strides to the door. Suddenly, I wish he'd stay.

Hands shaking, I tear open the envelope.

"In the Matter of the Marriage of Oliver Adam Morrissey and Juliana Carmen Morrissey… " The black letters wave across the page.

Oliver clears his throat loudly. "Not that you need it, kiddo, but here's a little advice." He takes a long pause. "I don't negotiate from a place of weakness."

I cut my eyes to Dr. Phillips. She's staring, ghost-eyed, mouth open. Like she wants to speak but can't form a word.

The red light blinking on the wall means her next couple is here.

"I'll be that father you always dreamed about, Mrs. Morrissey. In my home with my children. Be gone by five o'clock," Oliver says. "Sharp."

"It's not just your house." I say. "You said your parents gave it to both of us before we got married, remember?"

"That never happened. It's called separate property," he says. "I just wanted you to think they liked you." He gives me his megapixel smile. "Even my old man thinks you're a tramp."

"The twins won't stand for it!" I scream. "Not in a million years!"

"Now, that's where you're wrong," he says. "They know everything is all your doing. They deserved to know the truth. Sons can't help but idolize us and there's nothing like little girls and their daddies." He bats his eyelashes. "You, of all people, should know that."

He counts ten crisp hundreds from his wallet and presses them into my palm. Then, as if he's sacrificing the last, salty French fry from bottom of the sack, he plucks out a single dollar bill and it floats to my lap like a feather. Then with no see-you-later, no nothing, he takes three giant steps to the door and pushes it open.

The entire lobby gawks at me. A frizzy-haired, older woman sits on a sofa with her dog-faced husband. Looking at me with intense clarity, her eyes swallow mine, then drop to the floor.

The cushion beside me sinks down. There's a warm hand on my arm.

"Everything's going to be all right." It's Dr. Phillips.

Leaning into her, I look down for a place to throw up. There's only her black, pointed-toe pumps.

"I'm sorry, Mrs. Morrissey." Her tone is peaceful and kind.

"My name is Juliana Birdsong."

Did I speak the words, or are they lodged somewhere in my brain?

She guides me to the lobby. "Just call and I'll fit you in."

Don't hold your breath, is what I want to tell her. Then, I remember. The twins are just getting on the bus. Their family's falling apart and they need their mother to comfort them.

I have to get to them. Now!

Bursting through the door, I nearly trip over their roller blades.

Catching myself against the mahogany entry chest, I call out to them.

"Adam. Lindsey. Where are you?"

My high heels clack on the polished oak floors down the long hallway toward our kitchen. Through the living room, I get a glimpse of myself in the antique mirror above the carved limestone fireplace. My curls are a wild mess. A line of sweat trickles down my jaw.

Standing in the kitchen doorway, red blasts up my neck to my cheeks. Even my scalp burns. I can't stop my eyes darting around the room, from the paisley drapes on the bay windows, to the twins' kindergarten pictures pasted on the fridge, to the faucet dripping water into a glass of milk. My coffee cup left an ugly brown ring on the granite counter this morning. My lipstick's on the rim. Instinctively, I lower the door to dishwasher.

Lindsey is slumped on a barstool with her blonde braids at her shoulders. She's frowning at the television mounted above the oven, licking Easy Mac from a spoon. She's kicked off her Mary Janes and her pleated skirt meets the yellow socks stretched up over her knees.

"I need to talk to you and your brother, Lindsey," I say. "Would you mind turning the TV off, please?"

Her clear blue eyes don't leave the screen. Without even looking at me, she's able to glue my arms to my sides to keep me from hugging her. Today of all days.

Adam's cooking at the stove, sliding a quesadilla from the buttered skillet. His tight, brown curls stick out four inches in every direction. Hearing me, he misses the plate and the quesadilla falls on the floor. Stooping to pick it up, he inspects it, then puts it in his mouth.

"Oh, hey Mom," he says. "Dad called laughing and sounding all weird."

There's a Diet Coke on the edge of the sink. I take a sip and it's hot. That damn Sponge Bob on the television is driving me nuts.

"Oh, your dad's just hilarious," I say. "What did he tell you?"

"I answered it, but he wanted to talk to her." He motions his head in Lindsey's direction. "As usual, she won't tell me anything."

She stirs her macaroni and puts a bite in her mouth before turning up the volume a notch.

I snap my fingers like you would to a dog. "Turn that damn thing off."

"Make me," she says, lisping slightly.

She's grounded right now for back-talking me. So much for that.

Adam knocks her with his arm. "Come on, Linds. Quit being a jerk."

She swats him away like a mosquito. Elbowing her way out of my womb two minutes and forty-nine seconds before Adam, she never stops lording it over him.

"So, Mom, what's the deal?" he says.

Big tears are welling in Lindsey's eyes. She knows.

"Kids, I don't know how to say this." Combing my nails through my hair, I look at Adam. "Your dad's divorcing me."

"What?" He blinks behind his black square frames. "You guys aren't always smoochy-smoochy, but come on, Mom. You can't do that."

"Well, Dad said you're crazy if you think you could kick him out," Lindsey says, flipping through the channels. "And, you have to be gone by five o'clock."

The green-lit numbers on the coffee maker say 4:32.

Adam's low voice turns high again. "Holy crap, Mom. You mean today? Like right now?"

"Looks like it," I say. I'm sweating. I can smell it.

Adam's face falls. "Why do you always do what he says?" He tugs my arm. "Where would you even go?"

I hadn't thought that far ahead.

"Your Uncle Richard and Wally's, I guess."

Lindsey drops her metal spoon and it tings the inside of the bowl.

"Listen to me, kids," I say, looking between them. "If I had to leave, it would only be for a couple of nights," I say. "Any longer, and I'll come get you."

Lindsey whips her head in my direction. Her heart-shaped earrings catch the light. "Dad said if you tried that, we'd have to get all new friends because they're in a different school district," she says. "But he said you could forget it, because they'd turn Adam into a fag and me into a fag hag."

Adam's eyes grow wide. "They would?"

"Lindsey, that's such a hateful thing to say I can't believe you'd repeat it," I say evenly.

She wipes a tear with the back of her hand. "Well, isn't getting divorced what you wanted?"

"Sweetheart, of course it's not what I want," I say. "Your dad, he's divorcing me."

"Well, what was he supposed to do when you broke his heart?" she says. "And, you think if he moved out instead of you, it'd be okay?"

I reach out my hand to touch her arm, but she'll have none of it. "I'm your mother," I say. "I never want to be away from you two for a single minute."

"Maybe you could go stay with your boyfriend," she says.

I stumble on my words. "Boyfriend? I don't have a boyfriend."

And it's the truth.

"Dad said you do," she says.

Adam's wrinkling his dark, heavy brows. The look on his face. I can't stand it. "When have I ever lied before?" I search his eyes. "You tell me."

Looking away, he hooks a thumb in his belt loop and says softly, "When has Dad?"

Try half an hour ago in the therapist's office.

And, in Las Vegas when he held me tight, said he loved me and that everything would be okay.

Lindsey raises her chin. "We're fourteen, so we get to choose where we live. Dad said so." She backs toward Adam and drapes her arm over his shoulder. "And we're staying here."

The red roses on the table—I hear their petals drop.

My babies. My darlings.

The clichés that people use to describe feeling this horrible, like your heart's being ripped out of your chest? That's exactly what it feels like, but it's worse. Your heart feels so cold it shivers.

I watch their backs as they leave the kitchen.

The doorbell rings and I jump. Making my way to the entry, my legs ache.

I peer out the glass panels by the door. It's a smooth-skinned young man wearing a brown tweed jacket leaning against my copper mailbox with his arms crossed over his chest. He looks like one of those snotty fraternity brats who's had the world handed to them gift-wrapped and monogrammed since the day they were born. Definitely one of Oliver's junior associates.

I yank the door open.

He straightens up and smiles. "Mrs. Morrissey? I'm Bobby Lyle. Your husband told me to stop by and see if you need help packing your car."

"Leave," I say. "Now."

Still smiling with his perfectly straight teeth, he doesn't move.

I glare at him using all the firepower my eyes possess. I feel the actual pain of them bulging from their sockets.

"Get my husband on the phone."

I watch the neighbor boy across the street throwing the Frisbee for his Rottweiler. The dog springs high in the hair and latches onto it with his sharp teeth.

Hearing the phone ringing and finally Oliver's voice on the other end, I yank the phone from the young man's hand and scream into the mouthpiece. "You're not throwing me out, Oliver! I will not leave Lindsey and Adam!"

He takes a moment to answer. "I pray you'll make it easier on them and leave of your own accord," he says drolly. "You know how bored Mrs. Arnold next door can get with nothing to talk about, so please don't make a scene."

"You can't do this, Oliver," I shriek. "It's my home!"

"Too bad you didn't get that law degree, sweet britches," he says, then switches to his authoritative lawyer voice. "Assets belonging to a spouse before the time of marriage are separate property. It was given solely to me and you are welcome to look at the deed."

Bobby's fingers tug at his starched collar like it's too tight.

"I'd rather not get a forcible detainer," Oliver says. "But if that's the way you want to play it, there's still time for me to swing by my boy Judge Speed's chamber before I come check on you. You never gave him much of a chance, Juliana, but he really is a great guy." He stifles a laugh. "Now, put Bobby back on."

My wrist goes limp and he barely catches the phone as it slips from my fingers. Heart pounding, I look across the street again. The neighbor boy and his dog are gone.

Bobby backs up but he doesn't step off the porch. "I'm sorry, ma'am, but you must be off the property by five o'clock," he says gently. "If it were up to me, you could take all the time you need. I promise."

31

How many times have we rehearsed it in our minds? The proverbial your-house-is-burning-down moment, when we can only take what matters most before the place goes up in flames?

My mother said to always return things in better condition than I got them, but then I don't see her anywhere around here today.

Ready, set. My watch says 4:43. Go.

Our long hallway is lined with portraits of Lindsey and Adam. I leave only the hooks on the wall. Silver frames that clutter the piano: Photos of my parents, ones of Richard and me, the twins as Raggedy Ann and Andy, Minnie and Mickey. I rake every single one into a laundry basket. You better believe I grab every photo album. Oliver can kiss my ass if he thinks I'm leaving those. Think, Juliana. Think. The ceramic elephant Adam made me. Lindsey's Flat Stanley. The home movies.

I'm nauseous. I look around me. Think.

I run to the master bath and open Oliver's pristine closet. He's adamant that his clothes not touch each other, or else. I push aside his fresh golf shirts and turn the combination to his wall safe, 36-24-36. His emergency two grand is replaced with a hand-written note that says, "Fuck you, Juliana." It's signed with a smiley face.

After dumping every suit, dress shirt and tie on the floor, I leave a smiley-faced note of my own. "Not in this lifetime, buddy. You'll never get to do that again." I toss in the ruby horseshoe bracelet and slam it closed.

No time for a plan. I sweep my arm across my smooth marble vanity. My makeup, skin products. Pomegranate candle. I toss them in a wicker basket. I cram my toothbrush in my pocket and reading glasses on my head. My dresses, shirts and jeans. Shoes, purses and belts. My goddamn underwear.

Adrenaline, panic. On my hands and knees, I look under the bed like I'm checking out of a hotel.

When can I come back? I can't breathe.

I shuttle back and forth between the house and the driveway. Passing under the wrought-iron chandeliers, over the Persian rugs, and beside the fine paintings gracing the plaster walls, my possessions seem to hug me close. Finished, I stand on the front porch. My car's stuffed full as a pillowcase with no way to see out. I look down at my hands. They're shaking. I've broken three nails.

I swallow hard. My watch says 4:56.

I push the front door open to go back inside for the last time. It feels hot to my touch. The twins are all that matter. Like I'm surrounded by hot licking flames, I check behind every door, inside every closet of my frantic mind. When I find them, I'll snatch them into my arms. Then run like the devil.

"Adam, Lindsey, it's time. Come tell me you love me?" I stand in the entryway listening, but there's no answer. I rush to the kitchen. The television's still on. Stepping through the French doors, I check by the pool.

Winded, calling their names, I climb the stairs, two at a time.

Adam's collapsed in the computer chair, his long legs stretched out in front of him, his bony arms dead at his sides. Lindsey's cradled on his lap, squeezing her arms around his neck. He shakes his curls to hide his tear-stained face. I kneel down and kiss his forehead. He lets out a soft moan.

I tug one of Lindsey's braids. Her shoulders, delicate as a bird's, begin to tremble. Falling against her back, I wrap her in my arms and smell her hair. Adam leans up and digs his quivering chin into my neck. I feel his warm breath. I squeeze them more tightly than I ever have before.

"I don't want to go," I whisper. "I love you both with all my heart. Please change your minds. Come with me. Please."

The muscles in Adam's neck flex slightly as he readies to stand from the chair. Then he stops. He could never leave his twin. Their bond is that strong. And I love him for it. She needs him more than I do.

Lindsey sobs. "Dad called. He's almost home and said you better be gone." Her blonde lashes sparkle with tears. "I'm sorry, Mommy. Just go. You know how he is when you're late."

I kiss them both. "This is temporary, I promise you. I'll be back."

Adam looks up. His eyes tell me, "I know you will, Mom."

For now, all I can do is bubble-wrap them in my love. To keep them safe.

Oliver's young enforcer respectfully holds open the door. I push past him, slide behind the wheel of my car and turn the ignition.

I drive up the long, paved driveway that splits our two acre-lot in half. At the top, I throw it into park, hop out, and open the back. I drop to my knees and dig up the yellow verbena I planted years ago. The roots are tough but surprisingly easy to pull from the ground. I scoop scads of them into the recycling crate from the curb using a Styrofoam cup from Sonic. I rub the sweat from my forehead with my dirty hand, lean through the driver window and take my pink Swiss Army knife from my purse. Kneeling in front of the rose bushes, I grasp the largest, most luscious red bloom and a sharp thorn pierces my thumb.

Looking back at the house, I raise it to my mouth and taste blood.

As I turn onto the street, a strange, sudden wind sucks the divorce papers out the window.

Driving away slowly, I cry the silent kind of cry where the back of your throat shrinks tight and burns to your tonsils. Then, the pain clots and scabs so you can't swallow.

The gate sweeps closed behind me.

Oliver, you sonofabitch.

Five o'clock.

The sign on the door reads: "Welcome Cinnamon Dolce Latte," with a whipped cream curlicue standing tall and proud as a Dairy Queen dip cone. A woman wearing a green coat swings open the heavy glass door on her way out. A young guy steps from the parking lot onto the sidewalk and catches it. There's no laces in his tennis shoes and he's not wearing socks. Barelegged, my dad used to call it. Peeking from the cuff of his jeans is a dragon tattoo with red eyes, a long tongue and sharp teeth above a skull and cross bones. His navy T-shirt has the word "FUCT" in yellow block letters.

It's been thirty minutes and my hands are still shaking. My knuckles are black, smeared with mascara. I never take my eyes off my car while I stir in my sugar.

Asking for help has never been my style, but drastic times, drastic measures. Three nights at the Four Seasons and I'd be tapped out. Plus, trusting practically everything I own in their parking garage? Forget it. It's bad enough in the Starbucks lot, a hundred yards on the other side of the plate glass window. Everyone knows that any carjacker seeing a forty-ish woman chasing after her Lexus with a latte in her hand would stop for sure.

A little girl with blonde, flyaway curls in a pink sundress waits behind her father. Rocking on her rubber heels, she holds the back of his wooden chair. I punch in the number.

The most insulting word in the English language. Selfish.

I wipe my eyes. Eight rings. He picks up.

That's right. Selfish.

"Hugh Birdsong."

He still answers the phone like that in his mellow, Morgan Freeman voice. I think of the old green phone with the rotary dial. He couldn't still use it, certainly.

"Hi, there. How are you?" I try to sound upbeat.

"Fine, fine. Just fine." It's clear he has no idea who it is.

"Thanks a lot. It's Juliana. Birdsong. Remember me?"

"Oh, sure. Sure. I know you."

"Did I get you at a bad time?"

"I have company just now."

He sounds muffled. Like his mouth's not up to the phone.

"Then I won't keep you." I take a deep breath. "I need to ask a quick favor."

And he's silent. My eyes dart to the little girl, then back to my car.

"Are you there?" I can't wait any longer. "Can you hear me?"

"Yes. What?"

"What are you doing?"

"I'm entertaining a young woman."

"A young woman? You are? Who?" I'm not watching the car anymore.

"You don't need to be privy to my entire goings-on."

"Does she have a name?"

"Yes. Of course." He's searching. "She's dark-headed. Not wearing any clothes."

"What? Who's with you?"

"She's smoking one of her long cigarettes."

"You're saying she's naked *and* smoking?" I say. "You hate people smoking in the house. She must be really pretty."

"Pretty as a picture," he says softly. "So pretty, I'm holding her in my hands."

"You're playing with me, aren't you?"

I listen carefully for another voice. I check and we're still connected.

"Are you there?"

It's like he set the phone down, or dropped it. What in the world?

I call his name several times, then finally hang up.

Perfect. He never helps me when I ask him. Just perfect.

It's not like he was my first choice. I only called him at all because I couldn't chance Oliver thinking I'd be taking the kids to Richard's.

I shift the phone to my other ear, return my wallet to my purse and check the parking lot again for hoodlums. I mean, crap—everything I own is in there.

Times more drastic. I'd give anything if I could just leave a message but I have to talk to him. Obviously.

Richard picks up.

"How about we skip the part where I have to get ugly?" he says. "Save us all some trouble, finish the job and take me out of the loop."

The last time I heard my brother this pissy, it was with me.

"Hold on," I say. "What are you talking about?"

He pauses. "Just Wally's store. I thought you were the contractor."

When did Wally get a store?

He recovers quickly. "To what do I owe this honor, your majesty?"

I shake my head, thankful for a smile.

"Shut up, smart ass, and finish your story."

"I can't afford a nervous breakdown right now, but Wally feels like he can because he has more time than I do. I told him, 'First things first. Let's finish the job and then pick out the Italian chandeliers,' but he just doesn't get it."

Richard's always been talkative. Our dad used to offer him five bucks if he'd just shut up until dinner was over. And to stop burping the damn alphabet.

"Good God, Richard. Why can't the contractor have more clients like you?"

"No, the question is, Jules, why can't we be like some poor white trash family in a pop-up trailer and only have to worry about putting the Schlitz and Parliaments on the table?"

"You're breaking my heart."

"Listen, Jules. You called me, so out with it."

I suck air through my teeth. "I have a weird question to ask. Is it okay if I sleep at your house tonight?"

After a long pause, he clears his throat. "Excuse me, what did you say?"

"Can I spend the night tonight?"

"Why on earth would you want to do that?" He enunciates each word.

"I can't go into it right now. Painters, you know." I bite the inside of my cheek. God, why did I say that?

"Just you?" Then in a baby voice, he asks, "Is Dorothy running away from home?"

"Why are you being such an ass?"

"Think about it," he says.

"I have no idea," I say. "Help me out."

Silence.

Slowly, I say, "Yes or no?"

"We're in San Diego, so I guess it's cool. Oh—you'll want the code to get in. If you have a pencil, write this down." He's enjoying this. "It's my birthday."

"It's still branded on my ass with your picture, sadly," I say. "When are you coming home? Why are you out there?"

"Several days and business. I have to take another call."

"Wait. Can I use your wheels?"

"Seriously, Jules? I don't like the sound of this."

He wants me to beg. I wait him out.

"The convertible keys are on the ring in the kitchen," he says.

"The Mercedes? It's running?" Death buggy, old as hell from 1973. "How about Wally's car?"

"Left it at the airport. Quit being such a girl."

I watch the customers in the parking lot milling around my car.

"And listen up, Jules, because this is important," he says. "Don't go in my room."

"Jeez, how many times do I have to tell you I didn't swipe your baseball?" I say, and hang up first. I wish I could see the look on his face.

Pushing the heavy glass door on my way out, I raise my keychain, hit the red button, and the black Lexus SUV across the steaming asphalt starts to beep.

It's not long until I'm pulling into his driveway and punching the keypad. The house is an updated 1940s bungalow. It's the same general idea as the house where we grew up in Hyde Park, but Travis Heights is decidedly more fashionable and only two seconds from downtown. Richard's owned it for years and had it refurbished in the contemporary-trendy warehouse style with air conditioning tubing and water pipes exposed. The walls are sleek museum white and scattered with hip and happening art work. A charcoal sectional flanks a pair of lime green wing chairs sitting atop an authentic zebra rug. Not my thing but truly spectacular, nonetheless. What's wrong with me? I'd take this house in a heartbeat because mine isn't mine anymore. Guess it never was.

I kick off my heels and head for destination number one: the kitchen. Moving the horrid pink wine coolers out of the way, I uncork the bottle of Kendall Jackson in the fridge, pour myself a glass, then head for destination number two: the master bath. I plop my purse on the vanity and open the medicine cabinet. I'm searching for Motrin to ease my aching head, but like any responsible citizen I check the expiration dates on the plastic, amber bottles. It's gratifying to know Rich is living the good life with Adderall, testosterone, male growth hormones. Oh, and a little Vicodin.

I avoid my eyes in the mirror as I butt my ashes in the toilet and drain my glass. Squeezing my eyes shut, I snag the keys to the Mercedes and I'm gone.

The smell of tacos and fajitas welcomes me, and I feel better. Taquería Pepe. *Su casa es mi casa.* Pepe's has a certain magic that's made it the West Austin social club for decades. The ancient waiters know our families by

37

name and everyone's order by heart, down to which kid will throw a hissy fit if one measly onion touches their enchilada.

We haven't sat at the same table with our kids since they got out of high chairs. You know how teachers separate certain kids because they bring out the absolute worst in each other? That's us, the Morrisseys, Magruders and Evanses. Pepe's is the highlight of our existence, the time we reserve for each other. Better be on time or you'll miss the sparkling conversation. Miss it altogether and you'll be the conversation.

I breeze past the line of diners without a standing reservation and scan the dining room for Mary Ellen and Cheryl. They're in the booth against the far wall with their heads together. Mary Ellen looks up and waves her arm with a sweet expression. I snake through the noisy tables, nodding at several people I know.

I slide across the red, vinyl cushion next to Cheryl. Her auburn hair is pulled into a two-inch pony tail, held in place with several bobby pins. Her sleeveless blouse shows off her tan, toned arms. Wrinkling her brow, she touches my forehead like she's checking a child for a fever, and her cool palm is a relief. They've already ordered me a margarita. I stir the skinny straw and take a long sip. Brain freeze.

Mary Ellen squeezes my hands across the table. "How are you, sweetheart?" she says.

"Juliana, tell me what happened," Cheryl says quickly. "I thought y'all worked things out on your trip."

I take a deep breath. "Me, too. I bought Oliver's promise that we'd work it out today in counseling. He made me leave the twins. Just leave Adam and Lindsey there." My voice raises an octave. "He's Satan."

Cheryl bangs her fist on the table. "Oh, my God. He did not. Oliver taking care of the kids? Give me a break," she says in her tiny voice. "This is unbelievable. Even for him."

I fan my face, trying to keep it together. None of us says a word for several moments.

"You're going to be okay, honey, I promise," Mary Ellen says gently. "It's Lindsey and Adam we're worried about. They're the big losers in this thing."

"Don't you think I know that?"

I wonder what they're doing now. If they're still upstairs. If Lindsey's still crying. If they're all right. I roll my head back and rotate it, hoping everything will return to focus. It doesn't.

Mary Ellen clucks her tongue to soothe me. "Well, I know the $1,000 walking around money Oliver gave you won't last long,"

I tilt my head to the side. "Where'd you hear about that?"

"Mike," she says.

I shoot her an exasperated look. "He and Oliver have been talking?"

She nods. "Why is that surprising? They're business partners."

Eyeing her, I pull my fingers through my curls and tuck them behind my ears.

A waitress in a bright orange peasant blouse wipes down our table and leaves the requisite salsa, *queso* and a red basket of chips. She's drawn thin, black arches over the plucked skin where her true brows once were, and brown lip liner circles her mouth like chocolate.

The woman's scarcely left the table when Cheryl raises her brows and puckers her lips. "Oh, my God. What's going on with her makeup?" she says. "She really needs some wax for that moustache. But she does have those Latin genes."

"Cheryl, quit it." Mary Ellen pushes her arm, and salts the chips.

I can't help but watch her forehead when she talks. It doesn't move. Fresh Botox. Her peach tennis visor is pushed back high on her head like sunglasses, exposing her black roots. She catches me looking and picks at them with her red sculpted nails.

"Don't worry," she says. "I have an appointment with Fronz tomorrow."

"What are you talking about? Your hair always looks great," I say.

Cheryl peers over my shoulder. Reaching for her purse, her large, sapphire dinner ring catches the light. She rolls bright pink on her lips and blooms in an instant.

"Paul! How are you?" Lifting her face expectantly, Cheryl's tiny brown eyes open wide as she blinks her short, brown lashes. She and Paul have known each other since high school. Why he thinks he is so hot remains a mystery, standing there in his purple jersey and silly ball cap with the BMW emblem.

He leans down to kiss her cheek. "Ladies, ladies," he says. "Enjoying us a Little Margaret this evening, are we?"

"Yeah, Paul." Mary Ellen winks. "You know us wild party moms."

Did she just push her boobs together?

Paul rests his hand on my back. "Juliana, luscious as always. You looked lovely at the Hospice Ball recently," he says. "I'm auditioning new mistresses tonight. I saw Oliver in the parking lot and he said you're available for a try-out."

I look him in the eye. "Very funny. Don't ever say anything like that to me again."

He gives me a shaky smile. "Lighten up, Juliana. Oliver wasn't being serious," he says. "At least I don't think he was."

"How about you saunter over to Kimberley Singleton's table? She's probably more your style." I motion to the table against the wall where Kimberley is sitting with her daughter, Amber, who's Lindsey and Adam's age. Paul casts a lustful gaze in her direction.

"How are you, girl?" Mary Ellen calls to her.

Kimberley smiles at our table and tickles the air with her pinky.

I am loving her black scoop-neck blouse. And how come my hair never looks like that?

"You won't believe the latest Kimberley story," Cheryl says. "You're going to just die."

I raise my brows. "Do you think we could talk about it later?" I say. "My life's kind of falling apart right now."

She presses her lips together and looks heavenward. "Well, it's about her daughter's karate instructor, so don't let me forget." Turning back to Paul, she says in a flirty voice, "So, where's Laura tonight?"

"Book club, so I'm babysitting. Evan's soccer team is still undefeated." Walking toward the table of noisy boys in matching uniforms, he calls over his shoulder, "Tell the hubbies I said hello."

Mary Ellen stirs a chip in the *queso*. Sliding it in her mouth, she lazily watches his butt from the corner of her eye.

Mariachis dressed in red, sequined matador costumes circulate through the dining room crooning "El Rancho Grande."

"Shit, I hate those guys," Cheryl says. "Don't look at them and maybe they'll leave us alone." She balances her menu strategically and ducks behind it, accidentally knocking over her water glass. It narrowly misses my purse.

I scoop it up and rub my hand across the bottom to make sure it's dry. "That's Vuitton, okay? And I won't be buying any more."

They swap looks as I rise from the booth and head to the rest room.

I walk through the door marked "Señoritas." Leaning against the Talavera tiles, I soak a paper towel and press it to my cheeks. What's happened to my life in the three hours since I entered the therapist's office?

When I return, there's a fresh margarita at my place. Raising it to my lips, I scan the tables for my friends, finding them at the round one in the middle of the room sitting with Mike and Glen. What are they doing here? My breath catches. And Oliver. It's like my face was clipped from the picture and his is taped into the hole I left.

I glare at him, homicidal. He knows I'm watching him, and that I'd never confront him here. Humiliating me is more important than being home with the twins right now? I take my phone from my purse and dial the house. It goes to the machine. Why don't they answer?

He scoots his chair closer to Cheryl's and rests his head on her shoulder. Oliver looks like a moist, lumpy frog when he pretends to be grief stricken, but I know all too well the vampire hiding underneath. The table never looks my direction. But plenty of other people in the restaurant do.

Mary Ellen and Cheryl eventually make their way back to rescue me.

I dig my teeth into my lower lip. "What did he say?"

Mary Ellen raises one perfectly arched eyebrow. "That you two would be happy campers if only you weren't out of your fucking mind." She smirks in his direction. "But don't worry. He said it's nothing that *The Proper Care and Feeding of Husbands* by Dr. Laura wouldn't solve. I wanted to slap him," she says. "We're going to help you, honey. Cheryl and I both, and it's going to work out. "

I look back to the men's table. Oliver's talking with his hands while Glen nods. Mike leans back in his chair with his arms crossed over his chest. Staring straight at me, his eyes well with tears. I quickly look away.

"Then," Cheryl says, "Oliver said that the only available men you'll have to choose from are fat old goobers like Fred Stanley." She wraps her hands around her neck like she's choking. "But I took up for you, Juliana. I said you'd become a lesbian before you ever went out with him."

I press my hands on the table. "That's it. I'm going over there."

"This isn't the time, Juliana," Mary Ellen says. "Or the place."

"She's right Juliana," Cheryl says. "Don't."

I pick through my wallet and toss my money on the table.

Mary Ellen takes hold of my arm and I yank it away. "Sit back down. Come sleep in our guest room. Forever, if you want."

"Thanks," I say. "But, I'm staying at Richard's."

Even though I barely ever see him, and he's not even home tonight, being at my brother's house is what I need.

I walk to the men's table, feeling Mike and Glen's eyes on me, but it's only Oliver I'm looking at. He throws me an innocent smile. My cheeks burn, but I don't break eye contact with him. How did I ever find that ugly-souled man attractive? I guess love does that to a person.

I grip the edge of the table. "You're not getting away with any of this."

"To what are you referring, Mrs. Morrissey?"

"How could you tell the twins I have a boyfriend?" I say. "You better tell them the truth."

"We should probably talk when you're calmer, Mrs. Morrissey." He shakes his head ruefully. "Besides, I can't imagine you'd come clean with the children."

For a man with a hair-trigger charisma who plays people for a living, his children are easy to snow. He'll make me look like shit, no matter what I say.

He mouths the words, "Don't cross me." Then winks.

My fury has turned into panic.

"Take away my money, the house, anything, Oliver. Just not the kids."

His eyes scan the room. Catching the waitress's attention, he points to his empty margarita glass.

Watching her head toward the bar, I whisper, "I'm out of here." I can barely choke out the words,

I call the twins when I stop for gas. Lindsey answers the phone. She says her dad stopped in, changed clothes, and was off again. I tell her I'll be by to take them to school in the morning. She says their dad has it handled.

Before I can fill the tank, the pump denies my card. I scream.

Oliver must've canceled every card in my purse.

I drink what's left of the bottle in Richard's fridge.

And, one more.

# CHAPTER THREE

### ◈ ◈ ◈

---

"Is Mr. Birdsong there, please?" says a professional voice.

Loud, too loud. And bright. I've left the overhead on and the clock says nine-thirty.

"I—I'm sorry. No, he's not."

"This is Seton Hospital calling and it's important that I speak with him."

I sit straight up in bed. Crap, my head.

"This is Juliana Birdsong. I'm his sister. What's wrong?"

"I'm calling about Hugh Birdsong."

I swing my legs over the bed. "Was he in an accident?"

"I don't have that information. Just that he came here by EMS."

"I'm coming. And thank you."

All my clothes are in my car. Richard won't know if I use his toothbrush. Or steal a shirt. I've had plenty of hangovers, but this one's a mother. God, what I need is a greasy burger.

### ◈ ◈ ◈

The first thing I see is my father's curved, white toenails, cut straight across with the clippers of his old leather manicure set. He yanks on the intravenous tube that's connected to a bag of fluids hanging from a tall pole. His foot sticks through the bedrails, and the hospital gown is pushed up his thighs.

I'd been just fine not having seen my father's testicles until this point in my life.

I rush to steady the pole and free his legs. "Stop. Let me help you."

I can tell he's surprised to see me. He looks terrible. His face is red. Feverish. He needs a shave, about four days' worth.

"Get this damn thing off me," he growls.

"Hold on. I'll call the nurse." I punch the red button on the wall.

Neck muscles flexing, he cranes his head from the pillow and kicks the squeaking rails. His gray-blonde curls stick straight up from his forehead, and the scruffy sides hang long at his ears. White tape has peeled from the needle in the back of his hand.

A short, heavy nurse ambles slowly down the hall, untangling the chain of her reading glasses from her stethoscope.

"Please, ma'am," I call out. "My dad's going to wet his pants."

He grunts. It's too late. His eyes shoot to mine. My heart catches and I give him a sad smile. He glares at me like it's my fault and I turn away.

The nurse pushes past me to the side of his bed and pulls a pair of gloves from the dispenser on the wall. Looking down at him she says, "Did we make a puddle?"

Because you wouldn't move your fat ass, I want to say.

I back into the corridor and pull the door closed. A dry-erase board hanging on the back has Hugh Birdsong scrawled in black marker. The last patient's name is still visible underneath.

A woman in baggy sweatpants walks high on her toes, pushing her husband's wheelchair. He's slumped down, staring at the pale blue blanket draped over his knees.

"How far before you get to the elevator, I wonder?" she asks no one in particular.

I can't help peering into the room across the hall. "This place is a torture palace, huh?" the patient says. His wife gives me a disgusted look and yanks the privacy curtain closed. I lean my back against the wall and close my eyes. I'm so deathly hung over I could puke.

The nurse opens the door and nods me back in. A short man with coarse black hair and a sunburned face steps in behind me. Frank Alden, MD, according to his nametag.

"I'm Dr. Alden," he says importantly, as if MD stands for Minor Deity.

"Nice to meet you. I'm Ms. Birdsong," I say. "What's wrong with my father?"

"We need to set his left ankle. It's broken in two places. Hit his head, too. We know that much." He trains his eyes on me like I'm a criminal. "No one's been helping the man with his blood pressure medication. He's dehydrated, his blood sugar's through the roof, and he has an enlarged prostate."

"What? Is he all right?" I try not to sound defensive.

"Clearly, he is not. We're ruling out a stroke, but we're running tests to see what else is out of whack." He flips the sheets on his clipboard.

"A stroke?" I lean in, careful he doesn't smell my breath.

With one foot on the floor, he stretches to the hand sanitizer hanging on the wall and pumps it twice. "Has he had one before?"

"He's fine," I say, not knowing if I'm lying or not.

"He was very disoriented when he came in and couldn't answer a lot of the questions we asked. Has he been diagnosed with Alzheimer's?"

"Of course not. He's only seventy-four." I look at my dad. Nothing. "Maybe he forgets things, but Alzheimer's? No way."

"Age may have nothing to do with it," the doctor says matter-of-factly. "Sometimes conditions can be exacerbated by strokes and head injuries. Maybe you'd like to see what I'm talking about?" He takes a pen from his pocket. Modern Healthcare is printed on the side. "I wonder if you could answer some questions for me, Mr. Birdsong."

My dad looks distrustful. "I'll do the best I can." He shifts his rear in the bed and adjusts the sheets.

"Are there any tragedies in the news right now?

Hurricane Katrina. I want to blurt out the answer.

"Not that I know of," Dad answers slowly.

"He's never watched much television," I say.

Dr. Alden respectfully consults his clipboard. "Can you tell me the name of our president, Mr. Birdsong?"

He starts to answer, then his face goes blank. He looks to me for help.

I flinch. It's like an electric shock goes through me.

"It's George Bush, sir." Dr. Alden pauses. "George W. Bush." He emphasizes the W.

My dad snaps his fingers. "Good God. Of course it is." He looks like a little boy.

Dr. Alden acknowledges me with a quick nod. He poises his pen. "Sir, is our country involved in war?"

"Probably," Dad says. "With a Republican in the White House."

Man-to-man, Dr. Alden looks him in the eye. "Mr. Birdsong, what year are we in?"

"Come on. You know this one." I touch his knee. The sheet is cold.

Dad's eyes are cloudy and his mouth is set in a straight line. He turns his head and stares at the wall.

Dr. Alden takes his pulse, checking his gold watch. I feel every tick of the second hand. He drops Dad's wrist and looks at me. "Why don't you give us a minute?" he says.

I walk out, leaving it open a crack. I peer around the edge. Dr. Alden unfastens the blood pressure cuff from Dad's bicep, taps the intravenous tube, then presses the stethoscope to his back. He moves it to another spot, and listens again. Satisfied, he helps him ease back onto the pillows.

It's time to get Richard on the phone. I swallow hard and dial his number. I'd really give anything if he wouldn't pick up this time. If I could just leave a message. Dizzy, I close my eyes and lean my arm against the wall and my head on top of that. That hospital smell suddenly fills my nostrils.

I jump at the sound of Richard's deep voice.

"Did you wreck my car?" he says.

"Hell, no. It's Dad. He crashed his cycle and broke his leg. He's at Seton."

"Is he okay?" he says quickly. "What the hell happened?"

"I'm piecing it together. EMS picked him up. And there's more than the leg. He might have hit his head. He's not remembering his meds. Or much else, for that matter," I cry. "Rich, he can't remember jack shit. We have to take his keys away."

I'm startled when the door to the next room slams. I look to the nurses' station and they're raising their fingers to their lips to shush me.

"You're hysterical, Jules," he says. "So, Dad has memory problems. He's never mentioned anything to me about getting lost."

"If he can't remember he's getting lost, he probably wouldn't be telling you about it, now would he?"

He exhales loudly. "Now suddenly you're the expert?"

I imagine Richard's dark eyes. His comments cut me cold.

"You better take good care of him, Jules."

"Rich, how dare you say that? You know I will."

"I have to run. My taxi's here. Keep me posted." He clicks off.

Hanging up, I feel so tired. An orderly collects plates off the floor and stacks them next to towels and toilet paper on his cart. I'm struck by the similarity of hospitals and hotels.

"Ms. Birdsong, may I have a word?" Dr. Alden joins me in the hall. "We'll keep him here and run some tests."

"Tests?" I say. "This is all coming so fast. Is this normal?"

He takes off his glasses and rubs his eyes. "What's normal? If you find out, I hope you'll enlighten me. In any case, I'll make a list of professionals you may want to talk to," he says. "I told him that driving is out of the question."

"I would think so," I say.

Dr. Alden looks down, making a couple of quick marks on the chart. "He wasn't happy to hear his current living arrangements are no longer workable either."

My eyes tick across the trees in the courtyard just outside the window. Their falling leaves. The branches sway.

"I'm sorry, what did you say just now?"

He frowns over his clipboard, like I'm the most clueless person in the world. I raise my hand to my mouth. My father can't live by himself. That's what he's saying.

He slides the clipboard into the metal rack on the door, then pokes his head back inside. "Thank you, Mr. Birdsong," he calls.

"Come back and see us," Dad says in a friendly voice.

I start to say something when Dr. Alden pivots and starts down the hall. I want to pull him back. But, if I did, what would I even say? That I'm married to an asshole? That my kids don't have a mother? And now this?

Watching his starched, white coat until he turns the corner, I don't expect it when he turns around and strides back toward me. He stretches out both hands and takes mine. "It's a sticky wicket, no doubt about it. But your father's getting good care here. Take comfort in that." His face somber, Dr. Alden drops my hands gently. And he's gone.

The patterned linoleum under my feet seems to swell. Then, dreamlike, as if I'm floating on the ceiling watching it happen, I read Hugh Birdsong on the door, afraid that by touching the knob, it will fall off in my hand.

I force myself through the door and inch toward the edge of the bed. Dad reaches for the plastic cup of water and I place it in his hands.

He clears his throat. "He doesn't look old enough to be a doctor."

"They never do." I shake my head. "Listen, they'll take good care of you here, okay? He said so. You take blood pressure medicine? Are you eating right?"

I wonder if I can trust what he'll say.

"As far as I know," he says, his voice getting thinner. He fiddles with his gown.

"Are you in pain? Have you had a stroke before?"

"I'm not a doctor."

"How did the accident happen," I say. "Where were you going?"

He coughs phlegm into the cup of water and looks at it. "I feel like death."

"I know, and I'm sorry," I say. "Give me that." I toss it in the bathroom trash and fill another cup.

Has he had accidents before? How many? I study him. He looks so small here, although he's six foot two. I drag the side chair to the bed and pull my hair brush from my purse. Before I can raise it to his head, he grabs it and drops it on the bed. I shrug and take it back, then lift my fingers to my throat. Remembering, I hold them out and look at them. My three broken nails. The twins. Oh, the twins.

"I know it's not the greatest time," I say slowly, "but I've got a problem."

"Me, too. Stand in line." Pressing his chapped lips together, he blinks at me through his smudged glasses, lenses barely large enough to cover his eyeballs. I motion for him to hand them to me. I wipe them clean, hold them back out to him, and he ignores them.

"What's that smell on you?" he asks. "Is that gin, for Christ's sake?"

"No, but thank you for asking, Detective Birdsong."

He lifts my hair to his nose, and I pull from his reach.

"You're not smoking, are you?" He wrinkles his nose and the crease between his brows deepens. "What a nasty, disgusting habit."

I start to say that I only smoke when I drink.

"I didn't get the impression you thought it was a disgusting habit last night."

"What the hell are you talking about?" he says gruffly.

"The woman who was in the house when I called last night?"

He squints at me. "Woman? There hasn't been a woman since your mother died."

I try staring him down but he doesn't waver.

"Just forget it," I say. Probably not the best choice of words.

He wads up his tissue and throws it at me. I jump.

Well, what was going on, then?

I continue watching him as he tries moving his leg. After a few moments, he touches the needle on the back of his hand.

"When can I take this damn thing out?" he says.

I thump the bag of liquid with my finger. "When they're finished pumping you full of whatever's in here, I guess."

"Yeah, so I can piss it all over these lousy, cheap-ass sheets."

There's a television remote on the side table. He frowns at it, punching several buttons to no avail. "Damn thing," he says.

I grab it from his hand and hold it as far from my face as possible, but I still can't read the buttons. Hurling it at the television suspended from the ceiling, the remote clatters to the floor. I squeeze my hand over my mouth.

Dad slides on his glasses. "What's wrong with you?"

Like air escaping a balloon, I say, "Oliver and I are getting a divorce."

He sucks air through his teeth. "Oh, my stars. What do you want to do that for?"

"It's complicated," I say slowly. "He's difficult."

"The man is a beast," he says angrily. "I could smell it a mile away. I never liked the way he looked at you."

I never much liked the way he looked at Mother, either.

"Can I come to your house? Not for long, I swear," I say. "Until I get things sorted out."

He eyes me, rubbing the cleft in his chin, as if he couldn't be more surprised at what he's hearing. It's not at all what he expected his daughter to say.

"Here's the thing. Oliver kicked me out of the house."

He grips the rails vigorously. Rising up in bed, he winces in pain.

I press my fingers to my tear ducts, but it doesn't help. There's only gray. The walls. The dingy sheets. His hair. His messy beard. And now, his eyes.

My mouth crumples. "It feels like crap having to crawl here asking you for help."

"That's what I'm here for, Jules."

"No, it's not." My voice cracks. "Thank you, but it still feels like crap."

It sounds like such a minor thing, but I've never spoken like that to him before. From my deepest heart. I rest my head on the rails. I can't look at him. He pats me tenderly on the head like you would a puppy and it sends me over the edge. My shoulders begin to shake.

"You come stay with me," he says.

I peek up at him and he's smiling.

"We'll have fun," he chuckles. "I'll put you to work."

We stay like that for a few minutes. His hand is warm on my head. Soon, he's drifted off and I'm grateful, because I can't break down again.

I jot a quick note telling him I'll be back. Setting it on the nightstand, I see a message for me to call Sammy Sanchez, his old boss from the CPA firm. Alongside is my dad's key ring. I stare at it long and hard.

Someone has to get his motorcycle off the street and back in his driveway. Yippee. Looks like it's me.

# CHAPTER FOUR

◆ ◆ ◆

Peeling the black Chanel sunglasses from my face, I stare up my childhood home. Overgrown branches tent the house, dense with round, gray moss balls that hang from spindly limbs like tangled, tendriled Medusa heads. The tin roof is ochre with sap and pollen, though I don't remember it ever being shiny. Completely covered with ivy, I could swear the house had shutters once, but it's impossible to tell.

Two stories straight up and down with a high front stoop and a porch that wraps around the front, the house measures sixteen hundred feet, tops, hardly enough to hold the jagged memories of growing up here. Shrunken tight, it always felt like the walls were closing in. When reality was monstrous. Jump and the net will be there. People say that, but it's bullshit.

I take a deep breath. Climbing the steps, I notice the cracked stucco columns are crusted with dried cicada shells and spider webs. Standing on the porch, I peer through the rusted tear in the screen, and it's as if sticky fingers are pulling me inside. The screen slaps shut behind me, followed by a tiny echo. I'm a grown woman and I'm moving back home.

Swinging my hand over the newel post, I glide my palm up the smooth banister. Catching myself at the landing, I look down at the dark living room. The floral sofa, coffee table and side chairs seem eerily like doll furniture. Sun from the windows casts leaf-shaped silhouettes across the worn carpet.

Upstairs, I cross the hall to mine and Richard's old bathroom, ugly as it ever was with its pink speckled tile and worn grout. You've got to be kidding me. The same toilet brush holder is behind the pink toilet. My Clairol Kindness hot rollers are on the counter with my Hollywood makeup mirror. I open the vanity drawer. Noxema in a blue jar. Corn Silk powder and Big Lash mascara with the pink tube and green wand. Charlie cologne. Charlie? What was I thinking? I pull back the dingy shower curtain. No whirlpool jets or hand-held shower on this tub. Is that seriously Herbal Essence shampoo in the soap dish?

I'm in hell.

Now my room. Even better. The purple shag carpet, still spongy like an old bath towel. My violet drapes with the little yellow daisies, how I remember those. I'll be sleeping on my little twin bed under the poster of Danny Zucko from *Grease*.

There's my old Pioneer stereo I used to think was the coolest thing ever. I run my fingers across my old Stevie Wonder albums. Doobie Brothers and Elton John. Yearbooks and class composites, and a homecoming mum. A metal Slinky ready to walk down the stairs. Things left behind I didn't remember I'd missed. It's a diorama of me, stopping at age eighteen. The age of my arrested development.

I think of Lindsey. She and Adam are forever stuck in the front of my mind. What am I doing here in this room? I'm in hell, all right, and I'll be roasting there for eternity for leaving my twins. Screw you, Oliver.

Seeing the center drawer of my nightstand, I turn away and focus on the dinky closet that's scarcely big enough for my shoes. Since Dad's never been a clothes horse, I'm sure finding space in his closet won't be a problem.

I push open the door to his room.

It's like a cyclone hit.

Dirty cups and plates are everywhere, and I mean everywhere, plus silver Pop-Tart wrappers, a couple of quart-sized Neapolitan ice cream cartons and a can of Hershey's. There's no sheets on the bed and a week's worth of newspapers is wadded in the blankets. Dad's blue striped robe is at the bottom of the bed with a house slipper sticking out underneath. A mountain of dirty clothes is heaped on the chair and the rest of the closet is on the floor. The television's blaring. I switch it off.

I brace myself against the door frame to the bathroom and flip the switch. Cloudy water stands in the sink, clogged with hair and whiskers and the mirror is splattered with years of toothpaste. Bending down, I pick up stiff, mildewed towels and toss them in the tub. Soap on a rope hangs from the shower head. The huge bowel movement in the toilet takes three flushes to go down.

Seeing her sanitized, clean-room like this, my mother would come unglued. Maybe this is Dad's passive-aggressive way of giving her the finger.

51

Oh, gracious. What about the kitchen? I trudge downstairs.

From the doorway, I can already smell rotting food. A couple of roaches crawl up the side of the refrigerator. The big kind.

I peer over the edge of the cast-iron sink. Fritos and roaches are swimming in a bowl of—is that milk? A blue china mug is caked with black, and there's a chicken pot pie and a half-eaten can of Wolf Brand. I check the backsplash for a disposer switch and hell no, he hasn't put one in. I pull down the squeaky oven door, and I've never seen anything quite like it. Yes I have. It's called a barbeque pit. There's no telling how long the meatloaf has been in there. Assuming that's what it is.

Opening the cabinet under the sink, I cup my hand to my mouth. Spoiled fish sticks are spilling out of the garbage. There's a half cantaloupe with its slimy seeds and a carton of rancid onion dip.

Ants drip single-file to the floor.

I start scraping rotten food into the can. Retching, I think I may heave. I yank the bag out of the can and fuck it! The stupid thing splits open and vomits all over my cute sandals.

Good God. Are there rubber gloves? Tongs? A toilet plunger?

Aren't there usually housekeepers for situations like this?

Oh forget it. I kneel down and use my hands. Ants bite me from my knuckles to my elbows and I wildly brush them to the floor.

"Dammit, Oliver!" I scream. "Screw you again!"

I kick the door open and carry the can down the driveway, dump it in the trash cart at the end, horrified that Dad's the only tacky neighbor with his still on the curb. Dragging it back to the house, I see a stiff cotton mop hanging over the wooden fence. I peel it off and slivers of paint come with it. I throw it in the dirt.

I step onto the porch and drop to the hanging swing. A breeze blows the wind chimes and I remember their split personality: Maddening sirens or calming church bells, it all depends. I lean back and close my eyes.

"Ivy will strangle a house if you let it," my dad said. "It will seal off the windows, burst through the roof, and overtake everything." Then a cross look came over his face. "You'd love that though, Carmen, wouldn't you?" But, Lord knows he always left every damn chance he got. And, since home was where I was, it meant he didn't want to be with me.

I'm the one who brought the ivy home. Knowing ivy thrives in the shade, my mother said to plant it on the east side of the house, the side without the sun. By the time my dad discovered it, it was too late.

When I came home from college that horrible summer, I needed him more than I ever had, but he'd wrapped himself so tightly in grief, there was no room in his arms for me. Everything about it pissed me off. Seemed like a total act to me—too little, too late. His same M.O.—selfish. That's right, selfish.

I find myself wondering what my mother would think about what I'm doing. She understood how it feels to be born female. An outsider. She understood being married to a man who ignores her feelings. But would she approve? Would she be proud of me? I seriously doubt it.

My dad's prophecy was right. Strong, tangled vines encased the house and boarded-up the windows. But, how is it now that he's the one left behind the ivy, and I, after being ripped feet first from my comfortable existence, am hurled back here with him?

Today, I wish it was the maddening siren of a fire truck I heard, coming to rescue me to take me away from this place. But, it's clear I'm not going anywhere, and no help's on the way.

# CHAPTER FIVE

❖ ❖ ❖

---

The mahogany desk is large enough to seat a family of ten. It holds not just a telephone, but a multi-buttoned console, a Rolodex the size of a toaster and an adding machine the size of two, plus a pair of mechanical typewriters. But, no computer. Loose papers and green ledger sheets are towered sky-high, and on the top floor, like a cannibal's trophy on a stick, is the brown, shriveled head of Sammy Sanchez.

His tortoiseshell glasses blend seamlessly with his mottled cheeks. Instead of a necktie, he wears a leather bolo with a tigers-eye slide to hold his collar together. Under his Roman nose is a moustache that's as white and thin as dental floss and twirled on both ends.

At last, I have a face to put with the stern, heavily-accented voice that would call our house night and day, summoning my dad to the office like he's now done me, as if I were on his payroll or something. I try doing the math on the 1938 Harvard diploma on the wall and give up. Well, I don't care what age the old buzzard is, I'm not taking any behavior off him. My dad wouldn't want me to. I just know it.

"Good morning, Señor Sanchez," I say.

He scowls at his watch, then me. "Good afternoon, Juliana."

He pronounces my name with an "ah," just like my mother. Really pisses me off when people do that. It's pronounced Julie-Ann-a, with a short "a" in the third syllable. I mean, it's not that big of a deal—why can't people just get it right?

"It's Juliana," I correct him. And, being that I'm two minutes late, not two hours, I ignore his good afternoon crap and look him straight in the eye.

Like doing the breast stroke, he parts the tall stacks of paper, extends his hand through the middle, and no smiles, we just shake.

Taking the seat opposite him, I smooth my pink, silk skirt and return my sunglasses to my purse. Looking around the office, I note the drab, uninspired color palette. File cabinets, walls, switch plates, upholstery and carpet, all the same. Like oatmeal. And, a chair this uncomfortable means he prefers short meetings. It's probably past his naptime already. The pompous old raisin.

"So, tell me, how is that divorce of yours coming along?" He looks over his glasses. "I presume that you keep a watchful eye on your finances."

I don't have to tell him shit. But, like undressing in the doctor's office, I'd rather not, but I do it anyway.

"We're not exactly hurting for money, if that's what you mean," I say stiffly. "My husband is a very competent money manager."

Whistling through the gap in his front teeth, he scrawls blue words on a legal pad, tears off the page, creases it precisely, and slides it under his crystal paper weight.

"Exactly the reason you may wish to call in a forensic team," he says.

I blink.

"Husbands have refinanced the family home and moved the equity into their business. Quite often, they will set up separate bank accounts with separate mailing addresses. It is called insurance." He pauses soberly. "You would think more women would do it, instead of being stupid, trusting imbeciles."

Looking at his purple-veined hands, I ball mine into fists. It's all I can do not to snatch the paper weight and bop the old fart on the head with it.

"Well, let us get down to it, what do you say?" he says.

"Let's."

Loosening his bolo tie, he takes a deep breath. "Hugh came to me to prepare for when he became incapable of making decisions. He said, and I quote, 'I don't want to be a wart on anyone's ass.'"

That sounds like my dad, all right.

There's a black and white photograph on the credenza behind him.

Señor Sanchez follows my gaze. "We have no choice who we fall in love with, do we? The third Mrs. Sanchez divorced me ten lifetimes ago, and it still hurts. Right here." Wincing, he shoves an imaginary knife through his chest.

When I don't react, he coughs uncomfortably and turns back to the photo. "Good looking kids, don't you think?"

I read the caption: *Company Picnic 1956, Carmen Mata & Hugh Birdsong.*

He hesitates, then carefully hands the silver frame across the desk. "You should have it."

"Are you sure?" I say.

"I have plenty of their pictures." He taps his temple. "Up here."

My dad is standing behind my mother in the photo with his hands on her shoulders. It must have been a breezy day because his hair is flying. Wearing a pale suit and dark tie, he grins at the camera like he owns the world. Smooth waves swept back, my mother's lovely face is upturned and she's smiling, clearly flirting with him.

Seeing her look so happy makes me sad somehow.

"They asked me to keep an eye on her, your grandparents. When they shipped her up from Monterrey for The University of Texas. Poor, homesick señorita."

"You knew my grandparents?" I'd never met anyone who had.

He nods his head and purses his lips. "They would not let her come home, like it was a test or something," he says. "Then they went and died on her."

Not exactly meaning to, I stroke the glass.

"She had learned perfect English before she ever got here, but she never could get the hang of the slang, as they say. The universal language of numbers was her comfort zone. There is always one correct answer." He taps his pen on the adding machine for emphasis.

"Your mother started here when she was about twenty-one. I was ninety then, I believe," he snorts. "She had more smarts than every woman in the office, and definitely, the men. Maybe even your old man, but you did not hear it from me." He smiles knowingly. "Tall and handsome, he had an inflated ego as it was. Every secretary was loco for him. But, your mother being a confident, competent woman, they were not always so friendly to her."

He must have my mother confused with someone else. Competent? Okay. But, confident?

Seeing my expression, he draws an X over his heart. "Their same house on Avenue C? She put the money down from her savings. The down payment, you understand. Earned every penny herself."

I've never met the woman in this picture he's talking about.

He motions to the picture. "Here, let me see that again."

I raise it toward him.

56

"Not accepted so much back then to marry a Latina, but your father always follows his heart." He smiles to himself. "The day I caught them in the supply closet." His chuckle turns into a coughing fit, but he manages to choke out, "Ay Chihuahua!"

He pours himself a glass of water, chugs it, and does it again. Raising his eyebrows at me, he points to the pitcher.

I mouth "no thanks," hoping he'll hold off dying until he finishes the story.

"Carmen was the best employee I ever had, although she was much more than that. She was my goddaughter, you know."

Yep, I heard that a time or two.

Shaking his head, he continues, "It was the time of the traditional family and a wife working meant a husband could not support his family," he says. "Besides, for Latinas, home and family are number one." He slaps his desk. "Not negotiable."

Okay, that's more like it. That's the woman I remember.

I look down at her face again. She's so beautiful.

Sifting through the files on his desk, he runs his nimble fingers across their perfectly-typed tabs. Finding the right one, he hands an envelope over the desk. "I have here what I would like to call Hugh's Letter to the Future."

My dad's handwriting, all right, I open it and begin reading.

It begins, "When I was diagnosed with Alzheimer's disease, I cried and said goodbye to myself."

Oh, Dad, I didn't know. I didn't even try.

Swallowing hard, I slip it back in the envelope and into my purse. Not here, I prefer to read his words in private.

At the next file tab, my heart falters. It says Funeral Home. Oh, no.

I imagine Dad walking through the doors of that awful place. Down the long hallway with the pink carpet. The same room lined with caskets. The gruesome task of choosing his own.

"It is all paid for. But, we are probably getting a little ahead of ourselves." Señor Sanchez says matter-of-factly. "You will want the neurology report. Trust me, you do not want to start from scratch."

Cheeks hot, I begin skimming it. Is this true? Hugh Birdsong's name is on top, so it must be.

"There is something else, Juliana." There's that incorrect pronunciation again. "Your father gave you decision-making authority over his affairs."

I look up. "Me? There's got to be a mistake. Managing his money and investments?" I say. "What about Richard?"

"There is no a mistake." Opening his mouth like he's about to say something else, he shuts it again.

The next file is marked Sagecrest Alzheimer's Facility.

"He's not that bad," I say.

Señor Sanchez pours me the water after all, and slides it in front of me. "Yet," he says.

I turn to the next page. "There's a deposit receipt and a contract with his signature," I say loudly.

"Ready to pull the trigger when it is time." He doesn't blink.

"The trigger?" I tilt my head to the side.

"It was his way of telling you that he would understand your choices, whatever they may be," he says gently. "He wanted to let you off the hook, knowing what he himself would do in your position."

"Put him away?" I shake my head fiercely "No. I won't do it. Ever."

Señor Sanchez' voice is grave. "We had disagreements over the years, but I know Hugh better than anyone," he says. "He knew that by giving you his Power of Attorney, it would force you back into his life."

There's a box of tissues on the edge of his desk. Taking one, I begin separating its thin layers. It's how I feel, myself.

"These arrangements speak to his state of mind, I am sorry to say. For obvious reasons."

"Being?"

He clears his throat. "There being no money for it, of course."

I scrutinize his face, the crazy old coot.

"His substantial monetary investment in your brother's South Congress condominium complex?"

Waiting for my recognition, he wrinkles his brow.

"What are you talking about?"

"It was not a project I would ever recommend to a client. I did not like it from the start." He runs a smooth hand over his thin, white hair. "I would not want to speak out of turn, but you may wish to have a sit-down with Ricardo. In many ways, it was a rough time on him, as well."

I take hold of his desk. "Since he's not here right now, how about you tell me?"

"Real estate bust. The condos went south. A bad partnership. Being a man of pride and principles, he refused to declare bankruptcy."

"My dad is broke? You can't be serious."

I'm getting the feeling that he is.

Señor Sanchez uses a monogrammed handkerchief to wipe his lips. "Your father's house is the collateral on his loans and he will lose it, too, if his creditors are not paid." He grimaces. "To the tune of about thirty-two hundred dollars a month. Right now he is three payments behind."

I wave my arm across the paperwork. "I'm expected to pick up the ball now? Pay for everything across the board?" It's impossible to keep my voice down. "I can't anymore. What am I supposed to do?"

He stares at me, pity on his face. "I could not say, young lady."

Torch me.

I pull my purse over my shoulder with my parents' photo sticking out the top and stand to go.

"Did you get a ticket from the garage?" Señor Sanchez says softly.

He validates it with his parking stamp, then plants his cane firmly on the carpet and slowly rounds his desk.

My shoulders are limp when he hugs me. He pulls a handkerchief from his pocket, shakes out the folds and hands it to me. But I don't cry in front of people. I don't.

He looks at me closely. "Your resemblance to your father is so striking that up until now, you had not reminded me of Carmen," he says, his accent more pronounced.

I jerk my head away. "I'm nothing like her."

As I head to the door, I hear him mutter, "It is not fair. None of it."

Walking down the corridor, I tick off the names posted on the doors. Not expecting my father's name, my heart catches. I crack the door, and like a little girl, I peer inside the still darkness, hoping to find him there. The stranger, in his life I never knew. I flip the overhead switch, but the bulb's gone out. Heading to the slatted blinds at the window, I bump into my father's chair. I'm tempted to sit down, but it seems wrong. Like disturbing the room of a child who's died.

A sliver of sunlight from the blinds hits the crystal prism nameplate on his desk and makes a sparkling rainbow. Reflecting to the space above his desk, a painting that hid in the shadows now glows.

I stumble in and stumble out when the elevator doors open, close and finally open again. Stepping from the Littlefield Building to the sidewalk, I shield my eyes, and search Congress Avenue for my car until I remember it's in the damn garage. Entering the crosswalk up ahead, of all people to see, it's Kimberley Singleton, wearing a bright, turquoise suit and dynamite strappy sandals. There's a wiggle in her walk.

"Hey Kimberley," I call above the noisy traffic.

Turning, she smiles and tickles the air with her pinky.

"Know a good divorce attorney?"

She's the perfect person to ask.

"Stephen used Anabel Brock. I hate her."

"Thanks," I holler back. "I'll give her a call."

# CHAPTER SIX

◆ ◆ ◆

---

The tiny woman sitting alongside me on the plaid sofa in the lobby of Sagecrest Alzheimer's Facility is named Mrs. Calloway. Her blue eyes magnified comically behind her thick lenses, she stares at me intently. Her Christmas tree pin is the same one Oliver's mother wears, but Christmas was months ago.

Hearing a male voice in the front foyer, she looks up expectantly. Not him, she turns back to me.

"My son's taking me to lunch," she says.

"Where's he taking you?" I ask.

She smoothes her lap with dainty hands. "He knows good places to eat."

I start to speak, but she looks again to the foyer. Still not him, she takes my arm and leans in like she's telling me a secret.

"I fall asleep all the time," she says. "I never used to, but lately I do it even when I'm in the middle of talking to someone."

"You do?"

"Oh, yes." She smiles brightly. "I'm asleep right now."

"Really?" I'm not sure what else to say.

"Not everyone here is bad off, dear. I'm what they simply call 'out to lunch,'" she says. "But, for many of the residents, unfortunately, it's breakfast and dinner, too."

Hearing another male voice, we both look up this time. Pushing fifty, bearded with a long lion's mane and large, white teeth, the man could pass for the tall, good-looking Bee Gee from *Saturday Night Fever*, sans the unbuttoned silk shirt.

He introduces himself as Mr. Read, the Sagecrest director there to greet me. When he says he's looking forward to seeing my father again, I want to tell him he can take a big flying leap. But, I agree to his fifty-cent tour. Self-punishment, I guess. Dad suffered through coming here, so I can, too.

Down the corridor, I begin sniffing the air like a Glade commercial. If one of these places smells like urine, it's probably time to kiss it goodbye.

Mr. Read points out the collages on a resident's door—a happy bride and groom, a handsome young man in uniform, a young girl on a bicycle. He seems nice enough. I guess they wouldn't hire an asshole for his job.

"Research shows a residential setting is soothing to the residents." He smiles with his big, white perfect teeth. "We do our best to make Sagecrest warm and cozy. Like home."

I try to focus on what he's saying, but I'm distracted by a loud mumbling in the lobby. Checking over my shoulder, I realize it's coming from a big man with reddish stubble slumped low in a corduroy wing-chair. Staring straight ahead, his eyes are lined with drippy red. Dressed in a cheery yellow sweat suit, the man's sneakers seem to weigh down the floor like bags of cement.

Anguish on his face, he suddenly begins yelling, "Lord, help me be a better me! Lord, help me be a better me!"

As his haunting voice follows us down the hall, I wonder who the man was before. And what he did or didn't do.

The past is alive in this place. Yesterday is today.

We pass a woman in a wheelchair holding a lifelike, rubber baby. Her hands are gnarled and her nails are thick and long. Catching me looking at her, she clutches the baby to her heart. Another woman with long, gray braids coiled around her head looks straight off *The Waltons*. I wink at her and she winks back. A youngish, dark-haired man doesn't when I smile at him. Groping his pocket, he brings out a bent cigarette with much of the tobacco fallen out. He pokes it in the corner of his mouth and puffs.

I try to block the image of my dad living here from my mind. Looking at the newspaper, then again, brand new each time. The easy-chairs in the lobby have crocheted doilies on the armrests and the walls are papered in gingham, but this could never be Dad's home. How do these people do it?

Don't stare too long or their sadness will swallow you, and you'll be sitting face to face with them, then directly across from your own reflection. It's scary as hell.

I hover next to Mr. Read. He's the only shield between me and my emotions. We stop in the recreation room. Men and women are playing bingo, grouped together at small tables.

I wonder what it's like, having to make new friends at their age, like kids dropped off at summer camp. They probably don't feel like it. Especially in a place like this where people's hearing isn't so great. Not only that, but no one can remember you and you can't remember them.

Along the wall, is a long table scattered with bingo cards. In the middle, a large-boned woman sits alone. Her hair is faded charcoal, and her pale skin is smooth and waxy. She has no eyebrows at all. I imagine her penciling them in each morning in her bathroom mirror. When she was who she was. Three cards are spread before her, like she's playing solitaire. She carefully lifts each one. Then, as if she's placing a stamp on a letter, she tries her damndest to put each one back where it was before, but it doesn't work that way. She tries again.

The bingo leader reaches into a clear, plastic air machine of dancing Ping-pong balls. She calls out the lucky number, "B-15" She glances across the tables like a kindergarten teacher. "B-15. Anybody got a winner?"

I watch a wrinkled man run a slow finger down each row of his card. The next man over grunts, slides him a red checker and taps the proper square.

Mr. Read says, "The residents come here every day to play this game. Sometimes twice."

"Looks like they're darn serious about it, too."

He smiles broadly. "You better believe it," he says. "Winning means a peppermint stick."

Recognizing his voice, smiling women look up from their cards and wave. As if taking an encore, he bows theatrically and throws them kisses.

I take in a large, grand photo that hangs on the wall of a stately judge in long black robes swinging a gavel in front of the U.S. flag and seal. Mr. Read touches my elbow and points to the woman turning the bingo cards. I'm still watching her over my shoulder as he guides me out the door.

One last room on the corridor.

"This is where the residents eat their meals."

I force a smile.

Serving tables are lined cafeteria-style against the far wall, their dull, metal chafing dishes stacked on top. And, the glasses aren't glass. They're that thick, hard plastic kind. The plates, too, in that awful putty color. Each table has a lonely vase of carnations.

"And while I'm thinking of it, if your father has medications, we administer them, too." Mr. Read checks his watch. "We bring everyone down around five o'clock. The menu's not exactly four-star, but it's balanced and has the nutrients they need."

"So you're saying the food's pretty poor, then?" I ask.

"You can try it," he says pleasantly. "Be our guest for lunch one day."

I force another smile.

Highly unlikely, since I plan to forget I was ever here.

I really wish we'd skipped the living quarters. White walls and naked mattresses. Bare-bones like a college dorm. Mr. Read flips on the bathroom's overhead fluorescent. Ammonia stings my nostrils. Stand-up shower has fiberglass walls, a grab bar and a bench. Toilet is seat only. No lid.

"We help them bathe them every other day. Or more." He lowers his voice discreetly. "Depending on the circumstances."

I whisper, "I think I understand what you mean."

It's all I can take.

Down the hall to his office, I watch my shoes.

Once inside, I begin listing all my dad's problems. Knowing he's not going to get better, it's a bitter pill. Alzheimer's. You can fight it, but you can't beat it, and that's the ugly truth.

I'm feeling numb, somehow detached, like a canvas tent snapped loose from its stakes. Kind Mr. Read must've seen it a hundred times, but you'd never know it. He speaks slowly, but I only get bits and pieces. Things like, Denial is Potent, and Master Plan.

A leaf blows against the window. Flat against the glass, it's the size of my hand. And, like a fist, it hits me hard.

I could get it one day.

And, Richard, too.

What about Lindsey and Adam?

Mr. Read's final words are the hardest of all to hear:

"It will be like leading a frightened horse out of a burning barn."

This falls to me. How will I take care of my father?

Hugh Birdsong, the stranger he's always been.

I grip the arms of the wooden chair.

Lord, help me be a better me.

# CHAPTER SEVEN

❖ ❖ ❖

---

I'm punching the doorbell on Richard and Wally's front porch with a bundle of roses in my arms. Their music's cranked up so loud inside, I doubt they even hear it. Wally called before they boarded their plane from San Diego and invited me to dinner. Deciding I needed a break from driving past my house, excuse me, *Oliver's* house, I said okay.

I finally give up and walk on in. Wally's adjusting the knobs on the living room stereo, rocking his skinny hips to the Latin beat, wearing starched khaki shorts and spiffy violet button-down.

Even though we grew up together, him across the street, somehow it's like I'm seeing him for the first time. I've been by several times, including sleeping here the other night. But Oliver, the kids and I have never been invited for dinner. I hadn't really thought about it much. Until now.

Hand on the switch, I flip the lights off and on a few times.

Wally quickly spins around and begins dancing toward me, shaking imaginary maracas in his hands. Laughing, I do the same, the best I can with roses in my arms.

"A girl after my own heart," he says. Sniffing them deeply, his fair lashes sparkle behind his black-framed, Buddy Holly glasses.

Maybe Wally's not conventionally handsome with his close-set eyes and weak chin, but his eyes are bluer than colored contacts and his red goatee is trimmed to perfection. Just like Sting may not have the best voice on the radio, you'd never change the station on Wally either.

Hand at the small of my back, he ushers me into the kitchen.

It's one of those modern, Photoshop kitchens. Sleek, black lacquered cabinets, a glass-tiled backsplash and nothing on the marble counters but a bowl of fruit. A mod crystal chandelier hangs over the island. It's bright pink and I love it.

Wally unfurls a linen tablecloth onto the breakfast table.

Guessing correctly, I open the drawer by the dishwasher and find the knives and forks. Heavy, gleaming silver. The good stuff. As I begin setting the places, he comes behind me with a pair of candlesticks.

"Want to tell me what's wrong, Jules?" he says.

Adam needs help with his research paper. It's due tomorrow, and when I proofread Lindsey's on Tuesday, he hadn't even looked at the assignment sheet yet. I check my watch. I wonder if they found the silly lunch boxes I snuck in and left on their beds earlier—Scooby Do for Adam with M&M's inside and Hello Kitty for Lindsey stuffed with Skittles. I might know if they'd call me back.

"Maybe over dinner, then," Wally says.

Smiling weakly, I lower my eyes.

"I hope Mexican's all right, since that's what we're having."

He steps to the island where Diana Kennedy's *Cuisines of Mexico* lies open. He flips the pages silently, mouthing the recipes to himself.

One of those faux Andy Warhols hangs on the wall—the types with the four identical photos, each washed in a different pastel. The subject is Richard's yappy Schnauzer, Fritz who springs straight in the air, an inch from my face.

"Yikes. Hey buddy," I say.

Richard rounds the corner into the kitchen and hands the little shit a treat. Rewarding him for almost taking off my nose.

"Let's use our company manners, Fritz," he says. "Remember how we talked about that?"

People who act like their pets are children gag me. Especially when it's an over-indulged, only child. I lower my hand grudgingly and scratch the mutt's pointy ear. He growls.

Richard holds out his cheek to be kissed and his thick, "spent the night in jail" stubble scratches my lips. He keeps it scruffy on purpose because he thinks it looks cool, and it does. Lucky him got my mom's shiny, dark hair which he wears longish and combed straight back. He got her gorgeous olive skin, too, and keeps it that way using every face product available. Standing 6'2" like our dad, he also got his square jaw and cleft chin. It's so true when women say he's too good looking to be straight, and, many have tried to change his mind. I've always hated him for being prettier than me, especially now that I'm about to be back on the market.

"Get you a beer, Jules?" He also got Dad's cool deep voice.

And, did I mention I got our mom's one crummy feature? Measuring barely five-foot-one, it's why I'm always in heels.

He leans into the Subzero. "Wally, seriously, what's this pink crap? It's embarrassing." He picks up a wine cooler like it's a dead ferret.

Wally glances up from the cookbook. "Please ignore him," he says. "I only keep him around to lift heavy objects."

Richard rummages around in the door. "I thought we had some wine in here somewhere."

Nope. And, those wine coolers suck.

"Just give me a beer," I say.

He does, then leans across and snaps Wally's cookbook closed. Clearly peeved, Wally pops him with a kitchen towel.

"Sorry, dear Wally, but I haven't tasted my mother's cooking in years." He knots an apron around my waist. "So, let's get after it, sister."

I chop the onions and chilies while he busies himself frying the tortillas. It's been a while since my brother and I worked side by side, like our mother taught us. The enchiladas will be perfect and so thick with garlic we'll have bad breath for a week.

Wally balances Fritz on his hip and proudly tells me about the retro-vintage shop they're setting up in an old house in the trendy shopping district on South First Street. Everything sounds great until Wally says he finds the inventory on eBay. Okay, I'll reserve judgment until the grand opening, but I predict less Shabby Chic than Shabby Shit.

Richard contributes little to the conversation. Highly unusual for him. After hearing about the South Congress condo debacle, I know he wasn't kidding when he said it's Wally's shop. Having begun amassing distressed properties in his early twenties, Richard has too much pride to admit that he lost everything. His and Dad's everything, too. Hard to take as he can be, I like the old, cocky Richard much better.

He closes up the tortillas in the warming drawer, then suddenly whips around to face me.

"Spill it, Jules," he says.

Ugh. I knew this was coming.

I stall, pointing to the bite of cheese in my mouth. "What?"

"Oh, I don't know," he says. "Maybe start with why you slept here the other night and borrowed the convertible? And, thanks for bringing it back dirty, by the way."

"Did not," I say. "I ran it through the carwash. And, I filled it up."

"How about the bird poop on the windshield?"

"Don't freak out, Rich," I say. "Besides, I can't imagine why you'd want that car in the first place."

He takes a long pull off his beer. "It means something to me. And, I refurbished it, okay? Myself."

"Did you, now?" I say. "Impressive."

Wally nods. "He's done several. He's actually quite good."

Richard twirls his finger in the hurry-up motion. "So you were saying, Jules?"

I continue stirring the enchilada sauce. "Oliver and I are splitting up."

"Figured as much," he says. "So, why is this the first I'm hearing of it?"

"I couldn't admit that I'd failed, Rich." I hesitate. "Not to you."

With everything we've been through, the way he looks at me, I know he understands.

Wally opens me another beer and tosses my empty in the trash. "So, how's Oliver taking it?" he asks.

I try not to tear up. "Just great," I say. "It was his idea."

He reaches for the phone. "Give me his number," he says. "I'm going to kick his flabby butt."

And, he could, too.

Richard crosses his arms over his chest. "It's about time somebody did. I hate the heartless douche-bastard."

Since when? He could've fooled me.

Wally shoots him a look and draws a line across his throat. "Zip it, Birdsong," he says. "Tonight's not about you."

Richard gives him a stiff salute.

I lower my eyes, unable to hold it in any longer. "Oliver kept the twins there with him."

Richard quickly wraps his arm around my shoulder and helps me sit on a bar stool. Not knowing what to do, Wally plucks one of the roses from the vase and sets it on the island in front of me.

"I can't be away from my kids." I put my head in my hands. "Why can't stupid Oliver just leave in the morning before I get up and not come back until I'm in bed? And, leave me the hell alone?"

"You should know that's not how it works," Richard says quietly. "It never does."

I level my gaze at him and he shrugs.

"So, where are you staying," Wally asks gently.

I exhale loudly. "Dad's."

Richard smiles. "Mrs. Morrissey schlepping back to the Hyde Park bungalow?"

I smirk. "Any time you want to come share the bathroom again, feel free. Besides, Dad could use my help, Rich. He's worse than you think."

"And, you're paranoid, like I told you on the phone."

"I don't think so, and neither does he since he made plans to move to Sagecrest," I say tentatively. "With a deposit and everything."

Richard's shocked. "He told you that?"

I shake my head. "Señor Sanchez."

His eyes flash. "Why are you talking to that old bag of assholes?"

I left him an opening to tell me. He didn't take it.

"Señor Sanchez sent for me when Dad was in the hospital. It must have been his cue to hand over his directives," I say. "They're all laid out."

He and Wally trade looks. "Well, you can forget about Sagecrest, Jules," Richard says. "I'd never do that to him."

"Me neither. The thought makes me sick," I say. "Anyway, I'd never do anything without talking to you."

He raises his voice. "What's that supposed to mean? You think you could?"

"Well, yes," I say slowly. "That's what having Power of Attorney means."

His face goes white. "He put you in charge?"

"You didn't know? I figured that's why you're pissed at me."

Wally looks between us.

I slide off my stool and face Richard. "So, what is the reason?"

He shrugs. "Think about it."

I hurl the apron at him and turn on my heel.

Wally dashes after me. "What about the enchiladas?"

Slamming the door, I hear Richard holler, "Thanks for the fucking flowers, Jules!"

# CHAPTER EIGHT

❖   ❖   ❖

It was my mom's office with windows looking to the backyard and two walls of matching bookshelves. Her desk doubled as her sewing table where she made my skirts, pants and dresses. Underneath are old McCalls and Butterick patterns, neatly folded away. Her Singer sits in the corner, collecting dust.

My dad uses it now. The desk, not the sewing machine. Papers are strewn everywhere, littering the desk and the floor. Unopened bills are late-stamped in red. I hate the expression, but it's all gone to pot.

Head spinning, I sit in the middle of the awful mess, not knowing where to begin. First things first. Take care of business. I crack a window and call an old friend. Great multi-tasker that I am, I begin untwisting the phone cord while Mike finishes up a call, since both things will take a while.

He finally answers. "So, I hear your dad's in the hospital."

"How'd you know so fast?"

He slurps his coffee. "Everything okay?"

"Not really. I need to get back up there right now, like I don't have anything else going on," I say. "What about you?"

"If I had a tail, I'd be wagging it," he says drily. "Sorry, but can you make it quick, Juliana? I'm on my way to court."

"Oh, Okay. Well, in case you hadn't heard, I'm getting a divorce," I say with a little laugh.

"I heard a little something about that, and I'm sorry, Juliana," he says. "It absolutely killed me watching you at Pepe's the other night."

"Yeah. Thanks, Mike," I say. "So, what do you think?"

"That talking to you about it would get me into nothing but trouble."

"Mary Ellen's a different story, but I'd never expect *you* to take sides," I say. "Although, if anyone understands what a jerk Oliver can be, it's you."

Waiting for one of his irreverent comments, I hear nothing but his pencil tapping.

"You hold a very special place in my heart, Juliana. You've always known that," he says slowly. "But the truth is, I've taken on Oliver as a client."

I'm sucker-punched.

My voice shakes. "I'm begging you, Mike. You know I don't want this divorce."

I hear him slapping his desk. "Don't you think I tried to change Oliver's mind?" he cries. "I'm the one who told him to get his shit together."

Squeezing the twisted cord in my palm, things begin coming into focus.

"I'm the new case you took on while Oliver stayed in Vegas."

There's nothing but silence on his end.

"Just so you know, Mike, Oliver's adultery accusation is a fabrication."

He exhales loudly. "Of course I know that, Juliana."

"Then, don't do this Mike," I cry. "Why would you?"

"It's called preservation." He pauses. "We're business partners, Oliver and I. Anything that affects the firm affects me."

I've heard at times like these, you find out who your friends are, but I'm not sure I wanted to know.

"I better hang up now," he says. "And, I really am sorry, Juliana. Take care."

Hearing a dial tone, I take the receiver and slam it against the cradle over and over and over and over. Breaking another fingernail, heart throbbing out of my chest, throat so tight I can barely breathe, I bend to put my head between my knees. Then, I jerk straight back up.

A young woman startles me. Leaning against the bookshelf.

I raise my hand to my lips.

Bewildered, I sit back and study her.

She's naked. Flawless. Exposing her perfect breasts. The woman is bent forward with one leg extended and the other drawn to her chest. Thick, dark hair frames her profile, covering her eyes, obscuring part of her face. Such shiny hair. It hangs to her elbows. Beautiful. There's a cigarette between her teeth. And, on her inside ankle is a pair of tiny, red footprints.

How could I not have seen this portrait of my mother before?

I step from behind the desk and crouch down. Gingerly, I put out my hand and touch her. She's smooth. Except the red footprints are slightly tacky, as if freshly painted. I run my finger across a slightly raised scar that stretches diagonally from one corner of the canvas to the other. Flipping it over, I see it's actually a slice that's been patched. Expertly.

I suddenly get goose bumps.

This is the naked woman my father was entertaining the other night.

Just a painting.

What was it he said? Pretty as a picture?

So real, he held her in his hands.

# CHAPTER NINE

◆ ◆ ◆

---

Lindsey's curled up on her bathroom floor in front of the toilet. Only her blonde curls peek from the top of her tattered baby blanket. Her back moves up and down with every breath. She's in her Princess Jasmine footy pajamas she hasn't worn in years. Her toenails have punched through the bottom and they're painted bubblegum-pink.

Kneeling down beside her, I pull the blanket back.

Her eyes open wide. "Mommy, you came. I knew you would."

I put my palm to her forehead and her whole body seems to relax. "Absolutely, sweet pea. You're my little love bug."

She holds still as I wipe her tear-stained cheeks, then I wrap her in my arms. I feel the delicate bones in her back. I've missed touching her so much.

She quickly rolls to her knees. I guide her head to the toilet, take her hair in my hands and hold it out of the line of fire.

Nothing comes out.

I look into the bowl. "Have you been drinking anything, honey?"

"7 UP ," she says. "That's what you always give us."

I hold the cool washcloth to her cheek. "Since you haven't thrown it up, that probably means it'll be over soon, honey."

She swoons theatrically and leans on the side of the tub with a dramatic moan. Five silly fingers spider-walk all spooky-like across the lip of the tub. Bumping the gooey bar in the waterlogged soap dish, her spider-fingers seize up, then skittle back under the blanket.

"Where is your dad, little spider?" I ask, not a bit of irritation in my voice.

"I'm fine by myself. When people are sick, they just sleep all day."

Toilet tissue spools from the roll.

Her dad told her that.

She falls back on the fuzzy bathmat again and presses her pale cheek to the cool floor tile. I raise her head to my lap and stroke her hair. Her lids drop and I watch my beautiful daughter. The little gold studs in her ears. The freckles on her cheeks.

Someone clears their throat. Lindsey's eyes dart to the doorway behind me and she buries her head in her blanket. It's Oliver, briefcase in hand, tugging the knot of his pink, silk tie. He still wears his wraparound sunshades from the car.

"What are you doing here?" I say.

"I live here," he says dully. "What are *you* doing here?"

I peel back the blanket from Lindsey's head.

He looks at her like he's just discovered a litter of puppies living under the bathroom sink.

"What happened to Caroline's mother taking you to school?" he says. "And, you left the door unlocked."

Lindsey squeezes my hand three times, our old code for "I–Love–You."

"I started throwing up right before they got here, Dad," she says. "I told you those bananas with the brown peels were bad."

"That's probably it," Oliver says, squelching the irritation in his voice.

I smile up at him. "So, what are you doing here, then?"

"I might ask you the same question."

Lindsey sticks her tongue out at him. He raises an eyebrow at her.

"Meet me in the hall, Mother?"

Oliver leans against the oak banister. Behind him on the wall is a gold-framed portrait of the two of us. I'd like to use it to knock the smirk off his face. He tilts his head toward Adam's room. I follow him inside. He shuts the door.

"I'm going to look the other way this time," he says calmly. The kind of comforting voice animal handlers use. "Please don't force me to do something I really don't want to do."

I feel the color draining from my face. "They're our kids. Why are you doing this?" My voice trembles. "Can't we talk about it? Oliver, please."

"Since you got past the new locks and security code, I'm having surveillance cameras installed to keep this from happening again." Smoothing his lapels, he looks me up and down. "Don't steal anything on the way out."

"That's it? That's all you've got to say to me?"

"There's someone downstairs foraging for food in the pantry." He hesitates. "And, I love you, Juliana."

I know my husband, and he means it.

The sick bastard.

Deep dimpled megapixel smile, he turns on his heel, and that's the end of it. I hear the soles of his Italian loafers on the Oriental rug on the stairs.

Lindsey's soft baby blanket frames her face. The pajamas are so small the elastic pinches her precious slender wrists.

"He's bouncing you out of here?" she says.

I nod. Eyeing the knob, I consider locking us up inside.

Her face falls. "I didn't mean to get you in trouble."

I can't let her see me cry.

It's not Lindsey's job to take care of me.

I give her my best smile. "I love you, baby doll," I say. "I'll call and check on you later. Get some sleep, all right?"

She looks lost.

Wrapping my arms around her, I feel her sharp chin bobbing up and down on my shoulder. "By the way, Linds, there's black Oreo crumbs in the corners of your mouth."

"Oops. You knew I really wasn't sick?"

"I had a feeling," I say.

She giggles and pulls the blanket back over her head. "Bye, Mommy."

Now I can cry.

Hearing my footsteps in the kitchen, Dad pokes his head out of the pantry. He offers me a vanilla wafer, but I shake my head.

"It's time for us to go home, Dad," I say.

He hops after me on his crutches, a bag of Cheetos between his teeth. As we make it through the living room, I slide a fine Lalique vase from the bookshelf under my sweater.

Out to the car, I guide him through the front door and down the limestone steps that lead to the driveway. Raising my wrist to wipe my nose, the vase slides from under the hem of my sweater, and it explodes.

Sparkling crystal shards on dull, dingy concrete.

# CHAPTER TEN

❖   ❖   ❖

---

Adam is a man-child of fourteen with new stubble on his chin. A melancholy surrounds him, but he swears he's not unhappy, just laid back. I'm projecting my feelings onto him, he says, but there's no way he came up with those words himself.

Adam's not into being spoiled rotten. His needs are simple, he says. He's flip-flops-only and likes his jeans split at the knees. Lying on a stone bench with his arms crossed over his chest, he moves rhythmically from side to side, drumming two pencils on his thighs. He wears a thick leather braid with a single blue shell on his wrist. Always the little white cord connecting his ear to his pocket, even when he's playing the guitar. Especially when he is. He's played since first grade. John Mayer or the "Malagueña," he picks and strums equally well. The sound does something to my heart. I know it's where I am meant to help him most.

Recognizing my honk, he rolls up and lugs his gargantuan camouflage backpack over his shoulders.

Oliver can lock me out of the house, but he can't stop me from picking my children up from school.

Adam covers a yawn with the back of his hand and begins walking toward me, long arms swinging at his sides.

My heart tugs. Make this squeezing in my chest go away.

"Hello, Baby Bear," I say. "Hop in."

I reach to hug him. His face says, "Don't even think about it."

"Oh, excuse me, Mr. Cool." I say, offering him a frozen Snickers bar with the wrapper peeled back perfectly. I hold it while he bites off half. He swallows it quickly before leaning his head back for me to steer more into his mouth. With the shell cracked, the melted ice cream runs down my wrist.

Watching him chew, I notice his nose has a huge, scabbed-over, volcanic zit. I wasn't there to run the needle under the hot water, poke the damn thing, and squeeze the puss out with a warm washrag. That's the way you do it.

I'm marking time by the rising and setting of a zit?

I take a baby wipe from the console to wipe the sticky off my hands before pulling into traffic.

"How's school?" I say.

He licks his lips. "Big, stupid project tomorrow. We need poster board."

"Of course you do," I say. "I ran over here to grab you while Grandad's at his doctor's appointment. You'll get to see him when I come back." I check my watch. Plenty of time.

Raising the visor, Adam looks straight through the windshield. He's not wearing the St. Christopher medal I gave him. He rarely, if ever, takes it off.

I look to the seats behind me and there's only his backpack. His guitar's not there.

"You forgot it?"

"Not really, Mom. Well, you might call it that." His voice trails off.

Great going, Oliver. You have to remind him. He's only fourteen.

"We'll be cutting it close, but there's time to get the guitar at the house, get you to the lesson and pick up Grandad before they set him on the curb."

Ugh. Why did I say that?

I rub the last sticky brown from my fingers. "I'll just call and tell the doctor's office we're running a little late."

"Don't worry about me," Adam says. "You should spend time with your dad. I mean, he's at the doctor, Mom."

Such sudden concern.

"I'mnotdoingitanymore."

"Excuse me?" I look at his face. His cheeks are pink. "I'm talking to you," I say. "Pull that cord out of your ear."

He doesn't. "It's a hassle, Mom. I have better things to do."

Tsk, tsk. I've heard this before.

"Adam, you love guitar."

"Not really, Mom. You love guitar," he says. "Dad said I could quit."

"Dad said? Did he, now?"

"He got me my own set of sticks. MacGregors," Adam says, like the brand's supposed to mean something. Then, with a new assuredness, he says, "He said when you're done pitching your shit-fit, to give him a call."

I dial Oliver's number. It goes straight to voice mail.

"Give me your phone," I say.

"No."

"Hand it over, buster."

He sighs and does it, then looks out the window.

Pick up, Oliver. Pick up. At last, he does.

"This is me. Pitching my shit-fit," I say. "Forget it on swapping guitar for golf. Don't you know he's talented?"

"It's not a good time to talk, Mrs. Morrissey," Oliver says. "Just cancel the stupid guitar lesson because that Paolo person? He works for us, not vice versa."

I speed through the orange light.

"And for your information," he says. "Adam's working with the new golf pro, Jimmy. It's his strict policy not to teach kids, but he's taking Adam as a personal favor to me."

Overhearing, Adam's eyes light up although he fights a smile. Oliver is showing him more attention than he did all of last year. But that's supposed to be a good thing, right?

"He needs to hit some balls, so just drop him at the club and I'll pick him up," Oliver says. "Like I always do."

Like he always does, my ass.

He hangs up. I call back. No answer.

Adam and I ride in silence. Well, I do. He still has his earpods in. I'm impressed at his willpower, keeping his facial muscles frozen while he's entertained by our little family drama.

I park the car in front of the music studio. "Paolo has an extra guitar. I've seen it," I say. "Borrow that for today." I punch the unlock button and I wait for him to get out of the car. "Do it."

Without looking at me, he pulls his backpack from the rear seat to the front like I've griped at him a hundred times not to do. It bumps my shoulder. Not hard, but it does. He climbs the brick steps to the studio and jerks open the door. For the short moment before it closes, I hear the tinkle of piano keys.

I pull to a parking space at the end of the lot. Before a minute is up, here he comes, strolling out the door. When he's out of sight, I bang the heels of my hands against the dashboard and scream. Not some little squeak like when you see a spider.

A long, full-out, makes-your-throat-hurt scream.

Then, I remember Dad.

I'm from one parking lot to another before I even know it. I hop out and round the car. Seeing the sky, I halt immediately. Transfixed.

Sunsets usually have a pale pink and orange sky.

Not this one. It's red and blue, stretched long and wide. Interspersed. Like red icing on a blue cake. Filling up the air.

I've never seen these colors in a sky before. They don't belong. The blue is thick and almost navy, yet strangely faded. And, what is that red? It's bright and muted all at once.

I concentrate until I finally know.

It's crepe-paper-blue. Not fresh out of the plastic. After it's been draped over a goalpost. And then rained on.

It's the red of glowing tail lights on a highway, traveling faraway into the distance.

At dusk, before it gets truly dark.

## CHAPTER ELEVEN

❖ ❖ ❖

Dad's leaning against the lip of his bathroom sink watching himself in the mirror. He opens the medicine cabinet. His eyes dart from Right Guard to Crest, settling on his black, little old man's comb.

He holds it up for me to see. "Well, I don't know whose this is," he says. "The last people who stayed in this hotel room must have left it."

"Do you want to see if it works?" I say.

He shakes his head like I'm crazy, "I want my own damn comb."

Hopping down the hall on his crutches, he calls over his shoulder. "And, I'm sure not using a stranger's toothbrush."

He's worked-up. Lord have mercy.

Coming to fill my coffee, I find him in the kitchen wrestling with the deadbolt on the back door. Finally swinging it open, he bangs it against his cast, cursing loudly.

"Hey, where are you going?"

"Work," he growls. "Tax season. Got lots on my plate."

"Wait." I set down my coffee mug and chase after him. "The office is closed today."

Out the door, he begins hopping toward his beloved 1950 Indian Cherokee Roadmaster, his only mode of transportation since I've known him.

It didn't take me long to find out the "Dad, your leg's broken so you can't ride that thing" excuse didn't go over so well. Who knows how many near-disasters he's had. The cycle has a fresh scratch or two, I've checked. Yesterday I told him it was out of gas. Tuesday, I said we couldn't find the keys. He thinks he's leaving, all right, but good luck, mister. I'll let the air out of the whitewalls if I have to.

The night I brought him home from the hospital, I didn't expect him to look around, checking his bearings. It's his house, not mine. He's the parent, not me. It was paralyzing, understanding in the space of a millisecond that's not how things would be shaping up at all.

I'm unsure of how he regards me. Is it as a grown woman? Or does he see a younger me who's locked in his memory? Does he wonder why I'm not in school? We've never had a relationship independent of my mother before. As much as he saw me back then, I never thought he'd be able to pick me out of a police lineup. Now, I sure don't.

My idea of housework is sweeping the room with a glance and it hasn't been much fun getting back into it, I'm not going to lie. Maybe cleaning the house wouldn't be so bad if it weren't such a pit, but actually, it would. So quaint and darling. That's what people say about old homes. The people who've never lived in one. The dripping faucet, running toilet and a few cracked windows aren't that big of a deal, but the AC doesn't work for beans. The sheetrock's crumbling. Water stains stretch from the ceilings down walls, which tells me the roof leaks, too. Things like that. The house is deteriorating. Like his mind.

We've gotten comfortable with silence. Parked in front of the TV, we'll watch *Wheel of Fortune* and *The Price is Right*. He's even got me watching *Bonanza*. I'm not sure he's able to follow the plot, not that there is one, but he sure likes having it on.

I'll try to talk to him and he'll roll his eyes like I'm total pea brain, even though he's the one who doesn't remember what we talked about two minutes ago. Sometimes he'll squint his forehead like he wishes I'd shut up. Other times, he'll ask, "Why are you still here?"

Well, shit, do you think I want to be here? Away from my children? That's what I want to ask him. If only he would turn to me and say, "I'm a big boy. Why don't you go home and be with your children? They need you more than I do." Even if he said it, I would stay. But I still wish he'd say it.

Let's say the new's worn off.

I'm in charge of his medications. The frequency and dosages. I help him dress. If I don't, his outfits are atrocious. He says it's all sixes and not to worry about it. It's not that I especially care that his plaids are mismatched, but he'll forget his socks. He'll try and walk out the door without his pants. And, he's started making messes. Most of them I'd rather not go into. I hold up the towel to cover him when he limps out of the shower. "Would you like some privacy, Dad?" He ignores me. The look in his eyes. He hates it, too.

It's not just the new deadbolts. It's nightlights. Little notes I've had to paste up—turn off the oven and close the fridge. I'm fed up with searching for lost things, but mostly, I'm fed up with spending money on new ones. Plus, his creditors are calling. His reputation's on the line. It may not register with him anymore, but he's my father, and it does with me.

The fucking cuckoo clock needs to knock it off. Every quarter hour. I can't take it anymore. As I climb the footstool to rip it off the wall, it occurs to me to just stop winding it.

Sometimes I tell myself that he'll be okay, that he was getting along fine before I got here, but it's ridiculous, crazy thinking.

Hugh, Jules, Hoss and Little Joe. Every day, just the same. No change.

I've got to figure this mess out.

Or I'm screwed.

# CHAPTER TWELVE

❖ ❖ ❖

"I'm selling my engagement ring," I tell Mary Ellen on my cell phone.

I move my finger back and forth on the steering wheel, watching how the diamond catches the sunlight. Three and a half carats set in platinum. Jeez, I need to have my nails done.

"Don't do that," she says. "You should make it into a necklace for Lindsey someday. No, you should save it for Adam."

"It's way too big for a necklace. And for Adam to give his fiancé the ring from his parents' broken marriage?" I say. "Sends the wrong message."

"Gotcha. Have it reset into a dinner ring then? No, scratch that. It's totally obvious they're recycled when women wear brilliant-cut diamonds on their right hands. Like a red flashing sign that says you're divorced."

"Awesome. Just the look I'm going for."

"Maybe you will be soon." Her voice lifts at the end.

"Hm-mmm," I say. "Doubtful."

At the next light, I look over at Dad in the passenger seat, then take off my ring and thread it onto the chain around my neck, next to my mom's gold coin. Looking down at my finger, I notice it's indented. Like you've had a tight rubber band around your wrist too long.

"When are you going to start dating?" It's Mary Ellen's gossip voice. I've heard it a million times. I used to think it was funny.

"Please shut up," I say. "I'm married. Besides, the thought of dating, much less kissing anyone makes me nauseous." And I mean it. I'd rather get it sewn up down there.

"Why would you want to sell it?" she says.

"I have to get money from somewhere. My dad's house needs a ton of work, plus he owes thousand to his creditors every month, not to mention the money I need to hire an attorney so I can get the kids back," I say. "It's not like I could ask Oliver for it."

I wait for her to say, "Oh, my God, Juliana, my best friend, I'm horrified that my husband, the asshole, is helping your husband, the dickhead, screw you in your divorce."

Instead, she says, "Who are you using?"

"Anabel Brock." I wince.

"Honestly? Why on God's green earth would you use her?"

We both know Mike can grind her into the pavement like a cigarette.

"She's priced right," I say. "Plus I got her name from someone who should know."

She waits for me to tell her.

"Kimberley Singleton." I wince again.

"You're talking to her?" she says. "You can't be serious. She's a realtor now. You heard the scuttlebutt, right?"

"Oh, now what?"

"When she shows homes to male clients, she has them meet her there. Her car is parked out front, but no Kimberley. They search the whole house, only to find her in the master bedroom. Under the covers. Or in the shower." She pauses for dramatic effect. "Naked, of course."

"Naturally," I say. "Well, it's not like we're best buds and hanging out."

"All I'm saying is that if you roll around with shit, you're going to get some on you."

I hate her know-it-all comments.

"Hey, what about the rest of your jewelry?" she says.

"I keep it on my vanity but it wasn't there when I left."

"Your two carat studs? Your armful of 18k bangles?" she says. "Your huge ruby pendant and long dangles?"

"Mmm-hmm."

"Even your Yurman?" she breathes.

"Yes, Mary Ellen," I sigh. "Everything. Including all of my dinner rings, too," I say. "Oliver stashed them somewhere."

"That Oliver's such a prince." She exhales loudly. "You and your pop aren't exactly close, so how's it going being roomies?"

"He's with me right now, actually, riding shotgun and taking a siesta."

Long forearms crossed over his Madras shirt and his mouth wide open, he looks dead to the world, but behind his dark flip-up shades, you never know.

"I want to make an appointment with Anabel for Tuesday morning," I say. "Could you come by and stay for a couple of hours?"

"She can't even leave him alone for that long?" It's Cheryl's voice in the background. Thanks for telling me I'm on speaker.

"Hey, Cheryl," I say.

"Hi, Juliana," she calls. "How are you?"

"Fabulous," I say. "Never better."

"I'm glad you didn't say the next day," Mary Ellen says. "That's when we play doubles. Wednesdays at nine, as you very well know."

Boards, committees, all my volunteer, I've canceled everything. Even things that have to do with the twins.

"We figured since you're sidelined, we filled your spot with Joanie," she says. "It was actually Oliver's idea."

"Joanie Johnson? That's weird. I wonder where Oliver ran into her."

"Just tell her. It's okay." It's Cheryl's voice again.

"She, Andy and their kids have been sitting with us at Pepe's," Mary Ellen says quickly. "She said she had to ask you to step down as Symphony League President. Were you okay with that?"

I squeeze my eyes shut.

"Sure."

"Speaking of Oliver, he said to tell you that Adam needs an ortho appointment. His top brackets are loose or something," she says. "And, Lindsey's due for the dermatologist."

My hands choke the steering wheel.

"I'm on it," I say. My voice is wobbly. They must hear it.

"Don't be sad, sweetie," Cheryl says. "Hey, maybe y'all could meet us at Pepe's later. Does your dad do happy hour?"

Something tells me that's not the best thing to get started, but trust me, I've thought about it.

I put on my blinker and turn into the grocery store. "I better scoot, you guys," I say.

"Okay, then," Mary Ellen says. "Let us know."

I pull as close to the entrance as I can, then scurry around and yank Dad's crutches from the backseat.

"Pull yourself up," I say. "Now, push this foot out. You can do it."

"Keep your shirt on!" he barks.

He rubs his hands down his cast like it's bothering him. At the inside of his ankle, there's a set of tiny red footprints. I reach down and rub my fingers over them. He kicks my arm.

I throw up my hands. "Fine," I say.

He tucks a crutch under each arm. "Got that door?"

"Got it." I slam it with my elbow and lock it.

Keeping a respectful distance, I follow him through the automatic doors, past the lotto machine and *USA Today* rack. Outside the men's room is a college boy in khaki shorts and Birkenstocks.

"Excuse me," I say sweetly. "Could I ask you a favor?"

He raises his hand to his heard and looks behind him. "Me?"

"My father's having trouble." Enlarged prostate. "Would you mind helping him in there, please?"

The boy looks horrified.

"That's a little—awkward," he says and pushes past us.

I put my hands on my hips. "Dad, I can't believe that little pipsqueak wouldn't help you."

His left eye is pinched in anger. "Move," he growls. "I have to go!"

"Okay," I say to his back. "Meet you here at check-out."

I'm comparing prices when I see Kimberley Singleton traipsing down the aisle wearing thigh boots and a leopard mini. I step behind the cabernet.

Why can I not get away from this woman?

"Hello, Juliana," she says.

I do a quick inventory of the other shoppers. She's notorious. With her big boobs and light blonde hair, she makes me think of Marilyn Monroe, the seductive voice and everything.

"Hello, Kimberley," I say, setting chardonnay in the cart, clinking glass on metal.

She looks at me with soft brown eyes. Are those lashes real?

"I want you to know I'm sorry about your situation. I didn't get to tell you that when I saw you downtown. When I heard about your daddy too, I hurt for you so bad."

I fuss with my hair. "Oh, I'm fine. It's all good," I say.

"I was where you are," she says. "I remember how much I needed someone to tell me that I'd get through it and everything would be all right. That there really is life after divorce." She smiles, but her eyes are sad. "Not many people understand it or even want to. It's all very unkind."

I can't explain it, but I almost cry. Her words are the best thing I've heard in days. Weeks. She hugs me. Embarrassed, I pull away, but she holds on to my arm.

"Listen, Juliana, if you'd ever like getting together to talk, I'd love to. About anything."

"Oh, sure," I say. "Let's do that."

Next time I'm in Sri Lanka.

"Good," she says and sashays up the freezer aisle. She puts a couple of Cool Whips in her cart. I can only imagine what she uses *those* for.

Down the paper aisle, I toss in toilet tissue and think of Adam throwing vegetables and everything else he didn't like out of the basket while Lindsey sat on top of the bread. Just when I was about to throttle them, a little old lady would invariably sneak up behind me and coo, "It goes so fast. Enjoy those precious dumplings while they're little." I knew she was right, but I really wanted to say, "Then how about switching carts with me, Grandma?"

Now I wish I'd listened.

I make my way to check-out, but there's no Dad.

Pushing past all the aisles, I look up and down. Where the hell is he? If he's in the ladies room, I'll kill him. Starting to run behind the basket, I round the frozen foods toward check-out again.

Good gracious. There he is, bent over his crutches in front of the TV Guides, talking to a checker with cropped white hair. She nervously glances at the customers in line.

"Dad," I call, waving my hand. "Hugh Birdsong!"

He turns his head in every direction. Finding me, he gives me the high sign.

Getting closer, I pop my hand over my mouth. His faded jeans are navy from his crotch to his knees. He's wet himself and he doesn't even remember.

What the fuck, God, are you laughing up there? Do you think this is funny? I tell you what. You owe my daddy a huge apology.

Vision blurred, I lean my head all the way back and shake the tears off my eyeballs. I rush to his side. He smells like urine.

"Dad, are you okay?"

The white-haired checker is barely younger than Dad. She touches my arm. "My mom had it, too." She holds my gaze several moments. "Just love him," she says.

I put my head down and rifle though my purse so he won't see anything's wrong in my face. A canister of Quaker Oats spins on the conveyer belt, and the customers are tired of waiting.

"Let me pay for those groceries," he says and tries the back pocket of his Levis for his wallet. Thankfully, I hid it in the freezer.

"Where's your cart?" the checker says.

I can barely concentrate past the fluorescents reflecting off her glasses. Finally, I point and say, "It's by the Mountain Dew."

She muscles it to the front of her line. If anyone has a problem, they don't dare mention it.

"Take your time," she says. "We'll have them ready."

I mouth the words, "thank you," and take Dad's elbow.

He negotiates the narrow check-out line, knocking metal baskets along the way. Seeing his soaked pants, a pimply-faced sacker jumps out of the way.

"Look, there's the car." I steer him to my Lexus.

Winded, he balances on the passenger door. I slide his crutches across the backseat, then round the car to the driver's side. I start her up and switch on the AC for him. There's the sound of his seatbelt stretching across his chest. He snaps it closed.

"I'm just getting you situated, okay?" I touch his knee. "Be right back with the food."

He fidgets in his seat. "I'm sick of riding in this damn car."

Paid up, I push the rickety cart across the hot pavement, pop open the back and load in the bags. The pimply-faced grocery boy redeems himself by returning my empty cart.

I step to the driver's side and pull the handle.

He's gone.

I check for him in the rearview as I back up. I roll through the lot, looking between the cars.

"Dad," I call. "Dad, where did you go?"

The sun's too bright. I scan the other storefronts. There's a boy on a scooter walking a dachshund.

"Dad. Daddy." I keep calling his name. "Where are you?"

A woman dressed for a luncheon turns and looks at me.

What was I thinking, leaving him alone?

I wheel onto the street. I check the library parking lot, the bus stop, in front of the video store where they're having a sidewalk sale.

Panicking will only make it worse. Calm down.

"Have you seen an old man on crutches?" I ask the gas station attendant, the bicyclist, the kid in the crosswalk who wears a backwards baseball cap.

They haven't.

This is exactly what I deserve.

No way he could've gotten this far. I take a left on 45th and another on Speedway. I'm hysterical, crying his name out the window. The more time passes, the less chance I'll find him. The trees and houses are a blur.

I pull over. Idling. Stay in one spot. He can't be too far. Help me, God. Help me. I squeeze the steering wheel. I crane my head in every direction, tears running down my face.

Finally. Under the striped awning behind Quackenbush Coffee. He's safe. Thank you, God. He's stooped over in front of the newspaper racks, beside a blue, weathered mail box. Pretty as you please, he drops the door on the mail box and looks inside.

Rolling down the window, I pull up beside him. Steam seems to rise from the pavement. Hearing the engine, he slowly tilts his neck to the side. The sun has turned his nose pink.

"Have we checked the mail today, Jules?"

He's fucking serious.

I watch my shaking fingers punch in the lighter. I tap a Marlboro Light from the pack in my purse and raise it slowly to my lips. I guide the angry orange torch to the tip.

"Stop that," he says. "It's a nasty, disgusting habit."

"Get over it."

# CHAPTER THIRTEEN

❖ ❖ ❖

Anabel Brock is macho.

When she plays football, I'd say she's the center. Baggy gray suits like hers are usually only found in the men's department. Her coarse, shoe-black hair looks more mowed than trimmed, and against her freshly ironed blouse, her face looks straight out of the hamper. Bless her heart.

She's on her telephone headset. Nodding at what's said, she hums into the mouthpiece. Seeing me in the doorway, she points me to her guest chair. With one hand, she forms the "just a minute" sign and with the other, she makes the "talk-talk-talk" gesture.

As she swivels her red tufted chair and looks out the window, I take the opportunity to check out her "I Love Me Wall" that's hung with diplomas and certificates. Hmm. The posed photos with crusty male dignitaries and politicians, I'm sad to say, it's hard to pick out Anabel.

Her shelves are stacked with books: *What Women Need to Know About Untying the Knot, Love Your Kids More Than You Hate Your Ex-Husband.* There's seriously an orange-covered *Divorce for Dummies.*

Throwing a match on my marriage? My impulse is to cut and run.

I picture myself looking into the bathroom mirror one morning, and yikes, there I am, a thrice-divorced waitress living in a fleabag apartment. I imagine driving Adam to college. Oliver's in his Jaguar and there's me following in my purple PT Cruiser. And there's Adam saying, "Yeah, meet my mom and dad..." Then, heads turn as I'm being escorted down the aisle at Lindsey's wedding on the arm of her future-husband's nephew. They're all thinking, "Awwww. Look. There's her mother. She used to be pretty, but God bless America, look at her now....she screwed everybody up." There's

Oliver all grizzled sitting in the next row. The photographer's shooting the pictures after the ceremony. "Okay," he says, "let's get a shot of the bride and groom with the bride's mother. Good. Okay, got it. Now let's get a picture of the happy couple with the bride's father."

Give me strength.

In a husky baritone, Anabel signs off on her phone call. "Tell Dad I love him, too."

She steps hurriedly from behind her desk to shake my hand. As she does, shoes poke from her gray, cuffed trousers. They're stripper shoes with four-inch, clear heels. Gold, with ankle straps. When we shake, her hand is silky smooth.

Not what I expected at all.

"Maybe you've heard I used to be a big cheese before I was invited to rehab," she says. "I drank so much then, I'm still hung over."

"Yes, Ms. Brock, I have heard that," I say.

Which means she's affordable.

"Kimberley Singleton referred you?"

I nod, embarrassed.

"If half of what you hear about her is true, she's got to be exhausted." She shakes her head. "But say what you want, that woman's got guts."

She settles back behind her desk and reaches into a jar of Jelly Bellies. Chewing them quickly, she reaches again for the jar. "All righty. Let's get down to it. How are things between you and your husband?"

"I keep trying to convince him we're not on speaking terms."

Anabel doesn't miss a beat. "Spouses become so much a part of you, they're like a tattoo," she says. "The good news is that although it's costly, time intensive and the pain is excruciating, you can get rid of them."

I like this woman. Not enough that I want to date her, but I like her.

"Do you work?"

Not outside the home.

"I was formerly my husband's legal assistant."

"So, you know your way around these things. Makes my job easier," she says. "Anything he has on you that could get dredged up? Drugs busts, DWI arrests," she lists them on her fingers. "Felony convictions or babies?"

I shake my head.

"Infectious diseases? Anyone damaging he could call as a witness? The smallest thing can make you look like a serial killer."

"No, Ms. Brock."

"Okay, here's my first bit of advice."

Oh, shit. Here it comes. The new-kid-on-the block speech.

"Don't broadcast your business," she says. "Folks ask, 'What happened?' and you think, well, these are my old pals and they really care. I'm not saying they don't like you, because they probably do. But Mrs. Morrissey, they will trash-talk you. No need to set it out on the curb."

Oh, shiver me timbers. No one's going to do that to me.

"A concise sound-byte is your friend. It's your public relations strategy. And here's my second bit of advice," she says. "Move."

"Let me get right on that," I say. "I'll just pick up and head for Dallas."

"Not literally. Go to a different dry cleaners. A different coffee shop. Change your flight pattern."

She takes another handful of jelly beans, picks out the blacks ones and tosses them in the trash. "When everything around you changes, the comfortable parts of your life seem like all you have, and holding on seems like a good idea until people start treating you differently." She pauses to raise her eyebrows. "People act like divorce is contagious because it is. Personal contact increases their chance of infection, and they sure don't want a beautiful divorced woman forcing them to look at their own marriages." She looks straight into my eyes. "You will be treated like head lice."

I frown at her.

She takes a frilly, feathered fountain pen from its holder and makes notes on a yellow pad. "Have you had sex with anyone in the past fifteen years?"

She watches whether I blink. Supposedly the telltale sign someone's lying.

"Just Oliver," I say.

"Bummer." She begins writing again. "What about him?"

"It's possible, I guess," I say slowly. "Let me ask you something, Ms. Brock. Why would a man who wants to sleep with his wife be interested in having an affair?"

"Simple. Men will risk everything to get laid. They like having a warm place to put it and they're usually putting it somewhere." She leans back in her swivel chair and looks up at the ceiling. "Plus," she says, "there's no shortage of available women for a man who's breathing."

One day, Mary Ellen and I are taking Home Girl here out to party.

"I'm not doing my job if I'm not on the lookout for chains that need untangling." She tosses back another handful of jelly beans, shrugs, and begins writing again. "Okay, let's change gears," she says. "How are you looking financially?"

Before I can answer, she puts up her hand.

"Stop. Forget I asked that," she says. "We'll talk about that at your next appointment, Mrs. Morrissey, and make a plan of action."

"My name is Juliana Birdsong."

She nods approvingly. "Good plan," she says. "A forward thinker."

Yeah, I hear that a lot.

"Ms. Brock, I'm not living with my children right now," I say. "My husband kicked me out of the house."

Her large nostrils flare.

My heart falls to my knees. "It's his separate property," I say. "He can't do that?"

"Of course not. That's absurd. It may be his separate property, my dear, but it's the marital home." She makes more notes on her pad. "You cannot believe anything your husband tells you. He's a personal injury attorney," she says. "Hello!"

I'll kill him.

And, I'll enjoy watching him die

If Anabel sees my eyes beginning to tear, she doesn't show it.

"Ms. Brock, are you married?" I ask her.

She looks up. "Fuck, no!" she says loudly.

"Do you have children?"

"Double fuck no."

"Don't think I'm ambivalent about my financial settlement, Ms. Brock. I assure you that I am not. But my children? They're the reason I'm here."

Her eyes travel to my left hand. "I see your finger is bare. Does that signify something?"

I raise my chin. "The ring is diseased and was infecting my finger."

"Don't sell anything to pay me. It should come out of your joint funds. I guarantee that you're paying for Mike to make a pretty penny off you."

I raise my hand to my throat and rub the diamond between my fingers.

"I appreciate everything you're saying, Ms. Brock. I do."

"Your children are the most important thing to you, Ms. Birdsong. You told me that."

"Damn right," I say.

"What else do you want?"

Is this a trick question?

"I want to be happy."

"What are you waiting for?"

I shrug. "For my divorce to be final, I guess."

Throwing her legs on the desk, she shows off those stripper shoes.

"Let's get you a head start."

# CHAPTER FOURTEEN

❖ ❖ ❖

I keep thinking that murderously attacking the yard has got to quell my anger. Stabbing the hard, stubborn earth with my shovel, I imagine Oliver's neck at the end of the blade. The dirt clods are his head. I flatten his skull with the back of the shovel. The powdered dirt is his brain. After wiping the tears from my eyes, I start again, even madder than before.

At least living with my dad keeps from being a complete homicidal maniac. If I got arrested, I think he'd be pretty pissed. He's behind me on the porch right now. I bring him out here with me most mornings to keep him out of trouble. After propping up his leg on the hanging swing, I'll hand him over the sad, withered geraniums that I found in the greenhouse that Richard built me out back. It was a high school graduation present. His, not mine. He thought I deserved something special for being left home without him for a year while he got to escape to college. Anyway, Dad's been trying to bring the geraniums back to life.

I'll listen for his voice as he tells himself things, like how to jump a battery. I've heard him change a tire. I think he does it so he won't forget how. It seems he stretches his mind as far as he can, but he can't always find what he's looking for. Something he can't find on Monday might show up on Tuesday, but maybe not. His brain is farsighted. The more distant the memory, the more in-focus it is.

The chain squeaks, which means he's easing off the cushion.

"Did we check the mail today, Jules?"

I throw aside another heap of Oliver's brain. "Yes, but I have no idea what you did with it."

Squinting behind his tiny lenses, he looks down at me. "Are you crying?"

I brush my tears and turn my head away. "No, of course not."

"Sure looks like it."

"I miss my kids," I say softly. "They're all I think about."

"You've got kids?" he says. "Where are you hiding them?"

It makes sense that he wouldn't have the kids in his memory bank. I didn't bring them around him much, not that he was making such an effort to see them on his own, but I do wish he remembered them. I used to see his expression in their faces. Now, it's their expressions I see in his.

"We pick them up after school every afternoon, remember?"

"I must have misplaced that."

He says that a lot.

"Did we check the mail today?"

That, too.

I have to get them back, but I can't do it without Oliver. I'm afraid that without him, there's no kids. It's an awful feeling, needing someone you hate.

I toss my work gloves on the steps and plop down on the porch.

Dad pokes at the cicada shells at his feet, disturbing a layer of brown rocks underneath. They look oddly like baked potatoes.

"Damn, nasty, disgusting yard. Putting in this rock garden was one of the stupidest ideas your mother ever had." He hits the rocks over and over, then drops the crutch on the sidewalk.

"Don't you dare say ugly things about Mom."

He grabs the crutch back and begins hitting the rocks again.

What he said about the yard is true. Tree roots claw their way across the dirt like gnarled fingers. Fallen limbs, brittle as bones, lean against the trunks, and leaves layered at the base are bleached from the sun.

It's like a Tim Burton movie.

I'll never make any decent progress without my old gardening tools in the garage, and there's no telling where Dad put the key. The tools are the iron and forged-steel variety, not that crummy Home Depot crap you can only get now. I bought them with my employee discount at the plant nursery in high school, when the smell of dirt was irresistible and I had the most gorgeous tan of my life. Every day I'd tug the mammoth hose across the gravel and coo to the bougainvillea—back then, along with mood rings and pet rocks, talking to plants was all the rage. The day the bougainvillea exploded in sheer, pink blossoms, I was hooked.

I straighten tall and look at the porch. "Dad, what would you think of working on this old door?" I say. "It needs sanding, but if we got a can of paint and a couple of brushes, it might look pretty nice."

He looks up. "You said paint? All right."

He struggles to his feet, swatting me away when I try and help.

"Soon as I get me a nap, that is."

An hour or so later, I'm standing in the flowerbed nursing the yellow verbena that I've transplanted from my old yard when I hear a car pulling up to the curb.

Oh, joy. It's Oliver.

He pushes open the gate and looks up the wet walkway. He judges the time between the rising and falling of the sprinkler, then goes for it. Scowling, he whisks droplets from his gabardine slacks, then stamps his feet as water spits from his alligator loafers. I'd laugh, but I don't want him to notice me. I sniff my pits. Fantastic, I smell like a goat.

He uses the comb from his back pocket to comb back his auburn hair, then widens his stance, like he's going to the bathroom. Now, his eyes tick slowly across the house as he adds up everything that's wrong with it. It takes a while. I know because I've made the list myself. Making it halfway up the steps, he wraps the column and begins picking off chips of stucco.

"Stay off the porch."

Startled, he follows my voice. Finding me, he looks me up and down and whistles. I'm wearing frayed cut-offs and a stained tank top I found in Richard's closet. The bandana in my greasy hair completes my adorable look.

"Nice outfit, Ellie Mae." He smiles, twirling his finger. "Turn around this way."

I drop to my sore knees and shove the spade in the earth.

He comes down the steps and squats beside me. "Thought I'd check and see how you're doing over here," he says pleasantly.

I nestle dirt around the roots and press it down hard, trying to keep my hands from shaking.

"Love what you've done with the place," he says, all cute and jokey-jokey. I don't respond and he rubs his moustache. His old self-calming technique. After a moment, he picks a few acorns from the flowerbed and lines them up next to my knee. Scraping my hands through the soil, I begin covering the next verbena. Raising up, he brushes my bare shoulder with his fingers. I bite my tongue to keep from saying something we'll both regret. The ugly words are the ones people always remember.

He kicks over the clay pot filled with cigarette butts, all with my pink lipstick on the filters. "Hey, Ms. Closet Smoker. Didn't take you long to get into the swing of things," he says. "With your suspicions, I'm surprised you'd feel safe staying over here."

"I don't know why you'd say that."

"Save it for someone who hasn't lived with you for the past umpteen years," he says. "Your father's never helped you and he's not going to start now. Especially since he's hit the skids," he says. "Since your brother bankrupted him, I should say."

My eyes fly open. "Where did you hear that?"

"He came crying to me for a bailout after his condo fiasco. What a nimrod." He picks an Altoid from the tin in his pants pocket and pops it into his mouth. "I told him to beat it, of course."

"How could you? They're my family."

"Fuck them. They're not my family and they're sure not sucking off my tit."

I stand to face him. "That's all you're about, isn't it?" I say. "Money."

"That's right. So don't ask me to do anything over here, either, because the answer's no."

I tap a Marlboro Light from the pack, light it, and blow smoke in his face.

He holds out the Altoids. "Here," he says. "Take several. Smokers can always use a breath mint."

I wonder how he'd feel if I put this cigarette out on his forehead.

"I did some checking, Oliver. It's illegal for you to throw me out of the house," I say evenly.

"Ha. Surprised even you fell for that one, kiddo. Thought you'd at least learned it on *Judge Judy*," he says. "But, it's irrelevant, since you're stuck here at the Hotel Californa. You know, where you can check in, but you can never leave?"

I scream in his face, "I'll never forgive you taking my babies. Give them back to me, Oliver. Please."

He laughs. "You think they'd be caught dead staying at this little house?"

"Oh, I'll get them back. You just watch," I say. And I mean it.

He puffs out his chest. "The kids aren't exactly choked up that you're gone, but bring it on, sister," he says. "Mike's ready to go. Anytime you are."

"You make me sick," I say.

"You make me horny."

He reaches his hand down my top. My necklace pops out. Seeing my diamond ring dangling from the chain, he yanks it off my neck.

"Not for sale."

Smiling in triumph, he slides it on his pinkie and drops my mother's gold coin on the ground.

I slap his face.

It turns red. His eyebrows, too.

"Oh, I'll see you on the courthouse steps, all right," he yells. "All of our friends think you've lost your mind, but I told them you'd go crazy. Just like your mother."

The screen suddenly swings open and thwacks the side of the house.

Oliver and I jerk our heads to the door.

"You leave her out of it!"

Oh, shit. It's my dad. And, man, is he pissed off.

He's hopped to the door on his good leg, red-faced and winded. Sweat shines at his temples, and his top lip is quivering. I've never seen this side of him before, but I like it.

Oliver's eyes cut to mine and in that instant we communicate like husband and wife. I see his shock at how much Dad's changed. His eyes tell me, "Juliana, I'm sorry," and I sense it's for more.

Dad waves me into his outstretched arm and pulls me to him. I lay my head against his chest. It feels good.

He lifts his chin and stares Oliver down like a gunfighter. "This is your chance to run, young man." He pauses. "I suggest you take it."

Shamefaced, Oliver steps forward, and slowly offers his hand.

"Hugh, I meant no harm."

"No one hurts my daughter!" Dad yells. "Understand? Now get the hell off my property!"

Oliver looks to me innocently, like I'm going to bail him out or something. I throw him a la-de-da expression and he slinks off the porch.

Dad's eyes drill a hole in the back of his head until he's inside his creampuff Jaguar and his tires squeal around the corner.

Dad turns to me and says, "Who was that?"

## CHAPTER FIFTEEN

❖ ❖ ❖

Lumber is stacked outside the entry to Wally's shop. A few paint cans and a split bag of cement with gray powder spilling out the side. Old fashioned, double-hung windows face the parking lot. Or, what will be the parking lot. That's where the Mercedes convertible is parked which means Richard's inside, unable to tear himself away from griping at the contractor long enough to come see Dad.

Pushing open the door, I'm hit with smell of fresh-sawn pine and the aching whine of a chainsaw. Careful not to ruin my suede pumps, I circle the room, checking the progress. The walls are primed but not painted yet. Hand-hewn display shelving lines the walls, and thick, yellow cords drop from the ten-foot ceilings. The center one must be for the Italian chandelier Richard was fussing about.

The scuffed hardwoods need refinishing, but I'm sure that's the last thing the contractor will do before he folds up his tent. For now, they're marked off with blue masking tape, intended to divide the living room into different sales areas. The space by the door will be the cash register, I bet, where Wally will ring up his first of many sales.

I follow the three-step crown molding to the room in the back. Richard's sitting cross-legged on the floor nailing down baseboard. A blue bandana is knotted around his neck. Hunched over like that, his back's got to be killing him.

"Where's your fancy contractor?" I say.

He glances up at me. "So, we're speaking now?" he mumbles through the nails between his lips. "I can do a better job myself. Plus, I'm free."

"Nice work, Rich," I say. "It's beautiful."

He tosses aside the hammer and crawls to his feet. The leather tool belt clatters around his waist. "You find yourself doing all sorts of things you never thought you'd do when you're broke." He strides to the sawhorse in the middle of the room. "Guess you're finding that out."

A dustpan full of sawdust catches sun from the window and sparkles in the light. I dump it in the metal trash can.

"This poverty thing isn't exactly your bag, now is it?" he says.

Mom had a word for when Richard acted this way.

*Malhumorado.*

"Oliver said you asked him to help you and Dad out."

He cuts me off. "Like I said, you find yourself doing all kinds of things when you're broke."

"That's why you're mad at me, isn't it?" I say. "You assume since he turned you down, I was in on the decision?"

"No shit, Sherlock. You could've snapped your fingers and maybe Dad and I wouldn't be in such sad shape." He centers a two-by-four on the sawhorse, lines up his T-square and marks the board with the pencil from behind his ear. "I wasn't asking for a bailout. Just some breathing room."

I try not to raise my voice. "Oliver doesn't ask my opinion on anything. You should know that. I only heard of the condo project from Señor Sanchez."

"How would this family ever survive without Señor Sanchez?" he says sarcastically.

The old goat will survive us all. Like a Twinkie in a landfill.

Starting up the skill saw, he maneuvers a long board under the blade. Finished, he tosses it aside and centers another.

I grab it with my hand. "So, I guess you've been too occupied to come check on Dad?"

He bucks his chin. "Are you the pot or the kettle, Jules? None of this would be a surprise if you stayed in better touch yourself," he says.

"We're not getting anywhere fighting, Rich," I say. "Can't we put this down and move forward?"

He bends to pick nails from the ground and I take his face in my hand and turn it toward me. We stare each other down for several moments, but I'm a mom now and I can do this all day. I've gone pro.

Looking away first, his dark stubble catches the light. "Dad's emotionally constipated, but I still wanted a relationship him and I couldn't wait for him to come to me anymore," he says. "So, I was going to impress the shit out of my dad."

"I doubt you held a gun to his head," I say slowly.

"He thought building the condos was a cool idea in the beginning. Said for me to go for it, because what was he doing with the money in the bank?" Richard barely takes a breath. "But things changed after they went belly-up. He changed. Soon he forgot where they were even located. Every conversation, I'd have to start from square one—Dad upset, me upset. The disaster was always brand new." He shakes his head. "Putting you in charge of his stuff, he's made his feelings quite clear, and it doesn't feel so great."

I kiss his cheek. Sometimes it's better to say nothing.

There's the sharp toot of a horn. Hearing screeching brakes, we bolt to the window. Fritz stands in the middle of the busy street, looking side to side. Like out of nowhere, Wally dashes to the curb. Waiting until the traffic clears, he claps his hands. "Fritz, come!"

The pooch tucks his tail and trots to his side. Wally scoops him up, presses their noses together. "Bad dog, Fritz. You know better than that."

Richard rakes his fingers through his dark hair. "Thank God," he says. "I couldn't take it if I lost that dog." Seeing Dad out the window, he shrinks from the glass. "Why did you bring him here?"

"Don't be dense," I hiss. "He's sick and he's your dad."

"Hey, you guys," Wally calls. "Give me a hand. Your dad wants to come in."

I lean out the window. "Okay. Be right there."

"Stay out of it, Jules," Richard says. "You know I can't face him."

"How about you give it a shot?"

His face twists in pain. "You don't understand."

I step toward him. "No, Rich, you don't understand how it feels when your child won't pay attention to you. How it feels when they pretend they don't need you anymore."

"You want to talk about hurting Dad? You came back from Houston with twins. We didn't even know you got married," he says. "Didn't we deserve to be included in your plans?"

How about what I deserved?

I brace myself against the window. "You coming or not?"

"Not."

I stomp to the door. "You're acting like a child."

He calls after me, "Takes one to know one."

On the porch, I freeze.

Dad's at the convertible. The driver side. The soft top's down. Wally comes behind him, drops Fritz' leash over the side mirror and begins patting him on the back.

Dad grips the steering wheel and leans into the car. I expect him to begin checking the gauges, when he quickly reaches for the seat and begins running his hand over the smooth, tan leather. At the headrest, they stop.

I glare at him.

Just back away from there, you fraud. You phony. You have no right doing that.

Fritz begins pulling against the leash, trying his darnedest to unloop it from the mirror. Springing in the air, he knocks Dad's elbow and his crutch slips in the gravel. Before Wally can catch him, he crashes to the ground.

I tear across the parking lot.

Dad's flat on his back, crutches splayed beside him, color drained from his face and lips. His elbow's scratched and bleeding, grit embedded in his skin.

I drop to my knees beside him. "Dad," I cry. "You okay?"

I lift his hand and squeeze it. Limp. His chest's not moving up and down. I press my fingers to his neck, then drop my ear to his heart and listen.

Dad bats my head.

I jerk up and look down at him.

His lids tremble behind his crooked flip-up shades. I brush his gray curls off his forehead with my fingers. He grunts loudly and swats them away and runs his hand down his thigh, checking for his keys.

Fritz pants by his side, saliva dripping from his long, pink tongue. If Wally weren't standing right here, I might swat that dog. Oh, I definitely would.

His eyes spring open and zero-in on Wally. Some kind of man-code, I guess, Wally wedges his hands under Dad's armpits from behind and hoists him up. Dad immediately leans his hips against the door and cups his palm around the headrest.

I tug his shirt, all dusty on the back. After a moment, I say, "Come on, Dad." And he doesn't fight.

Wally on one side, me on the other, we shepherd him toward my Lexus. Dad grips the roof, pulls himself up into the seat and Wally helps swing his legs onto the floorboard.

"It's sure been nice seeing you today, Mr. Birdsong," he says.

Dad puts his hand on his arm and looks at him carefully. "You, too, little neighbor boy, Wally Wallace," he says.

Wally's blue eyes become wet and glossy.

It tears your heart out, I know.

Turning to me, he says, "Jules, think I can talk you into doing some landscaping over here?"

I've already surveyed the situation. Zero street appeal. Charlie Brown trees hug the house. Not to brag, but I've been told I have two green thumbs.

"Sure, Wally. I'll see what I can do."

"What's the real reason you're leaving?" he says.

I motion my head toward the shop. "Rich won't even come by the house to see Dad," I whisper.

He shoves his hands in his pockets. "Oh, he's come by. He just hasn't stopped," he says. "How else do you think I know about the dynamite work you're doing? He says you're really super-duper talented."

Well, doesn't that just my warm heart like brandy?

"Talk some sense into him, Wally," I say.

He brushes a tear from my cheek. "Your brother's always felt unlovable. Always."

I glare at the door. "If he acted a little nicer, maybe he wouldn't have that problem."

"Did you know that when people act unlovable, that's when they need it the most?"

"Humph," I say. "Then Rich must be ultra-needy."

He squeezes my hand and walks through the door, leaving it open a crack. Richard's on the floor, twisting the yellow cord around his power drill. Wally pulls him to his feet and wraps him in a hug. Richard rests his chin on his shoulder.

# CHAPTER SIXTEEN

❖ ❖ ❖

I remember being a fourth grader, standing outside my parents' bedroom door knocking. I knew she was in there. I'd seen her go in. I yelled, "Mom, Mom, Mom!" I needed her to help me with something. At least I thought I did. After a couple of hours, Richard got the screwdriver and opened the door. She was sitting on the floor in the dark. He slammed the door shut.

We'd seen her drive one time, probably a few years before that. We were waiting in the parking lot outside Dad's office. It was dark outside, I remember, because she bopped Richard on the head when he opened the door and the light came on. Outside her driver door, I also remember seeing a mountain of cigarette butts on the pavement. By the time Dad walked out the door, kick-started the Indian and wheeled out of the lot, Mom didn't peel onto the street until his cycle was out of sight, and we still beat him home.

Never the homeroom mom, the Girl Scout leader. Never made a performance at school or a parent-teacher conference. Take us to the park to play on the merry-go-round? How about just meet us at the stupid bus stop? It wasn't possible for her to leave the house she said. She was like a dog on a chain.

We'll see about that, Richard said. Besides, we never got to go anywhere, so we had to make our own fun. The game was called "Make Her Come Outside."

Richard found a snake in the yard, caught it in a bucket and slipped it into the bathtub, and then he faked a frenzy fit, begging her to get it out of the house. She'd have to go outside for that, wouldn't she? Negative. She took one look in the bathtub and closed the door behind her, then hauled us into the laundry room where we stayed until Dad came home. And Richard got a spanking.

Round one went to Mom.

Smoke her out. That'll do it.

He got her dust rag and squirted Endust on it, lit it with matches and chunked it in the sink. It set off the fire alarm, all right. I ran and got her. "Mom!" I screamed. "The kitchen's on fire!" And it was, too. The curtains over the sink ignited. She yanked the red fire extinguisher off the wall and sprayed the whole smoking kitchen until white foam covered everything, then she ripped down the curtains and sailed them out the window. The look on her face.

She shook the shit out of him. "Tell me, Ricardo. What did you do? You awful little boy."

But, Rich wasn't one to buckle. He screamed right back. A long, loud, piercing monkey scream. And later, when Dad spanked him, he laughed.

Okay, technically, she didn't have to go outside, did she?

Round two went to Mom.

Try another fire, but be smarter about it this time. Richard took a tennis ball soaked in lighter fluid, lit it and catapulted it to the yard below with a serving spoon from his second story window. If the yard was on fire, she'd have to come outside and extinguish the flames before burned the house down, right? She thought it could wait until she found us. Hiding in the closet. Richard torched the yard, all right, and he also got the pleasure of dousing it with the hose.

Even bigger spanking for that one. More laughter.

Round three absolutely went to Mom.

She'd leave the house for a gas leak. Definitely, if we lit a match.

Okay, we weren't that stupid.

Next was the ultimate. What if I was hurt? Serious-bad hurt. She'd have to come out then, wouldn't she? Richard had me stand in the driveway and scream my head off. Like someone was cutting off my arms and legs with a chainsaw.

"Mom. Help me! Mom!" I yelled. I looked around, hoping the neighbors didn't hear.

"Ricardo, help your sister!" I could hear her even outside. She called on him for everything. Being the oldest, it was his curse.

He stood watching through the dining room window. Like a ghoul, he pressed his face to the glass. I remember thinking how mad Mom would get with him for making a greasy nose spot on the window like that. And, she did.

"Ricardo. Hurry. Your sister is dying!" She was frantic.

My throat felt like blood. I couldn't believe the horrible sound was coming out of me. I was petrified to find out what she'd do when she saw I wasn't hurt at all.

Time to throw in the towel. I gave it one last scream.

She shoved the door open. I could see the fear in her eyes, the utter panic, but her feet didn't budge. Her house dress hung to her knees. It was blue, dotted-Swiss. Somehow, I remember things like that. Then, all at once, like Wonder Woman or something, she flew to the driveway. I'd never seen anyone move so fast.

She felt my arms, checked my legs. Put her hand to my forehead and the back of my neck. Her face was chalk-white until she saw I was fine.

Then, it turned purple.

"Why would you do that, you naughty, bad, bad child?"

Then she stopped herself and fell to her knees.

She wrapped her arms around me and squeezed me tighter than ivy. I don't know which of us cried harder, her or me. With my head clamped over her shoulder, I couldn't move or breathe, but I managed to focus on the window. I expected to see my brother there, dancing and raising his arms over his head in victory.

But it was Rich who cried hardest.

He hadn't expected that round would go to me.

Thinking Mother loved me best.

## CHAPTER SEVENTEEN

❖  ❖  ❖

Lindsey hyperventilates at the thought of performing with the dance team. When the curtain rises, it's deer in the headlights time. It's hereditary. My mom let fear kidnap her brain, too.

She warned me of the many horrors that could befall me. If you don't behave yourself, the Chupacabra will get you. That's the fat animal with red eyes and a tail who sucks goats' blood. Don't treat your family well? *La Llorona* will teach you a lesson. She's the wailing woman who searches the night for children and steals them. Don't stay out after dark because the night air has evil spirits. Going outside was rare for her anyway, but she'd never dream of it without a *rebosa* over her nose and mouth. As if a little piece of fabric could protect you from a mean old evil spirit. Afraid of the world, she'd see to it that I was, too. Mean people out there will laugh at you, she said. There's too much to risk, too much at stake. If your own mother thinks you can't do anything, that's what you become used to.

This afternoon, Lindsey's in ballet class with eight other girls. They're basically her age, some a little younger and some a little older. They're doing their practice warm-ups. Each of them is fresh and lovely. Especially her. And here, now, it's all joy. I love to see her happy.

I'm watching her through the one-way mirror. Inconspicuously. Secretly. Like the interrogation rooms on the police shows. I feel sketchy, like the father who lost visitation with his kids and became their school crossing guard just to see them. Imagining myself raising the flag at the crosswalk wearing a nifty orange DayGlo vest and cap, I shudder.

Lindsey points her arms out straight to the sides. She snaps her head to the right and her profile follows the same line. She did a good job slicking her curls into a tight bun, the required hair-do for ballet. She wears the Danskin black leotard and pale pink tights I picked up for her at the beginning of the school year. The left knee is torn and smudged with black. She must've dug them out of the dirty clothes hamper. I'd never let that happen.

She spreads both hands on her stomach, lowers her torso and bends at the knees. With her lips pressed together in concentration, in her face I see elementary school-Lindsey sitting in her little wooden chair behind her little wooden desk. Her pigtails, I braided them every morning.

Ballet is over. Now it's Jazz class. Fluid movements replace ballet's tight positions. Shoulders move in circles and the girls are animated. "Funky Cold Medina" comes on the stereo and they all shake their little hips. I start to cry. I miss her so damn much. It's selfish, but I'm also mourning my own loss of never having anything that was mine. That I was good at. I had no more choices. Chances. I'd gave it all up. My potential is nowhere.

The mirrors aren't completely impossible to see through. If you stand in just the right spot, from the other side, you can tell who's watching. Lindsey squints and looks at the mirror straight on. My initial reaction is to duck so she won't see me. How kindergarten. She moves closer and puts her face directly opposite mine. Realizing it's me, she rolls her eyes.

When the class is over, she comes straight out.

She watches me from the corner of her eye. "I'm working on a solo," she says. "Miss Regina is giving me private lessons."

I try not to look shocked.

"Honey, that's wonderful. You're definitely talented enough," I say. "When did you decide to do that?"

"I didn't."

"Oh. Your dad, then?"

She looks away and nods.

"How's it going with your dad at home, Lindsey?" I say.

I hear the words come out of my mouth and the neck of my blouse seems to vibrate. The feelings, like shrill gusts of laughter, are here so suddenly that I can't get my breath.

"Dad needs me now. I'm cooking," she says proudly. "And not just grilled cheese."

My heart shakes, rattling like china.

Stop it. Just quit. You can't go home with her.

"That's great, honey. I bet they're delicious," I say.

"I'm doing the stuff you used to do, like the wash and taking out the trash. But when Dad asked me to shave his neck I told him it was gross and disgusting." She rolls her eyes.

I completely understand.

"He wants to know if you liked the flowers," she says.

If he sent flowers there'd be Anthrax in them.

How dare Oliver involve Lindsey in one of his mind games?

"He said for me to ask if you've been lonely for him."

She waits for me to answer. She can forget it.

"He doesn't know what's wrong between you guys. I don't either, Mom." She doesn't break eye contact. "And, I deserve to know."

"Our problems are grownup things. They're personal and private between your dad and me and you have no business hearing about them.".

"Whatever, Mom. I knew that's what you'd say. Dad treats me like a grownup. He calls me his buddy," she says, just so happy to be telling me this.

Oliver, you're an idiot. Lindsey has enough friends. What she needs is a parent.

Her backpack bag rings. She dramatically raises a gleaming Nokia cell phone to her ear, making damn sure that I see it. She's been riding me to get her a one since fifth grade. Of course, I said no. It's the new bells-and-whistles model. Costs way more than mine. She turns her back to me and answers it.

"Hi there," she says. Her cheeks dimple. Deep ones, just like Oliver's. "Get real, Daddums. I'd never lose your Visa."

It's all I can do to not wrestle the damn phone out of her hand, but I'd never give her the satisfaction. I'd die first.

She hangs up.

"Let's go, honey. We'll get some ice cream, okay?" The only time I get to see her is after school. "Grandad's waiting in the car," I say.

Looking down, she slides the phone in her backpack. "I'm late," she says. "Spanish Club meeting."

Lindsey wouldn't be caught dead in Spanish Club. She says it's for nerds.

"I'll take you wherever you want to go," I say. "We can go get manicures together." It's her favorite thing.

"I've got a ride," she says. "Don't worry about it."

Before she can get away, I grab her and hug her hard. She smells like peaches. Avoiding my eyes, she pulls away and starts down the hall. She stops and her head drops. I watch her face in the two-way mirror. Her chin's trembling. I think she's going to turn around when she bolts down the hall.

The studio door swings open. A cold rush blows through the hallway. And, she's gone.

I cross the parking lot for my dad. I watch him napping through the passenger window. If it weren't for him, I'd make it work. I'd get my family back.

It feels like I have two hearts. They're swollen, on both sides of my chest.

A single heart can't hold all the pain.

# CHAPTER EIGHTEEN

❖ ❖ ❖

I tighten the sash of my robe and peek out the drapes.

It's my mother-in-law, Olive Morrissey. That's her pink Cadillac on the curb, the eighth she's scored selling Mary Kay Cosmetics and she looks just like her style icon of the same name. Olive's bleached, lemon curls are ratted tall and airy as meringue, and she's drenched in bright pink—lipstick, to her toenail polish.

I pull my hair into a quick ponytail using rubber band from the newspaper and crack the door. Damn, I wish I'd brushed my teeth.

"I had to see this for myself."

I hold the screen open. "Then you're just in time, Olive."

She steps inside, expression on her face like she smells broccoli cooking. "I'd have made it sooner, but I had a hard time finding this place. You understand what I'm saying."

Olive wasn't always a rich snob. She got that way, wanting the best for Oliver. Speech and acting lessons. Tennis, squash and golf. Extras weren't happening on Pete's salary. Now she's at the top of a 400-woman pyramid earning a percentage of their sales. That's a sweet deal, and I say kudos to Olive. That bling on her ample bosom is real, too. "Top Producer" written in diamonds.

She kneels down and flips over the rug, checking for knots per square inch, I suppose. Standing upright, her eyes dart side-to-side, as if she's suddenly aware she's in a trailer home.

I hold a cup of coffee out to her. She likes it black with two sugars.

Ignoring it, she places a book in my hands. "You need to read this from cover to cover," she says. "And then read it again."

I check the title. *A Purpose Driven Life.*

I open the cabinet behind me, put the book inside and close it.

"Why, Olive, I'll cherish it always."

She stiffens, pressing her hand to her throat. For some reason, I can't stop watching the wiggle of fat under her chin. I'd kill to see how she looks without makeup.

"Oliver came all the way over here to reason with you," she says. "Pitiful that he's raising the twins now because you're an unfit mother."

I back up. It's like she slapped me.

"You know me, Olive. You know who I am. What's wrong with you?"

I lean in close and search her eyes. There's no one home.

"Oliver's lying. Can't you see that?"

She wags a pink, sculpted fingernail in my face. "You treat Oliver like an old shoe because marriage isn't always wine and roses? Pete and I have stuck it out for fifty years," she says. "And, you don't leave the kitchen, no matter how hot it gets in there."

"Do you want to bet?" I say.

I take her elbow and steer her from the room. She yanks it away and looks at the green wine bottles in the recycling bin. Counting on her fingers, she starts to say something else when she notices the child-protection knobs on the cabinets under the sink. Her eyes drift to the floor.

I retrieve the book from the cabinet and hand it back. "I have a purpose in my life. It's being Lindsey and Adam's mother." I raise a toast with my coffee mug. "Now, good day, Olive."

She marches toward her pink Coupe de Ville. Tears welling in my eyes, I shut the door. Oliver only interacted with his mother at my urging, and her gratitude has always floated in the air between us, and this is how she's treating me? Is it wrong of me to think she'd support me? I'll never forget her telling me, over spiked holiday eggnog, "Check out how a man treats his mother, dear." She paused, then whispered slowly. "How he treats her, is how he'll treat his wife."

There's a knock on the door. I crack it open.

She reapplied her pink lipstick. It's on her teeth.

"You need a facial, dear. And probably some Botox. I'll make you an appointment and tell them to put it on my card."

I sink behind the door. "Thanks." I think.

I turn and look at my face in the entry mirror. Strange that my beauty has ceased to be a priority. My skin. It does look dull. And my curls, they're shoulder-length now. I haven't worn makeup in days.

She takes my hands in hers and squeezes them tightly. "It's been eating me up inside, knowing how much you must be worrying about the twins. Especially with the hard time you've been having with your father."

I hug her tightly.

"There's something you must to know, but you may not betray my confidence," she says, face inches from mine. "You know I love you Juliana, but Oliver is my son. Do I have your word?"

"Of course."

"He's never been a mother before," she says mildly. "He's always working late. Going out of town. He's in over his head and he knows it. The twins fix their own meals most of the time. His secretary, Carol, can only do so much. He even asked me to come to Austin and stay. Can you imagine that?"

I squeeze my eyes closed.

"Pete wouldn't stand for it." She purses her lips. "When I said no, Oliver mentioned getting an Au Pair."

My eyes fly open. Over my dead body.

"And, you know how he is, dear. He gets set on something and that's what he's going to do."

She forces the book back into my hands.

I'm thumbing through it as her Cadillac pulls from the curb.

# CHAPTER NINETEEN

❖ ❖ ❖

---

I'm grateful for the nights my warm childhood bed shelters me from the rain and I can find sleep. But most nights, I lie awake listening for the music of Lindsey's laughter and Adam's guitar. Instead, there's only the sound of rain drip-drip-dripping into the stagnant puddle under my window.

Each night I see the same thing. Me leaving the house and the looks on their faces. Their reflections in my rearview mirror as I drive away. They never cry, not that I can see. I imagine them doubled over after my car is out of sight.

I hate myself for being away from them. I think of how they don't deserve any of this, and how they need me even if they pretend they don't. Being separated from Oliver, I expected to be half a couple. But being separated from them, having other people tell me things about my own children that I didn't even know, I'm half a parent.

The lonely rain is relentless. It doesn't let up.

Could this be how my father became an insomniac? Shifting the weight of his guilt from side to side as he tossed and turned in his bed? Countless times when I was growing up, I'd hear his footsteps on the stairs in the middle of the night. In the morning he was gone. My mother would cross her arms, saying who stays up that late and gets up that early? It seemed like he was actually hiding at the office rather than be at home with us.

This week I checked into finding caregivers to help me with my dad. It's a ridiculous notion, but I'm so damned exhausted. I see the twins less and less because I have to stay home with him more now. Hauling him around isn't working out like it was. It's not just his bathroom problems. He becomes more difficult now as the day wears on. They call it Sundowners.

If only I could stop thinking of following his ultimate wishes. It heaps another dose of guilt. Some people would condemn me for doing it too soon and others for doing it at all. I know in my heart that the only person's permission I should need is my dad's. I have it. But, it's worthless. Now, hearing his footsteps in the middle of the night, it's not only guilt that I hear. It's my own resentment.

No sleep coming, I throw back the covers and crawl out of bed. Stopping first at the refrigerator, I head outside to tend to the pitiful yard. I uncoil the old hose and yank the sprinkler across the brown grass. The patches it won't reach, I water by hand. Going through my rounds with a glass of wine in one hand and a cigarette in the other, no one to socialize with anymore and isolated as my mother, I have my own cocktail party on the lawn.

I still refuse to give up on the yellow verbena from my own yard. No matter what I do, their shallow roots won't take hold. I've never seen plants die so fast. Maybe it's too much water or fertilizer. Dad's house faces a different direction altogether. That's probably it.

I've barely finished my wine when a strong breeze kicks up and the clouds burst. Tugging the hose behind me, I squish across the yard. The wet, soggy ground gives slightly under my bare feet. I stoop under the dripping eaves to spray the grass off my feet. Steadying myself against the house to my hand disturbs the ivy, and its brittle, dusty leaves drop to the ground.

I switch off the hose and step through the back door. The smell of tonight's pot roast lingers. The kitchen is pitch black. I feel my way to the fridge.

Pulling the handle, a tall light breaks from the door. I take the wine from the shelf and refill my goblet. In the instant before the door sucks back closed, I see Dad's dark profile outlined against the pale cabinets.

He's seated at the table with his hands splayed on the tablecloth. There's peanut butter, graham crackers and Hershey bars in front of him.

"Dad, what's wrong? Why are you sitting here in the dark?" I say.

I flip on the light.

"No," he says forcefully.

I turn it out. "It's after midnight. Shouldn't you be in bed?" I say.

Sitting down beside him, I watch him from the corner of my eye. His tongue licks a glob of peanut butter stuck to his top lip. He's focused on the black knobs of the stove. Robotic, like he's unaware he's doing it, he gives me the last graham cracker spread with peanut butter and a couple of chocolate squares stacked on top.

I put the whole delicious thing in my mouth and slowly chew it up. When I reach for my wine to wash it down, he slides the glass away and pushes the open milk carton in front of me. I look at him with pursed lips, then take a big swig from the carton, Richard-style.

The daughter. I forget sometimes

He rests his head on his hand, and I absently watch the lines on his neck as he breathes. Suddenly he presses his palm against his forehead. Like he means to push it through his brain.

It must hurt, he's pressing so hard.

"Don't understand," he says. "Why. To me."

"I'm right here with you, Dad. You're in the kitchen. Here on Avenue C."

It's the only thing I can come up with to say.

"You hate me." The pain in his voice, the anguish. "Parents shouldn't be problems."

I take his other hand and hold it to my cheek. "I don't hate you. You're not doing this on purpose."

I feel helpless. He's counting on me.

He rubs his palm from his forehead to his crown and holds it there, pressing down. I guess he's trying to keep his brain still, keep it from coming out. Or maybe he's meaning to punish himself.

A strong gust of wind hits the window. Limbs thrash. I turn my head and peer through the rain that sheets down the glass. A bolt of lightning cracks. A flash. I squeeze his hand. Outside the storm spirals the leaves of ivy in a circle.

He squeezes back.

# CHAPTER TWENTY

◆ ◆ ◆

I couldn't stand the thought of people coming to my Dad's rundown house for the sale. No way. I live in this town. If Wally hadn't let me use the shop, I don't know what I'd have done. It's nowhere near open yet, but today's the only time that would work since Dad's at the hospital running diagnostic tests all day.

I'm tired of smiling at people. I'm tired of them smiling at me. The ones whispering to each other about what they suspected is true. Juliana's having the "Lifestyle Adjustment Sale." How about the "My Dickhead Husband Tossed Me Out on My Ass and I'm Broke as Shit Sale?"

People are stacked six deep in the parking lot, waiting to get in. I watch them from the folding table where I have my calculator and cash-box set up. It's by invitation only. Or, so I thought. I didn't think about the car traffic. The directional signs and colored balloons I tied to the fence must've brought them running. It takes everything I have not to hide in the bathroom.

Life's a bitch sometimes.

Wally's lifting a silver Louis Vuitton shoulder bag from the glass case. He handles it with reverence of the King James Version and the care you'd give a newborn. My Gucci baseball cap is on his head. The pink one with the interlocking G's. The tag dangling over his ear reads $45.

His clear voice is somehow audible over the crowd. "It's just one of her little lunch-y bags. Her closet's full of them, but you can have only so many," he says. "It goes for $1550 at Saks."

When the woman doesn't pounce on it immediately, he takes a felt cloth from his pocket and wipes away a speck of dust.

She tugs his arm. "How can I know it's not a knock-off?"

He whisks it back into the case, like a chocolate bunny that would surely melt in the sun. "This isn't Chinatown, baby girl," he sniffs. "People who own the real thing can tell."

The woman rifles through her purse and produces a credit card.

"It's cash and checks only, ma'am."

"But it's American Express," she says.

Her eyes are desperate. I recognize the look.

"Juliana, so you're working now?" someone says. "You're having garage sales for a living?"

I'd know that obnoxious voice anywhere. It's Suzette Smith, the president of the Junior League. In my red Prada sunshades. She turns her head from side to side, appraising herself in the mirror. She slips them off, checks the price tag, and sets them back down.

I want to snatch her bald headed.

Picking through the basket of silk scarves, her fingers find the Hermes toward the bottom. "What's up with you and Oliver?" Her voice lilts at the end. "I heard you learned he was divorcing you in the therapist's office, but I want to hear your version."

Sound byte. Sound byte.

I lean in close.

Her eyes brighten, like I'm offering her a cookie fresh from the oven.

"Oliver is the father of my children and he loves them as much as I do. Neither of us would want to say anything that could possibly get back to the children." I smile sweetly. "I hope you understand."

Would it be laying it on too thick if I folded my hands in prayer?

"Hmm-m," she says.

It's occurred to me that going through a divorce is similar to being pregnant. Like a big swollen belly that people just can't keep their hands off of, your life becomes public domain. With going through both pregnancy and divorce, there are the same questions: "How far along are you? Was it planned?" I'll be happy just so, "My husband screwed me and here's what I have to show for it," isn't also the punch line of my financial settlement.

Scoping the room for shoplifters, I see Richard organizing a stack of belts. My fabulous belts. Looking in the mirror, he tries a few on. He's wearing his hair gelled and combed straight back. He looks cool today in his faded, denim western shirt with pearl snap buttons. What am I saying? Richard looks cool every day.

A stocky woman with a blonde bob holds my black linen, knee-length shift. She looks vaguely familiar.

She puts her face an inch away from his. "Where's the dressing room?"

"In the back next to Alterations," he says dully.

She gives him a nasty look. He unzips the dress for her and helps slip it over her head. When it won't go over her wide hips, he pulls it right back off. She squeezes her eyes closed.

"I hear the down-on-her-luck society matron is Juliana Morrissey," the woman murmurs.

Richard slides the shift back on its hangar. "We don't disclose the names of our clients," he says. "It's not professional."

"You just gave me my answer," she says. "I had to see it for myself."

He says noncommittally, "See what for yourself?"

"What she's been up to, other than selling her things on the sidewalk. But, she must have plenty of time for it, though, what with abandoning her children like she has."

He screams in her face. "What is wrong with you, woman? Were you raised by wolves?"

Her eyes fly open.

"You don't deserve to know my sister. Much less wear her Fendi."

Richard tries yanking the pants from her hands. She won't let go.

He raises his hands over his head and claps them twice. "Mr. Wallace?" he calls over the crowd.

Wally looks up.

"Security, please," Richard says curtly.

Wally straightens tall like a wrestler and strides toward the woman. He takes her elbow and she pulls it from his grasp.

"Oh, girl, don't be making me take off my shoes and go Ninja on you," he says. She drops the pants.

As he's escorting her to the door, the woman waves a hundred dollar bill in his face. Checking that Richard's back is turned, he raises his finger to his lips, and then slinks back for the pants.

Shaking my head, I turn away only to see a skanky woman trying on my Jimmy Choo knee boots. Without sox. Good grief, what her feet must smell like.

"They look good with your butt," her hairy husband says. "But not good enough for *that* price."

The woman shrugs and kicks them against the shoe rack, and most of them tumble to the floor. Bending down to put them back, someone pinches my rear. Incensed, I turn around.

"So, lady. Where are you hiding the good stuff?"

It's Cheryl. Mary Ellen's standing beside her.

"I'm so glad to see y'all," I say and hug them hard.

Finally. People who remember how good I looked wearing these things.

"I didn't know things were this bad," Mary Ellen says. Looking into my eyes, she squeezes my wrist so hard it hurts. "Why didn't you clue us about this?"

"I might've lost my nerve if I talked it to death."

She nervously flicks her blonde hair off her shoulder. From the crooked expression on her face, she doesn't know what to say.

Cheryl gives me a shaky smile. "When did your hair get so long?"

"Does it look awful?"

She tilts her head, critiquing it. "I like your regular chin-length better, but your curly hair's beautiful no matter what."

That was nice of her. I smile.

She looks toward the rack of gowns hanging in front of the picture window. "Isn't that your red strapless from the New Year's Gala over there? I just loved that dress. The Symphony Ball's this weekend." She blushes, realizing what she's said. "But you knew that."

No shit. I'm not brain dead.

Now she makes a big show of casualness, taking off her cardigan and tying it around her skinny waist. "Why didn't you use a resale shop?" she says. "At least that way you'd be anonymous."

"Seriously, Cheryl? For resale, you only get peanuts," I say. "Besides, Wally's helping me. He does it all. Estate sales, art auctions, you name it. He's the best in the biz."

Okay, I made all of that up, but after this he'll have the savvy to do it. Not to mention my killer mailing list.

"He'll be sending out invites for the grand opening. This is the pre-grand opening extravaganza. He has an amazing eye," I say. "That's him over there."

They follow my finger. He's sifting through a stack of my "skinny pants" I've long outgrown. There's a whole table of them.

An old friend taps me on the shoulder. Old friend? I don't even remember her name. She points to the sunglasses on my head.

"How much for those?"

I pull them off and look at them. My black Chanel with the gold C's on the hinges. I search my memory for how much I paid.

"Fifty dollars," she says quickly.

"Fifty dollars? Really?" I say.

She tries taking them from my hands. "Seventy-five. Firm."

Mary Ellen's eyes flash. "Go to Neiman's and get your own pair."

As she backs away, Mary Ellen waves exuberantly at a couple of elderly women breezing in the door and they wave back. "No matter how much money they have," she says under her breath, "people love to haggle. It's part of the garage sale experience."

Cheryl elbows her. "Not that this is one of those, of course. It's just that some people won't accept a fixed price."

I sigh loudly. "That's fine, because I'm not giving my stuff away."

"Seriously, Juliana," Mary Ellen says softly. "How are you holding up, girl?"

I finally can't hold it in anymore. "What do you think?" I say. "This is what I'm reduced to, now that *someone* told Oliver that I was selling my engagement ring."

Her face turns tomato-red.

Damnit. I didn't want to believe it was true.

Cheryl blinks her little eyes. "Mike must have said something."

Mary Ellen glares at her, stumbling on her words. "Juliana, I am so sorry. I wasn't even thinking. I'll never tell Mike anything you said again."

"Why would you tell Oliver's lawyer anything I said in the first place?" I scream.

Nosy women look my direction and whisper.

Cheryl wraps her arm around Mary Ellen. "It didn't happen on purpose, Juliana. It's not like she told Oliver herself."

This isn't happening.

I return the sunglasses to my head. My hairline's wet. I touch my palms to my face. It's clammy. The room's suddenly stuffy. No moving air. I look down the hallway toward the bathroom. It's gridlocked.

I steady myself against the check-out table. A slender woman tries handing me a twenty. I snap up the cashbox and head toward the back door.

"Juliana," Mary Ellen calls after me. "You all right?"

I shoulder through the door and collapse on the wooden bench. Putting my head between my knees, I take several deep breaths.

I may slit my wrists.

Something touches my back and I flinch.

"You're going to be all right."

I look up.

"You really are, you know that?" Wally says gently.

I let out a soft moan and rake my nails through my curls. "These people suck. I just want them gone."

"Let's hope they don't leave just yet." He chuckles. "Let's just get through the next couple of hours, okay?"

He gives me a quick hug, then ushers me back through the door. I watch him weave through the crowd. Locating Richard in front of the leather jackets, Wally whispers something in his ear. Richard's eyes scan the room. Finding me, he pumps his fist in the air. I smile.

Wally is right. After a couple more demoralizing hours, the sale winds down and we roll up the sidewalks. Sapped and sweat-stained, I plod through the parking lot, untie the balloons and pull up the yard signs, then drag myself back inside and kick off my heels.

Wally's already consolidated the remaining dresses onto a hanging rack and begins folding the last of the sweaters. He still has hat hair from the pink Gucci baseball cap that finally sold an hour ago. Richard sits cross-legged on the floor sorting through the sneakers nobody wanted. He ties the laces together and tosses them in a wicker hamper.

Tallying up the take, I keep punching the numbers into the calculator. I do it again. And again.

"Damnit, this can't be right," I say. "I must have priced things too low."

Wally stands over my shoulder. "You're being a little negative. I think that's a good number. Plus," he says in a perky voice, "we got to meet all your cool friends."

I glare up at him. "This money isn't shit in the scheme of things and now I don't have any cute clothes. The house is bleeding me dry. The roof collapsed. I told y'all, right? Plus, the creditors are losing their sense of humor. What if they take the house?"

Richard unzips his money belt. Finding several large bills he'd forgotten, he adds them to the till, then slides his watch over his wrist and drops it in.

After checking the time first, Wally does the same.

"In case you didn't know, Jules," Richard says. "Chinese culture defines a crisis as danger and opportunity."

# CHAPTER TWENTY-ONE

❖ ❖ ❖

Lindsey's waiting at the bus stop, shaded beneath the sloping metal overhang. Her hair isn't flat ironed in its usual braids today; she's wearing it natural, like mine and it swirls around her shoulders.

I signal, check both mirrors and pull into the dedicated teachers' lot. Mindful of the thick, sloping fenders, I swivel the wheel and pull into the last visitor spot. Straddling the vinyl seat, I plant my boot on the pavement and read the enormous changeable letters sign:

PARENT-TEACHER MEETING
WEDNESDAY 4:00 P.M.

My brakes squeak, and Lindsey looks up. I can see from here she's chewing gum. With her retainer in. Raising her hand to her brow, she looks hard in my direction.

I pull off my helmet, white and shiny with a black strap under the chin, like Speed Racer.

Her eyes open wide, then they fall to the ground as if she dropped something. After a few seconds, her eyes look up like there's no recognition. I beep the horn. Then they narrow. She makes a beeline across the crosswalk, turquoise hoodie sweatshirt knotted around her waist and cute little shoulder bag bouncing on her hip. Stopping several feet away from me, she looks me up and down with a disgusted sigh.

"A motorcycle, Mom? Really?" she says. "Where's your Lexus?"

I loop my helmet over the left handlebar. "I have lots of responsibilities and things to pay for. I had no choice but to sell some things," I say defensively.

I planned not to sound that way.

"Thanks a lot, Mom." she says. "You're embarrassing me."

"If I'd known your social standing was on such shaky ground, I'd have rented a limo."

She checks over her shoulder. A girl in tan shorts is bent at the waist leaning into a puny yellow Hyundai. She's talking to a boy with greasy brown hair combed down his forehead. Blinding glare bounces from the windshield.

Lindsey's eyes are wounded. "Everyone's watching," she says.

She's exactly right. A couple of mothers I remember from her elementary school, one of them raises her hand to whisper something. About The Morrissey Twins' Mother.

"Mom, what's wrong with you?" Lindsey says. "Don't things mean anything to you anymore?"

"Young lady, stand here. Put your arms down. If your skirt comes higher than how long your fingers extend down your leg, it's too short," I say. "And, what's with all that eye makeup?"

She kicks my front tire with her toe, narrowly missing the spoke wheels. "Trilby Jackson said her mother came home from your garage sale wearing your red coat, and I saw one of the moms in the front office carrying your tan Gucci purse," she cries. "I knew it was yours from the lipstick stain on the strap."

What have I done?

She cocks her hip to the side. "Dad said you should get a job instead of selling everything that reminds you of your old life," she says. "And he never stops bugging me to tell him everything you've said about why y'all aren't together anymore. I told him nothing, since you told me nothing."

She searches my face. "He says you're going crazy like your mother." When I still don't respond, her voice gets higher. "Are you? Or, are you just being weird on purpose?"

There seems to be a film between me and everything else.

I don't react to anything the way I did.

It's like I watch things happen, so I can tell myself about it later.

If I knew what to say, I'd say it.

All I know is that none of this is her fault. None of it.

# CHAPTER TWENTY-TWO

❖ ❖ ❖

---

Mr. Read says my dad's despondent. He doesn't seem to care about anything. Hand him a book to flip through? He puts it down. Magazine, same thing. Playing dominos with the other residents? Bingo? Forget it. Not the thrill of his existence. He pretty much just sits there. I brought his brass floor lamp from the living room at home. It's the one he uses to read by. His fluffy, plaid bedspread and his maple bedside table, too. I'd have brought his four-post bed if they'd have let me.

Mr. Read helped me realize that checking him in here was the right decision. Where Dad really needs to be. It's best, he said. I tried to tell myself the same story, too. To see if I would believe it.

My dad, or Lindsey and Adam.

I had to choose. They won.

Putting him here was the only way I'd have the time and energy to fight to get them back.

I'd never get them to live with me at Dad's with the house in such pitiful shape, so I patched it up the best I could. I got the roof fixed, put in the new heater and AC, had the phone turned back on. I paid the first two months here at Sagecrest, got Dad's creditors up to date and made payments for two months in advance. And, now there's no money to pay Anabel.

School's almost out and I'm picking up the twins. I stand to leave.

"I have to go now, Dad."

"You're going?" He pushes up on the arms of his chair. He begins to get excited. "Can I come with you?"

My twisting heart burns in my chest. I'd like to take him with me, take him back to the house, but I know he'd want to stay. Every time I dissolve, I read the letter he wrote. I know he doesn't realize it, but it's what he wanted when he was rational. Knowing I couldn't be in two places at once, that's rational, too, right? Oh, Dad, that letter. Will he ever forgive me? Will I ever forgive myself?

Now when I need to go, I've learned what to say. And what not to. I tell him to wait here. That I'll be right back. He'll stop looking after a couple of minutes. He won't remember in a while.

But I will.

He can't see me crying. He can't.

Watching my feet, I slink down the narrow hallway lined with wood-paneled doors, one after the other. An elderly woman tries one of the knobs. It doesn't open. Her sparse eyebrows are blackened with a pencil, drawn in a jagged line. She raps the door with the meat of her hand.

I try the knob, and it opens.

She tilts her head and asks me, "Is this my house?"

I don't know, so I stand behind her and study the old pictures taped to the door, in hopes of recognizing the younger her. They're glossy black and white photos with black processed edge-frames. We study them together. There is one particular image of a handsome young man in uniform.

I point, careful not to touch it. "Is this your husband?"

"Where?" She looks closely.

Her delicate blue eyes are lovely. Like moonstone.

"I have no idea," she says. "But my husband, wherever he is, I wish he would come and get me right now."

She shuffles into the room and sits on her bed. The look on her face is so sad. She's probably way past remembering why, so I sit on the bed and cry for her.

# CHAPTER TWENTY-THREE

◈ ◈ ◈

Turn off Mixmaster. Raise the beaters. Pop them out, lick off the batter.

It's for Adam. German chocolate cake. His favorite. He's spending the night tonight. I fill the first cake pan. Just as I start on the second one, the phone rings. Cradling the mixing bowl in my left arm, I pick up the yellow wall phone, and balance it under my chin.

"Hello. Birdsongs." Stretching the cord as far as it will go, I bend down to switch on the oven. Can't believe I forgot to preheat it.

"I'm calling for Hugh Birdsong, please." It's a woman's voice. Slow and southern.

"May I help you?" The last thing I want to do.

"It's a business matter," she says. Annoying sales people. "When do you expect him?"

"I'm really not in the market for anything new right now, but thank you ma'am," I say, and hang up the phone.

I pour the last of the batter into the second pan, then scrape the last bit from the mixing bowl with a spatula. I put it in my mouth. It's fantastic. I set the bowl in the sink and run water in it. And the phone rings again.

"Birdsongs," I say, exhaling loudly.

"Forgive me for calling back again," the woman says.

"Maybe you have the wrong number."

"This is the number I have. Is this Mrs. Birdsong? Carmen?"

"This is her daughter." I run a pink sponge around the bowl. "She's gone to the other side."

The woman stammers. "You mean she's dead?"

This is obviously a dear friend calling. "That's right."

I check the thermostat on the oven. One twenty-five.

I move toward the wall to hang up the phone.

"I had no idea. I'm sorry," she says, her voice almost a whisper. "When?"

"About twenty-two years ago. Don't worry about it." I push down the door to the dishwasher and load the beaters on the bottom shelf.

"Thank you, Jules," she says softly and hangs up.

Jules?

## CHAPTER TWENTY-FOUR

◆ ◆ ◆

I finally broke down and called the cranky old locksmith, because hell, no, I never found where Dad stashed the key to the garage. But sixty dollars and four months later, I still put off rescuing my old gardening tools inside, sure that exposing the doors will take forever, and I'm right. With thick layers of brittle leaves, impenetrable as a tomb, the garage is encased in vines like sticky fingers that won't let go.

Finally satisfied, my fingers raw and bleeding, I carefully ease down the ladder, and look up at the sagging doors. Silhouettes, like rusty skeletons laid end-to-end, are etched into the wood like fossils.

Looking through the cracked, dusty windows, my nose pressed against the glass, it's dark as a coffin, a cavernous two-car garage with no cars. I gingerly force the doors open. Rolling along the corroded, metal track, the screeching sound is a shrill, haunting echo.

Against one wall sits the old, splintered work bench with a plastic milk crate on top. I'm relieved to find my pinking shears and some green, gardeners' tape inside, but that's it. I toss aside a rusted metal tool box crammed with metal tubes rolled up like toothpaste and thin-bristled brushes, and a grimy, caved-in gasoline can in favor of a cardboard box with its top flaps folded over and under. Perfect. A sturdy, oscillating sprinkler. Pliers. A hand-rake and clippers. It's a start, but nothing close to being everything, and I'll be damned if I'm giving up yet.

Using a wooden stool, I pull the metal chain that's suspended from a lonely light bulb.

Light.

A chill runs across my scalp. Just above my head is the ceiling hoist. The cement floor has faded oil drips in the center of a ghostly outline.

Like striking a match, it all comes back. And, I remember.

Dad wouldn't have it back in here.

My heart beats faster.

The most horrible of days.

I'd lived here my whole life. The kitchen cabinets were still yellow. Their knobs were white. I threw open the doors and looked inside. The canned goods were alphabetized. Glasses lined up, tallest to shortest. SOS and Top Job under the cast iron sink. I lowered the oven door and checked in there, too. Nothing was out of the ordinary. Still, I looked around me, as if it was the first time I'd seen it.

I guess I hadn't. Not like this.

I'd never been alone in the house before.

Getting my bearings, I searched for my mother's old recipes. But, I knew the ones she'd never written down. I knew what she put in them. The chiles, the onions, the cheese, tomatoes and masa. I cooked homemade tortillas on her old comal. I knew I should be doing something for her and it was all I knew how to do. Richard stood by me at the stove, putting his hands on my shoulders and rubbing them. The whole time I cooked, I cried.

For her never leaving the house. For not being there when I came back. And, I hated myself for feeling relief.

Then I held Richard. He did some crying of his own.

I pulled out her lace tablecloth. Set the table for four with her china and polished silver. It was all beautiful, all perfect. Just as she'd like it. At her place, Richard lit a candle. Dad entered the kitchen. Absently clasped her gold coin around my neck. It felt cold. I remember that. And how it warmed immediately on my skin. Then he took his place at the head of the table.

He was so distraught. Just a mess, really. He looked awful, like he'd aged ten years. Richard and I shrugged at each other across the table. After never having seen him show his emotions before, we were shocked at our father acting that way. He'd always been disinterested, as if he was the only one that mattered, so that was consistent, I suppose, but this was weird.

Then, Richard loomed over him as he slumped in his chair. Picking at him. Asking things like, why didn't he look after her better? And, where was she going all the way across town? Dad wouldn't answer. Just looked up at him with something like fear on his face.

There were things I wanted to ask but wouldn't dare. Like what about me? Would a little sympathy for me be out of line? I'm the daughter, remember? Look what I lost. Pull your head out of your ass for once, I wanted to scream, and notice me.

Richard's navy pea coat hung over the easy chair. He roughly pulled on one sleeve, and then the other. It was a cold night. I remember that. Freezing, in fact. He took his gloves from his pocket. Pretending not to care, he put them on and buttoned his coat to the neck. So young. But, twenty-three seemed so old then.

He bucked his head at me. "Let's go, Jules."

We were like Lindsey and Adam. Him, Lindsey. Me, Adam.

"Wait," I said. "I have to ask him something." Dad must've felt my eyes on him, but he didn't break eye contact with Richard.

"I got accepted to law school, Dad. Here at UT." When he didn't react, tell me congratulations or anything, all I could say was, "I have to get the payment in for the semester."

He was still locked-eyes with Richard.

"Did you hear me, Dad?" I said. "Mom said the tuition was handled."

"Like hell it is." He didn't even look at me when he said it.

"But, I studied so hard to get in," I stammered. For years. Since I could remember. Graduated fifth in my high school class. On scholarship at Rice University, I made the Dean's List every semester but one. "What am I going to do?"

"Work for it," he said gruffly. "If it's important enough, you'll move heaven and earth to get it. And, the backbone you get along the way will be a bonus."

Cold wind rushed through the living room. Richard was straddling the door frame, one foot in and one foot out. He'd wrapped a wooly muffler around his neck by then.

"I said let's go, Jules," he said. "What's it going to be?"

He was blazing mad. I was, too. But, I'd never been allowed to show that I had feelings. I felt robbed. My mother gave me a gift and my father took it away.

Then, Dad turned and stared at me, fiery eyes rimmed in red. The look in them scared me. As if he didn't love me at all.

I turned and walked toward the door. Slowly as I could.

And he didn't stop me. The selfish jerk.

Richard ushered me through the door and kicked the screen shut behind us. I followed him off the porch and down the slick, frozen sidewalk. I was shivering. I'd left my coat inside but I wasn't going back in. Never. I looked over my shoulder at the house. Now, completely draped in its ivy. Like a shroud.

Richard opened the passenger side of his Mustang, but I got in my own car. My Chevy Nova. He slammed his fist down on the frozen windshield. With an anguished cry, he kicked the door shut as hard as he could.

If I'd known then how splintered the night would leave my cherished brother and me, what would I have done differently? Anything? How I've wondered that over the years.

Taking the keys from my jeans pocket, I started the engine. Turned on the defroster, my excellent LSAT scores languishing on the other seat. No thanks, I said to a student loan or owing anybody for anything. I drove back to Houston. I'd go to work.

I woke in the morning, safe in my lonely, efficiency apartment, curled up on the couch, still dressed from the night before. The television was blaring. Switched to MTV. It was brand new then. On top of my purse was a receipt from the Gulf station in Columbus. I hadn't remembered stopping.

After that, I didn't move. I didn't turn the volume down or change the channel. I just lay numb on the couch watching every imaginable music video in a continuous loop. I memorized every word, every note, every beat.

Knowing I was left for dead.

Finally putting the phone back on the hook, I remember flipping through the calendar, amazed at the days I couldn't account for.

The stages of grief those enlightened souls talk about? I have no idea what they even are. But, mine were denial, blame and anger, guilt and sadness. They're in a continuous loop, too.

## CHAPTER TWENTY-FIVE

◆ ◆ ◆

I'm straightening up the living room when there's a knock at the door.

I stumble on the floral side chair as I run to open it and bang the crap out of my thigh. I jerk the door open. Expecting Richard, my gaze lifts to six feet-two and immediately drops more than a foot.

It's Señor Sanchez. Smoking a Tiparillo.

"I closed the office early to get here," he says. "Traffic this time of day? Not so bad."

I take his arm. Cashmere blazer. Rico suave. And, is that Hai Karate I smell? "Come on inside," I say. "I have a Diet Coke."

"Hot dog," he mutters under his breath.

He begins inching through the door in polished black cowboy boots. I move to help him, and he shoos me away with his cane. I stand clear.

"Why didn't you just meet me at Sagecrest?" I say. "I bet Dad would want to see you."

"Doubtful. With the exception of having me pull his documents together, he will not speak to me."

"I don't mean to sound insensitive, but he probably forgot he's mad at you," I say.

"Your father may not know what he had for dinner, but he would remember why," he says brusquely. "It is not the kind of thing you forget."

"Why is that, sir?"

"It is nothing for you to be burdened with."

In the entryway, he grimaces and stands upright. Leaning forward on his cane, he looks past me into the living room. Seeing the tall crates stacked against the wall, his eyes narrow behind his tortoiseshell glasses. "The chink in his armor." He mutters and quickly snaps his fingers. "The one from over his desk is still in the car. I intended to send it with you that day, but you flew out in quite a rush."

He inches back down the steps to open the trunk of his car, an immaculate, chocolate brown 1975 Monte Carlo. The cool ones while the hoods were still long.

"Watch it, watch it. You do not know what you have there, Juliana," he cries. "She has clients itching to get their hands on these."

"Oh, come on, Señor Sanchez. You mean that Jan James woman?"

"When she closed her account at the firm, it did not exactly break my heart," he says, then his eyes sparkle. "Except her money was good to have."

"Then, she was your client?

"His."

We lower the painting to the ground and tilt it carefully against the bumper and I stare at the signature: Hugh Birdsong in block letters in the lower right corner.

He shrugs. "I thought maybe he had talent, but what would I know? I'm a numbers person. A dull, old CPA."

Exactly. That's what I'm saying. Just like my dad.

"I'm having a hard time wrapping my mind around all of this, Señor Sanchez. Richard and I knew nothing. My mother either."

He looks at me like I'm a dim-wit.

"You're saying my mother knew?"

"They were husband and wife."

I put my hands on my hips. "Then why weren't his paintings hanging all over our house?"

"According to the fifth Mrs. Sanchez, marriage is compromise."

I wait for him to theatrically shove another knife through his heart like he did at his office. He does.

"Excuse me for saying so," he says. "But perhaps you are learning the same lesson."

Watch it, old man. I was just starting to like you.

I kneel down and begin studying the painting. Glimpsing it for only a moment that afternoon, I don't recall it looking anything like this.

"How come I never saw Dad working at it?" I say.

"I could not say, Juliana," he says. "Still, it seems curious that this comes to you as a surprise. Did no one ever speak in your home?"

I tilt my head and stare up at him. Stooping forward, he inclines his mottled ear, awaiting my response.

133

I turn back around. "Tell me, did Ms. James say how she got her hands on the other paintings before she shipped them here?"

"When her gallery was new, she needed something to cover the bare walls," he says matter-of-factly.

Hmm.

"I wonder why she just returned them now."

"She read about Hugh's regretful financial situation."

I look up at him. "Where? In the *Wall Street Journal*?" I say sarcastically.

He gives me the dim-wit look again. "You may have heard of the Internet?"

I blush. Okay, that was pretty stupid, but for a little Podunk condo complex in Austin, Texas, she must have been Googling him. I wonder what else I should ask.

"Why did Ms. James contact you?"

"Questions after what you told her."

"What I told her?"

He knits his sparse brows. "You told her Carmen was dead, did you not?"

Ohhh. So, that's who the weird telemarketer woman was.

"I'm sorry, who is she again?"

"I told you. Jan James," he says. "You would never guess she was affluent. She was not always that way. A fortuitous inheritance from her elderly neighbors who she looked in upon. An artist, Bohemian-type. She referred to herself as a 'hippie chick,' as I recall. But nobody's fool."

He blows his nose, and it's pretty gross. "My apologies," he says. "So what are you going to do with the paintings?"

"Split them with Richard."

He wipes a monogrammed handkerchief under his nose. "That is it? She said they are valuable."

"Oh please. For the $500 or so they'd all be worth, I'd rather keep them."

"You are sentimental."

"Absolutely." I smile. "They're my dad's."

Señor Sanchez twinkles.

Still squatting in front of the painting, I run my fingers across the canvas, feeling its textured surface for several moments. He rests his hands on my shoulders.

"You spoke to Ms. James last....?" I say.

"1982."

"How do you remember that?"

Uncharacteristically sing-songish, he answers, "I just do."

Richard and Wally squeal up in Wally's Ford F-150. Richard's behind the wheel with Fritz on his lap. He slams on the brakes and throws it in park. Leaving Fritz looking out the window, he sprints up the sidewalk. About to step onto the porch, he notices Señor Sanchez in the driveway.

"Ricardo." Señor Sanchez breathes evenly, trilling his R's.

Richard does a formal bow like a bullfighter. "Señor Sanchez," he says gravely. "*Mucho gusto.*"

One alpha dog sizing up another, Señor Sanchez puffs his chest and leans forward on his cane. "*El gusto es mio.*"

My brother, young, muscular, and being on his home turf, narrowly triumphs. Relishing his victory, he steps stiffly into the house.

Carrying Fritz in his arms, Wally comes to stand beside Señor Sanchez and me. He quickly looks down at the painting, says, "Nice," and follows Richard inside.

Only a couple of minutes pass before they come back out.

Richard throws up his arms. "What the hell?"

I laugh at his expression. "Told you," I say. "Let's pack them back up and high-tail it down to Sagecrest. Dad's got to see them."

The canvases are large. One measures probably five feet by five feet, and the others are about six by six. As Richard and Wally file out of the house and load them into Wally's truck, Señor Sanchez appraises them each. "He improved," he says. "I like them very much."

Stubbornly declining to come along, Richard hands me the keys and Wally, Señor Sanchez and I crowd together on the bench seat.


The lights are out. The room is dark. Dad didn't have a good day and bedded down early for the night. Careful not to wake him, Wally and I prop the pieces gently against the wall as Señor Sanchez, who was kind enough to remember it from the office, arranges Dad's crystal prism nameplate on the bookshelf. Hearing Dad stirring, I turn to check on him just as moonlight shining from the window makes a rainbow on the prism and bounces to the painting from above his desk.

Once again, it glows.

## CHAPTER TWENTY-SIX

❖ ❖ ❖

His gray brows bunched together, Dad leans forward as far as possible without toppling from the chair. Reaching out tentatively, he gently touches his palms to the canvas and holds them still. Then, spreading out all ten fingers, he begins moving them lightly across the surface, as if he's reading brail. Bringing his face in close, he presses his nose to the canvas and a sparkle of recognition comes over his face. Nothing stirs a memory like your favorite smell.

Soaking up his talent, amazed that my own father painted something so beautiful, my eyes begin to tear.

He begins waving one hand anxiously while squeezing his eyes shut for several moments, then his eyes pop open and he stares straight above him, as if he's recreating the paintings on the ceiling. He carefully stands and walks in a circle, the best he can on his bum leg. Moving clumsily to the window, he looks to the courtyard, seeming to collect his thoughts with a distant look on his face. Distant but so present.

I touch his shoulder and he shudders slightly. His skin feels warm, like there's an electrical charge surging through him.

Finally, unable to hold it in, I say, "Why don't you paint anymore?"

He seems almost irritated when he answers. "It's not necessary to put a brush to the canvas. I form the composition and paint in my head."

A deep voice at my shoulder startles me.

"Why, Mr. Birdsong, you were holding out on us, weren't you?" It's Mr. Read. "After all these years, to have people admire your work must be the culmination of all your dreams."

Dad shoves his hands in his pockets. "Not really."

I nudge him. "Hey, Dad. Why did you stop in the first place?"

He begins looking out the window again. "Try going back inside a burning house," he mutters. "You'll die."

# CHAPTER TWENTY-SEVEN

❖ ❖ ❖

---

Adam plays air guitar.

"A new band asked me to join," he says. "Okay, it's just an audition, really. But they need a strong rhythm guitar. That's me. I'm a blues man."

I want to squeeze him, but I play it cool. No way I'm getting invested. My heart's still bruised from before.

"Open jams, rehearsals, gigs," he says. "All that stuff." He fancy finger works while watching me from the corner of his eye. "With a new Fender Stratocaster?" He looks to me hopefully.

"Oh, absolutely," I say. "Let's buy two."

So much for him not being spoiled.

He shrugs. "I have to audition with a certain song."

I nod my head. "I'm sure that's true."

"It's by Stevie Ray Vaughn. I thought I knew all his stuff, but I've never even heard of it," he says. "Plus, Mom, once you're in, there's new songs to learn all the time. It's fierce." He shakes his head. "I need the music."

"What you need is Paolo," I say.

He exhales, like he's glad the truth's out in the open. "I didn't tell him I was quitting, Mom," he says. "He's probably so pissed."

"Yes, he is," I say.

Adam's face falls.

"Paolo's a good man and he invested a lot in you. He thought he deserved the courtesy of a good-bye, especially from his star student," I say. "And the chance to talk you out of quitting."

His eyes are serious behind his square glasses. Desperate. "Will you talk to him for me?"

Adam's getting too old for his mommy to come to his rescue. If I keep it up, I'll still be doing it when he's forty.

"I'm happy to drive you over there," I say. "But the rest is your baby."

The apples of his cheeks flare. "I knew that's what you'd say." He slings his backpack over his shoulder and pulls out his spiffy new cell phone, just like Lindsey's. "No way I'm staying here."

Great. Which means she never will either. I know her.

Pulling back the curtains, I see him yank the flimsy gate off its hinges. Flustered, he throws down his backpack. The breeze catches the loose papers and blows them across the yard.

I start to bang on the window but stop myself. Watching my son chase the papers down and catch them under his feet, I'm amazed at the change in him. Gone are his holey jeans and striped, faded blazer from Goodwill with the rolled-up sleeves. Adam Morrissey in a pink Izod, pressed designer jeans and topsiders? I'll die if he cuts his hair.

Picking something off the ground, he suddenly stands, does a wind-up and throws it with all he's got, then jerks his head toward the house and pops his hand over his mouth.

I throw open the front door. "What did you throw?"

His reddened cheeks are streaked with white. "Golf ball," he chokes.

I push him aside and tear down the sidewalk. A white Volkswagen SUV is stopped in the middle of the street. The license plate reads SINGLE.

I tap the driver's window. It rolls down. "Are you all right?" I say.

Her low-cut sweater is wet down the front from her can of Fresca. Adam stoops down as she's mopping it from her cleavage. "Sorry I ruined your car," he stutters, not looking at her face. "I'll mow your lawn to pay you back."

"I'll take you up on that," she says brightly. "You know Amber Singleton, don't you? I'm her mom."

Adam blanches like he found out he just made out with his cousin.

Kimberley presses her palm to her hairline. "I'm not bleeding, am I?" She flips down the visor and checks.

"Whew! But it looks like it's time for a new one of these." She reaches over the dashboard and touches the cracked windshield. There's a bud vase with an orange daisy in the cup holder.

"I can't tell you how sorry I am," I say. "I'll write you a check right now."

"It's no biggie," she says. "It won't cost anything. My friend owns the dealership."

Ed Hastings Volkswagen-Audi? He's married. Oh.

"Hey, what are you doing on our street?" I say.

She points at two foil-wrapped casseroles on the passenger seat. "I brought you my scrumptious chicken spaghetti, fresh out of the oven." On top she's written in calligraphy, "Love ya Loads, Kimberley."

"It's what I used to bring to friends having a baby. Now I bring it to friends going through a divorce. And since you've also moved, Juliana, I brought you an extra. As a housewarming gift."

I blush. She's the only person who's gone to the trouble.

"And, we say thanks by cracking your windshield," I say. "Why don't we all go inside and we'll dish it up?"

Her hazel eyes and high cheekbones slant upward. "Well, sure. I'd love that," she says.

"Dad's coming to get me," Adam says. "I'm eating dinner with him."

"You know what?" she says. "I should probably go, too. It's getting late."

I squint my brow. "Adam, did you talk to him?"

"Carol said he's in a meeting."

The long-suffering Carol. Bless her heart.

"She always comes, except she just got back from dumping Lindsey at the mall and she has to grab her kid from daycare."

"Lindsey's at the mall with no adult supervision? It'll be dark soon."

"She's always up there," he says. "I figured you knew."

I take a deep breath and blow it out slowly. "I most certainly did not."

Kimberley leans forward pretending to search for something in her glove box. Adam can't help sneaking another peak at her cleavage. "She usually gets a ride home anyway," he says.

"Your father has Carol come back and get her, too?"

He shrugs.

"I'll go get her and while you study for your history test," I say. "You can spread out in the breakfast room."

He crosses his arms over his chest. "I told you I'm not staying. Especially since I need the review sheet off the school website. There's not even Internet over here, Mom."

He says it like there's no indoor plumbing.

Kimberley pats the seat next to her. "Hop in, Adam. I'll run you home. We'll swing by the mall and get your sister, too."

Adam says, "Where's Amber?"

"With her father. She only lives with me half the time."

There's a blade in my heart. She and I exchange looks.

Adam rests his hand on her side mirror and begins scanning the street.

I point at the storm drain, more than a little irritated. "Maybe you made a hole in one," I say. "Way to go."

I open Kimberley's passenger door to take the casseroles off the seat and Adam crawls in.

I put my hand to his cheek. It's still flushed.

"I don't know how to tell Dad. I hate golf," he says.

"We'll work it out, Adam," I say. "With Paolo, too."

He gives me a hairline smile.

I reach across and touch Kimberley's shoulder. She squeezes my hand, then puts it in gear.

I blow Adam a kiss as they drive away.

# CHAPTER TWENTY-EIGHT

❖  ❖  ❖

Dad hasn't noticed the new easel yet, or the canvas I put on it. When I stopped by Asel Art, the salesman said I just had to get M. Graham paint, so I bought several tubes, plus palettes to mix the colors. I even sprung for the fine Kolinsky sable brushes.

Dad resists when Mr. Read rolls him to the easel and sets the brake. Unable to turn the wheels, Dad twists his neck and scowls up at him.

Mr. Read points at the canvas. "Mr. Birdsong, look what we have here."

Dad eyes it suspiciously.

I'm paralyzed with anticipation.

"Are you going to give it a try, Dad?" I say. "What do you think?"

Dad's eyes travel from one edge of the canvas to the other, then he turns his head to the side and quickly looks back again, like he's checking to see if the canvas is looking at him.

I slide the old rusted toolbox from the garage onto his lap, in case using something of his own would make him more comfortable. It occurred to me that with the paint supplies inside, the only person it could belong to is him.

Irritated, he shoves it back at me. When I don't take it, he looks down. Seeing the metal tubes of paint, their plastic caps crusted with color, his eyes stretch wide. He takes the tube of red, expertly untwists the cap, raises it to his nose and inhales deeply. He hurriedly rummages through the box now, seeing which of his goodies are still inside, ignoring the worn brush on top with paint-stained bristles.

Pick it up. Pick up the brush.

There's noisy chatter in the hallway. Good news travels fast.

## PAINTING JULIANA

Mr. Read nervously cracks the door a few inches to shush the crowd of residents, caregivers and guests. Seeing my father at the easel, they elbow past Mr. Read and scrape through the door.

Dad turns to look behind him. Eyes like an overcast sky, his gaze stops on each anxious face. No one offers any words.

He yanks the new palette from the easel and hurls it against the canvas.

## CHAPTER TWENTY-NINE

❖　❖　❖

Wally decided on a name for the shop: Birdsong Boutique. It has a delightful ring to it, I have to say. The shop still isn't ready to open for business yet, but it's getting closer.

Built of sturdy, white limestone, the shop was originally a cozy residence with a big front yard and plenty of tall oak trees. Pulling up the grass in favor of gravel seemed sacrilegious, but they had to do something about parking. The trees will mean plenty of shade for the customers' vehicles, but also plenty of dirty windshields.

It's not a perfect world.

My hair's pulled back in an orange bandana and I'm wearing my Ellie Mae outfit Oliver likes so much. It's been a gorgeous Saturday, cool with a nice breeze, and now the sun's almost down, but I'm still up to my elbows in dirt. I'm nestling the ivy I brought from Dad's house into the shallow trough I dug around the shop's perimeter. Although I have mixed feelings about bringing it, this place needs all the help it can get, and ivy's the only thing that grows like whiskers.

Wally comes behind me, kicking dirt clods across the gravel. The look on his face says he needs to talk. I pat the tree stump beside me.

"Anything at all you need, just ask," I say. "We're family."

Reddish goatee perfectly trimmed, he slips off his Buddy Hollies and cleans them on the tail of his turquoise Polo. "Maybe I shouldn't admit to this, but I'm jealous of those kid's you've got. Call it biological clock, maternal instinct, whatever, but I've always some of my own."

More than anyone else I know, Wally is a kind person. Richard has better luck than I do with practically everything. Especially men.

"I was married for a time and I loved her, but not like she deserved," he says. "Her name was Lynn. We came close to having a child together and I'm not proud that it was my primary goal in marrying her." He sheepishly waits for my reaction. I give him a sad smile.

"When I told her that I played for the other team, she should've killed me, but she was a doll about it, really." He rubs his jaw. "A better sport than I'd have been."

"Whoa, me, too," I say. "I take it this was a few years back?"

"Ten. Seems like a lifetime ago."

Because I'm so nosy, I say, "Have you and Richard talked about it?"

"Ad nauseam, actually. He's scared to commit to a child," Wally leans forward and rests his elbows on his knees. "Maybe it's to me."

"I doubt that. I get the feeling he really loves you, Wally," I say.

And, I truly mean it.

"He's committed his heart to the relationship, but psychologically? I'm not so sure," he says. "Neither Hugh nor Carmen was a great role model."

"Nope. You were there for the whole ugly truth."

"Living across the street was entertaining." He chuckles. "But, I've told Richard none of that matters. If your childhood wasn't exactly dandy, you get a second chance when you start a family of your own."

"Oh, gosh," I say. "Your parents. How are they?"

His cheeks flare. "Call them and ask them yourself," he says. "Bunch of homophobes. They haven't spoken to me in years."

Wally stares at his lap and I drape my arm around his neck. We sit in silence for a few moments.

"If I could convince Richard, I'd want a formal commitment like other couples," he says. "I'd want to give our children that."

"You've already done so much for him, Wally," I say. "You took over his house payments when he lost everything, didn't you?"

He nods. "When you love someone, that's the kind of thing that you do."

"Underneath Richard's tough exterior, I wonder if there's not a pussycat inside aching to get out," I say.

"Sure there is, but what I told you before—well, he's afraid he won't measure up." Wally shakes his head. "But, I'll tell you this: I'll adopt an older child. Special needs. I'm not picky. Nothing's going to come between me and becoming a father."

Hearing tires on gravel, I turn to see Rich peeling into the parking lot in the convertible. The soft top's down, no matter what the weather. Fritz is beside him up front strapped into a doggy car seat.

"The best way for me to help may be for us to spend more time together, Wally. Adam and Lindsey, too, I mean."

I watch Wally's wheels turn.

Richard slams the car door and begins trotting across the gravel leading Fritz on a leopard-print leash. Seeing me, Fritz heads immediately for my crotch and makes a perfect bulls' eye with his nose.

I frantically brush him away. "Rich, how about teaching your dog some manners?"

He feeds him a treat from his pocket and pats his head. "You should feel honored the two of you have a special relationship," he says.

I hate my brother sometimes.

Wally bites the inside of his cheek, stifling a laugh.

I wait for Richard to ask about the paintings when he begins throwing the tennis ball. Fritz sprints across the gravel on his short, stocky legs and comes back with the slimy ball between his teeth, and his white tail sticking up straight in the air, waving like a windshield wiper. Just so precious.

"Can I can pick your brain, Jules?" Wally says tentatively. "I'm wanting to carve out a niche for the shop and I couldn't help but notice at the garage sale, I'm sorry, at your Couture Sale, your finger's on the pulse of the highfalutin ladies in town," he says enthusiastically. "They really like your taste."

Oh, I'm the flavor of the month, that's for sure. And, about as well-liked as licorice.

"Jules," Richard says. "This is the place where you're supposed to tell Wally, 'I wouldn't change a thing'".

Wally dismisses his comments with the flick of his wrist.

"Put in gardening section. That's what I'd do. Birdhouses and wind chimes, that sort of thing. Unique things you can't get anywhere else," I say. "Maybe a glass case for fresh flowers up front."

Wally scratches his temple. "You know, that's why I ask your opinion," he says. "You could be onto something there."

I shrug.

# CHAPTER THIRTY

❖   ❖   ❖

After taking no interest in anything since he's gotten here, now Dad sits admiring his paintings all day, entranced, scarcely saying a word. Some mornings, he'll have scarcely moved from the spot where I left him the night before. I'll ask him to explain them to me, but it's like he doesn't hear me. I'll catch him smiling. Other times I'd swear he's crying, but his eyes are as dry as the canvas.

Each of the paintings is produced in oil. On some, it's applied thickly and even-textured. Others, it's more like a delicate overlay; translucent as a misty shadow, or a pale lantern's glow. Highly-detailed, with expert execution, the paintings are so realistic it's eerie, the kind you can't help but touch to see if it's really a photograph—movement frozen in an instant, like captured time. But, stare at them a while and it's as if the movement goes on. How is it possible that his paintings seem alive, long after he's raised his brush?

Do they conjure up ghosts that will shake him out of his mental amnesia? If only they had hidden passageways leading to secret finding places for things he's lost. It bothers me when he looks at them with his eyes glazed behind their tiny, smeared lenses, as if he's asleep with his eyes open. Maybe he won't tell me anything about the paintings because he can't remember anything about them himself.

Now, he's moving his head from side to side, examining the canvases from different angles. Watching him, my emotions are so strong—joy in the beauty he's created—amazement and pride, but there's so much more. How did he steal the time to create them? What were they doing in New York? And, why did he never share them with me?

I want to ring his neck.

I decide I can't take it anymore. I'm going to do it.

I reach to turn the volume down on the radio, then squat down to his level. "Dad," I say slowly. "The paintings. They were shipped from a New York art gallery."

He cuts his eyes to me.

I keep my voice calm. "A woman named Jan James sent them."

His expression goes blank. I focus on his forehead. I try and look inside his brain and gather his mind.

"Why did she have your art work?"

Squeezing his lids tightly, the light catches his lashes.

"Did you hear what I said? Do you know her?" I wiggle his knee, but he doesn't open his eyes. I've often suspected that he uses his dementia to his advantage sometimes.

I sigh and turn the music back up. Maybe a change in scenery will dislodge something. Shake something loose. Dad doesn't seem to mind when I push his chair down to play a little bingo. Lord knows, I could use a peppermint stick.

We enter the rec room and the activities leader smiles at me with kind eyes. She's always grateful when I come up to help. Dad and I pull up to the friendship table in the middle of the room and join a lively group of residents.

I search the room for the judge. Her smooth face haunts me and I can't move until I find her. She's seated at the long table against the wall, with her same three tattered bingo cards lined up before her. When I wave at her, her eyes light on my face and her puzzled expression falls. For an instant, the real woman emerges from of the shadows, and it takes my breath away. The next instant, she's gone. And, continues her game of solitaire.

I slide a few extra checkers in front of the man sitting beside me. His brown hair is trimmed flat, only a half inch off his scalp. Not sure that he's getting the hang of it, I place a checker on the free-space in the center of the man's bingo card. Looking up, his expression tells me that he'd rather Juliana worry about Juliana.

Dad hasn't spoken a word since we left the room. I watch him closely, surprised that he's getting into it for a change. The leader pulls a couple of ping pong balls out of the air machine and calls the numbers loudly. Nobody yells, "Bingo," but Dad's card is getting pretty close.

Pretending that I suspect him of cheating, I lean in close and run my finger down each of his columns.

"Jan James." I say her name in his ear, slowly and deliberately. "Why were your paintings in her New York art gallery?"

147

## PAINTING JULIANA

He keeps his head down. His jaw moves. Just a little twitch.
I nudge his arm. "Were you living a double life or something?"
He looks up at me. The light bounces off his glasses.
"Who told you?"

# CHAPTER THIRTY-ONE

❖ ❖ ❖

"Glad you can finally get out," Mary Ellen says. "Now that your dad's handled."

She stands up and gives me a long hug. She smells good. Her hair is clean and her makeup is applied perfectly. Mary Ellen is a beautiful woman. It's been a while since I've seen her, and I'd forgotten.

One of the last times Mary Ellen and I were together was here at Taqueria Pepe. Not counting a few times in between when I picked up the kids from her house, or something like that. She looked after Dad for a couple of hours when I met with Anabel, but it's not like she made a special visit to come see how I was doing on her own. Oh, and of course my Couture Sale, but we haven't had lunch or anything. I've noticed before, but I really think of it now that we're sitting here face to face and she's telling me that my dad is handled. Whatever that means.

Our usual waiter, Felipe slides between the tables. He balances a griddle of smoking fajitas on his tray. They smell fantastic. Catching his eye, I give him an exuberant wave.

He smiles broadly. "It's been a long time," he calls.

I'll say.

It's crowded tonight. Even for a Friday. Lots of people aren't Pepe fans, saying their Tex-Mex is marginal at best. It's true that their chips are greasy enough to immobilize the contents of an entire salt shaker, but throwing back a couple of their margaritas will make a Pepe-convert out of just about anyone.

There's something dangerous in them, and it's not just tequila. They're laced with a potent substance more addictive than crack cocaine that causes subtle mind control. They're the real reason anyone comes to this place. After drinking one, you're sociable, two, you're quite animated, and three, you're at risk of embarrassing your family. A certain woman who will remain nameless—okay, it was Cheryl—fell from her car into her own driveway. She might still be lying under the sprinklers had her neighbors not seen her when they went for the morning paper.

Mary Ellen excused herself to go to the ladies room but she hasn't made it that far. She's chatting with a table of friends in the bar while I wait in the dining room. It's like I'm the visiting cousin from out of town who doesn't know anyone, so it's just peachy to leave them alone at the table. I was connected to those friends. I introduced them to Mary Ellen, in fact, and now she talks to them without me. I should get over it and join them, hug a few necks and kiss a few cheeks. Put on my social face—the one that used to fit seamlessly. But somehow, I just can't.

Trying to look nonchalant, I check my watch. It's been twelve minutes.

Kimberley is in a booth in the back of the dining room. Hair tousled perfectly, she's wearing long, coral chandelier earrings and matching lipstick. She's been watching me pretty much ever since I came in. Not staring, just glancing over every once in a while, making sure I'm still here. There's a handsome man I don't know at her table. He's leaning very close.

I take the bottle of La Crema from the ice bucket and walk toward her. I see her whisper to the man to beat it. I guess that's what she says, because he does. She casts her eyes down coquettishly. That must be how she draws people to her. Pure habit and instinct.

"I need someone to help me finish this bottle of wine," I say.

Kimberley moves her glass of tea and makes room. "Sit your little self down, then," she says with a smile.

"Listen, for the delicious casserole, I don't know how to thank you. And for taking Adam and picking up Lindsey? Well, Kimberley, that meant the world to me."

She self-consciously twirls the ends of her hair. "I've been thinking about her. How's she doing?"

"As much as I see her, I'm probably not the best person to ask," I say.

"At mine and Stephen's hearing, we got a parenting plan. Well, being a good parent isn't about winning a popularity contest," she says. "Or, at least that's what my mother told me."

She quickly nudges my arm and points to Mary Ellen who's standing by the table where she left me. "You better hurry," she says. "Your friend's waiting on you."

Seeing Felipe carrying a full tray of margaritas, Mary Ellen flags him down, gives him a big hug and takes one. She quickly licks salt from the rim and takes a long sip as her eyes scan the room. Spying me at Kimberley's table, she does an exaggerated double take and covers her mouth with her hand.

I linger at the table. "Kimberley, I had to put my dad in the Alzheimer's facility," I say. "Do you think I'll fry in hell?"

"I most absolutely do not."

"Really? How do you know?"

She puts her hand on my arm. "Somebody has to come first right now. I assume he's already lived a long, happy life," she says. "You? Not so much."

I consider whether this is true. In both my dad's case and my own.

"Do you want to do coffee?" I say. "At Jo's on South Congress? My treat."

"Oh, what a hassle. Why don't I come by the home so I can meet your dad?" She flashes her smile. "I'm sure he's a darling man."

I smile back. "That's right. He is."

I scratch down my number on her napkin and she tucks it in her bag.

"And, Juliana," she says. "If you really are going to fry in hell, you won't be finding out anytime soon."

Watching me leave the table, she tickles the air with her pinkie.

## CHAPTER THIRTY-TWO

◆ ◆ ◆

Mr. Read called saying my dad got no sleep again last night. I barely sleep myself. Strange, but knowing we're both awake, sharing the dark, lonely night comforts me somehow. When I can't be with him, I think of him lonely and wondering where I am. But does he know how much time has passed? Does he even put it together? I pretend to myself that he does. Believing otherwise makes it worse. After I hung up talking to Mr. Read, I walked to the kitchen and unconsciously began making the twins' lunches. Didn't matter that I haven't lived with them for months or that they've eaten in the cafeteria for years now. Since elementary school.

Standing in doorway to Dad's room, I check the blank easel. I've taken to leaving it set up in front of the window, ready for when the spirit moves him, if it ever moves him again. His signature is in the corner of every painting, but that's not good enough for me—I want him to prove that he paints, but like everything else with him, I must wait. The new paints and brushes are laid out so he can use them easily, but the canvas remains blank and the bristles have no color. His color seems to be fading, too.

Today, he's really zoned-out, in his own little world, pulled up in front of the paintings, doing that irritating thing again where he acts like he doesn't hear me. It's not like we were having deep discussions before, and I don't want to be weird about it, but it's been going on for weeks now and I'm starting to get worried.

What's he thinking, this man who's losing his mind?

He wears the same stained, ratty sweater every day. The top three buttons are missing, but he won't let me repair it, much less wash it. I hate seeing him like this, his dignity stripped away.

Why do people have to live so long when the end seems like one long, cruel, nasty joke? And that phrase "quality of life?" Well, I'm sick of hearing it, frankly, especially how it's never said without the words, "he has no," coming first. Having a high quality of life—what would that look like? Body-wise, it would be feeling super healthy, but in a broader sense, I'd say happy and fulfilled. And like what you do matters. And that you matter.

Checking my watch, I know I'll be late picking up Adam if I don't get going. About to tell Dad goodbye, I hear a loud noise at the end of the hallway.

A banging clatter.

A tall man in a tattered bathrobe stands at the door to the patio. A plaid porkpie hat is pulled down over his white, shoulder-length hair and his house slippers are broken down in the heel. Through the door is a little gazebo surrounded by potted geraniums. Beyond that is a sand pile with a yellow shovel and a pinwheel. A strong wind blows it round and round.

He presses his face to the glass and looks out, just a little boy who wants to go outdoors and play, but here, that's a big no-no. Who wouldn't want to escape this horrible place?

He puts all his weight behind the door, and the piercing alarm goes off. The man pounds his meaty palms against the glass. Panicked, he turns around. White hair frames his lined cheeks. His eyes are lost and frightened.

"Missy, will you open the door?"

He must be talking to me.

I nervously scan the hallway. It's deserted. What do I do? Play along with the cruel game that's in place here? I can't lie to a grownup. I was taught to respect my elders. Treat them with dignity.

"I'm sorry, sir," I tell him. "I don't have the key."

I don't.

My grateful heart jumps seeing an irritated male orderly turn the corner. Dirty sheets are wadded over his arm and he's clutching a large bottle of pills.

Eyes bright, the old man looks at him now.

Stopping, the orderly pulls his phone from the front pocket of his scrubs and calmly checks his messages.

Like a siren, the alarm's still blaring.

I don't take my eyes off him until he starts up again.

He does.

I'm in the clear.

Now, the poor, anguished old man balls his fists and beats the glass.

"I just want to go home!" he cries.

I turn my head away and wipe my cheek.

153

## CHAPTER THIRTY-THREE

❖ ❖ ❖

When I ask Adam about school, he tells me everything's good. But me being called to the principal's office, it can't be that good.

I'm not the first parent to squirm here, nervously reading the school menu taped to the wall. Today it's meatloaf and tater tots. Chocolate brownie for dessert. I doubt Oliver remembers to refill the twins' punch cards. I imagine them in the cafeteria line with only enough money to buy a Little Debbie.

Principal Murray sits in a maroon swivel chair, looking professional in her navy suit. She's new to the middle school this year, and I don't have an exact bead on her yet. She would seem nice enough reciting the pledge at assembly and she would always compliment the sugar cookies I'd bring to the office, but that's as far as it went.

Finishing her call, she faces a stack of papers toward me. I recognize Adam's handwriting immediately, tiny capital letters. After the unit for learning cursive was over in third grade, he never did it again.

"Your son's grades have slipped dramatically," she says. "In not just one class, but all of them."

Is it true? When I was here volunteering all the time, I had informants tell me if he was tardy to class. Flipping through his papers, heat rises to my scalp. D, C-, D, D+. A history test has a big red F on top.

Oh, he's history, all right.

It's hard to maintain my composure. "Shouldn't I have been informed of this earlier, Mrs. Murray?"

She straightens up in her chair. "We called your home many times but the messages were never returned."

Why wouldn't Oliver call her back? Oh, right—he's too important to check the machine.

"Had Mrs. Magruder not been in the office yesterday, I wouldn't have your cell number," she says, then threads her fingers together. "The truth is, Adam has been disruptive in class, always making a funny comment or finding some other way to get the kids' attention."

"That's not my Adam. I've never had a complaint about him. Ever," I say. "Certainly not a behavioral one."

"Mr. Peters the eighth grade counselor was able to wheedle from Adam that you and his father are separated," she says, then tops it off with a look that says, "Parents shouldn't be problems, but we see it all the time."

I want to sink into the floor. Looking down at the helmet at my feet, I'm reminded of how much things have changed.

"This Mr. Peters, may I speak with him?"

"He's in a training meeting this afternoon or I'd walk you to his office right now." She sifts through her drawer and hands me his card across the desk. It's thick, white card stock, embossed with the school's red and gold seal.

The person's card who steps in when a kid's parents are screwing up.

"I'd like to hear what my son has to say about this," I say. "Can you please call him out of class?"

"I don't see why not." She punches a few keys on her computer and pulls up his schedule. "He's in English now with Ms. Carter, but may I say something first?"

"All right." I scoot my chair closer to her desk.

"I think your son feels like he has no power and he's acting out to bring attention to himself," she says. "Negative attention is better than none at all."

Maybe Adam's not so bulletproof, like I thought.

"It's me who's not living with them right now." I pinch my leg, trying not to tear up.

She nods. "How are things between him and his father?"

A feeling of rage comes over me. "I really don't know."

"How would you feel about getting your son a tutor?" she says.

I shake my head. "He's never needed one before."

"Well, maybe now he does. We can see about getting him into one of our after school programs."

Has it come to that?

My heart jumps. "You didn't mention Lindsey," I say. "Are her grades doing all right?"

She smiles and shakes her head. "Nothing to worry about there, Mrs. Morrissey. Your Lindsey would do fine in the middle of a thunderstorm."

What a thing to say. It feels like that's what this is.

She reaches the bowl of Snickers on her credenza and offers me one. I absently remove the gold wrapper and pop the candy into my mouth.

"Forget about calling him out of class, please," I say. "Jumping on him in the middle of the school day is the last thing he needs."

Besides, I don't think I'm up for it.

# CHAPTER THIRTY-FOUR

❖ ❖ ❖

Calling Jan James is the last thing I want to do, but it's been ages now since she shipped the paintings—way past being rude. It's petty and childish and I know it, but I hate that this woman I'd never heard of knows things about my dad that I don't. And why did she keep the paintings from me? She had no right. Does she even have any idea how special they are?

"Jan James," she answers.

"Hello, Ms. James," I say. "It's Juliana Birdsong calling."

I hear her suck in her breath. "I'm so glad to hear from you," she says.

"Forgive me for being so late getting in touch."

And, I'll leave it at that.

"Ms. Birdsong, you don't know how sorry I was to hear the sad news about your father's health," she says. "How long has he been ill?"

"It's hard to say," I tell her dully. "He's gotten worse lately. My brother and I complied with his wishes and placed him in a home."

"Oh, my goodness. My thoughts and prayers are with him," she says, her voice no louder than a whisper. "And, you and Richard, too."

"Thanks," I say. "That's kind of you."

"Does your father still paint?" she says.

"Not that I know of," I say pleasantly.

"He's a very talented artist," she says. "And, I know what I'm talking about. For him to give it up would be a true loss. A terrible shame."

What is with that lazy Southern drawl? I'm from Texas, and Lord knows I have an accent, but isn't hers a little over the top? And, that she acts like she's so "in the know" really pisses me off, even if her fancy gallery is in the Chelsea district, on the West Side of Manhattan.

I did some checking. Damn sure did.

On to business at last, she says, "I'm glad you got the paintings in one piece. The shipping company said they were fine, but you never know."

That's right. You never know.

"It sounds odd, Ms. James, that my father entrusted you with his paintings over twenty years ago," I say, hoping not to sound irritated. "Señor Sanchez said you were my father's client. Did you come by them to settle a debt?"

"Oh, no. Quite the opposite. Your father's being an artist isn't his only talent. Hugh's investments made me all kinds of profit over the years."

"Then, what are you doing with them?" I say.

"I'd like the opportunity to do the same for him," she says, a smile in her voice. "I took the liberty of taking images of the paintings for sales materials."

No shit?

I figured she had them sandwiched between dusty stacks in the back.

"Your father's artwork has quite a following." Her voice lilts at the end.

Come off it, lady. At a New York gallery?

"If that's the case, Ms. James, you must have sold quite a few of them over the years."

"I haven't, actually," she says nonchalantly.

Zero? Which means these are all the paintings there have been?

I consider this for a moment.

"Being an art dealer, it seems highly unusual that you'd continue to carry an artist's work in your gallery if it didn't sell." I try and sound polite. "Your gallery is very successful, Ms. James, and business is business."

"They were part of the gallery's permanent collection," she says. "Several collectors have always been interested in his work. Quite desperate to purchase them, really. Now, the decision to accept the offers is his."

Wait a minute. Offers?

"Forgive me for possibly overstepping or sounding crass," she says. "But, there being only a limited number of Hugh Birdsong originals in the world makes them all the more cherished."

"Ahh-h," I say. "I see what you mean."

I wish I could look through the phone. See this woman for myself. See if she's for real.

"What offers are we talking about?"

"Upwards of twenty thousand, depending on the size of the canvas."

Say what?

"Ms. Birdsong, are you there?"

I do the math in my head.

"If this is the route you want to take, you have some emotional decisions ahead of you," she says, then pauses. "Such as which paintings you'd be willing to part with first."

She gives me a few moments for this to sink in.

"Thank you for sending the paintings, Ms. James. I'm truly grateful," I say. "But, there's no way I could ever part with any of them."

They're my father's legacy.

## CHAPTER THIRTY-FIVE

❖   ❖   ❖

---

Dad's pulled up in front of the wedding cake painting, oblivious to the leaves and acorns pelting the window. It's the one from the office that hung over his desk.

On a canvas measuring five feet square, it's an imposing cake, for sure, with several elaborately-decorated layers that become progressively smaller as they reach the top, like a high-rise office tower draped in luscious, glistening frosting. Gleaming, crystal plates wait alongside the cake, plus a dozen silver forks, a long-handled serving knife, and a pair of tall, slender champagne flutes with delicate lace bows tied to the stems.

With plastic blissful faces, the happy couple stands proudly on top, their tiny shoes planted in a fluffy foundation. I wonder what they'd say if I told them the truth—that with the slightest upset, they could tumble straight off. Put a lid on it, you crazy lady, because you're killing our buzz? It's what I'd probably say, right before gorging myself on a piece of cake.

Rising from my chair, I head to the bookshelf and retrieve Dad's old, rusted toolbox. He enjoyed looking inside it before. Maybe he'll do it again. I bend back the hinged lid and set it on his lap. He rests his hand inside.

I suddenly smell something yummy and delicious. How the wedding cake would probably smell if it were real. Funny, it looks so completely realistic that I quickly tap the image with my fingertip. Touching it to my tongue, I swear it tastes sweet.

The toolbox slides off his lap.

"Hey, what are you doing?" I say. "If you don't want it, just tell me." I squat down and begin picking up the tubes of paint. A wadded rag smelling of turpentine. A couple of brushes with green stuck in the metal band below the bristles.

There's the faint sound of his house slippers rubbing back and forth on the floor. I glance over my shoulder at him. Shoulders slumped over, he's leaning forward in his wheelchair, arms on his knees. My eyes zero-in on the paintbrush in his hand. He flutters his nimble fingers over the stiff bristles, and then he wraps his fingers around the handle and makes a tight fist. Muscles in his wrist taut, his veins are raised and throbbing.

I methodically load the contents back in the tool box, careful that I pack it correctly, or else the rusty lid won't close. I learned that lesson already.

*You know those bargains people make with God? Such as, if you save my child's life, I'll give everything I own to the Salvation Army?*

Surprised he's finally speaking, I raise my head. "Well, sure, Dad."

*That's the kind of deal I made with myself. When my parents spoke of "our son, the artist," it was in hushed tones. "The world is full of unsuccessful, talented people," they said.*

I laugh. "I wish I'd known them."

He cuts me off.

*They gave me two years to find financial success. The same two years they paid my tuition to the God-awful UT Accounting program. Failure meant my death sentence.*

I start to say something else, but he keeps talking. I look at his face. He looks different than usual. His brows are raised with his lids stretched wide open. Unfocused, unmoving, his eyeballs are glassy.

*If I became an artiste, we'd call it a wash. Otherwise, I'd suit up, plus repay the tuition. What did I have to worry about? Of the entire UT art program, I was considered the most promising. The professors said it, not me. I couldn't wait for the sun to rise. With coveralls over my school duds to keep them clean, I'd paint every morning for a couple of hours, capturing the images of early light and sky. Class breaks, I'd sit in the grass outside the library and watch the people go by. I'd sketch them. They must have thought I was either a cat or a square. Didn't matter to me.*

I realize he's not talking to me. He's in a trance, eyes frozen on the glistening wedding cake. I'm sure I'm imagining it, but the image seems to sway.

*I'd paint into the night. Never needed much sleep. I'd drop my paintings at galleries, enter art shows, hawk them at festivals and flea markets. Met the public. Like it or not, being an artist is a sales job. That's reality. I sold quite a few. Never enough to get by.*

*I fell on my face. And it hurt. A lot.*

Not taking my eyes off his face, I decide to go with it and just sit back and listen.

*I held my nose and took my punishment. I got a goddamn stupid job. But, I didn't shove the paints to the back of my closet.*

*Sammy Sanchez hired me at a campus job fair. Why, I'll never know. Before I could blink, I was on the fast track and I didn't even know how I'd gotten there, thrown into the dark, windowless bullpen along with a half-dozen other bulls. In my rumpled khaki suit, I didn't look like anyone else in the office. No chariot for me. I came in on my Indian motorcycle.*

*They were a tough, competitive bunch of jerks. One-upmanship was the order of the day. Each and every ever-loving, stinking day. Learning the office ABCs was murder. The damn protocol—who did what, who mattered, who didn't. There were twenty-five accountants, eight secretaries, a couple of gofers and the mail room flunkies. This was in the day before the big 8 firms.*

*It was as enjoyable as burned toast.*

*I'd had enough when lunchtime rolled around every day. Sketchbook in hand, I hopped the elevator and took my seat at the Sixth and Congress Avenue bus stop. Noisy cars pulled up to the parking meters, chatty women with shopping bags rushed between the storefronts, and confident businessmen walked with their suit coats folded over their arms. How could I waste my small portal of sunshine? Being an artist is a hard passion to break.*

*It's not like I was Picasso with some huge following, but I felt someone watching me. I didn't think I was imagining the woman who'd be ducked under the awning, the newspaper in front of her face. Dark headed, all buttoned up. I never let on that I knew she was there. I casually dropped my pencil one day and bent to pick it up. Raising my head to get a peek, I wasn't fast enough. All I saw was a long, shiny black braid before she slid through the brass revolving door.*

*The weekly presentation was Fridays at nine o'clock. Public speaking was never my forte, especially while being dangled over a shark tank. We bulls crowded around the conference table with overflowing ashtrays. I may have been the only person who didn't smoke in the fifties. At the end of the table was Sanchez, the stuffed-shirt, ball-busting, coolest of all customers. He hummed occasionally. Bored to tears or entertained, I never knew which.*

*One by one, we'd go around the table, detailing client situations, the implications of the tax laws, and so forth. All the crap I hated. The insufferable windbag, Geoff spoke ahead of me. The longer he droned on, the more nervous I became. To calm myself, I began counting backward from twenty down to one.*

*Sanchez's voice was like a sonic boom. "Look alive, Birdsong," he yelled. "You are up."*

*Twelve sets of hard eyes bore down on me, begging me to make an ass of myself.*

"Moron," Geoff said under his breath. A couple of men chuckled. One crumpled a piece of paper and made a basket in the trash can.

There was a loud rap at the door.

When no one looked up, Sanchez snorted and stepped to the door himself. "You fools could learn a thing or two from an old man about how to treat a lady," he said. There were several cleared throats.

A secretary backed through the double doors carrying a huge silver tray in front of her. She made her way around the conference table pouring everyone coffee.

I took several shallow breaths and started from the top. "Peterson Trucking is on the ropes," I said. "Poor suckers are being audited."

The secretary filled my cup. Her hands clutched the steaming percolator. They were tiny, like a girl's. She wore a slender black watchband with a gold face. No rings.

I took a quick slurp. It burned my tongue like a sonofabitch. Coffee spilled down the front of my shirt. I jerked up my head, to see who had ruined my short career. Huge, dark eyes stared back at me. Shiny, black hair was pulled off her face. She dressed like the other secretaries, but none of them looked like her. High cheekbones, olive skin. Exotic. A delicacy to her features, but behind them was a certain resolve.

I tried to stop looking at her. Me and every other man in the room.

"Nice job on those IRS letters, Carmen. Get them in the mail today, will you?" Sanchez smiled. I'd never seen that before.

"It would be my pleasure, Señor Sanchez," she said.

Nice accent. Just like his.

I nudged Geoff. "New secretary?"

"Big tickle-funny. She ain't no secretary. She ain't no executive secretary. If Ida wasn't out sick, she'd never be fetching us coffee. And dig this," he whispered. "Every chick in the office hates her guts."

I kept watching her. "Who is she?"

"Didn't you copy? That's who tallies our expense reports. She's Sanchez's assistant, for Chrissake ."

That's right. My checks came expertly typed. She must've rolled them carefully into the typewriter. Lined them up precisely.

She sashayed from the room, her shapely hips in perfect rhythm with the shiny, black braid that hung down her back.

Never less than perfect. Signed exquisitely in formal cursive:

"Carmen Mata"

I went back to Sanchez's office. Carmen was there. Seeing me, she looked away.

He took his fedora from the coat tree by the door and popped it on his head. "Carmen, hold my calls. I am meeting my dear intended at the jewelers," he said. "Here I go again."

"Which wife is this now?" Carmen said. "First there was Mitzi, next Georgette…"

"Thank you, Carmen. That will do. The new model is Betsy. The first one was Midge," he snorted. "Nice coffee stain on that shirt by the way, Birdsong."

I nonchalantly watched her lean over his desk.

"Are you ready for the ceremony?" she asked.

"I think I know what to do by now." He pulled on his cashmere topcoat. "We are doing it in the judge's office."

"Romance," Carmen smiled. "The way to a girl's heart."

Sanchez tapped the tip of his cigar on his silver lighter. "Okay, querida. What do you suggest then?"

"Roses, of course." I jumped in before she could answer. "Not the same boring red ones. They've been done. I suggest orange, violet and pink."

Sanchez put his head back and regarded me. "He is our artist, Carmen," he said. "Starving- artist, that is."

The first dig of many. Thanks, old man.

"Where are you taking her on the honeymoon?" I said.

"Niagara Falls," he said. "Georgette liked it."

"Dios mio," Carmen shook her head. "Whatever you do, please don't tell that to Brenda."

Sanchez waved his hands and raised them over his head. "It's Betsy!"

"So when is this shindig?" I asked.

"Nothing for you to worry about. Formal reception afterward," he said. "Senior staffers only."

Brushing my arm, Carmen gathered the files on his desk. As she headed for the hallway, I admired the slim curves under her polka dotted dress. Her beautifully sculpted legs. If I'd spoken Spanish, I'd have said, "Ay, caramba!"

"I have no one to escort me," she said softly.

"What?" I asked. "What do you mean?"

"Forget about it. Don't bother yourself," she said elbowing past me.

She was frosty after that. Meeting her in the halls, she'd turn on her heel and head the opposite direction. It was getting embarrassing.

Carmen was rolling carbon paper into her typewriter one morning when I got up the nerve to slide a pink message slip under her nose. I'll need your address, it said. And the time to pick you up. She wrote her answer in precise cursive, and slid it back across the desk. Before I could pick it up, she snatched it back. In all caps, she added, "Be on time," and underlined it twice.

She buzzed around the office now. When I came toward her she blushed. The most beautiful girl in the world wanted Hugh Birdsong? That's crazy, I thought.

*Tall, lanky, curly-headed, bespectacled me? The artsy guy on a motorcycle? I'd do anything she wanted and when she wanted. Are you kidding?*

She liked white gloves and funny little hats. Very Jackie Kennedy. Everything about her was just so. Never a hair out of place. Red lipstick, too. Nothing was more important to Carmen than fitting in. She had a plan for her life. Nothing done by chance. University of Texas Accounting Degree with 4.0 GPA: Check. Pass CPA exam: Check. Nail down position with Sanchez Financial: Check. Work as accountant, be respected and compensated fairly: Failure. It was 1955. Bookkeeper and assistant to Sammy Sanchez was the best she'd ever do.

Carmen's Mexican. So what? Didn't make a rat's ass difference to me, but it sure did to other people. Mexicans were considered capable of only menial labor. Speaking Spanish had to come with a wealthy pedigree or no dice. The only acceptable Spanish-speaking people to associate with were from Spain, South America or possibly Puerto Rico.

Let's face it, she was never a people-person. She came off as haughty and superior, but she was simply protecting herself the only way she knew how. When people treated her like she didn't belong, which was a lot, it hurt her feelings. She folded in upon herself. You could see it happening. She was like a little bird.

Carmen and I were lunching in the office break room one day when Geoff waltzed in.

"Looks like you're eating yourself some greasy taco, Birdsong?"

I knocked over the water cooler and pushed him up against the wall.

"Licking the red pepper from the crack of her spicy ass must have lit you up!" he cried.

His head thudded against the tile floor.

A crowd was forming. Senior staffers, secretaries, everyone. My pal Ed took my arms and held me back. "Cool it, Bird. Be cool, man," he said. "He's not worth it."

Our secretary, Deborah, knelt beside Geoff wiping the blood off his chin. All eyes were on Sanchez when he stomped into the kitchen. He looked to Deborah. He saw her as a safe bet, truth meter.

Her eyes traveled around the room. "Geoff didn't do anything and Hugh went berserk," she blustered. *I never cared for her much after that.*

I looked around for Carmen.

She wouldn't come out of the ladies room. Lousy Deborah was all I had so I sent her in. After calling her name over and over, Deborah finally inched under the stall in her dress and heels to find Carmen sitting on the closed lid, covered in sweat.

Stiff-jawed, Sanchez paced in front of her desk. As the hours passed, his concern bubbled into anger.

He cracked the door. "This has gone on long enough, Carmen," he called inside. "Have you forgotten what you promised the last time this happened?"

165

*I've never stopped kicking myself for not asking what he meant.*

*"Birdsong, my office," he said. "Pronto."*

*He slammed his door and scowled at me.*

*"Do not make Carmen your plaything," he growled. "She has enough problems without you becoming one."*

*"I thought you'd want me to protect her. What did I do wrong?"*

*"Office romance spells nothing but trouble. And, if you think you would ever be enough for Carmen Mata, think again, my friend," he said. "Think again."*

*Crazy old man. I kept my distance from him until his wedding.*

*So there we were.*

The Driskill Hotel ballroom in downtown Austin, a few doors down from the Sanchez Firm in the Littlefield Building. It was a tony affair, to say the least. You could hardly turn around without a waiter in a silly white dinner jacket filling your champagne. "Bubbly," they called it.

Embossed napkins read: Sammy and Betsy, February 14, 1955. Betsy was radiant in her white dress, matching gloves that stretched to her elbows and a trailing veil of fine, sheer tulle. She carried a bouquet of multi-colored roses just like I'd suggested. I was complimented.

They cut the cake and fed it to each other. Betsy smeared it on Sammy's face. Everyone laughed, except for me.

So fierce and stern at the office, with her, Sanchez was like a butterfly in his green brocade tuxedo jacket and a yellow rose on his lapel. I didn't recognize him, and at that moment, I didn't even recognize myself, standing next to this woman I didn't know. Just her smell intoxicated me. Filled my head with all sorts of evil thoughts. Her long, dark hair wrapped in an enormous knot, I wanted to bury myself in the curve of her neck. The gold of her chain with a bright clasp, if she unhooked it, would her head fall off? Odd, but that's what I wondered. And, how her skin would feel against my lips. Attraction paralyzed.

If Sanchez could have a woman like Betsy love him, why couldn't I? I wanted it, too. From Carmen. Hell, yes. I wanted her.

So, marry me, I said.

I thought she didn't hear me. The fine hairs on her neck caught the light. Answer me, I thought. No, don't. Am I crazy? I'm absolutely nuts. The glass of champagne in my hand was slippery in my fingers. I thought I might drop it. I raised it to my lips and finished it off. Would you like another glass, I asked Carmen. Yes, she said. A waiter magically appeared. I placed my empty glass carefully on his tray and took another. When I tried handing it to her, I realized what she meant. She was focused on the onyx studs of my tuxedo shirt, then, she leaned in close. She cupped her hand like she was telling me a secret. Lightly, like a little kitten, she licked the edge of my ear. And, I was gone.

*Sammy waltzed Betsy around the dance floor with his hand at the small of her back. It was his first dance with his new bride, but that didn't stop him from focusing on me. Flaring his nostrils, his expression demanded, What have you done?*

*I'm marrying to the apple of your eye. That's what my shrug told him. Take that, old man.*

Dad suddenly stops speaking.

I nudge his arm. "Hey, finish your story, Dad, don't stop."

Leaned to one side, his head drops on his shoulder. Relaxing his fingers, the paintbrush slips from his palm and rolls across the floor.

"Dad?" I shake his knee.

Puzzled, I pick up the brush and run its bristles under my nose. What just happened here? Is he only pretending to be asleep?

I place the rusted tool box on the highest shelf alongside his glowing prism nameplate, then turn back to look at the painting.

My gosh, the cake's been cut, with the lower tier half gone. Sugar-coated plates are stacked at the base. A silver fork has white frosting wedged between the tines. Crimson lipstick is smeared on the rim of the champagne glass. To the side is a multi-colored bouquet of roses with lace-wrapped stems. Betsy's.

Perched on high, the smiling bride and groom stare back. Stiff, plastic bodies tilted. Lopsided. Frosting hiding the edges of their shoes; their feet are mashed into place, but now they're crooked.

I think I've lost my mind. Oh, I definitely have. Maybe it's catching around here.

"Dad?" I say. He's quietly snoring.

I've got to get out of here.

## CHAPTER THIRTY-SIX

❖ ❖ ❖

I firmly tug the thin rope hanging from the attic until the door pops down. Something falls on my head. I release the rope and the door sucks closed with a thwack. I bend over and run my fingers through my hair. Thankfully, it's only pink wads of insulation. Caked in dried rat poop.

I return from the kitchen armed with barbeque tongs and a plastic trash bag. Holding my breath, I pull down the door, unfold the spring ladder and anchor it to the floor. As I climb the wooden steps, there's a distinct smell: Rodents have died up here, but no one thought to remove the bodies.

I hoist myself onto the rafters. Silhouettes of ivy over the dormer windows allow only thin straws of sunlight to break through. Stretching my fingers to the lonely light bulb, I can just reach the chain. Rat traps filled with hairy, blood-matted carcasses are everywhere. With a major case of the willies, I snag the nasty boogers with the tongs and drop them in the bag. A greasy, arrogant cockroach crawls over my foot and I scream! I look around me for little eyes.

Neatly-stretched tarps angle from the walls. There's a high chair, a baby swing. Our white flocked, Christmas tree from the sixties still in its stand, complete with lights and tinsel. Faded cardboard boxes are stacked three and four high. They're all labeled in my mother's hand. God bless her compulsive organization, but I'm still not taking the boxes at their word. I cull crate after dusty crate. Had she kept me, or thrown me out?

There's a hamper of worn accounting manuals and another with thick hardbacks on the Louvre and the Museum of Modern Art. Finding Richard's old track trophies, I smile.

I keep telling myself I'm looking for things of mine, but I'm not. I'm looking for her. She's here, like I knew she would be. Everywhere. Pieces of her. Now, her memory spreads to the corners of my mind, touching every last bit.

The next box is filled with her old books. I imagine her curled up with a Gabriel García Márquez novel on her lap. She didn't find it funny when I brought the first one from library, but how could I resist? *One Hundred Years of Solitude*. She could never get enough.

"Thank heavens no one outside the family calls you Jules. What a horrible name. It's Juliana," she'd say in her strong accent, drawing out the Spanish pronunciation I hated. But she sure never taught Rich and me Spanish. Didn't speak it herself. Except when she'd get pissed, here it would come. Her children were born in the USA, by God. Period. English only.

"I have no social invitations," she'd tell me. "No friends. No family, you're all I have. Your father never listens to me." So, I listened to her. For hours. While I would brush her hair. I was her best friend. She told me that a million times. I'd do anything to make her happy. She counted on me. My beautiful mother.

"You know better than to talk," she'd say. "*Perry Mason* is on."

Every afternoon. Courtroom drama in black and white. Especially around Perry's eyes. The man wore more eye makeup than his able secretary, Della Street. Each episode, Perry broke the case, having the guilty party break down on the stand. It's funny that back then Perry Mason was second only to Walter Cronkite as the most trusted man in America. My mother ate him up.

That's where she got the idea that I should marry a lawyer. She thought it was the most glamorous, prestigious and lucrative profession out there. My dad, being a CPA and financial advisor, you'd think we'd be loaded, right? More like the cobbler's children with no shoes. Oh, no one was exactly going barefoot, but she said he could always do better. My best chance of finding a wealthy lawyer would be attending law school myself.

A box is marked, "Special - Carmen." I pull back layers of tissue paper and find a dress of fine-spun silk with a blue diamond pattern. The tiny waist measures about twenty-three inches around.

When I left for college, I worried what life was like for her with me gone. I'm sure my father was there less and less. I imagined them moving about in utter silence, only rarely smiling in passing. Him sliding a pizza under her bedroom door. I knew that wasn't what happened, but I couldn't chase it out of my mind. I tried my hardest not to think of her. Sometimes I did a pretty good job.

Now, it's how my children treat me.

I loved her more than anything. I should've been kinder to her, more understanding. More grateful for what I had. Every birthday, I search the mailbox, pretending there will be a card. After seeing her nude painting downstairs, I miss her all over again. But not like that, of course. I stashed it in the back of my closet because I didn't want my father looking at her either. I know he was somehow involved and something sick inside of me wants to hear the truth about what really happened, no matter how bad it is. But, mostly, I like pretending it didn't happen at all. That my mother is still here.

But, I left her, too.

And now she's only memories.

# CHAPTER THIRTY-SEVEN

❖ ❖ ❖

Although Dad's speech was lucid and conversational, it didn't feel like he was telling me the story. It was more like he was narrating his own movie. A slideshow of his past. When the images eerily began to move, the paintings became the soundtrack, as if his words were set to music.

I tried asking him about it afterward. He didn't seem to know what I was talking about. It's impossible to know if he really didn't remember-remember or if he just didn't *remember* because he has Alzheimer's. Whatever, I have to see whether it was a fluke. Find out if he has anything else to say. But the more I push, the further he retreats, so I must wait.

The trance thing was too weird, so I got on the internet and did some research. A trance is an "altered state of consciousness," in other words, a different state of awareness than being just plain old "awake." A trance can be caused by tons of different things—intense mental focus for one, and Dad's got that down, staring at the paintings day and night.

And, here's something else: A trance can be brought on by sleep deprivation. Bingo again, since Dad never sleeps. Plus, some people go into trances on purpose with the help of a Shaman or something, with the specific intention of tapping into repressed memories, and to even tap into creativity and artistic inspiration. Mmm-hmm. Perfect, I know.

"Dreaming sleep" is also an altered state of consciousness. Of course I looked it up. Before, it seemed like Dad was asleep with his eyes open. Now I believe he's falling awake.

# CHAPTER THIRTY-EIGHT

◆ ◆ ◆

After burning my leg on the exhaust pipe a couple times, I realized that skirts and high heels don't cut it for us motorcycle mamas. Plus, open-toed sandals aren't so great for shifting gears with your foot. Dodging traffic. Getting honked at. The awesome helmet hair. When I have to stop at a light, I squeeze the clutch lever all the way in, ease off the throttle, let the bike begin to coast and slowly start to brake. Coming to a complete stop, I touch my left foot down and wait. I feel like an uber-goober with plastic grocery bags looped over my arm, mortified that someone I know will be in the next car over.

Lindsey's just super crazy about it, too. I brought her from school to the dance studio for her back-to-back jazz and ballet this afternoon. She'd hardly talk to me. No more than a sentence. Barely stopped in front of the studio, she threw her leg over the seat and bolted across the pavement.

It's classic for daughters to hate their mother and love their dad. I think it's because dads are on Mt. Olympus. Mothers are mortal—they're in the trenches. I know I probably shouldn't take it personally, but I don't know why it has to be that way for Lindsey and me. She's mad at me over the divorce thing. I get that, but how long will it last? Maybe forever. Maybe until just tomorrow.

I head down the hallway to the sales counter, count out eight dollars in quarters from my coin purse and slide them through the window to Miss Trish so Lindsey won't have to wear dirty, holey pink tights again. When she tries handing me the new pair, I tell her to just give them to Lindsey before the next class. Her comforting smile tells me she understands, but she doesn't. Miss Trish only has sons.

Class is over and Lindsey walks straight out. Trailing behind her, I read the dance announcements tacked to the bulletin board.

"How was school today? Did you get that paper turned in?"

She turns around. "Mom, do we always have to talk about that? Since this whole stuff started, it's all you talk to me about. That and dance, or whatever. You never ask about *me*."

I thought that's what I was doing.

It's one of the hardest parts about this shit. I'm not living with her, so it's an artificial closeness. True closeness happens when you wake kids up in the morning, tell them to not just leave their cereal bowls in the sink but actually load them in the dishwasher, yell at them to get their butts in the car, then watch their sullen faces in the rearview mirror on the drive to school.

"You can come live with me at Grandad's now, Lindsey. He's not there anymore, if that's what you're worried about."

"I'm fourteen, you know, and I can choose where I live without your permission at all." She raises her chin. "Check it out on the internet if you don't believe me."

I put my hand on her arm. "If you change your mind, I'll always keep the door open."

"Okay. If you want."

One of her friends knocks the mirror from the other side and calls her name. She reaches up and knocks back and her friend smashes her face against the glass.

Not looking at me, she swaps the ballet slippers on her feet for tennis shoes. "You don't even see your old friends any more, do you, Mom?"

"I still see them for lunch and things."

It's a lie.

"Mrs. Evans is so cool. I think it's weird you don't mention her name anymore," she says. "What about her?"

"Friendships don't always stay the same," I say slowly.

"No way, Mom. Mrs. Evans?" she says. "That must suck."

Yep. It sucks like a big dog.

She suddenly darts through the glass doors to the parking lot. When the other dancers crawl into the backseats of their mothers' Suburbans, I wonder how many sets of Chanel sunglasses are trained on me, marking an X right on my back. I'd love to throw my helmet in the bushes.

Oliver's silver Jag pulls into the lot. Spoke wheels, gleaming tires, its 518 HP engine purrs. "Take your Lexus to the dealership. They know what to do," he'd always tell me, pretending to know nothing about cars, when he very well does. He can take apart an engine and put it back together again, no problem. His father saw to it.

Pete wears long side burns and an Elvis curl. He never owned a car dealership like Oliver tells people, he worked on the engines. A grease monkey, Oliver calls him. Pete thought he was too big for his britches.

"Remember where you came from," he'd say. "No thanks, Pops," was Oliver's answer to that.

Even behind his dark wraparound sunglasses, I know he's looking at me. When he turns his head toward the Indian, I know he's dying to know how much money I got for my Lexus, barely three months off the showroom floor.

The window rolls down and he tilts his arm out the leather-padded door. "Why, good afternoon, Mother."

It burns me up when he calls me that and he knows it.

I bend down and lean into the cockpit. There's the ever-present new car scent and the AC feels heavenly. "I don't know why you wasted a trip because I'm driving Lindsey."

Coming behind me, she says in my ear, "Not anymore. I called him when we took our water break."

Adam cocks his head and looks at me across the dashboard. "Oh, hey Mom," he says, uneasy. Like he's not sure how to act

"Mother's going to join us for dinner," Oliver says.

Since when?

He takes my hand. I try pulling it back, but he raises it to his lips.

"We need to spill the beans sometime, don't we?"

There's a Santa Claus twinkle in his eye.

"Listen up, kiddos. I've decided to give Mother a second chance," he says. "Team Morrissey is back together again."

The twins' eyes dart to my face. Voice clotted, I nod vigorously to tell them what he said is true. But they know this jumbled, jagged expression means it's not. They know my face better than anyone, and I know theirs, too.

A look passes between them that says: Since Dad's lying to us now, does that mean he was lying before? The next look says: Even if they say our lives will be hunky dory again, from here on out, everything is up for grabs.

Oliver kisses my fingers and whispers, "Cat got your tongue?"

It starts to sink in. My heart jumps.

My babies. Oh, my sweet babies. I'm coming home!

Lindsey tugs his arm. "Daddy, I'm eating at Caroline's house. I already told you and you said okay."

He smiles at her. "You've become the little mother at home, haven't you, Lindsey? Keeping track of everything."

I'm coming home. I'm coming home. I'm coming home.

"And don't forget, you're dropping Adam at the country club, too."

Tossing her hair, she steals a glance at me. Her clear, blue eyes flash. She's warning me.

Oliver nudges Adam's elbow. "Sonny boy's been preparing for the Best Ball tournament. He's got quite a career started. The pro says he's a natural."

Adam sets his fuzzy chin and shrugs.

"But Daddy Bear, he's not as natural as your daughter, the dancer." Lindsey twirls gracefully in a circle, raising her slender arms above her like a swan.

"Lindsey, Mother and I are working it out and that's all you have to say?"

"Well, what if the kids don't want you to work it out?" She keeps twirling.

Adam screams at her. "Hey! Stupid!"

She doesn't stop. He fires his iPod at her through the window. It hits my chest instead and drops to the pavement.

Oliver roughly grabs her arm. "Stop."

Wounded, she looks at him earnestly. "After all the horrible things you told me about her, why would you take her back?"

"Now, simmer down, Miss Priss. Mother will say she's sorry."

"You said she'd rather take care of Grandad than me and Adam."

"That's Adam and me," he says.

"You might want her back, Daddy, but I don't." She pooches her lips out like she does. "No way."

Oliver turns to me. "Let's give them a little time, Mother. It's going to be fine." He rolls up his window while flipping down his shades. "Talk to you real soon."

His shiny tires crunch on the asphalt as Adam's liquid brown eyes stare at me through the back window.

I'm coming home.

# CHAPTER THIRTY-NINE

❖ ❖ ❖

I had a great idea. If there's a painting that will get Dad talking, I know which one it is. The nude portrait of my mother he was "entertaining" when I called him from the Starbucks after my jackass husband had me served at Dr. Phillips'. Oh, and how he relished blindsiding me in front of the kids, announcing he was giving me a second chance when I'm the one who did nothing wrong. But, I digress.

The painting is nothing like the others. It's sensual. Mysterious, with her shiny, dark hair provocatively draping her profile. If my mother hated it enough to slice it, why didn't she burn it in the fireplace or something, instead of having it repaired? If I looked that fantastic in the buff, I'd never put clothes on, much less ruin the proof.

Dad faces the windows, camel-backed in his new rolling chair. He likes it better than a wheelchair. It's more of a throne, really. Richard made it for him. He mounted an old office chair on a wooden disc with wheels so Dad can glide back and forth between his paintings and the window. As he awkwardly moves his casted leg, I watch the damn red footprints he painted on the side. They're symbolic of Richard and me, I guess, but broaching the subject? I'm not sure I can go there.

I slide it in front of him and remove the tarp. "This painting. Will you tell me about it?"

Nothing.

I move it a little closer and gently nudge his shoulder. "Isn't Mother beautiful?"

He whips his head from the window, expecting to see her there?

He follows my finger as I point to the portrait.

Grasping the edges, he devours it with his eyes. His fingers begin to flutter. Electric. I'd swear his hair does, too. He begin caressing my mother's body in such an intimate way that I have to turn my head.

On second thought, I think I might pass on hearing him talk about this one. Listening to my parents' sex tape? Ew.

Suddenly, he flips the painting over. His fingers trace the rough, diagonal tear stretching from one corner to the other, gracefully as skimming the rosin of a bow. As if he's done it many times before.

He deliberately turns the painted side back toward him and becomes very still. Barely breathing. The crepe skin around his eyes relaxes. He takes his thumb and rubs it around the tiny red footprints, making dime-sized circles.

So tender.

I step forward. He motions for me to back away.

When I don't, he jerks his head to me. His eyes flash. Lips trembling.

"It's okay, Dad. It's okay." I try to soothe him. "Just tell me who tore the painting."

"Carmen," he whispers roughly. "I tore her heart out."

I kneel in front of him. "Oh, Dad," I say. "I'm sure you didn't mean to."

I drape my arm around his shoulder. He slaps it away. Hard.

I fall backwards on the floor.

I wait for him to say he's sorry. Say something.

Rubbing the stinging red mark, I try not to cry.

Mr. Read appears in the doorway carrying red and white Chinese food take-out cartons. Seeing the look on my face, he continues down the hall.

"Wait, Mr. Read," I say. I pull myself up off the floor and dash after him.

He stops abruptly and turns around. I bump into his chest and quickly back up. My eyes aren't even level with the knot of his striped tie. Looking up, I notice his thick hair falling across his forehead.

"I'm sorry for intruding, Ms. Birdsong," he says uncomfortably. "I was just thinking you might share some lunch with me."

Head down, I take his arm and we slowly begin strolling toward the dining room.

"I know it's difficult when family members get cross," he says. "It's hard not to take it personally, but you really can't."

I shake my head. "You try making it sound so easy."

"It's common for the personalities of Alzheimer's patients to change. For some, traits from when they were younger resurface," he says. "Other patients change completely; kind and gentle before, they'll become ornery and spiteful. Downright mean."

We pause at one door in particular, covered in cherished family mementos. Mr. Read chuckles as he fingers the edge of the classroom photo of a young boy who looks remarkably like Adam. His smiling eyes seem to sparkle at me.

"Mr. Read," I say slowly. "I don't have any control over what's happening."

"Oh, but you do Ms. Birdsong," he says gently. "You didn't choose for your father to have Alzheimer's. What you can choose is your reaction to it." He pats my arm. "Handle it with grace."

Moving to the next resident's door, he taps it lightly. No response, he opens it a crack and pokes his head inside. It's the woman with the long gray braids and gnarled hands. Sitting on her bed, knitting needles at her side, she tries untangling a long strand of blue yarn. With tender eyes, he watches her for several moments before pulling the door to.

He turns back to me. "My mother was in a nursing home several years back. My father had been dead for many years, but she talked about seeing him all the time. One day, I told her, 'Tell Dad I said hi,'" he says. "The daughter of another resident was listening. 'How dare you mock your mother like that? So condescending and disrespectful,' she said angrily. 'But, why?' I asked her. 'We're connecting. It's where she is. It may not be this time—it's another time, but it's real.'"

I smile at this.

"Memories are some of life's greatest treasures that sustain us as we turn back to them in our minds again and again," he says thoughtfully, then chuckles. "However, some memories can be a blessing to forget."

I consider his words for a moment.

"When Dad tells me things about the past, it's not that I think he's lying necessarily, but how do I know what he says is true?"

He takes my arm and we begin walking again.

"A lie didn't happen, so it's not memory," he says. "The truth you remember. You don't even have to try."

## CHAPTER FORTY

❖   ❖   ❖

---

Dread takes me by the throat. I twist a wrinkled napkin between my fingers. A waiter wearing a black tie and crisp, white apron won't stop filling my water glass and won't stop smiling at me. I check the front entrance again. The mahogany-paneled walls are hung with perfectly-framed boxing posters. The smell of garlic bread is making me nauseous.

A young hostess with a freckled back and wearing a floral sundress leads a group of businessmen to their table. She's the one who hung my helmet between the Stetsons on the coat tree when I came in. Hugging thick, leather-bound menus to her chest, she swishes through the dining room.

The phone rang this morning and it was Oliver, telling me he's a changed man and to meet him here at Sonny's Steak House at noon. He likes their "man food"—aged beef, horseradish mashers and the wedge salad with crumbled blue cheese. This would be a great time for a cigarette but I quit. Not because I'm on a health kick. I'm poor.

The hostess waits until the men are settled comfortably around the table before passing around the menus. As the tallest man unzips his briefcase and spreads it across the tablecloth, she unobtrusively slides the vase of flowers against the Sweet'n Low. Heading back to the hostess stand, she looks in my direction. Seeing that I've changed personas, she winks, like it's our little secret.

That's right. After stashing my leather motorcycle chaps and lug-soled riding boots under the sink, I emerged from the ladies room as Mrs. Oliver Morrissey, decked out in one my few remaining outfits. If I know Oliver, he's expecting to see the St. John suit he found me at Saks last fall, but unless he runs into the woman in the hairnet and house shoes from my Couture Sale, that's not happening.

Why do the peaks and valleys of marriage have to be so brutal? Here's an idea: Husband and wife scale a tall mountain, plant the flag of love in the peak, then strap on their safety belts and repel down the other side. Touching down in the valley, they kiss each other's boo-boos and sip chilled water from a shared canteen. Instead, what we have here is face plant into a dumpster from the roof of a parking garage. And, it's me who's fallen from grace.

How do I volunteer to vulnerable again with a "kick-me" sign on my heart?

Where's that damn waiter who's in such a good mood? Mouth dry, I spot him coming through the swinging door to the kitchen, balancing a tray on his shoulder, but his water pitcher's not on it. Just plates. The thick, white restaurant kind. They rattle as he sets the tray folding stand. An irritating noise.

Suddenly aware of Oliver's cologne, *Eternity*, by Calvin Klein, I look up. Something's wrong.

There's his laughing green eyes. His deep dimples. But something major is missing. He rubs his fingers across his upper lip.

I blink my eyes. His moustache.

Completely shaved away.

"Quite a change, yeah?" He leans down and kisses me. "Smooth as a baby's ass, don't you think?"

I pull back and look closely. In its place is slick, never-seen-the-sun, anemic skin. No one's ever seen that lip before. Olive showed me a few baby pictures and he may have had it then, too.

He turns his profile from left to right, then faces me head-on. "When Dr. Phillips asked what changes you might like to see in me, you didn't think I was listening did you?"

"I didn't," I say.

It's all I can come up with.

"As I said on the phone, I'm a changed man," he says. "Guess Tom Selleck will have to carry the ball himself from here on out."

But, I like Tom Selleck.

Magnum P.I.?

Monica's fine, old man-boyfriend on *Friends*?

Oliver drapes his cashmere top coat over the edge of the tall, leather booth and slides in beside me. "Here, kiss me again."

Now that he mentioned it, it is like a baby's ass.

No doubt about it.

Craning his neck, he pings his water glass. "Let's get that waiter over here, chop chop!"

Heads turn. A man scowls in our direction. It's Jim Vickery, the contractor who built our pool house. Stocky man with a red gin blossom of a nose and a protruding dip-lip.

"Oliver?" he says. "Say, is that really you?"

"None other," Oliver says. "Five pounds lighter. Your thoughts?"

He pumps Oliver's hand. "That was one heavy moustache. Let's say five years lighter. How about that?"

Oliver abruptly hugs me to him and pulls me down into the booth. I watch Jim's ostrich boots under the table.

"Be gone with you, Jim," Oliver says loudly. "I must make out with my wife, now."

Batting him away, I come up for air. "Unhand me, sir!" I say. "I'm a married woman."

"Yes, well. Where are we on all of that, my sweet bride?" Before I can answer, he says, "I keep meaning to tell you how much better you look having all this weight off."

It's called the Divorce Diet.

"So, you dropped the suit, then?" I say.

"Don't be silly," he says. "I'm at the court house all the time."

My same smiling waiter approaches the table. "My name's Joseph and I'll be your server today." He graciously holds out the menu.

Reaching for it, I feel Oliver watching my hands. My gardening blisters have turned to calluses.

"Something to drink besides water?" Joseph says.

"Yes, my good man," Oliver says. "Gin martini. Dirty."

"Very good. And you, ma'am?"

"Just iced tea, please."

Oliver raises his brows.

"Get some appetizers started for you?"

Mmmm-m. Their Oysters Rockefeller are the best in town.

"A dozen of the Rockefeller," Oliver says, like he's reading my mind. "And let's get our food order in, too."

I order what I always have—the petit filet, medium rare. That's firm on the outside, soft and juicy on the inside. Oliver gets the twelve-ounce, aged rib eye, bloody rare. All but raw.

As Joseph backs politely from the table, Oliver smiles, stroking his naked lip where Tom Selleck used to be.

"What?" he says.

"I'm just wondering why you did it."

"I told you already. Doctor's orders."

"That's not what I'm talking about."

Gives me that megapixel smile. "Then, what?"

"I think you know."

"I'm here to make up. Tell me what to say, babe."

I haven't heard that in months and haven't missed it. I detest being called the same thing as a cheesy perfume they sell at Walmart.

"That was pretty cute what you pulled at the dance studio, Oliver. Giving me the news you wanted me back at the same time you told the twins."

"Our reconciling affects their lives as much as yours. I felt they deserved equal consideration."

I glare at him as he begins perusing the menu, slowly running his index finger down one side and then the other. Finished, he slides the menu under the pepper grinder.

"Oh, all right," he says, still not looking at me. "I couldn't take the chance of you saying no."

I exhale loudly. Sounds about right.

"It was almost as cute as what you pulled in Dr. Phillips' office."

"Oh, that? It was Mike's idea. The constable had to know when and where to find you," he says. "Papers are required to be served in person."

If I took this steak knife and shoved it into his neck, I wonder if he'd take it the wrong way.

He playfully tugs my hair. "C'mon, babe. Love me. I love you. Pretty please with sugar on top?" He strokes my cheek. "You're all I think about, lying in bed at night."

I'm sure.

"I never thought I'd say I miss your cold toes in bed," he chuckles. "Like ice cubes under the covers."

Why can't I make him love me. Really love me, like he says?

Joseph is back with our drinks. Nodding at a group of men at the bar, Oliver takes a long sip of his martini.

"Let's fast-track this thing," he says. "Put a period at the end of this sentence."

I'm moving home. I'm moving home. I'm moving home. I'm moving home.

"Then, I'll run by the grocery to make a special supper, pick up the kids on the way home." I can't stop smiling. "And, and we'll be better than before."

I'm moving home. I'm moving home. I'm moving home. I'm moving home.

"I'd love you to cook, Juliana. You can do that, but staying at the house?" He speaks slowly. "You know what I told Lindsey."

Lindsey? Who gives a fuck what Lindsey says?

I swallow. Try to stay cool.

"Let me move back home for good," I say. "It's important to me, Oliver."

"Don't pout, babe." He strokes my palm. I yank it away.

If he asks me to pick up his shirts at the laundry, I'll kill him.

The hostess circulates the dining room with the coffee pot. Pouring for the next table, she inclines her head, like she's lending moral support or something. I blink at her freckled back until she moves along.

"I'm making up the best way I know how," he says. "I'm tired of fighting."

"Okay. Then, I'll bring the twins back over to my dad's with me."

He makes a face. "Well, that sounds fine, except staying at your dad's little booger box? They're just not interested."

"Booger box?"

"You know what I mean," he says pleasantly. "But, can you imagine driving from Hyde Park and making it across town by eight a.m.? Easily forty-five minutes. More, depending on traffic. Besides, the kids like doing their own thing when they get to school in the morning."

Now, he's telling me what my own children do?

Calm. Deep, calming Yoga breath. I pick up the little table placard with today's dessert special: Chocolate Orgasm.

I watch him from the corner of my eye as he takes a call. I recognize Mike's twang on the other end.

Finally hanging up, he says, "I'm sorry, babe, but I really have to run."

"You do?" I say. "We haven't been served yet."

"Deep-pockets cry the loudest and there's a real titty-baby losing his complete cool in my conference room right now." He kisses me hard, then slides out of the booth. "Can we do this again?" he says. "Soon and often?"

I smile. "I'd like that."

He takes a hundred from his wallet. "Here's cash for the bill," he says. "And, listen, we both know how all this is going to wind up. Back at our cozy castle in Westlake, babe. Don't sweat it."

I smile weakly.

He takes a couple more bills from his wallet and slides them under the edge of my plate. "And, go get something nice for yourself, okay?"

I watch him stride from the dining room.

He pivots on his heel and points to his lip.

"Just for you."

# CHAPTER FORTY-ONE

❖   ❖   ❖

The air is charged and buzzing.

Rows of spectators murmur softly as they watch the jurors file into the jury box. Black robes trailing behind her, the solemn judge sweeps into the courtroom and the room goes silent. She adjusts her long hem, settles into her high-backed chair and looks over the gallery. Her full sleeve drapes across the leather-bound law books stacked at her elbow. The Texas flag on her left and the American flag on her right, the state seal hangs behind her on the paneled wall.

As I study the woman, I think of the Sagecrest judge with her bingo cards laid before her in the rec room. Wonder how long she was on the bench. I imagine her administering a packed docket with her own quiet grace, carrying out the mantle she was given. Before the cruel Alzheimer's stripped it from her back.

Edging forward in her seat, the judge regards my husband as he approaches the bench. Relaxed as playing nine holes, Oliver raises his polished, cordovan wingtip to the edge of the dais and rests his elbow on her desk. She removes her glasses and inclines her head toward him as she mulls over his words. Then, directing her attention to the opposing counsel, a colorless man with a strained expression, she beckons him with her finger.

The man advances quickly to the bench. The judge's lips move. Hand over his heart, he backs away. A satisfied Oliver slides a hand in his pocket and steps casually toward the counsel table to join his client, a clean-shaven man in a thick, white neck brace. I recognize the junior associate who pulls out Oliver's chair. It's Bobby Lyle, the young man he sent to harass me the afternoon he kicked me out. Clearly peeved that Bobby hasn't powered-up his laptop yet, Oliver drums his fingers on the table until the yellow Microsoft logo fills the screen.

It's been years since I've been in a courtroom. Fifteen, to be exact. I didn't know how much I missed it. It was Dr. Phillips' suggestion that I come here. Well, not here specifically, she just suggested that I take more interest in what Oliver's doing. He's making a good faith effort to follow her advice, so it's my job to get on board, too. Stop focusing on just the icky parts of Oliver instead of the old Oliver. My Oliver. He's got to be in there somewhere.

Composed, shoulders back, his stride confident, he approaches the jury box. His commanding stare travels to each face, settling on a male juror in a tan V-neck sweater. The man presses his hand to his cheek, eyes fixed intently on Oliver's every move. It's crazy, but I'd forgotten how superb he is. Through his precise oratory, his demeanor shifts from charming to benevolent to life-and-death.

Stepping to the counsel table, he soberly consults a document, then, as if outraged, he flings it on the table. All eyes follow his stiff finger as he points at the defendant. He holds the courtroom in the palm of his hand. And, I know exactly how they feel.

Back in Houston after my mother died, I had zero time to dilly-dally getting a job. I registered with a headhunter and nailed down a position with the Jamison Firm in short order. I was a paralegal there going on five years. Paid my dues, as they say. Didn't take long until I was the best paralegal in the firm, and for me, a nameplate on my desk didn't cut it. My name should've been emblazoned on the door: Juliana Birdsong, Attorney at Law. I wanted to be noticed for who I was. Oliver noticed. Word got around about me, I suppose.

When he approached me at the courthouse, I already knew exactly who he was. Everyone did. If not personally, by reputation. The insanely handsome hot-shot lawyer with the super-charged personality from the prestigious personal litigation firm, Bales and Ford. Oliver Morrissey was matchless. Aerodynamic. Cases no one thought could be won, he hit them out of the park.

"You'd make a fine lawyer. Why the hell aren't you one?" He may deny it now, but he said it many times, and I didn't disagree. It wasn't right away, but he said I was damn well going to law school and he was sending me.

When he lured me away from Jamison with a substantial increase in salary, I jumped in with both high-heeled pumps. Hell, yes I did. I loved the way his mind worked. His instincts were always right-on, analyzing cases to determine the perfect strategy. He was demanding and the work was often horribly dull and tedious—comes with the territory—but being on-hand for his high-profile, whirlwind cases made it worthwhile. Going to work every day was intoxicating. I felt so alive. I felt important. Like the work I was doing mattered because it affected so many people's lives. Our work chemistry? We were flat-out amazing together. With Oliver, I felt I could do anything. I believe I made him feel the same way.

I guess I had a little crush on him. Let's face it, I'm not the first woman to find power attractive. I don't believe I'm alone in that. Especially in a man who looks like Oliver. Plus, isn't there always a little sexual tension floating through the air at work, in social situations, and practically any time men and women interact?

I'd been working for him coming on two years. He was sitting on the maple conference table one day with a leg dangling over the edge. I was seated in a swivel chair at his side, hanging on his every word and writing most of them down on my yellow legal pad. He was wearing highly-polished tassel loafers and argyle socks. Charcoal and maroon. I remember things like that. He also wore a silly pink, polka-dotted bow-tie and matching braces. Not on his teeth. Braces was the cool thing to call suspenders back then. Not that I had any room to talk in my red Nancy Reagan dress with Alexis Carrington shoulder pads. Gotta love those eighties fashions.

Some fat toad of a lawyer whose name I've forgotten came in to discuss legal strategies. He and Oliver machoed, bantering back and forth, comparing notes on this case and that. They took turns throwing darts at the jumbo pizza-sized, black and red dartboard against the far wall.

Oliver's turn, he rested his Cuban cigar in the ashtray and squared up with the board. Lining up his shot, he motioned to me with his head. "I'm taking this one home." Then : one, two, three, he hit three bulls eyes.

Me? Seriously? My pulse quickened. It was the first I'd heard of it.

Toad looked down at me with a boner on his face. Remember, I was only twenty-eight. My head swimming, I kept my head down to hide my flushed cheeks, taking extra time with my notes. After a couple more games, Oliver told Toad he was dismissed. Tugging at his tie and sputtering on his way out, he quickly pulled the door behind him.

Hands shaking, I tore the top sheet from my legal pad and clipped it to the stack of documents in my lap. From the corner of my eye, I could see Oliver watching me in a way I'd never seen before. Looking me up and down like I was a piece of cheesecake.

"You're racking up lots of overtime, Juliana. Got way too many files stacking up." He pulled the feather-tipped darts from the board.

"Sorry, Oliver," I said. "I'll work faster and not bill so many hours."

"Maybe I could help you whittle them down," he said deviously.

In an instant, he spun my chair around and rested both hands on the conference table, one on either side of my chair, me in the middle. Slowly, seductively, he took his fingers and walked them up my arm. "How about I come by your house tonight. Call in some takeout?"

Before I could answer, he pulled me to my feet and kissed me.

It seemed like he appreciated the best parts of me. The smart side of me.

I kissed him back.

Not cool, I know. Falling for the boss.

He wooed me. It was deliciously irresistible. He became my everything. I fell in love. We both did. It was exciting racing to the moon in the cockpit. Beat the hell out of coach or even first class. It was fun being in love, being in love with Oliver. Oh, yes it was.

We can get it back, whatever it was we lost. I'm certain.

I'm jolted by the bang of the judge's gavel. I check the front for Oliver. He's starting toward the counsel table with a satisfied expression. His jubilant client raises his palm to high-five him and Oliver shakes his head. It's poor form to celebrate in the courtroom. Save it for when the check clears, he used to say. Grinning sheepishly, the man pumps Oliver's hand vigorously. His white neck brace jiggles up and down.

As if he knows I'm watching him, Oliver pivots his head and stares right at me. Seeing me, his eyes open wide. Hungry. I read his lips: "Let's talk."

On the dais, the judge says a few words. Court's dismissed.

The stenographer finishes tapping the keys and loads her little machine into its case. Agitated spectators file from the courtroom. Cell phones come out. People look at their wristwatches. Attorneys do the same with their laptops.

Three rows back on the left, I'm surprised to see my best friend. Mary Ellen lowers her dark lashes and covers the mouthpiece of her phone with her hand. I rest my arm on the back of the next seat, watching her. She runs her tongue over her pink lips and blinks. She flips a few pages in her calendar before returning it to her purse.

In a moment she skittles down my aisle, shimmying between the seats, bumping a few knees along the way. The flirty, ruffled hem of her skirt flounces. Reaching me, she rests her smooth hand on my shoulder. I glance down at her perfect red nails. Fresh manicure.

"Hey," she whispers in my ear. "You doing okay?"

She smells like face powder. Her breath, like Dentyne.

I wrinkle my brow at her. "Why are you here?"

"Oh, I had to bring Mike's briefcase."

So, there he is. Mike comes hustling down the center aisle, a thick, brown briefcase in his hand. Victorious, Oliver gives him a salute—his old signal for TD. Not "Touch-Down," but "Total Domination."

I glare at the back of Mike's straight, dark hair that's shingled up the back like tree bark. I always thought he looked like Bob Dole. A bald Bob Dole, of course. Mike should powder his shiny head.

When he stretches forward to shake the client's hand, Oliver punches him in the arm and points in my direction. Seeing me, Mike strides up the aisle with Oliver on his heels. His handkerchief peeks slyly from the breast pocket of his hounds tooth jacket. Reaching my row, his face breaks into a smile. Flashing canine teeth.

He holds out his cheek. "Come on," he tells me. "Let's kiss and make up."

To keep from slapping him, I bend to collect my things.

"Cease fire, Juliana," Oliver says with a laugh. Like everything's one big joke. "We're all friends. Let's all grab a drink somewhere."

"If you want to," Mary Ellen chimes in. I could kill her.

"You guys go ahead," I say. "I'm picking up the kids from school."

I pull my slick, white motorcycle helmet over my wild curls and tuck the long, scraggly ends inside. Like a rebel, I throw my shoulders back and head towards the exit.

# CHAPTER FORTY-TWO

❖ ❖ ❖

Kimberley keeps a manifestation board in her bathroom with big letters across the top that say: "Passion, Happiness & Physical Love." It has pictures clipped from magazines of exotic vacation spots. A big, white house. There's one of her in a lime green bikini. She also attends the Goddess Workshop at least once a year to get in touch with her personal power.

I'm sitting on the white velvet love seat in the middle of the elegant dressing area of the city's most posh and expensive bridal boutique. Every dress imaginable drapes from satin hangers. Long sleeves, cap sleeves, and strapless. Sweetheart necklines, silk organza, satin, tulle and taffeta. There's even a skirt of feathers.

Kimberley sticks her head around the changing curtain.

"Since the right man hasn't materialized yet, it's time to get serious and work with the laws of attraction," she says. "You know *The Secret*, and all of that? Choosing the perfect gown will help me send out the right vibe and draw him to me."

That's right. I'm helping her find the wedding dress of her dreams. No problem that she's forty-two, not to mention a little nuts.

She lifts the hem of the poufy skirt as if she's keeping it from dragging through a mud puddle. The dress has double petticoats and a ridiculous, two-foot-wide bow on the butt.

"Too prom?" she asks.

"There's a tiara on your head," I say. "Does the dressing room have a mirror?"

With a petulant pout, she yanks the curtain closed. I hear her laughing to herself.

The saleswoman's name is June. She's probably fifty years old. Dark headed, makeup applied expertly. Kind of Cleopatra-ish. Sweet as she can be. She's just come back with another armful of dresses. There's a yellow tape measure around her neck.

Kimberley pulls back the curtain wearing only a white merry widow, a garter belt and sheer, white stockings.

So, the lingerie story *is* true.

June hands her one of the lacier numbers. "Has he given you the ring?"

"Not yet." Kimberley bats her lashes and wriggles herself into the gown.

June begins shifting the bodice, then ties the satin sash. "Don't say yes until you see how big the rock is."

Kimberley says, "Don't worry."

"Ma'am, I hope we're not taking up too much of your time," I say.

"It's dull as dishwater in here today," she says. "Besides, this beats the hell out of folding the gloves."

"Gloves," Kimberley says excitedly. "I completely forgot about those."

"She'll want elbow ones, of course," I tell June.

"Naturally," she says. "Be back in a jiff."

Kimberley steps from behind the curtain. The smooth, satin dress shows four inches of cleavage.

"Wouldn't you rather save that look for the honeymoon suite?" I say. "There are other things in life than being a good-looking sex machine, Kimberley."

She flips her blond hair from her bedroom eyes. "Well, if that's the case, I don't know what they are."

I shrug and wait for the next dress.

"Okay, what about this one?" she says breathlessly. "Stephen would've loved me in this." She throws back her shoulders.

"Would it be about Stephen this time, or you?"

She artfully smoothes the waistline. "Me, I guess, since he was the love of my life and I ruined it. But I know I'll find love again. Why would I be in these circumstances if there weren't someone pretty special waiting for me at a destined moment?" she says. "Now, what do you think about the dress?"

The whole upper half is sequins over flesh-toned illusion fabric.

"You look like Tonya Harding," I say. "And, I can see your stomach."

She jerks the curtain closed and keeps talking. "This time, I need someone to look at eye-to-eye. As equals. Warts and all. Full disclosure. When that's all out on the table, if he still loves me—he's the one."

June comes back. "Sure thing, honey. Where would anyone find a man like that?" She holds out a dress with a sweetheart neckline. The full skirt is yards of tulle with pearls.

Kimberley shakes her head. "Sorry," she says.

"Don't be sorry," June says. "You need to have your dream gown." She leans down and refills our glasses of champagne.

"Won't you have some?" I say.

"Honey, if I got started now, I'd be on the floor by closing time. Trust me. It's happened before." She hesitates, then helps herself to my glass and takes a long swig.

"Listen, June. I know my friend's a bombshell, but can you find her something truly elegant?"

She holds up her index finger and winks. Soon, she's back with another gown, plus a pair of sexy ivory heels.

Kimberley opens the curtain for the last time.

It's a mermaid dress. Strapless. Tight from the hips through the knees. It accentuates her every curve. There's such a glow around her, it's ethereal. She's more beautiful than I've ever seen her. And that's saying something.

June helps her onto the raised platform, in front of the three-way mirror.

Seeing her reflection, Kimberley gasps. Puckering her lips while watching herself, she flounces the skirt and smoothes the lace.

"You know what my mother would say about you in that dress?" June says with a wink. "You're making a honeymoon baby."

"So which one are you getting?" I say.

Kimberley looks at June. "None of them," she says. "I'm sorry, I just wanted to get wedding dress shopping out of my system."

"As I said, this beats the hell out of folding gloves."

"Juliana, don't you want to try one on?"

"Gee, I would but I left my corset at home."

"Well, we're already here," she says. "Why not?"

"Because it's silly," I say.

June looks me head to toe. "I know what size you are."

Coming right back, she beams. "It's the prettiest one in the store."

Emerging from the dressing room, I put my right foot forward and curtsy. I fluff out the edges of the tulle skirt and twirl. "Do you think the train is too long?" I say.

"Heck no," Kimberley says and gently attaches the veil to the back of my head. "Is this as pretty as the dress you wore when you and Oliver got married? It must've been a big society to-do. Or was it on the Love Boat?"

I try my best to smile. "Hardly. It was a courthouse wedding. The judge officiating was one of Oliver's cronies."

Kimberley's face falls. "No way. With just the two of you, it must have been lonely."

It was. I wanted my mother there in that moment. And my dad to give me away. And Richard standing beside me as my best man of honor.

"So, what were you wearing?" she says.

"A dusty blue dinner suit."

"No veil, no gloves, no nothing?"

"No, that's it," I say.

And a nursing bra.

The result of too much alcohol, champagne actually, on the night Oliver told me he wanted to spend the rest of his life with me. Even if his wife wasn't especially keen on the idea.

Her name was Charlotte.

They didn't have a good marriage, he said. That they'd been separated for some time, and they had an "understanding." She was a career woman all the way—a big-time advertising exec who never wanted kids. A real women's libber, as he put it. Not willing to gamble, Charlotte insisted Oliver have a vasectomy and he didn't fight her.

I'd never heard her name spoken at the office, but now everyone seemed to be making a point of mentioning it. When her portrait came down, gossip reached hysterical proportions and the water cooler became the *Titanic*; the staff's collective shoulders were like an iceberg in August and they insinuated my talents weren't legit. Working Oliver's cases became virtually impossible while ducking the poison darts.

Then, I started showing.

Oliver said I was cute with my birthing hips. I wanted to snap his neck.

Kimberley steps on the platform and stands beside me. Avoiding my eyes in the mirror, I flip the veil over my face and she wraps her arms around me. Full of all these secrets, I can't hold in my tears any longer. I don't know this woman. Not really. But it seems she knows me as no one else has. Kimberley has a broken heart, too.

# CHAPTER FORTY-THREE

❖ ❖ ❖

---

Richard hands me a latte. Extra foam, just the way I like it.

"Well, what a surprise. And it's not even my birthday."

"Don't thank me," he says. "It's from Lindsey."

"Lindsey?" I check the Starbucks cup. "Richard" is scrawled on the side in black Sharpie.

He grins. "I bought it with the five bucks she paid me not to rat her out."

"Oh, Rich," I say. "What did she do?"

"Forgot that Wally and I were fetching her from the mall for dinner."

I dig in my jeans pocket for my phone and he grabs my arm. "Chill out," he says. "Just drink your latte and listen."

I try taking a sip, and the damn thing burns my lip.

"After we circled the lot about ten times waiting on her, I was ready to march inside to drag her out by her hair."

Been there, done that.

"Wally took one side of the mall and I took the other. When I finally found her at the makeup counter in Nordstrom's blistering Oliver's Visa, she said she'd already eaten." He smirks. "At Chick Filet."

I try pushing the cup into his hand. "Take it back, because I'm going to kill her."

He brushes me off. "You know I'm off caffeine," he says. "After we got past the pissy part, we all had a nice talk. She's a good girl. A cool chick, you know? She had all kinds of questions about you."

I raise my brows. "I'll bet."

Just to be annoying, he ruffles my hair. "I hate you means I love you," he says. "Where have you been?"

Right here, waiting for her to come back, I guess.

He hands me a fresh leaf bag, stretches out on the weeds and watches me scoop a pile of leaves inside. Second time I've raked this week, and the yard still looks like hell.

"Oh, and Adam's getting better with running the lake," he says. "Not overly-motivated, but he said it beats the wahoola out of golf, although that's not the exact word he used."

"I appreciate you taking him, Rich," I say. "You're a Godsend."

He leans up on one elbow and smiles up at me. "Just doing my job, being Mr. Wonderful."

"Then, hey, Mr. Wonderful," I say. "How about getting off that wonderful butt of yours and giving me a hand here?"

"I didn't ask you to rake leaves," he says.

I grab a handful of dirt from the flowerbed and throw it at him. Unfazed, he brushes it from his jacket and continues watching me.

After a minute, I say, "Seems like you're enjoying the kids, Rich. Ever think of having some of your own?"

He cocks an eyebrow. "Hmm-m. Sounds like you've been talking to Wally."

I shrug. "He's handing you an incredible opportunity. Just think long and hard before turning your back on something amazing that would change your life. That's all I'm saying. "

"Maybe I don't want a new life," he shoots back. "I'm good with mine just like it is."

Just as I consider grabbing more dirt, he climbs to his feet and reaches for the rake. Head down, he begins scraping up a pile.

"Honestly, Jules, I'm not against having a family. Really, I'm not, but can you imagine me pushing a stroller?"

I smile at the thought.

"And besides, gay-bashers are lined up around the block, ready to tell me that I have no right," he says. "It's pretty tough having people make assumptions before they've even gotten to know you."

I give him a sad smile. "Okay, but when was Richard Birdsong ever a chicken?"

He scoffs. "Me, a chicken? What about you, little sister? I leave you alone for five minutes and you're back together with Oliver."

"We're not together. Not as a family, that's for sure. I'm still living here."

He watches me tie-off a stuffed lawn bag and toss it on the curb. "That Jan James woman said the paintings are worth big bucks," he says. "And you better sell the suckers, Jules, or you'll be bringing Dad back home."

"I couldn't tell him I'm selling his artwork. Besides, until now, Dad was only someone to be mad at. Now I have something," I say. "Tell me I'm not crazy, Rich. Does that make any sense at all?"

"You don't have the luxury of being sentimental and I don't know what you're waiting on." He stares at me hard. "But then, maybe I do—Oliver's cash. Back together, your troubles are over and you'll have Dad's paintings decorating the walls of your mansion," he says.

I glare at him. "While that does sound spectacular, Rich, my goal is getting my family back."

Sitting down to shake the dirt out of my tennis shoes, I realize now is the perfect time to tell him.

"There's another reason I can't sell them," I say slowly. "It's hard to explain, but amazing things are happening."

He looks down at me and smiles. "Having them back, I bet it lightens his mood a lot."

"It does, sure, but they bring his memories to the surface. The only word for it is supernatural, really." I hesitate. "I'm telling you, they come to life."

His eyes widen. "What?"

"I know it sounds crazy, but come to Sagecrest and you'll see what I'm talking about."

"Boy, you'll say anything, won't you?" he says disgustedly. "Build a shrine around them complete with votive candles and a kneeling bench, and I'm still not coming up there."

"Rich, I'm not playing a game, here," I cry. "I'm being real."

Stubborn, thick-headed, doubting Thomas, stupid moron.

"You want real, Jules? Selling them, at least he could bail himself out of the lousy mess I made for him."

I sigh roughly. "None of that matters anymore, Rich. Okay?"

He drops to the ground beside me and rolls over on his back. "I guess we're both scared about a lot of things aren't we?" he says.

I lay my head against his chest and stare up at the fluttering branches in the trees, and watch their changing leaves.

Green to red to yellow. At brown, they finally fall.

# CHAPTER FORTY-FOUR

❖ ❖ ❖

Motherhood?

Right, sign me up for that job, I thought. Why would I want to do that? Richard is afraid to have children. What, with our role model, frankly, so was I.

Once the cat was out of the bag with Charlotte, she didn't take it lying down. It soon got ugly, and all of her venom was spewed at me. When I said to Oliver, "Wait a minute—this isn't what I signed on for. You said you were separated," he replied. "Metaphorically speaking."

Having never once intercepted one of her calls before, all that changed. Did I prefer to be called a concubine, a consort or a gold-digging whore? The woman was damn scary. She even had me followed.

My true paralegal responsibilities dwindled, replaced with the tedious minutia of his existence. Persona non grata, what happened to the best paralegal in the firm? Help Wanted: Legal assistant for Bales & Ford. They filled it lickety-split. I made the unemployment line. Oliver made partner.

Who hires a pregnant woman? A cranky, tired, swollen-ankled lumbering load who's simply biding her time at the office until she can take maternity leave, from which she may never return? And even if she did, what new mother can put in a law firm's dreadful hours when there's a baby to be picked up from day care?

Oliver puffed out his chest and stroked my belly. "You really have to hand it to my macho seed. Against the odds, this little bundle really wanted to come into the world." I did a little research to find out what odds he was talking about. Here's the birth control failure rates: condoms 12%; the sponge 9%, the pill 5%; vasectomy, 1%.

"Kill me now if I ever have a conversation about diapers." That's what I told Oliver before the twins were born. But it was inevitable, with two sets of diapers, two sets of everything, it was wild and I loved it immediately. I could do it. And I did. I had no identity except "mother," so I became the best mother ever put on the planet Earth. Or, so it seemed to me. I loved Lindsey and Adam so much, I found out that "mother" was a pretty terrific identity to have.

When he was free, to his credit, Oliver put a ring on my finger, but I felt like a weight with a complete stranglehold on his star. The Juliana he fell in love with was the beautiful, young and vibrant career woman. The one who was going places. My eight years of professional relationships virtually severed, I was desperately lonely.

"Oliver," I said. "Let's move to Austin. Make a fresh start."

With Oliver's reputation, he could practice anywhere. With my reputation, all I knew was I couldn't stay in the Houston fishbowl because I wanted to raise my children in peace. Not only that, I could finally become a lawyer, too—make good on his promise to me and my promise to myself. The University of Texas law school had accepted me before, I told him, and they would again. My LSAT scores were current; having just taken it again, I smoked it. Oliver said he loved me and wanted me to be happy.

Austin's legal community had a whole different set of players than Houston. After talking with a few firms, Oliver determined he wasn't much of a team player and would be going out on his own. Establishing a new practice was an expensive undertaking, he said, and that he needed every last dollar to pour into the business, so the whole Juliana going to law school was off the table. Swallowing my anger, I understood when he said he uprooted his practice from Houston for me, after all, and it was a sacrifice I should be happy to make for the family.

But, where were the Oliver and Juliana from before? The old Oliver? Where was he? Nowhere on the premises. Okay, how about just Juliana? Absent and unaccounted for. I remember being hungry for the work he and I had shared. I missed the interesting discussions we would have. I was like a raspberry snow cone with all the red juice sucked out. He quickly tired of me pumping him for work details, such as whatever happened to this case, that client, and what kind of settlement did he make. "I don't want to talk about work when I get home," he'd say, and I could understand that because I didn't especially want to talk about the twins when he got home and he didn't much want me to, either. Definitely not.

He left the house before I was up in the morning and as he walked through the door at night, both phones would ring. I only learned the details of his high-profile cases when I read about them in the paper.

The nights I'd fall asleep with a hand on both of the twins' formula bottles, I remember thinking that my life was over. The life that I could do what I wanted. Just for me. I adored my children and wouldn't have given up being a mother for anything. I just wanted something more. Not something else.

# CHAPTER FORTY-FIVE

❖ ❖ ❖

Anabel's jelly bean jar has only a handful of black ones left.

Looking up from her computer, she checks her watch before reaching her big, soft hand across the desk.

"Hello, Ms. Birdsong."

"Thanks for seeing me," I say. "I promise this won't take long."

Arranging my purse on the floor next to me, I nonchalantly peer under the desk at her feet. Five-inch leopard platforms. With ankle straps.

"When you made this appointment, I made a couple of phone calls," she says grimly. "Lots of information about you and Mr. Morrissey flying around."

I smile. "I bet there is. Oliver and I are reconciling."

She digs the last lonely beans from the bottom of the jar "Well, that's exceedingly good news for you." Popping a few in her mouth, she holds up her watch.

"Ok, here's the situation," I say quickly. "When a friend of mine was divorcing, there was a hearing where she and her ex-husband got a parenting plan."

"I bet this was Kimberley, right?"

I shrug.

"They're called temporary orders," she says. "She got some other things, too. I was Stephen's lawyer, if you'll recall, so I was there."

"Oh, right. Well, I wondered why that never happened for me."

She stops chewing immediately.

I begin rifling through my satchel. "My dad hoarded mail like a squirrel. I found his stash and these were in it." I hand the envelopes across the desk, their green return receipt tabs still affixed. "They're a Motion for Default, and a Notice of Default Hearing."

She inspects the post marks. "They're from over four months ago."

"I know this last one's trash." I shake it from the envelope. "It came a few weeks ago. I remember because it was the day after Oliver said we were getting back together," I say. "Since it's dated the day before, the clerk obviously mailed it, not knowing Oliver decided to call off the divorce."

I hold it up. Notice of Final Default

"You're back together and he told you that he got the dismissal from the county clerk?"

"He said he dropped the suit," I say. "What's wrong?"

She looks at me closely. "You have a certified copy of that? Because nothing happens at the courthouse without notice."

I shake my head. "I gave you all the letters I have."

"Oh, Lordy." She sighs. "When you never came back months ago, I assume you found other representation."

I start to answer, but she cuts in.

Her piercing brown eyes bear down on me. "You've probably gathered by this point in our conversation that Mr. Morrissey didn't drop the suit."

"What?"

"Did you know a default divorce can be granted 61 days after the petition is filed, Ms. Birdsong?"

I glance at the wall calendar behind her.

"There is a mandatory 60-day waiting period between filing a petition, court judgment and divorce," she says. "In a default situation, the initiating spouse can waltz into the court on day 61 and be granted the divorce entirely on their terms without the other spouse being in attendance or even signing the decree."

"Are you just trying to scare me, or are you telling me the truth?"

She looks over her glasses. "If you knew me better, Ms. Birdsong, you'd know that I am doing both."

"What are you saying?"

"When a person is served a petition in Texas, they have 20 days to file a response," she says evenly. "You did not file a response, which makes you in default."

I wrinkle my brows at her.

"You missed your first hearing." Holding up the letters, she points to the Notice of Default Hearing. "At which time, you would have received temporary orders for the span of the divorce process mandating several things: spousal support and the payment of bills. Including mine." She pauses. "Plus custody, possession time and support of the children."

I blink. That's what Kimberley was talking about.

"Your opportunity to correct the default would've been to make a counter claim at the Final Default Hearing." She points at the next paper. "Which you also missed."

My eyes open wide. "You're saying that all this time, I could have had possession of my kids?"

She threads her fingers together and nods. "Had you appeared and made counter claims, yes."

I lean across the desk. "You knew these deadlines but didn't warn me when I was here before?" I cry. "What's wrong with you?"

She levels her gaze at me. "I didn't believe drawing you a picture was necessary since you were your husband's legal assistant." She pauses. "All suits require an answer, and I assumed you knew that."

My heart sinks. She's right. I know that. Or at least I used to.

"I've had a lot on my mind. I was preoccupied with caring for my father," I stutter.

"Avoidance, ostrich behavior? Some women are like Scarlett O'Hara." She raises her baritone to a falsetto. 'Oh, fiddle-dee-dee, I'll worry about that tomorrow.'" She looks at me with disdain. "Honestly. Some women are so accustomed to their husbands doing everything for them, they imagine he'll handle their side of the divorce, too. Moronic, but true."

I glare at her. "For your information, Ms. Brock, when I worked for Oliver, we didn't do family law."

"What you did or didn't know about family law is irrelevant because the deadlines, along with everything else, are covered in the divorce petition."

"The papers flew out of the car the day I got them, which was fine with me because I don't want this bullshit divorce in the first place."

She swivels in her chair and rolls up to her credenza. "Get with the program, Ms. Birdsong," she says gruffly. "All of this is public information."

Squinting, she punches several keys on her desk top. The Texas State seal eventually appears on her screen and she begins scrolling through the website. When I scoot up my chair and try reading over her shoulder, she puts on her full-out lawyer voice.

They all have them, it's just a matter of time before they pull them out.

"A divorce petition sets forth to the court the specific legal grounds and facts supporting the request for a dissolution of the marriage, the reasons why a couple is no longer able to live together as husband and wife, as well as requests to settle items like child custody, property division and spousal support."

Finally locating what she needs on the site, she hits print.

"That's your husband's petition coming up now," she says.

We both stare at the printer. Nothing.

Raising the thick tangle of cords, Anabel's eyes trace the one connected to the back of the printer to the wall plug. Seeing it's plugged in, she roughly tears back the cover on a fresh ream of paper and loads it into the printer.

As it finally begins spitting out pages, I watch my ugly future fill the tray.

Anabel has to speak loudly over the noisy machine. "Property in Texas can be divided unequally if a spouse is at fault." Finished printing, she pulls out the document and fans the pages, making sure they're in order. "And, the evidence of fault was presented by Mr. Magruder to the judge at the hearing."

"Stop!" I scream. "The hearing happened?"

"Yes, ma'am. And, he has quite a flair for revisionist history," she says, shaking her head. "He said your husband had to perform all the house work and that you were emotionally and verbally abusive to him in front of the children, yelling at him every time he came home." She pauses. "And that you shouldn't be allowed around them because you have a drinking problem and you've been having an affair."

"He's lying," I cry. "What about my rights?"

"I keep trying to tell you," she says impatiently. "You made all of this possible by not filing a response."

Please stop saying that.

I squeeze my eyes shut.

"It appears that your husband said he'd dropped suit to keep you away from the hearing to prevent you from presenting your side of the story," she says. "You not appearing entitled him to a blank check."

"A blank check? I don't understand."

She sets the document in front of me. "It's what they call a one-sided divorce. The division of property, child support and visitation—everything that Mr. Morrissey asked for in the divorce petition."

I begin screaming. "We're already divorced?"

"Looks like it," she says.

"And, Oliver gets custody of the kids?"

"Under this scenario, yes." There's pity in her eyes.

I collapse in my chair.

"You're like a little lizard that's losing its tail when your marriage is about to end and it's terrifying to imagine part of yourself lying on the ground." She sighs roughly. "But sometimes the only way to be free is having it ripped from your body."

I put my head on my hands. "Anabel. What am I going to do?"

"Appeal," she says quickly. "It'd require some fancy footwork to have the default overturned and get you some days to file your response."

I look up. "You could do that, right?"

She crosses her hands in front of her. "Landing in rehab by way of probation, I'm in Chapter Seven and my pro bono days are over."

Before she can say anything else, I snatch up the document and head to the door.

"I'm sorry, Ms. Birdsong," she calls after me.

I run through the reception area and make my way to the elevators in the hall. Heart pounding, I watch the lighted numbers above the doors, counting the number of floors left until they open for me.

Stumbling in, I punch "L" for lobby.

A great big hand comes through the doors, stopping them from closing.

Anabel's out of breath. "Juliana, listen to me," she says. "Being that little lizard that loses its tail?"

I glare at her. "Yeah?"

"You'll grow a new one, I promise you," she says. "From totally new skin."

## CHAPTER FORTY-SIX

❖ ❖ ❖

Richard is lying on his back on the pavement of the PakMail parking lot, cutting loose the thick twine from the undercarriage of the convertible. Wally's truck is in the shop and strapping the painting to the trunk was our only option to haul it up here for shipping. I've wrapped it carefully in bubble wrap, brown paper and black plastic sheathing, and I hope it's okay. It damn well better be, because if Ms. James is going to sell it, the painting's got to make it to her it in one piece.

After he eases down the bumper, I try hauling it inside myself, but when he grabs the other side and we begin carrying it together, I'm glad. It's really heavy, and that's part of the reason, but mostly – well, maybe it sounds weird, but somehow it feels like Richard's helping carry some of my guilt.

Once inside, we lower the painting to the ground, and both stare silently straight ahead. With easily ten customers ahead of us, I don't remember ever being glad that a line is so long before, never once in all my years on earth.

The young man in front of us finally takes his turn. I nervously watch the back of his brown suede jacket as he stacks bulk-mail on the counter—white envelopes with red ink in the corners from one of those postage machines from Pitney-Bowes. As he turns away from the counter, the young man raises his palms and he gives me an apologetic expression.

The clerk's eyes bear down on me; still I fill out the paperwork slowly, careful not to check a box unless I've read it twice. Even after signing my name and giving her what's left in my wallet in exchange for the tracking receipt, I still don't believe it when she begins sliding the painting across the platform. My fingers seize up, clutching the frame instinctively. And they won't let go.

"You paid for the sturdy crate and extra insurance," she says gruffly, and slaps her hand against the cash register. "I know you did, because I've got your money right here."

My brother puts his hand on my shoulder. He squeezes it tenderly and my fingers relax and uncurl. When I look up at him, he simply points his head toward the door, indicating that he'll be outside.

Back turned, the clerk gently slides the painting into a slender, wooden crate and leans it carefully against the wall. She writes the words, "Do Not Lay Flat," in large black letters, then peels a lime-green "Fragile" sticker from the special sheet in her drawer. I wait until she has it firmly in place before ducking my head and walking to the door.

Richard's leaning against the trunk of the convertible. His eyes are somber behind the blue lenses of his spiffy sunglasses as he tears the foil from a bottle of fine champagne.

"Imagine how happy Dad would feel, Jules, knowing his painting would fetch so much money," he tries saying in a cheerful voice.

He pops the cork and pours our glasses. We both try not to cry.

"To Hugh Birdsong," he says.

We clink glasses.

"Congratulations, Dad," I say softly.

We hug each other tightly.

To hell with the tears. We let them flow.

## CHAPTER FORTY-SEVEN

❖ ❖ ❖

As I'm watering the drooping verbena out front, I'm surprised to see Mr. Reynolds opening our front gate. He's the retired body-builder from across the street who drives the black TransAm just like in the movie *Smokey and the Bandit*. Every weekend he waxes it shirtless in his driveway. It's awesome.

He takes extra care to shut the gate behind him, then pulls back his shoulders and begins walking stiffly up the sidewalk. After spraying the grass off my feet, I drop the hose in the weeds and meet him halfway.

"Afternoon, Ms. Birdsong," he says, not meeting my eyes.

"To what do I owe the pleasure, Mr. Reynolds?" I say.

He quickly glances toward their driveway where Mrs. Reynolds is seated in the front seat of the TransAm, windows rolled up. She pats her bouffant and waves feebly.

"My wife loves roses," he says. "Yep, that she does."

"I've never met a woman who didn't, Mr. Reynolds," I say.

He wipes his brow. "She saw some real pretty ones while she was walking the dog a while back," he says.

I smile pleasantly.

"Not too long after you came to live with your dad over here."

And, he's telling me this because?

"I should've come by sooner, except I was scared you'd report the missus to the Neighborhood Watch," he says. "It can't happen again—we've been warned."

I lower my sunglasses and stare at him.

He clears his throat. "I guess what I'm trying to say is that she stole the flowers off your porch." He hesitates. "Guess you'll be wanting your vase back."

Looking to their driveway, I make quick eye contact with Mrs. Reynolds. She lowers the visor.

"Don't worry about it," I say.

He puts a tiny white envelope in my hand. The kind florists use.

"This fell out when she brought them home and it's been taped to our fridge ever since."

The man's eyes don't leave the tiny envelope. I clench it in my palm.

"Anywho, she can't live with herself. Got herself all worked up, thinking the card is like a message in a bottle," he says. "She swears it's a marriage proposal." He looks at me hopefully. "I bet her twenty bucks it's not."

I hand the envelope back. "Then you may have the honors."

He rips it open and raises the card to his face.

"'Just Kidding,' it says." He looks up to catch my reaction. "And, it's signed, 'Love, Oliver.'"

I rake my dirty nails through my curls.

"Tell your wife it's the easiest twenty dollars she ever made."

## CHAPTER FORTY-EIGHT

❖ ❖ ❖

---

"If it's important to you, babe, of course I'll be there."

I believe those were Oliver's exact words when I told him I made today's appointment with Dr. Phillips.

He's such a lamb.

We take our designated spots—the lumpy love seat for the happy couple, the striped wingback for the seasoned therapist. Without taking her eyes off us, she tucks her skirt under her as she settles into the cushion. She slips on her black glasses, determined to understand how two people could appear so happy after what happened when we were here before.

We're one sick, codependent couple.

I was barely functioning until I realized something. In Oliver's mind, I spurned him three times: When he sent the flowers and I didn't respond; when he had Lindsey prompt me about them; and in person when he came by Dad's.

And, his agony is my reason to live.

Dr. Phillips fumbles through her bag until she comes up with a SlimFast. "I was puzzled when you requested this appointment, Mrs. Morrissey." She cracks open the can and takes a long sip. "I imagined you two were divorced by now."

I lean forward and smile. "Oh, we are," I say. "Oliver went through with it. He just neglected to tell me."

"Whew." He dramatically wipes his brow. "I'm glad *that's* finally out in the open."

He casually turns his head toward Dr. Phillips, gauging her reaction.

Unflappable, she continues looking at me.

"I'm sure there's a real story there, Mrs. Morrissey," she says. "But just give me the basics."

"I missed the default deadline," I say. "He asked me to reconcile, said he dropped the suit, and took it from there."

Eyeballing him now, she says, "You're a little corker, aren't you, Mr. Morrissey?"

He straightens the knot on his pink tie. "And I don't even practice family law," he says proudly.

But, he's catching on real fast.

"Absolutely impressive." Dr. Phillips steeples her fingers under her chin. "So, humor me, counselor. Share your motivation."

He leans toward her, as if taking her into his confidence. "I did it for fun."

I feel my nails digging into my palms.

"Gotcha," she says. "But, certainly there's more."

He blurts out the answer. "When the dumbass didn't even file a response or even show up at any of the hearings, well, she left herself wide open."

He looks at me for a response. What would I even say?

She sits forward in her chair. "Certainly you know that your children aren't getting what they need."

Oliver arches his back. "Whoa," he says. "Where did that come from?"

"They need their mother," she says mildly.

I can't stay silent any longer. "She's right, Oliver."

He cuts me off. "Don't think this is easy on me either, Mrs. Morrissey. That Lindsey's a handful. Well, I don't have to tell you that." He rolls his eyes. "Hoo-boy, you should hear her bitch about you... Sometimes I have to tell her, Linds, just let it go."

Calm. Calm. I take a deep breath.

"Then, Oliver, you've got to be sick of them by now. Let them come live with me. At least part of the time."

"Frankly, ma'am, they're just not interested," he says blithely. "I told you that already."

"They're fourteen years old," I cry. "They don't know what's best for them."

"Keep your voice down," he says sternly.

He may have me on the ropes, but I'll get the kids back a little at a time. He'll never know what happened.

Oliver raises his index finger. "Excuse me a moment." He opens his suit coat and deliberately retrieves his phone. Checking the screen, he chuckles like it says something funny, and begins texting.

Dr. Phillips clears her throat. "I'm curious, Mr. Morrissey," she says. "What's in the decree?"

He leans down and prudently slips out a manila folder with a red tab from his briefcase. "The money, the kids—imagine the worst it can be, and that's about it. Basically, she doesn't get shit," he says. "Pardon my French."

She eyeballs him, and then uses her middle finger to slowly push her glasses back into place.

"Don't worry about it," she says. "When's it final?"

"All it needs is my signature," he says easily. "And, to be filed at the courthouse, of course."

My heart jumps.

I finally look at him, smiling. "I knew you couldn't do it."

"Yeah, sure you did," he says. "And don't think you're going to just show up on the doorstep because I'm not letting you in."

I check Dr. Phillips. She's begun flipping through her plaid appointment calendar. Settling on a paper-clipped page, she erases an entry.

"Mr. Morrissey, why are you here today?" she says. "Going through this little exercise?"

"I told you already."

"Come now, Mr. Morrissey," she says.

Carefully straightening his collar, he looks at her nervously. Like he could get in trouble for lying. Not that it's ever been a problem for him before.

"The real reason?" he says.

This should be good.

They lock stares for a moment. Then he whips his head around to me.

"I love you, okay?" he yells. "So, how about you try loving me?"

"Oliver, we're starting over," I say gently. "Everything's all right now."

Stroking his lip, he deliberately scans the pages, as if making sure they're all in order.

I try snatching it from his hands. "So, tear it up!"

He looks down and carefully begins sliding it into his briefcase.

"Not just yet," he says.

"Why not?" I cry.

"It's called leverage, dear."

## CHAPTER FORTY-NINE

❖  ❖  ❖

I kept getting more titles after my name. Assistant, Mistress, Mother, and with each one came increased responsibility. Now, I was Law Wife which entailed membership in clubs and charity groups. Good for business. Oliver said he wanted me to be his ruby. His jewel. And he bestowed them on me often. And, the most incredible clothes. Everything I wanted. I began hanging around with women I would have never imagined myself meeting, much less becoming friends with.

I was somebody for the first time in my life.

His emotional control now elevated to an art form, our interactions seemed more like job evaluations, him, modestly arrogant with implied accusations about how I spent my time, and how I spent the money he gave me, as if he doubted whether my answers were true.

No shouting matches, just a pleasant hell veiled in a façade of happiness.

My fantasy was to drive off the Congress Bridge over Town Lake going ninety miles an hour and sail up to the stars with all the bats under the bridge falling in behind. I read every book on relationships I could find. I was forever in Barnes and Noble sitting cross-legged on the self-help aisle, reading book after book, setting down every pretense that I was going to buy one of the damn things. How could I bring something like that in the house?

But, no matter how much Oliver hurt me, I never let him see it. That's a gift I was unable to give him. I had to keep a little something for myself.

I guess you could call my behavior passive-aggressive. It seemed like the only power I had. I got into the habit of staying up later and later. It was an unspoken game we played. Wrapped in a nubby blanket, hand gripping my wine glass, I would sit woodenly on the lounger on our back deck watching the stars twinkle over downtown. After enough time, I'd tip-toe down the wood-floored hallway to our bedroom, lean against the door and listen. Silence meant he was awake, and I'd head back outside. Snoring meant hopefully slipping between the covers undetected. I'd watch the glowing numbers on my digital clock, and like lying on a bed of broken glass, if I didn't move, maybe I could get some rest.

I often thought about the resentment and anger that swirled in our bedroom. He thought it was ridiculous to have a wife who wouldn't even have sex with him. He was steaming furious, seething, in fact. But, guess what? So was I. What was supposed to be the sexual prime of my life was wasted. It flat-out wasn't fair.

Some nights he'd reach over for me. I didn't always win. But, at least the wine let me lie there passive when he got aggressive.

Early one morning before I drove the kids to school, Oliver stood at the shower door naked, asking if he could come in. I wiped the fog from the glass and regarded him. I'd said no so many times it was pathetic. I said okay.

He waited until I squeezed the shampoo from my hair to wrap his arms around me. I held my body stiff against his. He upturned my face and kissed me. Like a vampire, he sucked the warmth from my veins; even under the stream of hot water, I felt cold.

I loosened myself from his grip and stepped from the shower. The thick, glass door sucked closed behind me. Still covered in soap, I wrapped myself in my robe and drove the kids to school, just like that.

I wanted to feel happiness as strongly as I felt pain.

# CHAPTER FIFTY

❖ ❖ ❖

The next painting is a quiet painting. Calm. Smothered in stillness.

Though completely realistic-looking, the painting's thin brush strokes have an unusual blurriness to them, as if they're under glass. And, it's blue. Varying shades of blue, edge-to-edge, from milky to cornflower and indigo, with a distinct, diamond-patterned overlay. You wouldn't think it would be, but when I glide my fingertips across the surface, it's perfect—glass smooth.

Seeing the diamond pattern for the first time, I knew it looked familiar, so I pulled down the squeaky ladder and climbed up into the attic. Laying my hands on the right box, I peeled back the delicate tissue and marveled at my mother's blue silk, diamond-patterned dress with the unbelievably tiny waist. It's been draped over a special padded hanger in Dad's closet waiting for the destined moment, which I hope is now.

I wait until Dad chooses a round-tipped brush from his old rusted toolbox and fixes his eyes back on the painting before spreading my mother's dress across our laps. As he cradles the brush in his palm and begins shaping its soft bristles, I watch him closely, because this time, I'm not going to miss his strange transformation. Soon, his shoulders droop forward and his eyes seem to lose their focus. He's in a trance.

There's a faint sound. A buzzing hum almost like bees. I feel a strange hypnotic pull, as if the painting is drawing me closer. At once, the air smells like my mother. Her individual scent. How does he do that?

I breathe it in, savoring her memory in my heart. Oh, Mother. Mother, please come back.

Please come back and stay.

Tears spring to my eyes as the image begins coming into focus.

Clearer now. It's my parents' bedroom.

A tarnished silver vase on her dressing table holds a single blue rose. I'm mesmerized, watching its stem bend slowly. The wilted bloom falls forward, humanlike. The petals are textured like lips.

Behind her dressing table is their four-post bed. Her wooden, ladder-back rocker is in the corner, deep blue in the crevices of the grain. Powder blue in the folds of the cushion are like dust. The buzz becomes louder now. The rocker slowly begins swaying. Shadow bands streak their pale bedroom walls.

All at once a fierce gust blows through the room. I whip my head to the door, the instant it slams shut.

Fluttering his fingertips across the bristles, my father begins to speak.

*I was crazy, nuts, insane for Carmen Birdsong.*

*We'd ride my motorcycle through the hills, her arms tight around my waist. How I loved hearing her laugh. She was my biggest pleasure in life. The most beautiful woman in the world, I made a promise to her, and now she shared my name.*

*Bodies intertwined, her soft hair against my chest, like husband and wife, we learned to know each other. Staying in bed all day long on weekends. Me, late to the office more than was acceptable. Sanchez made that abundantly clear. He also warned me more than once not to hurt her. There seemed to be an unspoken agreement between us that if I didn't take care of her, he'd plant his point-toed boot firmly up my ass.*

*"I'll make it worth your while if you'll come home from the office for lunch," she'd say. Tempting as she made it, we both knew I'd never make it back.*

*I couldn't wait to get home and see her. Swaying in her rocking chair, she'd be staring at the door when I walked through it at the end of the day, her hair tied back in a fresh ribbon. McCall's magazine said she should do that when her husband was coming home. Apply some fresh lipstick, too. Have a hot, delicious meal always waiting, and I appreciated the gesture.*

*Evenings she'd watch me paint. It took time away from the time I should be spending with her, she said, and it was clear her interest had waned. I can still imagine her there, smooth legs draped over the couch, her big dark eyes searching my face. It didn't take long until she was resentful, plus bored as hell.*

*Make friends and have them over, I'd tell her.*

*"You try being the Mexican in the ocean of blondes," she'd say. "I don't look like them, I don't talk like them. I don't do the things they do. I'll never be good enough."*

*When she became set on bleaching her hair, I told her, don't you dare.*

I would pull her to my chest and rest my chin on top of her head. My beautiful bride. I'd relax my skin and as calmly as I could, I'd breathe slowly, trying to pull the fear from her heart into mine.

I wondered if we should move to another area of town that wasn't so white and homogenized. In time she wouldn't go to the grocery store and stand in line. If I wasn't along, she didn't go out.

Carmen was happy when I met her.

Sanchez and I talked about it. He said he'd send accounting work home for her to do. It would give her a sense of accomplishment. Improve her mood, right?

He sent boxes of office supplies: Her old phone, her old Rolodex. Her favorite typewriter. Things like that. Plus, a mountain of paperwork. She converted the kitchen table into her desk. Pads and ledgers were stacked in the kitchen drainer. The drawer where we kept kitchen towels, hot pads and place mats was now brimming with her color-coded filing system.

I came in the back door one afternoon, my arms full of groceries. She heard me but didn't look up. Wearing a crisp white shirt and navy suit, pantyhose and high-heeled black pumps, she sat before a stack of papers, stamps and envelopes. Her fingers wildly punched the keys of the adding machine. Its white roll of tape puddled on the wood floor.

Confused, I asked, "Why are you dressed like that?"

She stood and looked down the length of herself, then twisted to check in back. "What? Is my slip showing?"

"Sweetheart, you could wear pajamas and no one would know," I said.

With the exasperated look you'd give a child, she sat back down, tore off the adding tape and compared it to her ledger sheet.

"That's the same spot I left you in this morning. Take a break already." Standing behind her, I worked the knot between her shoulder blades. She shrugged me off.

"Enchiladas are in the oven and rice and beans are on the stove," she said. "And, your cycle dripped oil on the garage floor. I rubbed sand into the spot."

Everything was basically going well. Too well, really. Now, to her, only home felt comfortable.

Then we became parents. Now what?

I got to walk out the door every day. She was saddled with the kids. In desperation, sometimes she'd push them to the park in a stroller.

"They did it again, Hugh."

"What?"

"At the park, another mother asked if I was Juliana's babysitter," she cried.

"Ignore them, Carmen. Who cares?"

"That's easy for you to say because they're not insulting you."

She had a good point.

*She wagged her finger in my face.* "How dare you not treat your wife well? La Llorona will teach you a lesson," *she cried.* "It's time for you to work on something important."

Until then, I told myself, "It's not her fault. She's doing the best she can."

The hell she was. This wasn't her best.

My father's voice stops. He leans back in his chair, and just like that, it's over. He relaxes his palm and the paintbrush rolls across the carpet.

Watching him sleep, I take the thin blanket from the bed and tuck it around his shoulders. Remove the glasses from his face and set them on the table, brush the curls off his forehead and stroke his cheek. I carefully pick up the paintbrush and return it to the rusty toolbox, and slip out the door.

In the hallway, I lean against the wall. Feeling so drained, I slide to the floor and drop my head between my knees.

If you're in the middle of the ocean, do you take the lifeboat or let the next person hang onto you and you both drown?

Hearing a sound, I look up. The rec room leader is walking toward me leading a female resident by the hand. It's the blank-faced judge.

Not breaking stride, the judge speaks faintly. "A plant in a closet doesn't bloom," she says. "Give it sun and it doubles in size."

I watch her wispy, charcoal hair as the goes past.

# CHAPTER FIFTY-ONE

◆   ◆   ◆

An icy shiver shoots up my neck all the way to my scalp, the kind that says it's not just a cold, but the flu.

Perched high in her striped wingback chair, her slim ankles crossed, Dr. Phillips has Oliver and me sitting on the carpet at her feet. Back-to-back, like a couple of escaped convicts handcuffed together in a lousy prison movie.

"In order to demonstrate how effectively you communicate with one another, I've given you each two identical bags containing building blocks in assorted shapes, colors and sizes," she says. "Without looking, you will each construct a building using the contents of your first bag. Then, using the other bag, you will replicate each other's buildings by following each other's instructions."

Smiling nervously, she pulls at the strand of beads around her neck. It's the first time I've seen her unsure of herself.

"So, Mrs. Morrissey," she says. "You will tell your husband how to build your building, and he will tell you how to build his," she says. "When that's done, you'll both turn around and see how you did. Got it?"

I nod.

Oliver exhales loudly. "I'm so glad I rescheduled a deposition so that I could play Tinkertoys, Dr. Phillips," he says. "Will this be over soon?"

"Please do humor me, Mr. Morrissey," she says stiffly. "Go ahead and empty your bags."

There's the hollow sound of the blocks hitting each other as Oliver dumps out his bag. I begin searching my purse for my glasses. Oliver, of course, had Lasik.

"You may begin," she says. "And no peeking at your neighbor's, please."

Working away, I glance up her. I don't know what to make of the look on her face. Does she think mine is stupid? Oliver's probably looks like the Taj Mahal.

"Finished?" she finally says.

"Mm-hmm," I say.

"Yes," Oliver mutters.

She claps her hands together. "Now who would like to go first?"

"Oh, ladies first," Oliver says. "By the way Juliana, I've been meaning to ask you something. Did you bring your riding crop this morning? Your jodhpurs look simply smashing tucked into your little riding boots."

Trying to psyche me out. Always so competitive.

"You should go first, Oliver," I say in a perky voice. "Age before beauty."

"Oh, goody," he says. "Start by taking all of the thin, square blocks and lay them flat in a square. Stand the thick, square ones on their sides in a square-shaped corral on top of that. Now take rectangular ones and put eight of them against the base, two on each side. Then do it again. All around the bottom, I want you to make a palisade, standing the square blocks on their ends all around, leaving a one-inch gap between the palisade and the building." He takes a quick breath. "Think you got that?"

I lay the last block.

"Got it," I say. "Okay—time for mine. Take eight flat rectangles for your base. Next stack eight flat squares. Next is the six square cubes, and then the four curved ones, edges touching, to form a square with the flat sides pointing up. On top of that, put the largest cube, and in the middle is the round ball. Voila."

"This looks like manure, Juliana," Oliver says.

Dr. Phillips raises her brows like she wants to laugh but wouldn't dare.

The suspense is killing me.

"Okay," she says. "Both of you turn around, please."

My jaw drops. Good God.

Two structures are just alike. Two bear scarcely any resemblance to each other. Guess which ones?

"Well, nice job there, Girl Friday," Oliver says, straightening up tall. "Looks like I trained you pretty well."

I eye the same crystal candy dish on Dr. Phillips' coffee table with the classic pink, yellow and white valentine candy inside.

*Kiss Me.... You're Sweet.... True Love.... Be Mine....* And the one in the middle: *Get Lost.*

Oliver stands and smoothes his pleated dress slacks. "Dr. Phillips, would it be acceptable for me to sit in a chair like a grownup, now?"

"Of course," she says.

When I clear my throat to get Oliver's attention, he puts out his hand and pulls me to my feet. Were Dr. Phillips not in the room, he'd sooner leave me sitting in a fire ant bed.

"Mrs. Morrissey, is there anything you'd like discussing today?" she says.

"I absolutely do," I say, looking into her eyes.

She sits forward in her chair and steeples her fingers under her chin.

"It's time for me to move back home with the twins," I say. "We owe it to them to try."

Oliver takes a pen and loudly drums it on the coffee table.

"With all of the ups and down between you two, you wouldn't want to rush things because it would be unfair to get their hopes up," Dr. Phillips says, as if she's reading out of a book. "When it happens, Mrs. Morrissey, it needs to be gradual."

I press my fingers to my forehead. Does this woman have any estrogen in her body at all?

I turn to Oliver. "Can they come stay with me some, at least?"

"Well, frankly, ma'am, it's not their thing. Like I told you before." He checks his Rolex. "Is there something else anyone wants to ask before I power down on this meeting and head to my next one?"

I stand to leave.

On my way to the door, I kick over his building.

# CHAPTER FIFTY-TWO

◈ ◈ ◈

Is that little old man snoozing away on the bed really my daddy?

Perched beside him, I watch his snoring nostrils. They're shaped like two plump raisins. With each exhalation, his lips quietly burst open like bubbles of boiling gravy on the stove.

He's in a totally different state of mind, and that I'm starting to understand it makes me worry. I'm here in this drama, paying more attention to his life than my own. Listening to the stories is an addiction, like not wanting to miss the *Guiding Light* or something, but soaps come on at the same time every day. With my luck, Dad will start spooling while I'm gone.

Getting him to actually narrate a painting is hit or miss. I wish I could just walk in the door, stick a brush in his hand and say, "Let's get this show on the road," but it's not that easy. He has to be awake, for one thing, and he also has to be parked in front of the right painting. The one he spends the most time looking at is my mother's nude portrait. Funny that. I guess what I'm saying is that it has to be the right time.

Time. It's what I think about all the time now. Like, how much is left until my life's back the way it was before? By the time I'm living with the kids again, will they still want me to? Will there be enough time for Dad to describe the next painting before the next round of bills come due? And, in that time, will he tell me everything there is to know? He can't see in front of him now, so how much time is left until he can't see behind him anymore?

How much time until he doesn't know me?

After narrating a painting, he's different for the next few days. As if the memories that spilled out have left him even more disoriented and confused. I'll try and comfort him in the best way I know how. I'll take his hands and massage them for him. I don't know if he realizes I'm doing it or not, but what I do know is that it comforts me.

I watch the shadow of his hair against the pillow. I study the creases the pillow case left on his cheek. The lines around his eyes and the dark circles under them. His lips are chapped, the bottom one peeling. I eye his chap stick on the dresser.

Okay, this is ridiculous. He's not waking up, school's almost out and I have to get going. The gray tuft of hair above his right ear stands up like a dog's tail. I wet my fingers and smooth it down before giving him a peck on the cheek and heading out the door.

Shuffling at the end of the hallway is one of the familiar Sagecrest couples. I've never seen them apart. Neither smiles. I've never seen them talk. Not to anyone, not to each other. The man's dark hair comes to a "v" on his forehead and he wears his shirttail un-tucked, hanging long. He's every bit of six feet five and the woman is easily a foot and a half shorter. She wears navy polka-dot slacks and a pair of matching Ked's, and red plastic earrings swing from her lobes like cherries. Favoring Katharine Hepburn, with the same tremor in her chin, too, it's clear the woman was a celebrated beauty in her day.

Eyes darting nervously, she hovers close to him clutching his hand. He watches anyone who comes near her. I wonder if he realizes there's not a chance in hell he could do anything to protect her. It's like they're holding on to each other for dear life.

A hand touches my back suddenly and I look up.

"Ms. Birdsong, is everything all right?"

Perfect. It's Mr. Read—just who I need to see. It's the fifth and I still haven't paid for this month yet.

"Can I do something for you?"

Waive the late fee? Crap, I can't ask him that.

Just so handsome, he smiles down at me with his perfect, white teeth. "Anything," he says. "Just name it."

Imagine my life with a man as kind as Mr. Read. Ha. What a laugh.

"Well, you know, maybe there is something," I say. "Perhaps I could get your take on something. Every time I'm here, I can always count on seeing Mrs. Calloway in the lobby waiting for her son to pick her up for lunch."

And, the bastard never comes.

If there's really a bastard at all.

He smiles again. "She's a special lady, isn't she?"

I nod and look over my shoulder at the sweet couple again. The man holds open the door to the women's restroom for the little lady. Once she's safely inside, he stands motionless, staring at the tall door.

"She may not be the most credible source, but something she said has been bothering me." I hesitate. "She said she heard voices coming from my dad's room late one night."

He coughs uncomfortably. "Ah, yes. We have a problem with residents visiting each other's rooms," he says. "We look the other way. They are grownups after all, and they deserve their privacy."

That's not what I was expecting him to say at all. I imagine Mrs. Calloway hanky-pankying with my dad and I can't get it out of my head. I try shaking it away, but it's stuck.

"In some instances, their spouses may be very much alive, and it's heartbreaking for the spouse that's left behind," he says. "The patients aren't being unfaithful on purpose, if you can even put it in those terms. They simply gravitate toward one another out of a need for closeness. At the core of each of us, we crave love. It's something we can't turn off."

I quickly glance over my shoulder again. The little lady pushes open the restroom door and the gentle man takes her dainty hand and hugs her to his side.

"Plus, as the saying goes," Mr. Read says knowingly. "There's a lid for every pot."

## CHAPTER FIFTY-THREE

❖ ❖ ❖

Kimberley's in charge of the snacks for this week's sales meeting. The head of the real estate company instructed her to bring three dozen mini-quiches and cheese blintzes from Upper Crust Bakery, but to not bother handing in the receipts. Seems there's some sort of a problem—something about Kimberley's ratio of homes shown versus homes actually *sold* is way off. Could be Mary Ellen was spot-on with her naked-under-the-covers story.

Balancing the cardboard boxes on her hip, Kimberley leans against the cash register. The chiseled twenty-something barrister wraps her thin, yellow Visa receipt around his business card and presses it squarely in her hand. Looking at him appraisingly, she flips open her mini-address book and slips it inside. "Damn, I love write-offs," she says.

Finished doctoring our lattes at the coffee bar, we look over the crowded tables. In her skintight, straight-legged Calvins, rhinestone belt and platform wedges, Kimberley heads to the only free spot, the dirty booth by the glass sandwich case. She's also wearing her light-blonde hair in a pouf today, bubbled at her crown. Wearing mine like that, I'd look ridiculous, but she carries it off with aplomb. I follow behind in my dumpy Levis, riding chaps and lug-soled motorcycle boots.

She watches a fifty-ish couple study the elaborate chalk board menu. They're dressed in matching red, white and blue bicycle getups, assuming people will mistake them for members of the Olympic bicycling team, I suppose. At last, they place their order with the clerk behind the counter, a Rastafarian with his nasty beard wrapped in a hairnet. It's good to know this place is so sanitary.

I can't think of a smooth way to ask Kimberley where her other friends are. Did she not have any others before I filled the hole? It's weird how she never asks me how things are coming with Oliver, although I'm grateful she doesn't because I'd rather talk about anything else. Maybe she doesn't have any women friends because she doesn't know how. She's just a guy's girl, I guess. Aside from her being a sex bomb, it's obvious men truly enjoy her company because she can never shake her former lovers even after they've moved into the "just-friends" category. Maybe men like her because she's not big on drama.

I tear the corner off my cinnamon roll and dunk it in my coffee. "How's that man hunt coming?" I say.

Wrinkling her nose, she fiddles with the thick, gold bangle on her wrist. "Oh, that," she says. "No takers yet. None that I'm seriously interested in, at least."

"Is that new? I've never seen you wear it before."

"It's from Bob." She slides it off and hands it to me. "Do you want it?"

I crinkle my brows. "What's wrong with it?"

"Nothing, really, except I haven't been able to find the Tiffany stamp on it even though it came in one of their fancy turquoise boxes." She frowns.

"Let me see." I slip on my stupid reading glasses and inspect it closely. Shaking my head, I hand it back.

"I know what you're thinking." She raises her chin. "It's only jewelry. Taking cash would mean I'm a hooker."

"That's ridiculous. I wasn't thinking that," I say gently.

I wasn't.

I touch her arm. "Why would you accept a gift from a man you don't even like in the first place?"

Narrowly missing my hot coffee, she quickly yanks the bracelet off her wrist and tosses it at me.

"Like I said, you take it."

Pressing fingers to her flushed chest, she begins watching the bicycle couple again. The man inspects a wheat bagel before passing it to the woman. She sniffs it and stuffs it into her backpack.

Funny thing about Kimberley, although she seems so confident, at the slightest embarrassment, her cheeks and chest turn bright pink. She takes a mini-perfume bottle from her bag, sprays some on each wrist and rubs them together.

"Why would you be in therapy with a man like Oliver?" she says. "Sounds like a personal problem to me."

The last customer left an *Austin Chronicle* on our table. I pull out the movie reviews and pretend to read them. Kimberley tears off the back page and begins reading the kinky personals. A rowdy little kid bumps our table. Our drinks slosh and neither of us looks up.

Unable to stand it any longer, I say, "What's that supposed to mean?"

She takes a nibble from her bran muffin. "Carrying Oliver's guitar case? How's that been working out for you so far?" she says. "Ever wonder what it would feel like to step up to the mic like Tina Turner, and sing?"

I pull back my chin. What a thing to say.

Using her knife as a mirror, she checks her smile for food. "I don't expect anyone to pay my bills and take out the trash," she says. "I'll do that myself, thank you."

I watch her circle several personals ads, fold the paper and slide it into her purse. "Oh, what am I saying?" she says breezily. "Y'all are working it out, so it's not a problem."

An hour later, I'm putting my quarters in a parking meter when I feel eyes on the back of my head, like someone's watching me.

Checking behind me, there's only a group of laughing college girls sitting on a rock wall dangling their tanned legs over the edge, so fresh and pretty, without a care in the world. If I still looked like that in a pair of skin-tight jeans, I probably wouldn't either.

Carrying my helmet in my arms, I take the grass-lined walkway leading to the tall limestone building. The University of Texas School of Law. That's what's etched in the thick, beveled glass on the double doors. I pull them open and a girl wearing a professional interview suit breezes through them ahead of me. A handsome group of guys carrying shiny laptops trots past me without even glancing my way. Probably because they're scarcely older than Adam and I'm old enough to be their mother. I'm probably older than most of their professors, too. Being older should mean I'm wiser. So, why don't I feel like it?

Standing in the foyer, I stare up the massive flight of marble stairs. I feel so small.

The eyes that seem to be watching me are the dark, fiery eyes of Carmen Mata Birdsong. It feels like they bore a hole from my gut, clean through my navel and come out on the other side. Oliver flashes through my brain. I swat him away. I always wanted to prove to my dad that I'd move heaven and earth to get what I wanted. More than anyone, I wanted to prove it to myself.

I bound the staircase and begin slowly down the hallway, glancing at the signs on the doors. Stopping in front of the one that reads, "Admissions," I quickly turn around.

And, I run.

# CHAPTER FIFTY-FOUR

◆ ◆ ◆

I've been drawing a landscape plan in my head—azalea shrubs against the house, with those fuchsia blooms that are so gorgeous in the spring. Rosemary draping from the front steps, mountain laurel and crepe myrtles galore, and a little arbor at the street that's dripping with wisteria. Purple pansies for the cold months.

I never thought I'd see the day that I was circling the back parking lots of high-end nurseries looking for rotting, throwaway plants stacked by the dumpster. My, how creative I've become now that I'm poor. But, I wouldn't take cedar. I don't want hawthorn. I learned my lesson with lugustrum in my old yard—their trunk decay is horrid. And, bamboo? No way. It takes over everything and I've got enough problems with the ivy as it is. I'll keep looking, but I'm not sure I could ever imagine myself asking for a freebie.

Poverty is *so* not my style.

This morning, I'm standing in the yard looking up at the sagging gutters. We had a real gully-washer last night and rain spilled over them like a waterfall. Now, they're close to buckling, and a deep muddy trough circles the ivy-strangled house like a moat.

I climb the wobbly ladder and look over the edge of the gutter. Yep. Filled with stagnant water and unable to drain, the downspout must be completely backed-up with leaves.

I circle the perimeter of the house until I find it, hanging about three feet off the ground. The bottom makes an L-shape, but rather than being angled toward the driveway, the downspout is pointed directly at house instead. Yanking back the ivy, I can tell immediately that the siding is waterlogged. I press my fingers into the wood and it's soft and springy to the touch. Maybe it's not a good idea, but I pull up hard on a board to see what's underneath. Rusted nails bend.

A dark, putrid smell. Peeking inside, all I can see is saturated insulation, like wet, pink Kleenex. What in the world is that? I pull the board back a little further. It's black.

Drawing back, I cover my mouth.

Black mold.

The twins. It will make them sick. Respiratory problems. Lung infections. Sinus. Headaches. Maybe worse. I'd never expose them to this.

Dammit, Dad. Why didn't you maintain this dumpy old house? Leaving everything a wreck for me to deal with?

Something's moving.

Tiny crawling ants. With white, transparent wings.

I know what those are.

Termites.

# CHAPTER FIFTY-FIVE

❖ ❖ ❖

Does Dad know his paintings are leaving?

It makes me sick that the only way to heist them is while he's asleep. Before I brought geraniums from the yard to help mask the lonely space on the wall. Something vibrant and alive to fill the void is the only thing that made sense somehow. The blessing is Dad's joy of discovery in experiencing the beauty of each new plant. A small consolation for having his work sold out from under him, I know. I like to imagine that he remembers when I'd place the pots of geraniums in his hands at home, and how he'd snap off the dead blooms, but, I know he doesn't. Still, the memory feeds my soul.

When I'm sure Dad's completely out, I pass the blue bedroom painting through the crack in the door. Wally takes it on the other side and positions it on the dolly as Richard holds it still. It's the closest he'll get to our dad—the entry to his room.

I take his arm. "Rich, I promise he's not awake," I whisper. "Take a look."

He anxiously pokes his head around the door, and his stern expression softens, as if he's watching a sleeping baby that he's yearning to hold. Just as I think he'll step inside and sit on the edge of Dad's bed, he slips me the tin of peanut butter cookies he made for him and turns away. Eyes downcast, he tilts the dolly toward his chest. I take Wally's hand and we follow him to the lobby.

Dressed in a lemon-colored luncheon suit, Mrs. Calloway's waiting on the plaid sofa. Peering over the top of *Oprah*, she studies us with interest. When we're past the lobby, she raises her narrow shoulders off the cushions and cranes her neck around the ruffled shade of the lamp on the side table, and watches us cross the foyer.

As Rich backs the dolly through the doors, its skinny, black tires bump over the threshold. Holding the painting still, I ignore Mrs. Calloway. It's the first time I haven't asked where her son's taking her for lunch, but today I just don't feel like it.

A Volkswagen SUV idles in the circle drive. License plate reads SINGLE. Kimberley hops out wearing a boa-print mini-dress and orange stilettos. She pops the hatchback and pushes aside a half dozen, wood-staked For Sale signs. Seeing my heavy eyes, she gently touches my cheek. As Rich and Wally load the painting inside, she and I stand arm-in-arm and gaze at the painting together.

It's hard toasting champagne when it feels like there's nothing to celebrate. But I try to remember that it's my dad we're toasting, celebrating his art and his creativity. And how blessed we are to experience it.

## CHAPTER FIFTY-SIX

◆ ◆ ◆

It's a little after midnight. The streets are black and deserted.

Mary Ellen called crying and said to come right away. My single headlight illuminates her white, stucco house as I swing into her circular driveway.

There she is. In front of her iron gate wearing her black leather jacket and tight jeans that look so great on her long legs. She's holding something white to her mouth. That's a towel. I lower the kickstand and rush to her side.

I hold both sides of her face in my hands.

Her eyes are wild. She smells like wine.

"Now settle down, sweetheart. You've got to hold still."

She lowers the towel. Her bottom lip's split vertically, like a sliced grapefruit. Her cheeks are black from mascara.

"Do I need stitches?" she asks.

"It's not worth taking a chance. It's your face and you've only got one."

"That's what I thought." She drops her Volvo keys in my hands and I pull it from the garage to the driveway.

She falls onto the front seat in a heap and flips down the visor. I whack it back up before she can look. Mary Ellen is so neurotic over the sight of blood, I've had to come over plenty of times and take care of her kids' most minor cuts.

"Mike needs anger management." Her voice shakes. "I hate him."

I've heard it lots of times after one of their fights. They make up, and it's as if their fight never happened. Until the next time. Some kind of weird foreplay, I guess. But I've never seen anything like this before.

She tries pulling down the visor again and I grab her hand. "Now, quit it. And, don't talk if you can't keep that towel on there."

"Hey, where are you going?"

I'm barreling across the low water bridge on Red Bud Trail and I better slow down, because the last thing I need is a ticket. Plus, having a cop see her like this?

"Not Seton Hospital," I say. "There's no telling who might be there."

"Well, where then?" she says. "Brackenridge would be tons worse."

"The Heart Hospital ER is always deserted. People think it's just for heart attacks, I guess," I say. "Now, what the hell happened?"

"We'd been fighting in the car." She combs her long red nails through her hair, then stops. "Oh, Juliana," she breathes. "I took you away from your dad, didn't I? Will he be okay by himself?"

"Honestly, Mary Ellen. You know I checked him into Sagecrest," I say. "A room just came free on his hall. Maybe we can get you in."

"Hmmmm," she says.

"Where had y'all been, anyway?"

She glances out the window. "Glen and Cheryl's."

Funny how a hostess can always slide in another place setting for a man, while I on the other hand, get blackballed because I might grab someone's dick under the table.

"When the babysitter left, Mike lit into me," she says. "Right in front of Ben and Alice. I opened the fridge to put the milk up. I didn't know he was throwing a coffee cup at the door and I shut it at the exact wrong moment."

I reach over and hold her hand. "I'm surprised it didn't break your teeth out."

"I stood over the sink and blood kept gushing. Ben had his arms wrapped around my legs and kept screaming over and over, 'I hate you, Daddy!' Little Alice clammed up and didn't say a word."

Mike should fry in hell.

Making it to the ER, the lot is virtually empty. Just a flashing ambulance and a red fire truck.

The triage nurse slides the window open. Her stony expression says she's seen it all. She swaps me a clipboard for Mary Ellen's license and insurance card. "The sooner you fill out the paperwork, the sooner you'll see the doctor," she says, and slides the window back shut.

The water dispenser in the corner has a large bottle upturned on top. I pour Mary Ellen a cup and tell her, "You're going to be fine, okay?"

Eyes vacant, she stares at the TV. *Cops* is on.

Her lip is still bleeding. I wonder if the wine's worn off yet.

Finally in an examining room, I tuck a blanket around her because she can't stop shivering. A doctor enters. Chalky skin, thick, rimless glasses and a stethoscope. I hadn't thought about what I would say happened until now. He doesn't ask.

I hold Mary Ellen's hand as he shoots her lip with a mile-long needle. She must be going through the roof but she manages to lie still. Her lip swells up twice the size.

Why doesn't he pull it out already?

Then, there's the stitching needle. He pokes it in her lip and threads it out the other side like he's hemming a pair of pants. My God. How does he use his hands like that? Don't screw up. Don't screw up, or she'll be scarred forever. Even a plastic surgeon can't pull a rabbit out of a hat. Mary Ellen cuts her eyes to me. I nod and smile.

The doctor says the most critical stitch is where the bottom edge of the lip meets the skin below. He knots the thread, tugs it tightly, and before her lip looks better, it's going to look a whole lot worse.

I smile grimly. "Thanks for what you did for my friend tonight," I say.

He hands me the prescriptions. "I hope we don't see her back in here."

I lower my eyes. "I do, too."

Mary Ellen's holding an icepack to her lip. I wrap my arm around her and shepherd her through the waiting room. By the time we make it to the car, the purple bruises have already come up.

Lowering the mirror, she sucks in her breath. "I'm so scared for Ben and Alice to see this," she says. "Mike didn't mean to do it. He was only trying to get my attention."

"You're already making excuses for him?" I say. "Their dad sent you to the ER, so don't act like it's not a big deal. Sweep it under the rug and they'll be more confused than they are now."

"Okay. I know you're right. What's Mike going to do?"

"Who cares? Fuck him."

Her face crumbles. "I wish he'd fuck me," she cries. "He says it feels like having sex with his mom. You've met her. She's completely disgusting."

"That's crazy. Did you have sex in Chicago a couple of months ago?"

"Barely."

"I can't believe that."

"You think I'm happy admitting to this? He was done six seconds after he crawled on top of me. He rolled his eyes and said, 'It's all your fault, not mine,'" she says. "What do you think it means?"

"Hell, I don't know. Maybe he's addicted to porn?"

She exhales loudly. "I'm sick of throwing myself at him," she says. "I can't live like this. Maybe you can, Juliana, but not me."

I ignore her comment.

"Other people's reactions are more important than Mike's right now. No matter what you say, people will assume he did it. "

"That's ridiculous."

"A woman gets murdered and the husband's the first suspect. Come on, Mary Ellen, he *did* do it. We need to come up with a legit-sounding story. And not the old 'I walked into a door.' And it has to be short and sweet. It'll sound like you're lying if it's long and complicated."

She rubs her eyes. "You're right. We've got all these parties coming up. The kids' teachers. The people at church. Dinner at Pepe's."

"Say you got your hair done. Anyone who goes to Fronz's shop knows about his slick stairs. Just say you slipped on your way in," I say. "Falling forward and hitting the higher step is the only way you'd bust your lip like that."

Plus, no one would buy that Fronz would let her leave with her roots looking like that. Why he doesn't book her appointments closer together, I'll never know.

After filling her meds at the 24-hour pharmacy, we pull into her driveway. The front of the house is dark.

"Hey, you never said what you guys were fighting about."

She lightly taps her finger to her lip. "It was stupid. Mike said I was talking to Oliver too much," she says. "But I told him it wasn't *my* fault, because without all this stuff happening between you guys, you'd be there entertaining Oliver yourself."

I swallow hard. "That's kind of difficult to do without Oliver bringing me to the party. And he farmed-out the kids rather than give them to me," I say. "No telling where they are."

"Spending the weekend with friends." She takes her purse from the floorboard. "When he said you missed the hearing, I wondered why you hadn't known about it on your own since I know you've taken the LSAT before."

My back stiffens. "You have it confused with the bar exam, Mary Ellen. The Law School Admissions Test judges your logic and reasoning skills," I say coolly. "And, if anyone should've warned me about the hearing, it was you."

"Mike doesn't tell me anything on purpose." She opens the car door and the light comes on. "We'll have lunch when I can chew solid food," she says. "How long did the doctor say until these stitches come out?"

I drop the keys in her lap. "Seven to ten days."

"Oh, no. There he is."

Mike just switched on the bright lanterns and stepped onto the porch. He's wearing a plaid bathrobe. There's a drink in his hand.

Mary Ellen wraps her arms tightly around my waist and keeps them there. If I didn't think he'd take it out on her, I'd shoot him the finger.

"I'll talk to him if you need me to." I say. Her chin wobbles.

The door cracks open. Ben's face peeks out for an instant before Mike reaches behind him and pulls it shut. Seeing Ben's face, Mary Ellen yanks her purse over her arm and begins racing up the walk. I've barely gotten out of the Volvo when she aims her keychain over her shoulder and locks the door.

I want my old life back.

## CHAPTER FIFTY-SEVEN

❖  ❖  ❖

When I enter his room, Dad's slumped forward in his chair, pulled up in front of the last painting. Eyes frozen, he's staring straight ahead.

The painting's not like the others. The wedding cake painting—now, that was a flashy painting. The glossy frosting, crystal champagne glasses, formal bride and groom. And, it's not lush and dreamy like the blue bedroom painting, either. This one is a pale, dull green. Matte finish, the paint has no sheen.

I creak open the lid of his rusted toolbox, so grateful when he takes a flat, stiff-bristled brush from the tray. With a somber expression, he rolls its wooden, paint-stained handle between his palms.

I pull my chair close to his and focus on the painting.

It's actually a ledger sheet. Just a standard ledger with vertical, uniform columns. Precise, penciled numerals fill the spaces—debits on the left, credits on the right. A nod to Dad's accountant's training, certainly, but why would a great artist choose a subject so sterile, ordered and uninteresting? As strange as his being an accountant, I suppose. Just like all the paintings, it's obvious that he crafted the frame himself, hand-cut the canvas, stretched it across the frame and tacked it down in back—the sign of an artist that truly cares about all aspects his work. The interesting part is that the edge of the canvas is loose in places, dark and singed, with a faint burnt smell.

As he begins rubbing the bristles with his thumb, Dad's head droops forward and his eyes become fixated on the canvas, then his posture relaxes so completely that I'm afraid he's going to shut his eyes and drift off to sleep. Looking at him closely, I notice his skin is strangely splotched and feverish.

"Dad, are you okay?"

I look back to the painting. Could there be something I'm not seeing? I scoot my chair closer. Smooth before, the dull, green paint looks bubbled. As if it's blistered.

I tap it lightly with my finger. Ouch! It burned the crap out of my finger.

All at once, there's a loud crackling sound and the room's like a furnace, as if I'm sitting on a fireplace hearth, too close to the flames. Pulsating heat waves begin rippling across my vision. I grip my chair.

A vibration engulfs my body.

The painting comes alive.

Penciled numbers topple from the ledger, free-falling, like frantic people jumping from a burning building. The stern, rigid columns have seemingly morphed into iron. Like prison bars.

Suddenly, the canvas sputters. Flashes and sparks.

It ignites. In a burst of fire.

Rolling loops of red eat across the canvas.

Hidden in the licking flames, something's moving. Dizzy, I squint, cupping my fevered brow. There. Behind the bars.

It comes into focus now. A crimson bird. Majestic.

More magnificent than anything I've ever seen.

A spike of orange feathers breaks from its skull, jagged like a saw.

Bathed in fire.

Crazed, frenzied. It thrashes its wings. Struggling. Beating them against the iron bars. Eyes wild in terror. Tortured.

Throwing back its slender neck, the firebird opens its golden, claw-shaped beak. It screeches, long and loud. High and piercing. An icy finger runs up my spine to the tip of my brain.

Then there's the back draft.

The bird explodes in a surge of fire.

Like paper, it burns.

My father begins twisting in his chair beside me. Heat emanates from his body. Flushed and twitching, he turns the brush handle between his slender fingers.

Voice rich and hypnotic, he begins to speak.

*Friday was trash day. That's how I remember what day it was. It was dusk when I pulled down our street. It was a hot, summer evening. My back was sweating through my shirt from the ride home.*

*The blue trash cart was at the end of the curb. Its hinged lid was swung open. I wheeled up beside the cart to pull it up to the house. As I took the lid in my hands, I recognized a familiar smell. My paints. Turpentine. I looked inside. Nothing.*

*I dropped my cycle in the grass and ran to the garage. It's where Carmen had taken to stacking my things on the cold cement slab.*

*Where were they? Everything was gone. She'd thrown them all out. Every brush. Every rag. Every last painting. It was everything I had.*

*I fell to my knees. I watched my shaking hands. I had to get a grip on myself or I would surely kill her. I remember taking deep breaths and reminding myself that little Jules was only in preschool, Rich was in Kindergarten and they really needed their mom.*

*I pulled myself up and walked slowly to the front yard and dropped to the grass. I rested my elbows on my knees. After a few minutes, I retrieved the cycle from the street and wheeled it to the house and deliberately pushed it into the garage.*

*I threw open the back door and hollered Carmen's name over and over. I found her in my old studio that was now her sewing room. I braced myself against the door frame.*

*It was the first time I remember hating her.*

*"I can't take the mess anymore. They smell horrible and I'm sick of cleaning up after your little boy games. I told you that you could continue to paint if it wasn't a problem," she said. "Well, it is."*

*She didn't look up from the sewing machine. She didn't even turn it off. Her mouth was set in a straight line like the creases on her forehead. But I knew that behind her severe expression, she wore a satisfied smile.*

*Proud as being crowned queen.*

Leaning back, Dad's shoulders fall flat against the chair. His lids droop heavily and the paintbrush falls from his fingers.

All this smoke in the room, we could be in for serious trouble. Heart pounding, I grab the handles and begin backing his chair toward the door. I hear a strong sucking noise, like switching off the gas flame in a fireplace, followed by a sputter. The smoke immediately dissipates. I quickly check the painting.

Expecting to see a clump of charred feathers and smoking, black cavity on the wall, instead, it's like someone switched the channel on the television. The canvas is a pale green ledger again. Perfect. Looks smooth as plaster. Incredulous, I touch it with my finger. Damnit! I jerk it back.

Sucking my fingertip, I look down at Dad sleeping peacefully. I brush the curls from his forehead, lean down and kiss his lined, flushed cheek.

What is the cost of sacrifice? The price of eating resentment?

After the burning anger dies, passion and desire come next.

It's much less painful to be numb to reality.

Death of his spirit equaled death of his mind?

Then something occurs to me. This painting, and the others, why didn't she throw them out, too?

An earsplitting clanging noise suddenly goes off in the room. Dad's body jolts in his chair and he instinctively cups his hands over his ears.

It's the fire alarm.

I put my arms around his shoulders to calm him. "Dad, it's a fire," I say close to his ear.

"Again?" he says. His voice is hoarse.

There's banging on the door, and Mr. Read throws it open. He yells over the blaring alarm, "It's a practice drill. Fire code requirement." He shoos us toward the hallway. "The drills are timed. You must clear out of here this instant."

I tuck the blue cardigan around Dad's shoulders. Taking the handles of his chair, I hurriedly begin wheeling him out the door.

"It's okay, Dad," I tell him. "I'm right behind you."

He checks that I am, eyes open wide behind his tiny, smeared lenses.

Confused, he watches the harrowing flurry in the hallway. Staff in doctors' scrubs attempt to maintain order, guiding patients from their rooms. The elderly woman in the wheelchair with the lifelike baby doll clutches it protectively to her chest, and an addled man with fear in his eyes suddenly drops to the floor and wraps his head in his arms. Mr. Read stands at the triage where the hallway becomes the lobby, reassuring the patients in a calm, clear voice that they're safe, but they'll need to come outside and congregate in the parking lot.

A frantic woman in a pink bathrobe barrels past another woman using a walker, almost knocking her down. Saddest are the patients oblivious that the fire drill's happening at all.

## CHAPTER FIFTY-EIGHT

❖ ❖ ❖

On Mondays, my mother phoned in her grocery order and the store delivered it. Everything the milkman didn't bring. Dad said he was through with bringing stuff home. He was too busy. The cleaners picked up and delivered his work suits. The drugstore delivered, too. Just about anyone would if my mom paid them enough. Back then, you couldn't get cute stuff online like nowadays, but there was mail order. Mom usually sewed everything she wore, except shoes and underwear. A coat wasn't especially necessary indoors.

Her hair was a mess. Hearing the grocery boy knock on the door, she pulled on her blonde Dynel Wardrobe Wig. Her hair used to be beautiful and shiny. She let it go gray, and it made her look so old. How I wished she'd dress up and go out. That I could sit on her fuzzy bathmat and stare up her as she curled her hair on hot rollers and put on blue eye shadow and rimmed her eyes in black, liquid liner. I wanted my mother to be like everyone else's. She was prettier than every single one of them. I didn't see what she was ashamed of. Not at all. But, here she stood in a faded housedress and slippers. It was afternoon.

She eyed the grocery boy through the screen. His name was Cliff. Tall and wiry with scruffy blonde hair.

"Put the bags on the counter and we'll compare what you brought to my list," she said. "Last week the lettuce was missing, so I'll be checking what you bring from now on."

Cliff followed her into the kitchen with three paper sacks in his arms. Bugles and a box of Carnation Instant Breakfast peeked out of one.

Swanson's out of another. Noodles Romanoff. Some Tang. She'd given up cooking everything Mexican by then. We even had an orange fondue pot with a little can of Sterno. Frozen fish sticks. Chicken pot pie. Totally disgusting. She said we didn't care if she went to extra trouble, so why should she?

"Sorry, ma'am," Cliff said politely. He knew better than to get on her bad side. "To make it up to you, the manager said to bring you an extra head of lettuce this week."

Finally letting him out the door, she said, "Why didn't you bring something I could use? I don't need an extra lettuce that will just go rotten in the refrigerator."

Why couldn't she have just said thank you?

Ninth-grade-Richard rushed into the kitchen wearing his sweat-stained track uniform and threw his cleats on the floor. He had no time for the craziness at home. Once he realized being on the track team gave him a means to run away, he took it.

He stood at the sink, filling ice trays to load in the freezer.

"Ricardo. I told you not to make any more ice," my mother said. "It gave you a cold already, and now you're trying to drink something with ice again? It will give you a sore throat, too."

What a bunch of crap. But it's what my mother would say.

Richard rolled his eyes and poured out the water.

She pulled the Tony's Pizza Rolls from the sack and held them up for me to see. "Juliana, I ordered these special for Friday when you have your little friend spend the night," she said.

With her back turned, Richard quickly refilled the ice trays and returned them to the freezer.

"Mom, didn't I tell you?" I said. "Marcy can't come. Her grandparents are in town."

It was a lie. I was in eighth grade now and I'd long-since stopped inviting friends over. I rarely went to sleepovers because it was considered rude not to reciprocate. They never said it, but I knew what my friends were thinking—that our family was weird. My mom was known as "The Mexican Boo Radley." That's what Richard and I had to live with. It was embarrassing.

On his way to the living room, he popped my bra and whispered in my ear, "They let girls go out for the track team, too, you know."

Her back still turned, Mom exhaled loudly and crammed the pizza rolls into the freezer, then slammed it back shut. She immediately whipped around and faced me.

"What's this *abuela's* name?"

"Mamaw," I said quickly.

She held onto the handle for a long moment as her breath became slow and deliberate. I must've passed the test since that's all she said.

When I would smell scorched cotton and hear the sound of aerosol mist every evening, that's how I knew my father would soon be home. At seven o'clock, my mother would set up her ironing board so close to the front door that he'd practically trip over it as he walked in. If that didn't work, the electric cord stretched to the wall socket might take him out.

Dad opened the door and dropped his briefcase inside.

She wiped her forehead and slid the back yoke of his wrinkled, white shirt onto the tapered end of the board, then flipped up the neck and ran the sizzling tip of the iron over the point of the collar. The combination of heat and pressure is what removes imperfections, she used to tell me, and for extra crispness, be sure to use the iron's hottest setting. That way, a starched shirt would keep its shape.

"It must feel good coming home with everything done for you. Knowing your clothes are clean and ironed," she said. "Leaving me here all day, knowing I am at your beckoning call."

I waited for his reaction. Occasionally he'd bite, but it was rare.

He bit.

"That's 'beck and call.' And besides, I couldn't care less about the clothes. I doubt Richard and Juliana give a big, fat damn either."

She opened her mouth to say something, but he cut her off.

"Go water skiing. Play badminton. Ping-pong. Try bowling, How would you feel about jogging?" he said. "You're ridiculous, Carmen. Just get out of the stupid house. That's what I'd do." Without even raising his voice, his words crashed against the walls like china.

My mother ate dinner alone in her room that night.

And lots of nights after that.

## CHAPTER FIFTY-NINE

❖ ❖ ❖

---

In the kitchen fixing dinner, I keep turning over the firebird painting in my head. Still no mention of what happened to Mother. But, he knows.

As I'm pouring dressing on my salad, a bright, orangey glow pulls me to the window; I press my fingers to the glass. Warm.

The moon is strange tonight. Too round. Too big. Crazy big. Like a juicy, ripe peach suspended at the tree line, it seems to bend the branches, too heavy to lift off. I raise the window sash and rest my elbows on the frame and the cool breeze fills my lungs. Presently, the peach moon begins to rise, surrounded by a glowing, silver fog. As it floats higher, the silver becomes rimmed with a bright crimson halo. I'll take it as a good sign.

I'm going down to Sagecrest. Maybe I can get him talking about the firebird painting again. I could get lucky. I pull on Dad's driving jacket, wrap my red wool scarf high on my neck and stuff my hair up in the helmet.

I grab the key to the Indian from the hook by the door, and I'm gone.

I creep through the entryway, checking for hopefully nobody. Now's not the time for polite conversation. Thankfully, the lobby's deserted and the lights in the corridor are dimmed. I pad quietly toward Dad's room.

A faint light spills from under his door. I hear a soft voice and an anxious pain spreads from my upper arms down to my elbows. I turn the knob and peek inside. Dad's plaid bedspread isn't turned down. I check my watch. It's too late to be in the rec room. Dinner was hours ago. Okay, the bathroom door's closed—mystery solved. Knowing he usually takes a while, I drop my helmet inside the door and pull it shut, then slide across his bed and settle against the pillows.

There's a bright glow across the room. My eyes drift to the open window, but it's not the moon. The shimmering city skyline is iridescent against a sky so purple, it's almost black. A towering skyscraper is a brilliant column of light with beams of silver stretching upwards from its peak. Like spotlights on a darkened stage, the silver beams dissect the night.

Now, I see Dad seated at the window, his masculine features outlined against the bright sky. There's a peaceful smile on his lips. I've never seen him look more handsome. The thin cotton drapes furl softly.

Hearing my footsteps, he turns his head just slightly. Light glints off the gold frames of his glasses.

"Come here, darling." His deep voice is low and easy. Relaxed.

I touch his shoulder. He takes my hand and holds it to his cheek.

Quickly averting his eyes, his expression changes.

"You're not..." He drops my hand.

"What's that, Dad?" I say.

"Where is she?"

I switch on the floor lamp. I hadn't noticed the easel before. He's in his rolling chair with his casted leg stretched to one side. The canvas is blank.

"Where... what have you done with her?" He braces his palms on the arms of the chair as his eyes search the room.

Maybe I'm crazy, because I search for my mother, too.

When I look back at him, his eyes are glued to the door. It's open.

I dash into the hall and check left and right. No one there. I sprint to the lobby. Hmm-m. Dark and deserted. I check the foyer, too. Not a soul. Taking my time, I walk back to Dad's room listening for noises just to be sure.

At the door, I step inside and begin to call his name, but the word catches in my throat. He's rolled closer to the easel. Veins bulge from his neck and his features are contorted. The expression of pain on his face is excruciating.

Sucking in my breath, I watch him pick frantically through the tray and seize a tube of red paint. He untwists the cap and squeezes its entire contents onto the middle of the canvas. Tossing the tube aside, he mashes his flat, naked palms into the glob of red paint, smearing it savagely from side to side, then uses the meat of his hands to grind it into the canvas. Eyes crazed, open wide, he stops to glare at his work, and suddenly rakes his nails across the canvas, and then his scalp, streaking his hair red. Then, chest heaving, sweat on his brow, he takes a brush in both hands, raises his arms over his head and shoves the handle through the canvas.

The red, clotted image is like a raw, bleeding heart that's been blown up with a rifle at close range.

## CHAPTER SIXTY

❖ ❖ ❖

"Come on, Mom," I begged her. "I'll never get my license if you don't take me."

"You took Drivers Education at school, Juliana," she mumbled through the pins she held between her lips. Her messy, gray hair was pulled off her face as she measured fabric with the yellow measuring tape in her hand.

"Everyone in the class had to take turns," I told her. "I didn't get behind the wheel enough for me to really be good enough to pass the driving test."

"Hold this straight for me." I did, and she used her sharp scissors to cut the fabric along the edge before she unpinned the flimsy pattern. No doubt it was Betsy McCall.

"Please, Mom. I know you can drive. Why can't you take me for once? You make Dad take us everywhere."

I knew she wouldn't do it in a million years, but I never stopped asking. I never completely gave up hope.

Dad knew she used to love to drive, so even though we didn't have that kind of money, he got her the Mercedes convertible after she admired it in a magazine, thinking she might drive then. Hoping she would.

"The garage needs finishing, please, Juliana. It's still a mess." She put her head down and guided the fabric under the bobbin before she started up the machine. "Thank you." she said, and I was dismissed.

I couldn't believe it when she actually came into the garage while I was sweeping. All five feet two of her. She was wearing a disguise—a blonde wig, orange scarf, big black Jackie O sunglasses and Dad's trench coat.

"More people will stare at you for dressing like a weirdo than if you just dressed normal," I said.

Looking over the sunglasses perched on her nose, she smirked at me and pulled the belt tighter around her middle.

I started lowering the soft top on the convertible and she wagged her pointed finger. "Don't push it. And keep the windows up."

Before I could make it to the driver side, she'd already collapsed in the seat, turned the key, and cranked up the AC, with all the vents aimed on herself. I tried turning on the radio, but she flicked my hand away and lowered the mirror. I watched her face in the reflection: Fear. So, I zoomed out of the driveway before she could change her mind.

Turn here, turn there, she'd say, consulting the wrinkled map she held in her lap. I was lucky as crap I didn't hit something because I didn't know what the hell I was doing. Or where I was going. Just a blur really, leaving behind every grocery store, street sign and shopping center that I recognized. Even the traffic lights seemed different. Flashier, somehow.

Come to think of it, even with the map, I couldn't imagine how my mother could know where we were going either.

"We're lost, aren't we?" I said.

"*Callate*, Juliana. Just worry the driving."

The MoPac Expressway was just ahead. Four lanes of cars, all going 70 mph. I'd never driven MoPac before. She hadn't either, she said, because it wasn't built yet the last time she drove, but she had no problem making me do it. Hands gripping the wheel ten and two, I put on my blinker, merged into traffic and crept along in the right lane.

"They're passing us. Drive faster," she kept saying and wouldn't stop until I was going as fast as everyone else. Every car was honking at me, especially the 18-wheeler on my tail.

"Here! Here! Here!" she shrieked.

Big green exit sign: Windsor Road.

A hairpin curve and exit ramp pointing straight down. I hit the brakes and jerked the wheel.

Any faster and we'd have sailed over the edge.

My mother pointed to our destination on the map. Clear at the end of Windsor Road where it ran out into Lake Austin. I kept going. Not long, we were trailing down winding, leafy streets where families cared way more about how their houses looked than we did. The stately, graceful homes were twice the size of ours. More like three times, and absolutely cost a bundle with their primo location. Most had four cars in the driveway, some with long, shiny motorboats.

Finally settling on Matthews Drive, she had me slow down as she began squinting and mouthing the house numbers. After a couple of blocks, she squeezed my knee and said, stop here and began surveying the big, fancy house in front of us.

"Who lives here?" I said.

With a sick look on her face, in a voice I barely recognized, she said, "Don't take your eyes off that house." Her parched words scraped in her throat.

Now, frenzied, panting like a dog, she peeled off her Jackie O sunglasses and ripped open the top buttons of her coat. Stripping Kleenex from the glove compartment, her trembling fingers wiped sweat from her face and neck. Black mascara had melted under her eyes and only the outer edges of her dry, quivering lips had any lipstick. Digging her fingertips under the front of the blonde wig, she tore it off her head and the orange scarf came with it. She draped her dripping hair in front of the air vents and began running her fingernails through the gray at the temples.

Her episodes were nothing new, but my heart was pounding. This must have been the greatly anticipated mega-meltdown that she threatened would happen if she left the house. Deciding now was probably a good time to leave her be, I smoothed the wig and scarf and hung them on the gear shift.

Taking several deep breaths, she whispered the word "relax" to herself over and over. When it seemed like she was finally settling down, I gently touched her shoulder. She screamed, long and loud, beating both her hands against the dashboard.

My eyes darted through the sealed-off windows, checking if anyone heard. All at once, our little white sports car felt like a flying saucer—a foreign spaceship hovering high above the safe neighborhood below where carefree, lucky children from normal families played on the perfectly-manicured lawns. The absurdity of the situation struck me hard. With no ejector seat in sight, much less an escape-hatch, I was quarantined inside.

With my alien mother.

I knew what she was thinking. My dad, a sex maniac? No way. Besides, where would he find the time? All my life, it had been Mom and me on one side. Him on the other.

I'd heard the girlfriend story before. Now I knew it was a crazy lie.

I watched her scrutinize the house until I couldn't take it anymore, I said, "I wonder where Dad is? He's probably hiding inside the mailbox, so as long as we're here, shouldn't we at least say hello?" I reached for the door handle.

She hit the automatic lock button, then grabbed my arm and squeezed it with her pointed fingernails. It hurt like a mother.

"So *cómico*, Juliana." She raised that one eyebrow. "The *Cucuy* takes bad little girls. I am ashamed of you."

I jerked my arm back. "*You're* ashamed? How do you think I feel?" I yelled it right in her face. "If Dad has a girlfriend, then prove it!"

I expected she'd burst into tears, bury her face in her hands and sob. Instead, she stared pleasantly at the tranquil beauty outside the windshield, as if I'd let the whole thing go if she'd pretend nothing ape-shit-crazy was going on.

Not so fast.

I wanted to force her. Like throwing a toddler in the deep end. Just what she needed to snap out of it.

"Why don't you drive us home, Mother?" I said. "I hear it's like riding a bicycle."

Sweat trickled down her jaw.

I turned on the radio, and this time she didn't stop me. I waited her out. She knew I wasn't budging.

"I never understood what that means," she finally snapped, then mashed the sunglasses back on her face and pulled the wig back over her ears like a helmet, completely lopsided with her wet hair sticking out on the sides. She flipped the orange scarf over the top with a messy bow under her chin and stalked around to the driver's side.

"I know very well how to drive, Juliana. You just watch."

Then, she slammed the door, put it in gear and drove home like the road was on fire.

She damn sure did.

That night at dinner, maybe I should have told Dad what happened. Just her leaving the house was mammoth, and he would have been thrilled to death she'd driven the car. But he'd want to know the rest of the story, and I couldn't do that to her. It was bad enough that I knew. So, I blackmailed her instead. But it backfired. Twice.

In a moment of sisterly love, I cut a deal with her to stop making Richard mow the lawn anymore. He was mad at me about something, I don't remember what, and I owed him one. Workers just appeared one day and yanked up the grass and put in a rock garden in its place, right up to the edge of the house. How was I to know that would be her solution? It looked horrible, especially when the rangy weeds came poking through. Everything was so stark and ugly, I couldn't take it. It's why I got the job at the nursery. I've always craved things alive and beautiful. And, yes. That's when I brought the ivy home.

I know it's silly, ridiculous thinking, but with all that ivy growing on the house, had I made her worse?

Years later, the accident report said the brakes failed. The car had been sitting for so long not driven, the fan belts had corroded and threw something off into the brake line. Now, that *wasn't* my fault.

But, I'm the one who made her believe she could drive again.

# CHAPTER SIXTY-ONE

❖   ❖   ❖

This morning, the Telefloral delivery man handed me a shallow white, three-foot-long box, expertly tied with a red silk bow. Beneath the heart-printed tissue paper were two dozen, long-stemmed roses. White with red-tipped petals, buds firmly closed. Vintage Oliver. The kind he used to send when he knew how to touch my love-buttons.

There was a cupid card inside. "Imagining your phenomenal cleavage," it read. Flipping it over, there was more: "When therapy gets dull later, let's duck out and head to the Four Seasons."

When I called to thank him, he had a better idea. Our therapy session would be immensely more fruitful if we met at the hotel *first* for a little sweet makeup sex, he said. Either that, or a good, old-fashioned grudge fuck. It was my choice.

At first I was a little hesitant to tell him what I wanted, but I've got needs, too, you know? Impressed, he said, "You got a deal, you sexy bitch. See your hot pussy between the sheets. And make it snappy."

Flushed with anticipation, wearing clothes with no buttons and zippers only, soon I was going up the plush hotel elevator, and trotting down the tastefully-appointed hallway. Of course I took the second choice; he was ready to make it happen, and so was I. But, standing outside the door to the suite, I almost began regretting my decision.

Oliver answered before I even knocked. Chest hair freshly groomed and white hotel towel knotted low on his waist, he swung the door open and let the towel fall to the carpet. Walking slowly to the king-sized bed, he knew full-well that he looked fantastic, and that I would follow.

Relishing my need, he cruelly teased me by inching slowly toward the center of the bed. Reclined fully across the mattress, he enjoyed having me watch as he took his hand and stretched himself out, just so.

Together fifteen years, we locked stares with no pretense, comprehending that what we both wanted was between the smooth, satin sheets.

He slowly pulled them back, revealing at last what was inside.

The dismissal papers stamped 30 minutes earlier by the county clerk.

That's right. A deal's a deal.

I tore up the papers.

And, he tore off my clothes.

Driving over separately, we meet in Dr. Phillips' lobby.

On the way, I believe we both came to the realization that we're starting over. I know I did. We're mates again. Partners. Parents. Lovers. And now it's sinking in. I know the road map. It's my job now to adjust the travel plans and destination.

Oliver and I settle in together on the lumpy love seat, Dr. Phillips in her striped, wingback chair.

As she cracks open a can of SlimFast, her monogrammed shirt cuff peeks from the sleeve of her charcoal, pinstripe jacket. Taking a long sip, she watches us carefully.

"I'm encouraged seeing you together, all smiles for a change. Therapy is immensely more productive when couples are in sync," she says. "Mindset and preparation are important."

Oliver's expression is thoughtful. "I'm with you all the way, doctor. Boning up for therapy is crucial."

I give him a blank expression.

"I don't want to rain on your passion parade, you two, but our purpose in here is to air out problems, and for today, let's steer clear of discussing the children." She turns to me. "Do you have anything this afternoon, Mrs. Morrissey?"

"Nothing special comes to mind," I say.

"If it does, let me know," she says and begins scrawling on her pad in her loopy cursive. She quickly looks up. "Why did you choose Mr. Morrissey?"

That's not a question I was anticipating.

"Are you sure we can't talk about the kids?" I say. "Or maybe play with those building blocks again?"

Oliver smirks at me.

"Oh, fine." I crinkle my brows and think for a moment. "He was, is, charismatic, dynamic and brilliant," I say. "Oliver's a star."

He chuckles. "Tell me something I don't know."

I jab him. "Well, why did you choose me, Mr. Smarty Pants?"

"Are you serious, babe? You were H-O-T. I fell for you hard." He fondles my thigh. "From the minute I saw you at the courthouse, I knew I was taking you home."

I think of early in our relationship. The tangle of sheets in the mornings. When he would send me those roses and it meant something.

"Mrs. Morrissey, could you expand on why you chose him?"

"We were perfect for each other, I guess," I say. "I wanted to help him succeed because he wanted it so bad."

"Good answer," he says under his breath.

She turns to Oliver. "What did you want from your wife, Mr. Morrissey?" she says. "Early in your relationship, I mean."

He gives her a dimpled smile. "I wanted her to want me."

Assessing him thoughtfully, Dr. Phillips twists her ballpoint pen between her fingers. "How did you make that happen?"

He takes a moment to choose the right words before he speaks. "As her employer, I had already won her confidence and respect—her allegiance." He steals a quick glance in my direction. "To win her heart, I had to win her trust."

Dr. Phillips addresses me. "And, did he?"

"I suppose. Sure," I say. "I did trust him. Since he was correct about everything else, if he thought our being together was all right, it must have been." I tuck my curls behind my ears. "I hoped that if I helped him, this amazing man who lit up the room would need me. And, some of his light would shine on me, too."

Oliver does the strangest thing. He reaches over and strokes my cheek. "I never knew you felt like that," he says.

I blush and look away.

Dr. Phillips doesn't waste time on tender moments. "What about your wife drew you to her in the beginning?"

He begins fondling my thigh again.

If he says my boobs, I'll kill him.

"I already answered that."

"Dig for depth, Mr. Morrissey," she says. "If that's possible."

He answers quickly. "If she were simply young, beautiful and vivacious, so what? Young women like that are a dime a dozen, but, Juliana was smart, too. The perfect combination."

Hell, yes I was. Still am.

The best paralegal the firm ever had," he says. "Seriously. I kid you not."

She raises her eyebrows at me, impressed.

He leans toward her, as if taking her into his confidence. "To tell you the truth, Doctor, she does such a crackerjack job shelving books at the middle school library, I don't know how they'd manage without her." He crosses his heart. "Honest to God."

Sending roses seems like such a romantic, heartfelt gesture when they're actually a mere phone call with a credit card from your secretary. As impersonal a gesture as you can get.

Dr. Phillips takes a sip of SlimFast. "Fair enough. In recap, you needed to be wanted. And, Mrs. Morrissey, you wanted to be needed," she says. "So, what came next?"

Oliver tugs my hair and motions for me to answer.

"This amazing man who lit up the room..." I pause and turn away. "He also sucked all the air out of it. After a while, I couldn't breathe."

He loosens my fingers from his arm. "I believe you still have the floor, Mrs. Morrissey," he says curtly. "Please continue."

"All right then, Oliver. I'll ask you a question."

"Shoot."

"Did you love Charlotte?" The words spring from my mouth.

His neck jerks backward. "Why would you ask me that?" he says. "Now, of all times. Here, of all places?"

I blink at him. "I just never have before."

Dr. Phillips writes words on her pad. No doubt, "Who's Charlotte?"

Oliver furrows his brow. "Isn't this line of questioning rather counter-productive?"

Dr. Phillips raises her pen. "Something you feel is counter-productive, Mr. Morrissey, is probably worth exploring."

Oliver throws up his hands boyishly. "Here, here. Objection!"

I tilt my head. "Why won't you answer?" I ask. "It's not that hard of a question."

His smile fades and his tone turns serious. "Sure, I loved Charlotte." He hesitates. "For a time."

Kissing my knuckles, he winks at Dr. Phillips. "Glad we got *that* one out of the way. Since I'm on a roll, is there anything else anyone wants to know?"

"Yes, Oliver. Answer me this," I say tentatively. "When you made partner and I was jettisoned from the firm, what did I get?"

His expression softens. His full lips turn down slightly at the edges. He seems vulnerable. And, tender. Touching his fingers to my lips, he holds my gaze for several moments.

"Well, me, Juliana darling," he says. "You got me."

As I searched under the sink for a flower vase this morning, I wished he'd have remembered that those particular roses aren't my favorite at all. I've never cared for the white ones with red-tipped petals, like a white shirt cuff accidently dipped in a hearty cabernet. Better yet, white cigarette filters with the lip-kiss of a red mouth.

"Me, Oliver. Remember Juliana Birdsong? What did she get?"

He shows his best dimples. "What any woman would want." He counts off on his fingers. "Ample time to be a mother." He raises two fingers. "Ample time to run the kids to all their activities and volunteer at the school." Three fingers. "The rest of the time, I don't know what you do," he says with a laugh. "Hey, sign me up for your job."

I glare at him. "If I'm not mistaken, Oliver, you took my last one."

He squeezes my knee playfully, trying to keep the mood light. "I already said you were fantastic at it, babe."

He never inquired, but I hate red rubies, too. He thinks they're the color of passion. Funny, that's not what springs to mind for me.

"You get to be supported in style," he says. "And I know you like that. Am I right?"

He waits for me to answer. I nod.

"Carrying the financial ball for the family—that's my job," he says earnestly. "And I think I'm pretty damn good at it."

"You must be a career mother, Dr. Phillips," I say softly.

Oliver cuts me off. "Now, just a moment. She's never had children," he says. "I checked."

Dr. Phillips bristles. "My life is not open for discussion in here, sir."

He gives her a charming smile. "Just stating the facts, ma'am."

She points her ballpoint at him in warning.

He shrugs. "You understand what I'm saying."

I wish I'd smashed his ugly-assed roses in the trash. Nothing says I can't the second I get home. Home. My dad's house isn't home. My home is where my children are.

"You changed the plan on me, Oliver," I say.

He looks back to me now. "Really? What plan is that?"

"You know what plan. Not the 'deal' you mentioned during the first time we were here," I say. "The one where after we had the twins and got married, you'd send me to law school."

"I wondered when that was coming back. After fourteen years never mentioning it again, to be honest, I thought you were kind of a sap." When I don't respond, he chuckles. "You know I'm kidding, Juliana, but tell the truth. You weren't too choked up at living the lush life. Not one single bit."

Dr. Phillips glances between us.

"Besides, becoming a lawyer, you'd be real sexy then. Be one of those dike lawyers, like Anabel."

Dr. Phillips finishes off her SlimFast and tosses the empty can in the wastebasket.

Oliver crosses his legs at the knee. "Jesus Christ. The man you loved and adored told you, 'I'll always take care of you, and you're going to be a wonderful mommy.' What's the crime in that?"

I glare at him. "The crime is, you punish me with the kids because you know how much I need them."

"Rules. Rules," Dr. Phillips barks. "No kids in here today."

He raises his voice. "You love them more than me, Juliana. Admit it."

"They're our children," I cry. "Why wouldn't you want that?"

As he rubs his bare upper lip, Oliver's eyes tick swiftly around walls, searching for something to settle on. Finding the clock, he checks the time against his watch.

"I'd like to interrupt and ask a question of you, Mr. Morrissey," Dr. Phillips says. "Why have you been torturing your wife all this time?"

He raises his chin and stares at her coolly. "She needed to see how much her life would suck without me," he says. "I wanted her on her knees."

"And that's exactly where you got me, with a rope around my neck, after selling everything I owned to be able to battle you," I say evenly. "I even put my dad in Sagecrest, you son of a bitch."

"Everything you owned, dear lady, was given to you by me."

I swallow hard.

He keeps the ball rolling. "Maybe it was my turn to change the plan for once," he says. "What do you think about that?"

Dr. Phillips slips on her glasses to get a better look at him. "I think I'd like you to expand on that a bit."

He flusters. "You want to talk about Charlotte in here? Then, by all means," he says. "We had a plan, and look how that turned out."

"How *did* it turn out, Mr. Morrissey?" she asks. "Wait, I bet I know." She pauses. "Divorce."

He flips his hand at her. "Charlotte became successful and for me, there was zero. Zilch. Nada. Just like my mother when she up and got herself a job," he says. "It didn't take long until she was looking like Dolly Parton, selling off-brand makeup for the immense honor and status of driving a pink Cadillac. The perks, as she put it. Said she did it to help me."

"Oh, for heaven's sake, Oliver," I say. "Your mother did do it to help you. She gave you acting and speech classes. She was so proud of how you could hold a crowd with your clear, expressive voice."

Dr. Phillips raises her brows.

"When Charlotte and your mother changed the plan, Mr. Morrissey, you stopped getting their attention?" she says forcefully. "Is that how you see it?"

He doesn't answer, but she's not backing off. "But, your present wife? Since you've been coming here, you've certainly gotten her attention."

He pounces on her. "If you're unable to approach these sessions in a collaborative fashion, Dr. Phillips, then remain quiet. You're a marriage counselor who's not even married," he says. "Divorced, in fact."

I open my mouth to defend her. She quickly raises an index finger to her lips and shakes her head.

Feeling stronger with her here, I keep my voice calm. "After you patted me on the head, knowing how important it was to me, Oliver, why would you make me that promise and never follow through?"

He threads his fingers and deliberately taps his thumbs together several times. "Now hear this: After today, this subject is aired-out and will never be spoken of again, neither inside these walls nor outside these walls, and is heretofore off the table." He motions his head in my direction. "See what I'm dealing with here, Dr. Phillips?" he says. "Well, I don't have to tell you—you're the professional."

Staring back at him, her eye twitches.

He sticks out his lower lip and looks at me. "Oh, poor little you doesn't get to support the family," he says. "You want to leave the house before seven and get home after seven? If you had to try cases yourself, cupcake, you'd have a meltdown. Last I checked, law firms weren't exactly clamoring for housewives who run carpool. Plus, at your age?" He bends over and begins pulling up his socks. "That train has left the station."

Dr. Phillips gives me a sideways glance and I duck my head.

Now, he faces her and bows out his chest. "Who'd have to listen to her? Me. Hold her hand through law school?" He smacks his chest with his fist. "Me! Who'd be picking up the slack with the kids?" He smacks his chest again. "Right again. Me! Forget it. Not interested. Hell, she'd probably expect me to give her a job again, too."

His words. They're like shrapnel.

My heart unspools. In rusted ribbons.

The expression on Dr. Phillips' face. Like she wants to say something nice. But nice words aren't the ones I want to hear. Nice words make me cry.

I quickly gather my things and head to the door.

Because I don't cry in front of people.

I don't.

Speeding, manic drivers are oblivious to the shivering woman in the woefully thin jacket. The digital thermometer on top of the bank reads 27; temperatures plummeted at least 30 degrees while I was inside. Missing every green light so far, I touch my left foot down on the slick pavement again and idle. In the next lane is my old friend Jenny Bates in her gold Toyota Land Cruiser. She pretends not to see me, but not her son, Carson. He knocks on his window and waves.

Moments earlier, only a fine mist was in the air. Now the air is solid—a hard sleet. Crystals stick to my nose and glasses, etching my cheeks like frozen tears.

Gas tank on fumes, I stop at the 7-11. I shove my freezing hands in my pockets and tramp toward the automatic doors. People without credit cards pay inside.

Waiting at the register, I glance over the glossy titles. *This Old House, Fortune, Mad Magazine,* and *US*. There's a loud beep when the boxed wine runs over the scanner. Oprah's smiling eyes sparkle at me as the clerk plucks a packet of Marlboro Lights from the overhead display. Back at the pump, I fill the tank, and the nozzle drips gas down my leg.

Finally home, sleet crunches under my tires as I wheel the Indian into the driveway. The trees have suddenly lost all their leaves and their trunks seem to shiver. The dead verbena in the flowerbeds is now covered in frost.

My fingers sting as I unbuckle my chinstrap and yank off my helmet. I climb the slick, icy steps and make my way across the porch.

Collapsed across the hanging swing, I have the sensation that I'm folding in upon myself, as if I'm sinking through a hole in the center and pulling the cushion down with me. My arm drops over the edge and it feels like blood trickles from my neck, down my shoulder, my elbow and my wrist, until it finally drips from the tip of my middle finger and pools on the hard cement.

If that's who I was, this is all I am?

I hug my arms across my stomach to keep my guts from seeping out.

Where's the rest of me?

## CHAPTER SIXTY-TWO

❖  ❖  ❖

I let the faucets drip, but the pipes still froze.

No running water, and Dad down to his last clean pair of boxers, I spent the morning at the Laundromat—seemed like a like fitting punishment for last night. My forehead is like a cracked windshield with a jagged line of pain breaking from one corner of my scalp to the opposite eyebrow. Plus, I can't stop burping.

Reliving last night's wine keeps me reliving last night. So, there you are.

Having wedged Dad's folded laundry in the cramped bureau, I turn and look at him, seated on his throne staring at the firebird painting. His ratty, blue sweater is buttoned up to his collar.

My phone rings in my pocket and I look at the screen. Oh, great. Of all people, it's Jan James. I hate talking to her, all bright and cheery in her slow, silly drawl. I step into the hall and take it.

"I've got an offer on the next painting," she says excitedly.

"Slow down, will you?" I say. "Don't you understand what I'm doing here?"

"I thought I did," she says. Her voice is bruised.

Oh, hell. Now I've gone and offended her.

I take a deep breath and try to compose myself. I shouldn't take it out on her. It's not her fault. Without Ms. James, I'd never have known Dad painted. And, she's my salvation.

"Both you and Señor Sanchez tell me my father paints, so why won't he do it for me?" My voice cracks. The last thing I wanted it to do.

I cover the phone with my hand for a moment.

"When they sell, there's no more. Worst of all, my father. With every painting, Ms. James, he's leaving me," I say. "Little pieces at a time."

Her breath is like she's blowing out a candle. "I'm very sorry."

I lean my head against the wall. "I just wish you'd quit doing such a good job, okay?"

There's nothing but silence on her end.

I squeeze my eyes shut and sigh. "I'll have it shipped soon," I say. "Will that work?"

"Just be sure I have the tracking number," she says gently. "And, listen. I'm always here for you, all right?"

"Of course, Ms. James. Thank you."

Hanging up, there's an uncontrollable shaking in my heart that comes on so suddenly I can't catch my breath.

# CHAPTER SIXTY-THREE

❖ ❖ ❖

"Surprise, babe," Oliver says. "Get ready to be impressed."

Hip cocked to the side, he rests against my screen door hugging a brown-papered bundle to his chest, as if it's a babe wrapped in swaddling clothes. He tips it toward me and I peek over the edge. Sadly it's just roses. About three dozen of them. Same ones as usual, white with the blood-tipped petals.

I'm in hell.

"Bet you have some water for these." He tries looking over my shoulder. "Aren't you going to invite me in?"

A vampire entering my domicile? I brace my foot firmly against the door frame. Inviting them in is the only way they can gain access. Learned that about 36 years ago.

"I'm sorry you got upset by what was said in therapy," he says casually. "It's all worked out now and since I was a good sport, you should be, too."

I stare at him blankly.

"You should follow doctor's orders. Dr. Phillips', that is," he says. "It was pretty uncomfortable after you took off, leaving us alone like that."

I bet it was.

"Especially when she made a play for me. A desperate play, actually." His voice trails off at the end.

"Oh, I'm sure," I scoff.

"Ha! Now that I've got you talking, aren't you going to say anything about the flowers?"

If I did, you wouldn't like it.

"If you'll quit pouting, I might have something else for you." He reaches into his pocket and out comes a red leather box.

With his megapixel, moustache-free smile, he creaks open the lid. "Please accept this with my most romantic intentions."

How can a man with such a brilliant legal mind be so obtuse? He thinks I'd actually want the bracelet from Vegas?

It sparkles under the porch light. I smile meekly.

He slips the tight cuff around my wrist.

"Why don't you check under the velvet?" he says.

I do. Blood-red rubies to go with the roses. Ideal.

"Carat and a half each. Pretty spiffy, huh?"

I look closely. Hey, I have a pair just like that. And, this is it.

So, where the fuck is the rest of my damn jewelry?

"Why haven't you said anything? Come here. Let me see your eyes." His face lights up. "Oh, ho! I know that look. You're well on your way."

And it's damn tough standing here trying to act sober, too.

He pops the ruby earrings out of the box. "Let me help turn you around." Moving in close, he kisses my neck. "C'mon, Mrs. Morrissey." He licks it. "We've come so far."

Something long and hard and pokes my hip. Believing it's him, I look down. Whew! It's a bottle of my favorite wine, La Crema Chardonnay.

He quickly elbows past me. "Let's get a look at this place," he says.

I follow him inside.

"Okay...Okay," he says slowly, looking around him. "It's not as bad as I thought it would be. Still bad. Just not as bad."

Thanks, dickwad.

"Buyers won't take it seriously it its present condition, so we might think about getting this house fixed up. Just the bare minimum. It's not worth putting any money into because we'd never get it back out."

"What?" I tilt my head and look at him.

"Hyde Park is a sought-after neighborhood. This place could fetch a good dollar, that's all I'm saying. Just something to think about."

"I'm not selling my dad's house."

"Let's check out this fine gourmet kitchen." Stepping inside, he eyes the corkscrew and wine on the counter.

Make that wine *bottle*.

He smiles, looking over his shoulder at me. "Didn't know you were that far along," he says. "Perfect."

He does the honors and tops off my glass.

"I get the impression you're still pissed, so let's do something about that," he says. "The Four Seasons that day? Curled my toes, babe. Some of your best work."

Not steady on my feet, I hold the lip of the counter.

He edges toward me. His fiery black pupils shine like bullets. "I'm going to have you coming like a pinball machine." He cups my ass with both hands. "How's that sound to you?"

About an hour later, Oliver's phone rings. He leans up on one elbow and takes it. I hear Adam's voice on the other end. Seems his pal Jordan ate some bad chicken wings and is puking his guts out, and his parents will have Adam home in about thirty minutes.

Out my bedroom window, I watch Oliver walk down the front sidewalk. Halfway to his car, he raises his stiff hand to his brow and salutes the night air. His old TD signal for Total Domination.

I untangle my girlhood sheets with the tiny purple daisies and pull them up over my naked body. Turning from the window, I reach for the sweating wine glass on the bedside table.

# CHAPTER SIXTY-FOUR

❖ ❖ ❖

I'll call Lindsey on the phone. When she does answer, she'll do that old game—you know the one where you pretend to have a bad connection by crackling a piece of paper in the mouthpiece?

Who does she think taught her that game?

I want her back to the Lindsey I knew, but it seems she wants to be someone else now. Someone I'm not sure I want to know anymore. But, I suppose my daughter's always been fearless. Like when she'd refuse to wear anything but her ratty Cinderella costume in preschool and would talk too loudly in restaurants. Oh, how she delighted me then. Even though I know I should probably back off and give her space now, I just can't.

Monday I was able to finally track her down at her friend Caroline's house. When I rang the doorbell, I couldn't believe it when she answered it and stepped onto the porch. I told her to gather her backpack and that she was coming with me.

"They eat dinner as a family here, with everyone sitting around the table together like we should have but never did," she said. "I like being here, but now you've made it where I can't feel at home anywhere." Then, she turned and reached for the knob and I grabbed her skinny arm.

Yanking it away, she turned to me with dead zombie eyes, all smudged underneath with black eyeliner and gloopy mascara. That's when I got the news that my daughter hates me. The words that spewed from her mouth were so ugly that she must've been saving them up for a long time.

She was such a wonderful little baby. She had a sweet little round head, the softest little cry, and those serious, blue eyes. Even then, it felt like she wasn't sure I knew what I was doing. Now, she realizes that she's finally the one with the power because I'm terrified of doing anything that could push her further away. Like one of those rubber balls tied to a paddle, the harder you hit it, the further it goes. Do it long enough, the elastic string snaps and the ball flies free.

Today I tried waiting for her after school like I did last week.

At five-thirty, Principal Murray's car was the last one in the teachers' lot. She watched me quizzically as she stretched the seatbelt across her chest and started the engine. Pulling up beside me at the bus stop, she rolled down her window.

"Children understand more than you think they do," she told me. "Even when you think they're ignoring you, they're really not. Learning from your actions, they're watching you all of the time."

If that's true, I hope Lindsey understands how much I love her.

I'm just grateful she's signed up for dance class. At least then I'm able to see her, even though I can't touch her through the glass.

## CHAPTER SIXTY-FIVE

❖ ❖ ❖

It's lunchtime, which means Mrs. Calloway is in the lobby. We're sitting comfortably on the plaid sofa together, reading *Oprah*. Finished with the Dr. Phil column, she nudges me to flip the page.

There's a tap on my shoulder and I turn around.

Richard.

He gives me a cold expression.

Mrs. Calloway's expression says, what an attractive man. She leans forward expectantly.

"You're finally here to see Dad?" I say.

"No, I'm here to see you. Thanks for returning my messages," he says pleasantly, with a stiff smile.

I open my mouth, but he cuts me off.

"You're hiding from me, aren't you? Thought you'd be safe here, the last place I'd come."

I can't tell him how I sit on the porch smoking and pouring back wine, knowing Oliver's coming. Pulling into his driveway, Mr. Reynolds used to smile and wave. Same for the neighbors walking their dogs. Not anymore.

Bless Mrs. Calloway. I'm so grateful when she speaks up.

"Why this must be that husband of yours," she says, batting her eyes like a little minx.

He takes her hand and kisses it gently. "Oliver Morrissey, Attorney at Law. Damn glad to meet you ma'am," he says smoothly. "May I borrow my wife for a moment?"

Nodding quickly, she purses her lips together, then leans her arms over the back of the sofa and watches intently as I follow Richard to the foyer.

I look up at him. "Rich, I was going to come by the shop after this," I say lamely. "I'm trying to tell you I'm sorry."

"Try harder," he says.

Tears well in my eyes. "If I weren't so ashamed, I'd tell you what I was really doing last night," I say softly.

Richard puts his chin in his hand and stares at me for a few moments, then turns on his heel. "I'm not your priest."

"Rich," I call after him. "Richard, stop!"

He doesn't.

Mr. Read rounds the corner from rec room at the far end of the hall. He carries a couple of green apples in one hand and a large bottle of pills in the other. Seeing me, he smiles broadly and quickens his pace.

Richard's shoulders rise up and down as he takes a deep breath. I rest my hand on his arm and he knocks it off before turning around.

"Nice hickey there, sis," he says. "Big man on campus is probably in the locker room now bragging to the rest of the football team about it."

I blush.

My eyes dart to Mr. Read who's now crossing the lobby in my direction.

"I have four words for you," Richard says, and he says them slowly. "Get your shit together."

From the corner of my eye, I see Mrs. Calloway tug the back of Mr. Read's khaki suit coat as he passes the sofa.

"Hey, they've got some decent coffee in the dining room." I motion my head that direction "Come on."

"It's almost noon, and all the residents, including Dad, are chowing down. But, nice try." He smirks. "I get plenty of pep talks from Wally. And, yes, I know," he says. "He's up here all the time."

"That wasn't my game, Rich. I just want to tell you how sorry I am."

He sighs roughly. "I don't understand what's going on with you, but I love you, Jules. And, your kids love you, too," he says. "Maybe rearrange your goals list. You have more power than you think."

I shake my head. "Like hell, I do."

He checks his watch. "Oops, I'm late picking up Fritz at the groomer. Dinner or something, okay?" He heads for the door.

As I look back to Mrs. Calloway, Mr. Read is gone, but a large man has taken the chair beside her. The resident with reddish stubble and red, puffy eyes who wears the cheery, yellow sweat suit. I jog through the foyer as fast as I can, but his anguished voice follows me, even after I'm outside.

"Lord, help me be a better me!" he cries. "Lord, help me be a better me!"

## CHAPTER SIXTY-SIX

◆ ◆ ◆

---

I step into my house slippers and peek out the window.
What the hell is that?

Beat-up, jacked-up camper-pickup with bald tires. Bondo patches on the fenders, and a muffler barely hanging on with twisted bailing wire. There's a "Baby on Board" window decal and a bumper sticker that reads, "You Can Have My Gun When You Pry it From My Cold, Dead Fingers."

Crawling out the driver door? Appears to be a man, finishing off a can of malt liquor. At seven a.m., I might add. He's smoking, and so is the engine. Jean cut-offs, hairy bird-legs and a sleeveless Rod Stewart T-shirt stretched over his pot belly. Oh, and a greasy mullet.

Ignoring the walkway, he tromps across the work I've done on the yard. On the porch, he stubs his soggy cigar in the potted geranium by the door. What a low-life.

I push open the door, but not the screen.

"Lady of the house at home?"

"Yes," I say, "but you're at the wrong home."

"That a fact?" He checks the house numbers. "Mr. Morrissey says his old lady lives here."

I cinch my robe tightly around my waist.

"The name's Smith."

I check his gimme cap. "Smith's Home & Landscape Design."

He belches malt liquor in my face and tosses his empty in the flower bed.

"Don't you know it's illegal to be drinking behind the wheel?" I say.

"If I can't drink and drive, how am I supposed to get to work?"

Lovely.

He punches his fist through the hole in the rusted screen. "First project we'll tackle. Right here."

My eyes fly open. "What's wrong with you? Cut that out."

"Don't worry, ma'am. Won't be no charge to you at'all," he says with a smile. "See, I got this barter situation set up with that fine Mr. Morrissey."

I back up. "I beg your pardon?"

"I done got sued by some piss-ant customer and your husband got the chicken shit off my back. Settled outta court. Four thousand smackers." He scratches his hairy underarm. "Gonna use the whole dang enchilada to beautify this here yard and house," he says. "Cause ain't nobody gonna want 'em like this."

Heat rises to my scalp.

"No upcharge for my ideas, neither, and from the looks of the place, you can use pert near ever one of 'em."

"Thank you, Mr. Smith, but your services are not needed here," I say. "This is not my husband's jurisdiction."

He whistles between his teeth. "Oh, Mr. Morrissey ain't gonna like hearin' that," he says. "Besides, ain't never smart to look a gift horse in the mouth."

He plucks his stogie from the geranium and heads down the steps. At the bottom, he puts his ear to the leaning support column and raps it twice with his knuckles. Starting to chase after him, I drop to the hanging swing instead and watch him tromp around the perimeter of the house, making notes on his hand with a pen. He stoops forward and checks under the eaves. Looking for wood rot, I suppose.

When he begins scrutinizing my yard work, I don't particularly care for the sour expression on his face. I look toward the street to memorize his license number and my eyes settle on the wet, dark gray sidewalk.

The sky's been clear for several days now, but you'd never know it; the soggy dirt under the concrete is saturated clear down to the roots. Water seeps up through cracks in the surface and stays puddled in the low spots, so on even the sunniest of days, the rain never truly goes away.

## CHAPTER SIXTY-SEVEN

❖ ❖ ❖

Señor Sanchez waits for me outside my father's room, dressed in a finely-tailored, double-breasted suit. The jade on his bolo tie matches his fedora.

"I knew you'd finally come up to visit," I say excitedly.

"This is not a social call," he says in his thick Spanish accent. His expression becomes suddenly stern. "I am delivering a message from the creditors that your father's payments are two months in arrears, putting him in grave danger of losing his home."

"I'm sorry, Señor Sanchez," I say. "It's his last painting and I can't bear to let it go."

His little white moustache tickles my cheek when he kisses it.

"Like your father, you have one of the most tender hearts I have ever known, and I have known quite a few." He clears his throat. "I am between wives at the present moment."

Gracious.

"You can put it off no longer," he says. "The time has come for you to act before it is too late."

I motion my head toward Dad's room and give him a challenging gaze. "I could say the same to you as well, sir."

He puffs out his chest and says staunchly, "Where your notions are unfounded, *mi dulce amiga*, it is inadvisable to intrude."

I quickly twist the knob and push the door open. He hesitates, then follows grudgingly behind.

Rather than studying a painting, I don't expect to see Dad rolled in front of the window staring at the blank canvas.

"Dad," I say. He doesn't respond and I repeat his name, louder this time.

He turns his head in every direction. Seeing me, he opens his mouth wide and draws a deep breath, vertical wrinkles above and below his lips.

It's his "I'm depending on you" expression. It gets me every time. He's the watered-down version of himself: Dad Light.

"Hello, Daughter," he says.

I bend to kiss him on the cheek. "Hello, Father," I say. "A special visitor is here to see you."

Señor Sanchez creaks forward on his polished cane, shoulders stiff as if bracing for a blow. Seeing how Dad's changed, his eyes become misty.

Dad stares at him blankly. Señor Sanchez slowly removes his fedora and tips it at him.

Suddenly gripping the arms of his chair, Dad raises himself from the seat. "You're not welcome here." Veins pop in his neck.

Señor Sanchez slowly wipes his lips with a monogrammed handkerchief. His nostrils flare.

"Got a hearing problem, old man?" Dad barks. "Leave. Now!"

Looking between them, I squeeze Señor Sanchez's arm. "Maybe you should do what he says, sir," I say tentatively.

"Perhaps that would be advisable. Let us have a word in the hall."

With his hand at the small of my back, he guides me gently and I smile at him over my shoulder. At the door, he swings it open wide, pushes me through it, and slams it behind me.

Well, my goodness.

Waiting for their voices through the door, of course I crack it open.

Señor Sanchez starts back in. "For your information, I do not take orders from a lying piece of dog shit."

Dad yells, "I'll make sure and carve it on your tombstone myself!"

"What is *art*?" Señor Sanchez spits out the word like dirt. "Nothing but a useless, meaningless, self-serving indulgence," he says. "Artists should have the skin torn off their bodies and be dipped in jalapeño juice."

The squeak of Dad's wheels means he's rolling closer.

"Anytime you're ready, old man."

"Do not tempt me, Hugh," Señor Sanchez says. "Because, believe me, she had better not show her face around here."

It's silent for a moment, then he knocks the door open with his cane and roughly pushes past me.

I watch him creak down the hallway.

## CHAPTER SIXTY-EIGHT

❖ ❖ ❖

Adam trots behind a blue, swaying wheelbarrow, balancing forty pounds of soil over the puny black tire. His dark curls bounce with each step. Losing control, the rubber handles fall from his grip and half the load dumps in the grass. Winded and red cheeked, he bends forward and puts both hands on his knees.

Adam's starting to fill out a little bit. The first day he insisted he didn't need gloves. When his outraged palms puffed, popped and oozed, that may have been the best thing that's happened. Being affluent saves you from doing this kind of work. Doing this kind of work saves you from being a spoiled little shit. We're playing catch-up.

When he gulps water from the garden hose under the pecan tree, he grunts and spits like a tough guy, all for my benefit. Hearing me laughing, he chases me down and sprays me with water. I yelp.

The new plants we're putting in the ground are from Sledd's Nursery. I finally got over it and asked for a freebie, and you know what? It really wasn't so hard. It was lots easier after I sent Mr. Smith away, his jacked-up camper brimming with oodles of plants. The man at Sledd's said they were tossing them out anyway, and it was no problem to deliver them for free. Seems they have a job in the neighborhood. Things are starting to look up.

I climb the dented aluminum ladder and begin trimming the ivy around the door. I swear, it seems like I just trimmed it yesterday. I really think I did. Like an army of marching ants, even killing off the front lines, there's always ample troops at the ready.

The lid squeaks as Adam opens the cooler.

"Son, is there an extra root beer for me?"

I hear ice jostle against the can. In a moment he touches my leg with it, letting me know he's there. Taking it from his hands, I see his fingernails are dirty. A mother notices things like that, and the all-too-familiar smell of his breath when he hasn't brushed. He's still not wearing the leather strap on his wrist with the single blue shell. Worst of all, the St. Christopher I gave him is still missing from around his neck. When I look at his legs, I see the hair's coming in darker.

"Listen, Mom," he says slowly. "I don't really want to tell you this. Lindsey would freak."

"Which is exactly why you should tell me," I say, and continue trimming the ivy. Poke too hard and Adam clams up. He's always been that way. Plus being a rat is hard stuff. I did it once. More, would've been hazardous to my health. Rich wasn't one for idle threats.

I wait for Adam to pick the skin off a few of his blisters. As he wipes the sweat on his face with the tail of his T-shirt, he watches me from the corner of his eye.

"Um, she's seeing this guy named Zac who used to work at the Chick Filet at the mall. Until he got fired," he says with a laugh. "And, he's in high school, if you can believe that. A junior."

I cup my hand to my mouth. "How long has this been going on?"

"Several months, I guess."

I quickly crawl down the ladder as Adam holds it still.

"Why are you only telling me this now?" I say.

"Because I didn't want to have this conversation."

I squeeze his bony bicep. "Spill it, buster."

"They hang out in the lot behind our school." He holds up his phone. "Here's his picture."

Squirrelly looking punk. Must be a real loser if he's hanging out with an eighth grader.

And, he's a dead man.

"Forward that to my phone," I say. "Does this Zac have a last name?"

Adam hits a few buttons and lets out a long sigh. "Zivley," he says. "It's him who brings her home sometimes."

"He drives?" I yell.

Adam throws up his hands. "Don't have a cow or I won't tell you things anymore."

Great parenting, Oliver. You're an idiot. She's fourteen.

"Your sister's not skipping school, is she? Tell me she's not."

He bites his lower lip. "We only have two classes together, and she's always at those," he says. "But yeah, she's ditching."

My throat's dry. I sip my root beer and then hand it to him. In a couple of swallows, he finishes it off.

"Thanks for telling me, Adam," I say. "And sweetheart, you're a good brother."

He rolls his eyes. "Sure doesn't feel like it," he says. "Don't say anything to Dad, okay?"

"You haven't told him?"

"He couldn't handle this, Mom. Lindsey needs you."

I know.

"I guess things are back on with y'all for good, now?"

His brown eyes say I better not lie to him; he wants the truth.

"I know you never wanted it in the first place, but I still couldn't believe you were coming by the house and, well, you know," he grumbles. "Especially after he was so mean to you."

It's like a million blaring alarm clocks going off at once.

"At first I made like I didn't see it on the bed, two feet from us, but that was stupid because you couldn't miss it." He scrunches up his face. "All black and lacy."

Oliver's a jackass but up until now, at least I thought he was *my* jackass.

"I asked Dad if it was his. You never know," he says. "I thought maybe he gets all kinky wearing your panties and stuff."

Over and over I squeeze the clippers in my hand. "What did he say?"

"He said, 'Good one, son. You betcha.' Then he twirled the thing over his head like a propeller and said, 'Your mother left it here.'"

I swallow hard.

Congratulations, Oliver. This may not be the shittiest you've ever made me feel, but it's up there on the list. Getting the tip-off from our son makes it even better. I should've sliced off his little dick when I had the chance.

"Was there anything else he said?"

Red streaks explode under his eyes like war paint. "That when women get used to having their chocolate sundae, you can't just cut them off."

Trying to catch my breath, I raise my hand to my brow, to shield my eyes. Adam drops to the step below and looks up at my face.

"Mom?" He shakes my shoulder. "Mom, are you okay?"

"Let's just be quiet for a minute," I say.

I watch his leather sandals as he climbs to the porch. He peels back the squeaky lid to the cooler and whacks it back shut.

"I smelled her!" He yells the words.

I jerk up my head. His face is white. There's tears in his eyes.

"Like, what's that flower?" he says.

"A rose?"

"No. They smell horrible. Like your white ones by the pool."

"In the blue pots? Gardenias?"

"Yeah. Those."

He flings the screen open, bolts inside and comes right back with his camo backpack. He throws it on the ground and begins unzipping it.

A fourteen-year-old's hands shouldn't be shaking.

He holds it up.

It's black, lacy and racy all right. I check the label. La Perla, Size Medium. Only Saks carries that brand in town as far as I know. It smells like it's been worn. I doubt for very long. Adam's right. Gardenias.

He breathes deeply through his nose. "Here, Mom. There's this too."

It's a Ziploc baggie with a Bobbi Brown lipstick inside. Not my brand. I've always been a Chanel girl. Scratch that. Now I'm a Cover Girl.

I inspect the label: Iced Pink.

What's the harm to Adam's heart in all of this? How must he feel about his father as a man and husband? And his mother as a woman and wife? I'm ashamed that we've failed him so miserably.

He stares at the ground. He can't look at me and I don't blame him.

"Sorry, Mom," he says.

"Honey, I'm all right. I'm just sorry you're in this."

I squeeze his hand.

He glues his eyes shut. "It's messed up."

The sun goes behind a cloud and we sit in silence.

So raw.

Rather than drive him home, Adam had me drop him at a friend's house. Now rocking on the porch swing, absently watching leaves trip across the yard, I couldn't tell you how I made it back here. I honestly can't recall.

A harsh wind kicks up and garbage cans roll down the street. Smelling rain in the air, and listening to the rumbling clouds, I pull Dad's leather jacket around my shoulders and close my eyes.

I've spent a lot of time on this porch in my life. I remember being a little girl dangling my skinny ankles over the edge of this swing, ignoring my mother's voice from inside the house when she called my name, as I wanted for Dad to make it home from work. Stomach growling, way past sundown, my eyes would search our lazy, lonely street.

My heart would jump when I'd hear the cycle's approaching engine, but I'd crouch down as soon as he wheeled into the driveway, too embarrassed for him to know that I was there. As he'd lower the kickstand and begin ambling toward the house, I never made a sound. Peeking over the cushion, watching how the chinstrap would dangle from his fingers, and the way his broad shoulders always tipped to one side, I can remember thinking that his shiny blue helmet surely weighed as much as a bowling ball. But now I know the man was just plain dog-tired.

Rain begins sloshing over the gutters; wind blows it up on the porch, and it soaks my jeans. I brace my feet on ground and push the swing back against the house, but it's no use. Giving up, I toss back the rest of my wine and start heading down the sidewalk. At the end, I drop to the wet concrete.

Hugging my thighs to my chest, I tilt back my head and let the raindrops pelt my tender cheeks till they're numb.

The lonely rain puddles on my tongue when I open my mouth.

And, I swallow.

# CHAPTER SIXTY-NINE

❖ ❖ ❖

The next evening, Kimberley and I weave through the tables at Pepe's as we follow the hostess to a booth in the back. I shouldn't have let her drag me here, but I couldn't stand the thought of facing Oliver if he stopped by the house. Besides, I need to vent about everything that's going on.

The old days, I would've cried on Mary Ellen's shoulder, but tonight it's Kimberley's blouse that'll be tear-stained—a slinky scoop-necked fuchsia number with fancy white embroidery. A waiter brings us chips and *queso* before we have a chance to order.

I look to my old table, not expecting to see the gang there, but then, maybe I do. There's Mike and Mary Ellen, Glen and Cheryl, plus their kids. And mine. Thankfully, no Oliver. Guess he took a dinner meeting and called to have Mary Ellen bring them instead of giving them to me. The waiter takes the kids' sodas from his tray and passes them around the table, and for once, none get tumped over. A woman with a froggy facelift named Margo who I've known forever is squatting next to Cheryl's chair. The woman's face is animated and she talks with her hands.

Lindsey gets up and heads to the ladies room. I tell Kimberley to order me the Guadalajara Special and that I'll be right back.

I push open the door marked "Señoritas" and lean against the hand-painted tiles. As I watch my daughter apply rosy lip gloss at the mirror, so young, tanned and fresh-faced, I can't believe something so beautiful came out of me. Just for a second, when she shakes her hair and bats her lashes, she looks like a grown up girl, and it scares me.

She looks up.

"Hi, honey," I say. "You look darling tonight."

She cuts her eyes to me in the mirror.

I run my hands under the faucet. "Kind of noisy in the restaurant tonight, don't you think?" I say. "And it's even more packed than usual."

"Mom, what are you doing here? You haven't come here in forever."

"Coming to Pepe's isn't the end-all, be-all of my existence."

The look on her face says, it used to be.

The towel dispenser is out and I dry my hands on my jeans.

"Mom," Lindsey says. "Do you think people don't hang out with you anymore because you ride a motorcycle?"

I put my hand on her arm and smile. "Oh, good grief sweetheart," I say. "Why don't you and your brother come with me when everyone's finished eating? I'll get you to school in the morning."

"Mrs. Evans invited us to spend the night at their house tonight," she says slowly. "And mine and Adam's junk is already over there. She's got to drive Thomas and Travis to school in the morning anyway."

I smile brightly. "Well, that's all right. I drove here with Mrs. Singleton and she won't mind taking us by there to get your things."

She rolls her eyes. "I'm not hanging out with Amber Singleton, Mom."

"Well, no one said you have to, Lindsey, but she's not even here tonight." I furrow my brow. "Has my little girl become a snob?"

"If I am, I got it from you. The old you, anyway," she says in a sassy voice. "I can't stand seeing you like this. Pretending you're this new person when I know you're not."

How dare she say that to me? Feel that way about me?

If I say anything back, punish her for dating a high schooler, anything, she won't love me at all. She will hate me for real.

When she sees the look on my face, she says, "I'm heading back to the table, okay? My *queso* is probably there already and it always tastes gross when it gets cold."

She starts for the door, then she stops and rests her hand on the tile counter. Watching her profile in the mirror, I see her chin is quivering. Wispy curls framing her face, she turns around and glances at the floor. Her little shoulder bag is at my feet. She stoops down to grab it and quickly reaches up for my hand. She squeezes it three times. I—Love—You.

There's the sudden sound of laughter and mariachi music when another woman steps into the bathroom. Before it has time to shut, Lindsey scrambles to her feet and bolts out the door.

From the look on my face when I return to the booth, Kimberley can tell something's different. Watching Lindsey sit down at her table, she says, "Is everything okay with her?"

I smile. "I think maybe it's better."

I can't help noticing a man whose eyes are glued on Kimberley. He's in his mid-forties. Pretty nice-looking, actually. Has his hair. Always a plus. Over six feet. Also a plus. He keeps finding a casual reason to come close to our table. First he needs a napkin from the wait stand. Next he helps himself to the iced tea pitcher. Tell me this can't be happening. It's so high school. And, it's like I'm not even here. Like I'm the ugly, fat friend. When he finally asks to borrow our salt and pepper, he rests his hand on the table. I do believe he's looking down her blouse.

"I've been thinking about you, baby," he says.

Kimberley looks straight at him in a direct, confident way. "I'm not your baby anymore, John."

Does she make her voice seductive on purpose? I imagine her practicing it in a tape recorder.

"I hear you're in real estate now," he says.

"You heard right," she says brightly.

"I've been wanting to get into some real estate," he says and she looks at him hopefully. "Preferably between your legs."

She sighs good naturedly.

Seeing I'm not smiling, Kimberley trips on her words. "John, meet Juliana Birdsong."

I glare up him. "What makes you think you have the right to insult my friend like that?" I say harshly. "Don't ever speak to her that way again."

He looks at me like I'm an insane, crazy bitch.

"Now, step away from our table," I say.

Kimberley's mouth falls open for a moment and then breaks into a smile.

Slinking away, the man narrowly misses bumping into Cheryl and Mary Ellen as they're coming from the bar with fresh margaritas in their hands.

"You remember what she said," Kimberley calls after him. "And tell your friends."

Cheryl and Mary Ellen hear it all.

And, I have no doubt that they will.

"Hello, single ladies," Cheryl giggles. "Just like *Sex and the City*." Taking Mary Ellen's arm, she gives me Kimberley's little pinkie wave that we all thought was hysterically funny.

Oh, I have a finger for Cheryl all right, and it's not my pinkie.

Kimberley presses her hands to the table and stares after them. "You know what my answer is to people who talk about me?" she says. "Get a life and stop worrying about mine."

Beginning to laugh, I almost buy her bravado until her eyes begin to water. I never knew how much gossip hurt until I saw it on her face.

After a moment, she slips her white jean jacket over her shoulders and begins sliding out of the booth. "How about we tell them to screw themselves and we find a new restaurant?"

I quickly pull my thin wallet from my purse.

"And, don't worry about the bill, Juliana," she says. "I've got it."

We duck out.

The lot is so packed, you'd think we were at a Longhorn football game. Cars are jimmying for the best spots by the door. After hearing two whole songs on the radio, the traffic hasn't moved an inch. I crane my head out the window to see what the problem is.

Perfect. There comes my esteemed spouse trotting across the parking lot. It's dark outside, but he still has on his black, wraparound sunshades. If it weren't for this traffic and the fact that I'm not driving, I'd run his ass down with the car and back up over his face a few times.

Oliver smoothes the breast of his Italian suit, and his gold cufflinks shine in the headlights. The car behind us honks and he turns his head in our direction, then begins swaggering toward Kimberley's car. Damnit.

He leans down and rests his arms on her open window. "Hey, where have you been hiding out?" Mega-pixel smile. "And did I ever tell you how much I dig your license plates?"

She casually flicks his fingers off her arm.

I clear my throat and he looks across her to the passenger side.

"Surprise!" I say.

"Well hi, babe." Giving me a sideways expression, he slides his sunshades into his pocket. "You girls having fun tonight?"

"Sure." We answer at the same time.

Kimberley pulls her brush from her purse and begins running it through her hair.

"I guess you saw the kids inside?" he says.

Jerk.

"They're all waiting on me, so I better get in there." Raising up from the window, he pats the roof of the car a couple of times. "I'll holler at you, Mrs. Morrissey," he says and trots across the asphalt. At the entrance, a group of noisy teenagers file through the door when he opens it.

Kimberley lowers her visor and flips up the lighted mirror. She flicks her hair off her face. The apples of her cheeks are pink. Her chest, too.

I look towards the entrance and see the back of Oliver's suit coat as the doors close behind him. I turn back to Kimberley and study her carefully. Her thick eyeliner slants upward at the edges of her hazel eyes, like a cat.

"You're fucking my husband, aren't you?"

Her voice cracks. "Juliana, you don't understand."

She leans across the console and puts her hand on my arm.

I yank it away.

"Juliana, listen to me," she says. "Juliana, please."

"I don't want to hear anything you have to say. Just shut up." I pull my purse from the floorboard and dig through it for my phone. My lipstick, something. Anything.

The car behind us honks. The angry driver leans his head out the window and yells. Kimberley shoves her arm out the window and gives him the finger. He lays on the horn and she does it again.

"Of all the betrayals, not you, Kimberley." I shake my head. "Not you."

"Hear me out!" She tries tugging my arm again.

"Don't touch me," I scream, suddenly livid. "With all your talk about how people shouldn't judge you, and now this? Mary Ellen is horrified that I'd be seen in public with you." I look her up and down. "Frankly, I can't believe it myself."

Her eyes go dead. Sleepy-dead. Like a mannequin. "So you *are* just like them," she says slowly. "Of course you are."

I pull my purse over my shoulder and reach for the door handle.

She hits the lock button. "Juliana, don't," she says. "Listen to me."

"Unlock the goddamn door."

She doesn't and I do it myself and climb out of the car.

Slamming the door with my hip, I'm suddenly overcome with a numbing sensation. Here in the middle of strangers milling past who mean so much to me, I realize how much my life has changed. But that I really haven't.

Seeing Kimberley's tail lights pull onto the street, and then finally swallowed up by traffic, my legs feel so tired that my thighs buckle. Crumpled on the curb, I drop my head in my hands and cry.

# CHAPTER SEVENTY

◆ ◆ ◆

Character is how you behave when no one else is looking. I tell the twins that, so what am I doing breaking into my own house? All right. Oliver's house, but I earned that damn stuff in there.

Thank you for being so lazy, Oliver. Trying my old key, it works just fine.

Lugging Wally's dolly behind me, I determine a plan for which pieces I'll take with me. Lucky for me, he said I could borrow his truck, too.

Once inside, priceless treasures that took me fifteen years to accumulate seem to hug me close. I'm like an addict running through a crack house, but I've got to stay focused.

Reaching the dark, lifeless kitchen. My kitchen. I stop.

Paisley drapes hang from the windows above the sink. My lavender hand soap sits by the chrome faucet. The fancy drip coffee maker is still plugged in. My ladder-back chair with the teal cushion is still scooted up to my desk. I run my fingers across the granite counter where my coffee mug would leave a brown ring in the mornings.

I lived here.

Now, it's like a movie set. Where nothing's real.

I take a cookbook from the shelf. Thumbing through the glossy, stylized pages is like leafing through my old life. I'm lint under the bed, now. A handful of pennies stuck in the couch. But, Oliver will always be smack-dab in the middle of my memories. Forever. I'd turn my head over the sink like a colander, if I thought it'd work and rinse every last one of them down the drain. But, we have no control over that kind of thing. My father's proof of that.

My eyes dart to the twins' kindergarten pictures pasted on the fridge. Would my Diet Coke still be in the door? Yep. I crack one open and take a sip. Hearing a loud ring tone, I freeze and look around me. It's coming from the bay window. And that over-stuffed black purse? I bolt across the room and frantically rummage through it. Keys, notepad, breath mints, hairbrush, pocketbook. I finally dig the phone off the bottom before the last ring. I stare at the screen and collapse on the padded cushions on the window seat. I squeeze the phone in my fist.

I'm startled by the sound of a sharp noise outside the window. Like a metal chair scooching across the tile. Hands shaking, I gingerly peel back the paisley curtain and peer through the double-pane glass, across the boxwoods and hawthorns, and past the tall fronds of palm trees in the yard. My eyes settle on the loungers by the pool.

There's a chisel to my heart.

My husband wears his black wraparound sunglasses. He's dressed straight from the office, wearing his navy silk-blend Zegna suit and a pink shirt with the French cuffs. She's in a skimpy leopard bikini that she has absolutely no business wearing. Plus gold, high-heeled sandals.

The two-faced whore.

He roughly pulls the cups of her swimsuit up over her breasts, not bothering to unfasten the hook in the back. He lowers his mouth to her large, pink nipples and she tilts her head back. A sparkle of sweat trickles down her long, graceful neck.

He roughly pushes her away. He unzips his pants and unbuckles his belt, then sits on the ottoman to untie his shoes. Watching, she pinches her nipple with one hand. Her other slides from her perfect belly button down her elastic waistband.

Eyeing her, he removes his pants and drawers, folds them neatly and lays them over the back of the wrought-iron lounge chair. She quickly drops to her knees beside him. Raising one foot to the granite coffee table, he tilts his pelvis forward, puts both hands around the back of her blonde head and pulls it to his crotch. She gives his bare ass a hard spank and it leaves a red handprint. He throws his head back and closes his eyes. His mouth makes a perfect "O".

After thrusting for a minute or so, he presses a palm to her forehead and motions for her to stand up. One leg at a time she steps out of her bikini bottoms, revealing her fresh Brazilian wax.

Knowing exactly what to do, with her arms outstretched in front of her, she bends completely over the back of the chair. She turns her pretty smooth face to the side. Diamond earrings glint on her earlobes. Her eyes are dreamy, lost and faraway. He comes up behind her, and still in his sunglasses, Zegna suit coat and black socks, mind you, wraps his hands around her thin hips and does her right there, doggy style, in the backyard. It's not sweet love making. Just red-faced and animal.

His loud groan is the only verbal communication between them.

I turn from the window. Woozy, I stagger to my feet. Shit, I have to get out of here. I slip her cell phone into my pocket. Then I remember the dolly. As I stash it behind the red chenille sofa in the formal living room, my eyes linger on my possessions—the reason I'm here in the first place.

Once inside Wally's truck, I peel down the long, winding driveway, checking the rearview mirror. The brown patches left in the yard when I dug up the yellow verbena the roots, well, they've filled in so beautifully you'd never know what happened. That is unless you were here that day.

Gravel crunches under my tires as I pass through the gate.

A yellow taxi idles across the street. Inside, a long-haired cabby is jamming to the radio, drumming the steering wheel and moving his lips. Pulling up beside him, I unroll the window and have a word. I slip him a fifty. He nods and slides it in his shirt pocket. I park in front of his cab, and all eyes on the house, we wait.

Ten minutes later, here she comes, traipsing down the driveway, with her black overstuffed purse over her shoulder. A flowing, black sun dress swirls around her thighs. Shielding her eyes from the bright sun, she cups her hand to her brow and gives the cabby the high sign. Smiling, she lazily crosses the hot, steaming pavement.

You betcha, she's smiling.

I roll down my window and call out to her. "Hey, girlfriend."

She halts and quickly looks behind her to the house. Nothing. She squints at Wally's Ford F-150. I tickle the air with my pinkie.

She's not smiling anymore.

"Oh, it's you, Juliana."

I lean my arm out the window. "Come, get in," I say sweetly. "I'll give you a ride."

I wave the cabby past. Giving me a toothy grin, he shoots me with an imaginary handgun.

She looks both ways for traffic and then, ever so femininely, she glides around to open the passenger door. She gracefully swings her legs inside, then takes extra care arranging her purse in the floorboard. You know, her lip doesn't look half bad. The swelling's gone and the scab has turned into a pea-sized divot in the center of her lip. Come to think of it, she does smell like gardenias.

And, sex.

She flips down the visor and checks herself in the mirror. Sifting through her bag, she brings out her Bobbi Brown lipstick. Parting her lips, she raises the little pink tube to her mouth and I'm reminded of Oliver's manhood on the patio.

"Can we go?" Mary Ellen says. "I have someplace to be."

"Did I ever tell you I'm half-Mexican?" I say.

She raises the visor and returns her lipstick to her purse. "No. I don't believe you did, though Oliver may have mentioned it recently."

"Hmmm-m. Okay. There's something else I wanted to ask you," I say. "Was that a new swimsuit?"

She squeezes her lids shut and threads her fingers under her chin.

"So let me get this straight, Mary Ellen," I say calmly. "You'd play tennis with me for a couple of hours, then swing by here and sex it up with my husband for a couple more, while I ran carpool with your kids in the car?"

She lets out a deep breath. "It didn't start until after you and he separated," she says dully. "The last time you played with us was before then, remember?"

I put both hands on my heart. "Well, that makes all the difference," I say. "I feel so much better now."

Gazing at her, it's as if I'm seeing her for the first time. Licking her lips, she runs her red nails through her blonde hair and stares coldly through the windshield. Like an ice princess.

"Mike won't touch you, so I guess that left poor, grieving Oliver. His head on your shoulder became his hand on your breast?" I say. "Friends share things, but this crosses the line."

She hasn't looked at me yet. I'm not sure she's going to.

"What was your plan, dear friend? For you and Oliver and our four kids to move into together?" I say. "Yours, mine and ours? How cozy."

"Of course not."

"This isn't you, Mary Ellen. What's wrong with you?"

Turning my direction, she gives me her slow, sexy smile. Her one that breaks hearts. "Oliver said you didn't want him, so what do you care?"

I want to slap her pretty face.

"Your roots are black, by the way," I say. Honest at last.

She wrinkles her nose. "I'm seeing Fronz on Friday," she says. "Think you could turn on the AC?"

"That day at the courthouse, you weren't bringing Mike's briefcase. You were there to watch my husband, weren't you?"

She rolls down the crank window and looks at herself in the side mirror. Harsh light bounces off the glass.

287

I grip the steering wheel, quiet for a moment. She doesn't have to answer. Everything makes sense now.

"This is why you and Cheryl dropped me, isn't it?" I say.

She hesitates before answering.

"No, it's really not," she says, her voice suddenly gentle. "I didn't set out to hurt you, Juliana. I can't exactly speak for Cheryl, but I know that *I'm* sorry it happened. Truly I am. Lots of friendships naturally fall by the wayside. It wasn't anything personal."

"That's bullshit," I say.

She exhales loudly. "Okay, Juliana. Did you ever think you let us down? Having each other to lean on, our friendship kept our marriages together. You broke our bond." She stares at her manicure for a moment. "Can't you see that?"

"Okay," I say. "But, I thought the test of friendship was standing by each other when times were hard. Especially when one of the friends is having trouble."

She lets out a little laugh. "Oh, that's where you're wrong. That's the easy time," she says. "When something wonderful happens for one of them, now *that's* the true test of friendship."

I furrow my brow. "What are you talking about?"

"You've always gotten what you wanted, Juliana. The rich life with a decked-out house, great car, and the best clothes and jewelry. Plus, you're gorgeous with a smoking bod." She smirks. "Poor you."

I flip my hand at her words. "How was I any different than you?"

"You changed. Your life changed." She peels off her sunglasses and looks at me straight on. "No more having to make it work for the children? No more having to listen to a stupid, asshole husband?" Her cold eyes cinge a hole through me. "I wished I could start over knowing what I do now," she says. "Who were you to actually get to do it?"

Having a momentary flash of the doctor shooting her lip full of nova cane, I feel a sudden pang of tenderness for her.

"Call it resentment. Call it jealousy, I don't care. Maybe I wanted to take something from you for a change," she says. "Even things up a little bit."

There's a sense of pride in her voice.

"You're in love with him, aren't you?" I say.

"You're just not getting it." She draws out every word.

It feels like we're trapped in a tunnel as we stare at each other hard, neither of us blinking. With lashes clumped thick with mascara, her eyes become misty and she quickly squeezes them closed. Lids quivering; a tear, fat and black, stains her cheek.

Sure she's about to lean across and hug me, she turns toward the door instead, and reaches for the handle. "Don't worry about the ride," she says. "I've got it from here."

"Not before you take this." I artfully arrange her black, lacy negligee on the console between us. "Adam found it on my side of the bed."

She flicks it away. Like it's hot.

"Oh, and I almost forgot, dear friend," I say. "Your daughter, Alice, called."

Eyes flashing, she clenches her teeth. Seeing her phone, she snatches it from my lap and turns it off.

"While you were inside, I used the time to transfer some numbers from your phone." I look at her with big, wide eyes. "Can you believe that in all the years I've known you and Mike, I've never had his cell number?" I say. "Or his private line at the office?"

"Juliana, you can't tell Mike," she breathes. There's fear in her voice. Total desperation. "I could never survive without him. You know that."

"Yep. Sure do."

"Think what he'd do to me." She points at her lip. "This or worse. You wouldn't want to have that on your head."

"Like the night you implied that it was me that loaded the coffee cup and put it in Mike's hand?" I say. "Maybe this time, he and I can take turns."

Mouth quivering, she swallows hard.

"I'll never speak to Oliver again." Her voice is almost a whisper. "What do you want from me, Juliana?"

I stare at her stone-faced for a good ten seconds, then buck my chin at her.

"Get the fuck out of my car."

# CHAPTER SEVENTY-ONE

❖ ❖ ❖

"How very nice to finally meet you, face-to-face, Juliana, after all of our phone calls and communications."

I'd know that Southern accent anywhere. She's much prettier than she sounds over the phone, still, I didn't expect her to be so old. In my mind's eye, she's in a backless, macramé halter. Señor Sanchez said she called herself a hippie chick, and all. I suspect her hair was deep brown before it turned gray on her. The front pieces are wispy and white.

"And, it's very nice meeting you, Ms. James." I lean forward to shake her hand, and she hugs me instead. My dad doesn't take his eyes off her.

I took extra care getting him spiffed up today, because I know he'd want to look nice. I gave his curls a fresh trim and twisted them with a little styling gel. He's even wearing a freshly-starched, blue button-down with a white undershirt peeking at the collar—I was shocked when he gave up his nasty blue sweater.

After glancing around the room, she gives me a tentative look. "Are there any recent pieces he's been working on?"

"Sadly, there's nothing to show you."

Continuing to look around the room, her eyes light on the canvas learning against the wall—all wrapped up for her and ready to go. It's the firebird painting.

Didn't ship it after all. Told her I couldn't afford it.

Pretty ingenious way to get her here, thank you very much.

"Your paintings hung in the front of my gallery, Hugh. Right by the door where every customer who walked in would see them," Jan says smiling broadly. Her teeth are crooked in the irresistible way of a child who needs braces.

"Gallery?" he says. "You have an art gallery?"

Seeing the hesitation on her face, it seems they've covered this topic already, since she beat me here. Her eyes dart to mine and I give her a tiny shrug.

It tears your heart out, I know.

Straightening up, she says, "Yes, Hugh. It's in New York City."

His face breaks into a smile and he claps his hands together. "You finally did it?" he says. "Well, good for you, Jan. Good for you."

"Absolutely. Told you I would," she says with a little laugh, as if hearing Dad's reaction again doesn't exactly break her heart.

As she comes beside him and squeezes his shoulder, I watch him carefully. His skin seems to warm at her touch.

"Excuse me, Ms. James," I say. "How is it that you and my father know each other?"

Her expression changes. Her light green eyes become serious. "Maybe you want to tell her, Hugh," she says. "Or would you rather it be me?"

He raises his palms and nods. I watch him carefully.

She leans toward me. "I would guess that Sammy's told you a little something?" she says.

"He told me a thing or two." I try and keep my tone neutral and pleasant.

"I just want you to know what your father did for me. Without Hugh, I'd have never become who I am."

My father sits taller in his chair.

She points at the firebird painting. "This is the one I always wanted to take home and hang it right over the fireplace." Coming up beside it, she rubs her hand along the covered frame.

"Your home, you say? I know you mean in New York, but I wonder where you lived here in Austin."

She hesitates before she answers. "Matthews Drive."

"Down by the lake, you mean?"

"That's right," she says.

There's a sharp tap at the door.

"Anybody home?"

Señor Sanchez sticks his head around the edge.

"Come in, come in. Please," I say.

"Look, Dad," I say. "It's Señor Sanchez."

He tips his fedora, while giving Dad a challenging stare.

Dad angrily rises in his seat.

291

I hustle across the room and whisper in his ear, "Please, Dad. Not today. Act like a gentleman while Ms. James is here."

Dad begins looking at her again.

Señor Sanchez follows his gaze. Seeing her, his eyes widen.

"Why, Jan. What a surprise to see you here," he says in his thick accent.

She regards him, her expression like an eagle's. Fierce and bold. Then, it instantly relaxes into her soft, lovely smile.

He creaks forward and takes her hand. He kisses it and releases it gently. "Enchanting as ever," he says. The old dog.

"It's been a while, Sammy," she murmurs. Fingering the gold beads at her neck, she appraises him from head to toe. "I must say you're looking well. Very well-preserved," she says. "How old are you now, Sammy?"

He twirls his thin, white moustache between his fingers. "Ninety-six."

And that's a very good thing. God bless him.

"I still have my eye on the ball, and everything else for that matter." He bares his teeth. "Why, my goodness. Excuse me for being so gauche. I have interrupted your conversation."

"Ms. James was about to start an old story," I say.

"Should be riveting. Please continue," he says graciously. "I will be delighted to help fill in holes or offer clarification."

I begin crossing the room toward the only painting left on the wall. The one that no matter what, I'd never dream of selling.

Jan looks suddenly feverish.

I make a big show of unhooking it from the wall, before carrying it to the easel and begin situating it on top.

"Ms. James, before you start your story," I say, and turn to face her. "I hope you could do a favor for me first."

"Yes, Juliana?" She tucks the thick, white streak behind her right ear.

"Take off those damn boots."

Her face cracks like an eggshell. She starts toward Dad, then stops and stares at me anxiously for a few moments.

"I said, take off those damn boots."

She slowly drops to the side of the bed. Bending at the waist, she unzips them. They're black leather, square-toed. Hitting just below her knees, they graze the hem of her red chenille skirt. She slowly pulls off each boot and lays them both on the floor neatly. She looks up and her thick, shoulder-length hair covers half her face. She stares straight at my dad. Like there's nothing else in the room. Nothing else in the world.

She slides down her left sock.

On her inner ankle, barely an inch tall, is pair of tiny, red footprints.

I deliberately run my fingers along the patched scar. "I'm curious as to how this painting came to be."

Reluctant, she says, "I haven't always owned an art gallery. I wasn't always a financial investor either, though that's how I met Hugh. I went to him for advice at Sanchez CPAs."

She narrows her eyes at Señor Sanchez. Raising his chin, he glares back.

"Learning he was an artist, I invited him to the community art school. When he showed up, he found out the class was life painting," she says.

Señor Sanchez opens his mouth like he's about to say something. Jan cocks an eyebrow at him, and he closes it again.

"In no time, the whole class came to stand behind your father. The group became larger and larger, until quite a crowd was forming," she says smiling. "Finally finished after a couple of hours, your father was curious to see who was the naked woman he'd been painting." She hesitates. "When I pulled my hair from my face, he was surprised to see that it was me."

Señor Sanchez clears his throat.

Jan unconsciously crosses her arms across her breasts.

Seeing my eyes grow wide, Señor Sanchez mutters, "As if sweet, innocent Carmen would ever expose her naked body in front of strangers like that."

Jan's eyes flash.

He holds up a finger. "Hugh tried hiding the sexy painting at the office. I told him that if it was not welcome in his own home, it certainly was not welcome there. Since Carmen did not know he was painting again, I asked him if it was worth it." Giving my dad a nasty look, he motions his head toward Jan. "That is when he began painting at *her* house."

She gives him false smile. "And, I welcomed him."

"Of course you did," I say dully.

"He deserved to be happy," she says. "He said he'd never felt more at home or more free to create."

Cutting his eyes to Dad, Señor Sanchez wipes his lips with his monogrammed handkerchief.

"I tried my best, but I was an abysmal artist, Juliana," she says with a little laugh. "And your father didn't disagree. He suggested rather than kick myself for it, I might try cultivating artists and bring them together with people who would appreciate their art. People with money," she says brightly. "A refreshing idea, I thought. But, when I tried convincing him to let me market his own work, afraid he would be found out, he refused."

Señor Sanchez scowls, shaking his head. "All of the hiding, all of the lies," he says. "All of the trouble."

293

She turns and points an angry finger at him. "Don't think I've forgotten your part in all of this," she hisses. "Hugh took the portrait home because of you. And, when Carmen discovered it, you're the one she called."

He places his hand over his heart. "Yes, her *padrino*. The one person who was honest with her," he says loudly. "But, she did not need a calculator to know whose portrait it was. She had known of you for years."

My anticipation is replaced with a gut-drop premonition.

Like a disaster's coming and that I'm helpless to stop.

"How?" Jan says.

Lowering his eyes, he looks away before answering. "I had put Hugh's client list in his briefcase." He pauses. "And you, Jezebel, were the only female on the list."

"You pious, pitiful old fool!" she cries. "You're the reason she got behind the wheel that day."

Seeing my pain at his betrayal, Señor Sanchez' eyes grow wide.

"Juliana, understand that I was merely trying to protect your mother. She deserved to know," he says quickly. "I regretted it the second I realized what she was going to do." He looks searchingly at my dad. "Hugh, that is why I called to warn you."

Looking at him, too, I realize his eyes are glued to the painting. Wasting no time, I open the toolbox across his lap and wheel him in front of the painting. Hands shaking, he chooses a small detail brush and flutters his fingers over the bristles.

There's a spasmodic, scintilla flash. So bright, I shield my eyes.

Followed by a gush of speed.

A giddy, frantic sensation. Like laughing and crying at the same time.

If only you could slap someone and they'd snap out of it.

The room takes on a steaming, bitter chill. Like that eerie, backwards phenomenon, scalding water so hot it's cold. Flaming ice that refuses to melt.

The thick smell of oily exhaust.

I cover my ears. I can't take the drawn-out screech of skidding tires. Or the violent impact when it stops. I knew it was coming, so I didn't flinch.

Top-of-lungs tortured screaming.

Last is the shriek of approaching sirens. That just keep coming.

The painting transforms. A band of gleaming silver springs up around the edges. Jarring, the nude image begins to fade. I know it's not my mother. Still I don't care. Don't go.

Reaching out to touch it, the figure evaporates in a mist.

Leaving the canvas smooth and clear.

Quick pop.

The sound of cracked ice.

Then, a tiny break in the surface, like a bullet hole dead-center.

The quiet sound of a crackling string of firecrackers, as the surface begins to splinter spontaneously in all directions. Spider-webbed in moments, like shattered crystal; the fissures are that delicate.

Thick, circular blotches of red emerge. Heart colors of anger, passion and danger. Grainy, piecemeal patches of graphite and slate. Abstract splashes of bright, glossy white. Jagged bolt of black.

Initially, the image appears chaotic and haphazard, as if the colors are propelled to the canvas in a reckless fury, but it's not that way at all. The movements seem choreographed—kaleidoscopic. Absorbing visual poetry. Beautiful, in a sick, excruciating way. And, the image glows somehow, strangely backlit by a golden, spectral light.

A dusting of ash. And the round Mercedes emblem seems to wash to the top and float upon the surface.

Heart pounding, unable to move, I stare at the painting. Señor Sanchez, Jan, my father. I want to strangle them all. The skin around my throat seems to shrink.

Without warning, the spectral light becomes an eerie red, throbbing glow. I quickly yank the blanket from my father's bed and throw it over the painting.

A muffled whirring noise. The easel shudders. And, the blanket stills.

The room is silent. Pin-drop silent. Not a word. No one speaks.

In a slow, measured voice I finally say, "Will someone please tell me what happened to my mother?"

Señor Sanchez reaches for my trembling hand. I don't take it. I watch the onyx stone on his bolo tie as he wipes his lips.

"She drove from Hyde Park, clear across town," he says thickly. "Hugh sped on that damn motorcycle from Jan's house on the lake, up Windsor Road. Racing to catch them, Carmen took the Windsor exit off MoPac. It was raining. The road was slick. Everyone knows that hazardous hairpin turn. Except, for Carmen, of course. She hadn't driven, much less been out of the house in years, so how would she?"

I close my eyes.

"She hit the brakes, and they failed. The little car went flying over the side and smashed into a tree," he says slowly. "An ambulance came. A fire truck was there and a couple of police cars." He begins to stammer, barely choking the words. "A limb came through the driver window. When I arrived, your father and a fireman were pulling her body from the car."

I fall to the floor and weep for my poor mother. It wasn't her fault. She didn't deserve to die.

Señor Sanchez bows his head. "If I could take back what I did, I would. A million times over." He drops his cane and tumbles to the floor beside me. Pulling me to him, he strokes my hair. "It is all right now," he murmurs. "What am I saying? It will never be all right." He takes a rough breath. "I loved her, too."

Unable to look at my Dad, I glance at Jan and stare at her hard. There are bags under her eyes. Crow's feet at the sides. She wipes her cheeks with both hands.

"You bolted from this room the night I came and the easel was set up in the window." I say. I'm not asking.

She nods.

"He was about to give it a try," she says. "After how upset you were, never having seen him paint, it seemed insensitive of me to be there."

My eyes travel to her ankle. "Tell me about the footprints."

She looks at my dad. "They're what I told you about the day I left, Hugh." She speaks so softly, I can barely hear her.

She sits in the chair next to him. He takes her ankle, lays it across his lap and runs his fingertips over the footprints.

Her voice cracks. "They're baby footprints."

"Hold on. Where's this baby?" I say. "I have a sibling? This is too much."

Jan shakes her head. "No, Juliana. Our baby daughter miscarried," she says, her heart clearly breaking. "I had her footprints tattooed on my ankle so I can keep her with me," she says. "She's always with me. Every moment of every day."

My father hangs his head and cries.

This is the other secret my father's been carrying for years.

I don't even know what I'm feeling. I don't know what to do, what to say. I just watch them. Señor Sanchez looks at Jan tenderly.

"I am sorry, Jan. I am sorry, Hugh. I did not know," he says.

"When you called, Ms. James, you didn't know my mother was dead," I say. "How were you unaware of that for all these years?"

"When your father left, I took my ticket and went straight to the airport, like I should've done years before. It was time for me to step out of the picture and leave your family alone."

"How did you get the paintings?"

"Your father sent them. How he found out where I was, I don't know."

Señor Sanchez raises his hand. "I sent them. Though what I would liked to have done to them…" His voice trails off. "It does not matter now. But it was impossible to destroy something so important that was a piece of my friend."

Jan takes my dad's face in her hands. "I couldn't believe you didn't want the paintings. I imagined you regretting that you had sent them to me, afraid to contact me and say you wanted them back," she says. "I never stopped loving you, Hugh. Not for a moment."

Dad looks at her with yearning.

She looks up at me. "I should go now, Juliana."

"Please, Jan," he says. "Can I get you like a glass of sherry or something?"

She unclasps her hand from his and he braces his hands on the arms of his chair to stand. "Take me with you."

She looks to me for something to say.

I press my lips together.

She puts her head down and walks to the door. She steps out and then puts her hand back inside and waves.

Dad doesn't take his eyes off the door.

I follow her into the hallway and find her collapsed against the wall sobbing. Her elbows rest on her knees and the meat of both hands is dug into her forehead. She's dropped her purse and her wallet and keys have spilled out. A silver tube of lipstick rolls across the polished linoleum.

I don't realize Mr. Read is there until he slides down the wall beside her and pulls her crumpled body to him and absorbs her sobs into his chest.

"I've got this, Ms. Birdsong," he says. "You can go back inside and be with your father."

I glare down at her. "Make it snappy selling *both* the paintings, Ms. James," I say. "And, your naked portrait, I expect it to be gone from my father's room today."

If my father led a double life, does that make him a liar?

Or does it make him a truthful man?

He lost three women he loved all in one day. My mother, Jan, and their baby. But, the fourth, he never even considered. I'd have gladly filled the gap in his life. If he'd only asked me. The woman who loves him that's always been here all along.

I keep walking.

# CHAPTER SEVENTY-TWO

◆ ◆ ◆

"Just one or two."

"Which is it?"

"Two."

The wobbly voice. It's mine. And the officer is a woman. Perfect. Her scowl says she just *loves* me. The official badge on her dark jacket. Silver with gold lettering. Shield in the middle. She holds my driver's license in her hand, illuminated by her long, black flashlight.

I watch the rain dripping from the stiff bill of her cap.

She looks me in the eye. "This is not a motorcycle license. Would that be correct, Mrs. Morrissey, is it?"

"No ma'am. Yes ma'am, I mean." My voice shakes. Pulse ninety-to-nothing.

"Ticket for that," she says. "What do you do for a living?"

I hesitate. "I'm a housewife."

"Where are you off to this evening, Mrs. Morrissey?"

Her black eyes bear down on me. The light bounces off her red lipstick. She looks about thirty. God, please let her be a nice woman. I check her badge again. Officer M. Lopez. What the fuck am I doing here?

I watch the rain dripping down the trunk of the police car. The flashing tail lights. The spinning, red lights on the top. Cherries, they're called.

"I was home and got an emergency call from my brother. He's out of gas on the upper deck of IH-35. He's waiting for me now in this rain. He's in trouble."

She begins writing on her pad. "Mmm-hmm. You may be in some trouble yourself."

Fuck!

"Mind hopping off that bike, please ma'am?"

I'm on the cycle and a cop drives the car? How ass-backwards is that?

Scared to look at her, I lower the kickstand with the heel of my boot. She's about my size. Same height. Wearing dark pants. Dark shoes. Rain droplets on the toes. Vehicles driving by. Does anyone I know see me?

There's a billboard overhead. "Morrissey & Magruder Count on Us. We'll Make it Right." Oliver looks presidential, arms crossed over his chest. Mike smiles down at me with his big feral teeth.

"Ever done a field sobriety test before, ma'am?"

Speak nicely. Don't smile. "Never."

"See that sidewalk beside us? It has a line down the middle. I need you to walk it for me. Heel to toe. Nice and easy," she says. "Think you can manage that for me?"

She raises her finger and points.

I can't look at her. Fuck. I nod and take a deep breath. I can do this. Look straight ahead. Focus on something. That tree. Heel toe, heel toe, heel toe, heel toe, heel toe. I will not fail. Heel toe, heel toe. I hear splashing rain from the passing cars. Brakes squeak. Heel toe, heel toe. Focus.

"That's enough. By my assessment, ma'am, you are driving impaired. I am charging you with a DWI. Do you understand?"

The car is white. A shield is printed on the door in black.

Red decal on the window: DWI, You Can't Afford It.

"Please. You can't. Let me do the alphabet backwards? ZYXWTV."

"That's not helping, ma'am. Have you taken a Breathalyzer test before? I'd like you to do that now."

Oliver said to never, ever do that. You're fucked, he said.

"I would rather not, ma'am."

"Your call. Refusing means immediate suspension of your license for six months to a year," she says. "Lean against the edge of the vehicle, please."

"What are you..."

"Face the vehicle. Put your hands behind your back."

I do it. Fast. There's a hollow click as she locks my wrists together.

Fuck, no. My one phone call. Has to be him. I begin to sob. Lindsey and Adam. What will they think? Richard's waiting on me. What's he going to do?

"Something about you says you really need some help." The back door swings open. "Bend your knees. Watch your head, please."

She pushes it down roughly with her strong hand. Shoves me inside. I slide across the smooth, black seat. I am now inside a police car. Downtown. The police station. Mug shot.

She slams the door. "We'll take care of your bike. Impound it. And I'll rest easy because, God forbid, it's ever my family out there driving that you run into."

"Officer, please. Don't do this to me. Please."

I twist in the seat. I look through the black grate between the back of the driver's seat and the ceiling. Barrier that separates the criminal from the law. My eyes dart across the front. A dash-camera. Black keyboard with a screen. Police radio with lots of silver buttons. Just like on TV.

I convulse. Metal cuffs pinch my tender wrists. I struggle to get free.

The officer climbs in the front.

Her radio makes a scratching, white-noise sound. Crackle. Crack. Fuzz.

I can't stop crying. Fuck.

"240, 273D, 246. Need officer," the radio says.

She grasps the black microphone in her hand and stretches the cord to her lips. "I'm there."

She whips her head around and glares at me through the metal grate. Burning, hateful scorn in her eyes.

I drop my chin to my chest. Start thinking about the kids.

My door's thrown open and she's screaming in my face.

"Go, go, go! Armed domestic dispute in progress! Move your ass! Now!"

She yanks me out by my arm.

I slip, and almost hit the pavement face-first.

She catches me.

"You've been shot in the ass full of luck, you worthless piece of trash," she says. "Someone needs me right now more than you do."

I lean against the door as she rips open the cuffs. Before climbing behind the wheel, she sails my keys into the street.

She shouts at me over the blaring siren through her open window.

"A woman could lose her life tonight!"

## CHAPTER SEVENTY-THREE

◆  ◆  ◆

Pushing the Indian home in the rain for two hours gave me time to think about a lot of things. One of which being how I'd make it up to Richard. He's not answering for several days now, and to tell the truth, part of me is relieved. I'm too ashamed to tell him why I left him stranded. I can't call Wally for the same reason, plus I'd never want to put him in the middle. His place is with Richard.

But I need someone to talk to so I called the only admitted drunk I know.

Anabel was kind enough see me again.

Looking across the desk at me with a confused expression, she waits for me to speak first. I swallow hard.

There's a sharp voice in the lobby. An agitated woman's voice. Getting louder now. Footsteps clattering up the hall.

"Excuse me, ma'am. You can't go in there." Anabel's receptionist blocks the entrance to her office, but the woman breaks past.

Tweed, turquoise mini-skirt, high heels to match, gold, designer belt swinging at her hips and holding a patent leather briefcase, the woman barges right in.

You got it: Kimberley.

Anabel's face breaks into a huge smile. "Always a pleasure seeing you, Nympho."

"That would be *Ms.* Nympho to you, Anabel." Looking her over from head to toe, Kimberley pulls a file from her briefcase. "If I hadn't screwed around on Stephen, you might still be drunk and unemployed, so how's about a little respect, honey child?"

Anabel gulps back air and pushes the jar of jellybeans toward her.

"And, love your shoes, by the way," Kimberley says. Green stiletto pumps with flowers on the toe.

Kimberley spreads the folder on the desk in front of me. Ignoring the folder, I give her a thirty-second eat-shit look.

Finally, she exhales loudly and says, "Well, of course, I fucked him."

"Slut," I say.

Her cheeks and chest turn bright pink. "About that night at Pepe's, you don't understand the whole story."

Anabel smiles and moves closer. "I don't know what you're talking about, but I know it's going to be good."

Kimberley shoots her a look. "I started with Oliver three years ago when he heard me say I played tennis. He made some cheesy comment about how I must look in a tennis skirt and asked if I'd like to play. That would be 'play' with a long, deep growl." She wrinkles her nose. "We played, but he had a pretty dinky serve."

"Oh, you poor thing," Anabel says.

"I know, right?" Kimberley says. "Oliver bragged about what he was doing then. Arranging everything in your lives, getting things in place in case you ever divorced." She checks my reaction before going on.

Anabel eyes the open folder like it's the last margarita left on earth.

"I always felt bad for you. I didn't tell Oliver the truth, but it's why I broke it off with him." She twirls the ends of her hair self-consciously. "When I ran into you at the grocery store that day, I wanted to make it up to you somehow. I liked you. And I wanted you to like me."

Wow.

Anabel sighs in exasperation. "Excuse me ladies," she says. "May I?"

I shrug.

She snatches the folder and begins reading the document, her lips moving silently. After a moment, she high-fives Kimberley.

"Nice work, Nancy Drew," she says. "It's an email Oliver sent to Mike, telling him about another one of his cases to keep off the books."

"So?" I crinkle my brows at her. "I think I understand, but tell me why it matters?"

"It's an under-the-table arrangement where Mike holds onto Oliver's fees generated by those cases in the event that the two of you divorce. After your divorce was final, Mike would then hand the fees over to Oliver."

Kimberley crosses her arms. "It's what's called 'Unreported Community Property.'"

"I don't know how many of Oliver's cases they've been handling this way," Anabel says. "But, I've seen this type of dirty arrangement before."

"Oliver is a pig," I say.

Kimberley nods.

"But that's not the only way you'd be screwed, Juliana," Anabel says. "Under community property laws, your divorce settlement would also include a percentage of the value of the Morrissey & Magruder partnership. With their arrangement, the hidden fees wouldn't show up on their books, meaning the worth of the partnership would be undervalued."

Seriously?

Anabel jacks up her leg and sits on the edge of the desk, and gets busy with the adding machine. The roll of tape puddles on the floor. I pluck the page from her hands and start reading the document myself.

I stare at Kimberley. "How did you get this?"

She checks her manicure. "I forwarded it to myself from Oliver's home computer this morning and printed it out."

I furrow my brow. "How early this morning?"

"Oh, it was pretty early."

Anabel hoots.

Kimberley shrugs. "If I could only get close enough, I knew I'd find something."

"You slept with Oliver to get this for me?" I give her a wry smile. "I appreciate the sacrifice, but Kimberley, it's got to stop."

She looks down the length of herself. "What am I going to do? My body's looked this way since I was thirteen. Men have been after me all my life." She hesitates and lowers her voice. "Juliana, no one's ever stood up for me the way you did. You've given me the courage to revamp myself."

"I'm glad, Kimberley," I say.

"But just so you know, I'm in treatment," she says. "But not retirement."

There's that blinding smile.

"I'd never throw you under the bus, Kimberley," I say. "Or make you my sacrificial lamb. Ever."

Anabel quickly looks up from the calculator and smiles. "We wouldn't have to because she already gave us the hard part—the answers." she says. "You know, I've never especially seen myself having kids, but the name Kimberley Brock? I like it."

"Forget it, Anabel," I say. "You know I can't pay you."

"Listen, dear heart," she smiles. "It's called contingency."

## CHAPTER SEVENTY-FOUR

❖ ❖ ❖

I don't know why lawyers always keep their conference rooms so cold. After three cups of coffee just to stay warm, I'm dying to go to the bathroom, plus I'd also love to puke my guts out, since every time Mike's assistant has passed around the Krispy Kremes, I've taken one. After the look of disgust on Anabel's face when I took the last one in the box, I put it back. Then, two seconds later, she snagged it and polished it off.

Depositions are such a bore even if it is my life they're discussing. With the introductions and preliminaries out of the way, Anabel says we should have everything wrapped up in few days. She is in fine form this morning. Looks like she had her hair freshly mowed just for the occasion. And, for the charcoal three-piece men's suit paired with canary-yellow, five-inch stilettos, I give her two thumbs up. When Mike smirks at her, she'll simply flutter her eyelashes at him. But for me, sitting across from him while he's smiling at me, just to piss me off for two straight hours? It's all I can do to keep from pulling his canine teeth out of his mouth and shoving them up his big, hairy nostrils. Oliver, on the other hand, hasn't even looked my direction. Not once. He'll make a grand show of professionalism by leaning back in his swivel chair, nodding sagely while stroking the skin where his moustache used to be, pause to jot down a few notes and nod again.

I counted eleven legal boxes with the Morrissey & Magruder logo stacked against the wall. Bringing reams of information is an intimidation tactic of Oliver's—his way of making the opponent feel like they're an ant up against a blowtorch. How I know this is because when I was his legal assistant, he made *me* stuff half of the boxes with paper.

One accountant already testified on value of our "estate," which came as excellent news since I had no idea we were so loaded. The next accountant up should be testifying about the value of the Morrissey & Magruder firm. Now's the perfect time to powder my nose and come back refreshed and ready to hear Anabel's questions, and I wouldn't miss it for the world. I wish Rich was here with me today because I know he'd be proud. Sweet Wally finally called me back since Rich still won't answer. He says it will be okay —to just give it time, but I'm not so sure.

I walk back in the conference room and everyone at the table looks up. Anabel gives me a crossways expression when I take my seat beside her.

Mike clears his throat and looks at her apologetically. "We've got to change the order because our out-of-town witness is on a tight schedule."

It's pin-drop-time when I look from face to face around the table. My eyes settle on the big-boned woman with the enormous smile who's sitting next to Oliver. Fifty-ish, probably, and not all that well-preserved.

She props her elbows on the table and laces her slender fingers together. "It's strange we never run into each other, Juliana," she says. "Especially when we know so many of the same people."

Suddenly, the room closes in.

Mother fucker.

It's Charlotte.

Seeing my face, Anabel pulls me to my feet. "My client and I would like a moment, if you would be so kind."

She pushes me through the door and kicks it closed. "If it's my birthday, it's okay, but otherwise, I don't like surprises," she says. "Now make it fast."

"Oliver's ex-wife," I sputter. "Bitch on wheels. They were still married when I had the twins."

Anabel raises her hand to stop me. "Wish I'd known that when I saw her name on the deposition list, except she uses another last name now—same one as a lady-accountant I know by reputation." Hand on the knob, she looks in my eyes. "But, she's not the first ex-wife I've run into, so be cool."

Back inside, Anabel settles down at the table and starts right in.

"So, Mr. Morrissey dumped you for my client here," she says pleasantly.

"Yes, he broke our vows. Yes, he committed adultery," Charlotte says.

A punishing wave of memories floods back in.

"Is that a yes?" Anabel says.

"It is," Charlotte says. "And we had a good marriage. A happy home for going on thirteen years."

Smiling demurely, she glances at Oliver. He bites his lip and winks at her.

"College sweethearts, Oliver and I were soul mates," she says. "I put him through law school."

"That sounds expensive," Anabel says quickly. "You must've been plenty steamed when he said, 'Honey, hit the road.'"

Charlotte shifts in her seat but doesn't drop her sweet expression. "I don't recall those being his exact words, but no, I wasn't pleased."

"I imagine not," Anabel says. "Especially when his beautiful, young mistress had a bun in the oven."

There's a box of tissues in the middle of the table. Anabel pushes it toward her.

"You're talking about Oliver, Miss Attorney, and he's a good man. He left our marriage because she tricked him. But there were blameless children involved," she says. "That's what he cared about."

Oliver shrugs modestly and she takes his arm. "*That's* what kind of man he is."

"I can only imagine how torn he must've felt, having to leave your children," Anabel says soothingly.

Charlotte hesitates. "We had none of our own." She lowers her voice. "I went to several fertility specialists. Oliver indulged me. We tried in vitro fertilization and all of that."

"That must've been rough, seeing as you were the one with the problem."

Charlotte blinks and swallows hard. "It was."

Oliver takes her hand and places it over his heart.

Even through his solemn expression, his cheeks dimple.

The lying bastard.

"Well, you're quite a woman. Especially when such a good man ditched you after all of that and never looked back," Anabel says. "Not everyone could be as forgiving as you, ma'am."

Charlotte glares at her, devil-eyed. "Forgiveness is one thing, Miss Attorney," she says, voice trembling. "The facts are another."

Now, she picks a tissue from the box and begins twisting it between her fingers. "For your information, Oliver and I keep in touch. He's told me time and again that Juliana has been a problem throughout the marriage. He's only stayed out of love and devotion for those kids."

"Hmmm-m. That's not consistent with the straightforward information I've gotten from my client."

"Well, Miss Attorney. Ms. Brock, is it? The thing you don't get about Juliana is that she's a sociopathic liar, a user, and crazy. Certifiably," she says. "She'll say anything to get what she wants."

I ball my hands at my sides.

Charlotte looks at me with loathing. "Bet you didn't know she's a drunk who thinks nothing of being wasted in front of the children."

"Wow," Anabel says. "Those are pretty awful things to say about a person. How do we know any of what you're saying is true?"

"If you don't believe me, why don't you check with Oliver's mother?" Charlotte sniffs. "She'll tell you the same thing."

I bolt to the door.

Anabel takes my arm when we reach the hall. "You've got to put on a brave face and pull it together," she says. "And, hustle it up because I have to get back in there and deal with Mike." She motions her head to the door. "He says there's *another* witness he's added to the list."

Feeling eyes bearing down on me, I turn around.

They're dark eyes, with pants, shoes and hair to match. And, red lipstick. I recoil as the woman regards me with disgust.

It's Officer Lopez.

---

I bend over to unzip my boots. My high-heeled, French calf, twelve hundred dollar Gucci boots. I'm sure the conference room was so dead-impressed, my boots were all they talked about after I left.

I've been telling myself that superficial crap means nothing to me, but if that's true, why did I just have to wear them today?

The trash under the sink's already overflowing, but I stack boots on top anyway. Bye-bye to the last remnant of Mrs. Oliver Morrissey. I don't have the luxury of being superficial anymore. It's too expensive.

And, wasn't Charlotte just delightful today? The stupid, naïve idiot, still falling for Oliver's line of shit after all these years. Me, too, I guess. What a fool he made of us both. Having an infertile wife, he swore to me there was no way I'd get pregnant because *she'd* insisted he get a vasectomy.

I really did love him. Especially then. Now, I hate his guts.

I light up a cigarette, because right now, having a smoke-free environment's just not all that important to me. Neither is the fact that I'm drinking cheap, screw-top jug wine from an iced tea glass.

So, I love getting snockered. What's the crime in that?

Good God, it's called a DWI, you stupid bitch.

I take another swallow from my glass and fill it to the rim.

How ironic that the person who made me a drunk in the first place used it to take me down. By this time tomorrow, all of West Austin will know what was said today. Even if the case doesn't make it to court, well, it's not only lawsuits that are public record. Depositions are public record, too, and the scandal will only get worse. It might not be this week or even this year. Maybe they'll hear about it from Oliver. Maybe they'll hear about it from someone else, but the twins will know everything I've done. And, my stigma will be theirs.

How are they going to get along without their mother?

I take another couple of sips.

Because I'm losing custody of them.

Lindsey. I've acted completely crazy. Embarrassing her in front of her friends. How could I tear down her world around her? It was all she had. She tried saving herself, but I wouldn't even let her do that. Contemplating the devastation of her family life, Lindsey's just a lost fourteen-year-old girl, wanting her father. And look who she found. That's who I was and I didn't even know it. What's that old adage? When a girl fails to get attention from her father, she seeks relief in the wrong places—alcohol, cigarettes. The wrong man.

And, Adam. My baby bear. My little boy. So lost and confused. Even with his own pain, he cared about me. He helped me and now in return, when he thought he could depend on me not to hurt him, look what I've done. All I've done is hurt them both, when what they needed was their mother's help.

Lindsey, she won't be surprised.

Going to sleep is all I know to do.

Climbing the stairs, I take another sip, swish it around in my mouth like mouthwash, and it tastes damn good, I'm not going to lie. As I round the banister on the landing, I take another sip – a nice big one this time – and I raise a toast to Oliver.

Cheers, babe! It tastes even better going down.

I slam my bedroom door hard and set the glass jug on the vanity, and sit on my stool with the daisy-print skirt and switch on my makeup mirror. Raking my fingers through my curls, digging my nails across my tender scalp, I watch my magnified reflection. Unable to take my eyes off my face. Giant pores. Cheeks pale, lips dry and peeling. Veins bulging from my neck. Wrinkles, too many to count. I guide a new cigarette between my lips and light it from the one burning in my other hand.

Just like my mother, I couldn't hold onto my man. If I'd had more sex with Oliver, I bet he wouldn't have run around on me, but once a cheater, always a cheater, they say. Maybe I should look at the bright side: At least he didn't give me herpes. I think I'd know by now—with all that itching and scratching, I've heard it doesn't take long. I take a big swallow. Maybe I have AIDS. Wouldn't that be a swell parting gift?

I could've held onto him if I'd have apologized. The next morning in the hotel room, all I had to say was two words: I'm sorry. That's it. I'd have my children. I had the power to save things every step of the way by just getting down on my knees and begging his forgiveness. It would've worked, too. I know it. He wanted me back. He told Lindsey but I didn't believe it. I could've made my life work.

I look to the windows but I can scarcely see out. The ivy boarded up all the windows and wrapped the house in such a heavy tangle of vines, it can hardly breathe. That's how it feels inside, too. Smothered. Like the walls are closing in.

I imagine my mother after I left, standing in the rock garden where the lawn used to be, her dark eyes studying the house until she sees exactly what to do. Her strong fingers guide each tender vine to grow with ordered perfection. With me not around anymore, she trains the ivy like she always trained me.

I have her to thank for Oliver. I got myself that rich lawyer, all right. Like an arranged marriage to my goddamned, preordained Perry Mason. When I abandoned my mother, she died and I couldn't abandon her again. What else was I supposed to do? I owed her that much.

And, in death, her hands were twice as strong.

I stub out my cigarette in the glob of toothpaste in the sink and gulp the rest of my glass. Pouring it full again, not much left in the jug, I take a nice, long swig. I took her advice on the key to happiness. Taking care of myself meant getting someone else to do it for me. That's what my mother taught me, because it was my job to take care of her.

Knowing you're in charge is an awful feeling for a ten-year-old. Hands shaking, I light another cigarette and finish-off my glass.

Why do I deserve to be fabulous when she couldn't be? I couldn't surpass her—that would be disloyalty. Our shared unhappiness is the bond that holds us together. It's all I have left of my mother. That, and my guilt.

I stare closely at my reflection in the mirror.

With my old life washed away, and my precious children, with no chance of getting them back, *this* is who's left.

Juliana Birdsong.

A pariah.

A stinking drunk.

Raising the jug over my head, I lean back my neck and pour the rest down my throat. It sloshes down my cheeks, my hair and my neck.

I suddenly knock over the stool and rip my blouse over my head, unhook my bra and yank it off. I cup a breast in each hand and squeeze hard. Fingers clenched like claws, until my nails break the skin.

I unzip my skirt and drop it to the floor. Kick off my panties.

And get a good look the skillful naked body that earned me an ugly scar of shame and deceit. Same as the one my mother carved across Jan's naked portrait.

A thief. I'm just like her.

I turn around. Bend all the way over and look at myself in the mirror. Rake my nails up each cheek. Skin under my nails, so they bleed.

A dirty slut.

Same as Mary Ellen. No better than Kimberley.

A filthy whore.

Handing over my body to get what I wanted. Even if it was to my own wretched husband.

This is who I am, Mother, and you caused it.

I hurl my glass at the mirror. It shatters into pieces. The biggest one, I watch my trembling fingers reach for it.

How would it feel, dragging this ragged shard across my face and body? Give myself a real scar for the world to see. More than I deserve. Slowly raising it to my cheek, I watch my dead blue eyes in the mirror. Flick the shard across my chin a couple of times. I hold it over my wrist.

Ha. I'm too much a failure to even pull something like that off. I drop the shard and reach for the jug instead. Damn thing empty, I turn to fire it at the windows, my foot slips on the wet glass, and it slices my fucking heel. With a loud grunt, I throw the jug and it bursts against the wall. Limping around the room, I just start grabbing things. The vanity stool. I slam it against the vanity. Rake all of my makeup to the floor.

Falling back on the bed, I think of Oliver thrusting inside me on this very mattress, how many times? I begin frantically ripping off the fucking daisy quilt, the sheets and matching pillowcase. Balancing on one knee, I squeeze my palms under the mattress, and shove it hard as I can. The nightstand tumbles and the lamp crashes to the floor. Turn around. Look. Crawl to the closet. Reach up. Start yanking clothes off the hangers. Out of breath, rip the cords out of the wall and bang my old stereo against the door. I collapse on the box springs and immediately heave over the edge. Drag the fitted sheet off the floor and wad it under my cheek.

I stare up at the windows. Dark. Just a sliver of light.

Now I'm the one left trapped behind the ivy.

A lonely ivy leaf inches through the window.

And, now it's coming inside.

Room spinning, I close my eyes.

Drifting off, I see my children's faces.

I jerk awake. Fear.

Heart racing. Can't catch my breath.

Horrifying images rush through my mind. I cup my hands over my ears to stop the roaring thunder. My bleary eyes dart around the room. Where am I? Sitting up, I suddenly remember.

My dream. And, it's back.

Stomach lurching, I throw my legs to the side and my shin bangs something hard. I sink back down and pull the sheet over my head. I'll pretend it never happened. The dream. Last night, yesterday, and last year. I'll shut my eyes and try to imagine that I'm curled up in a dark corner, because that's the best place to hide. Oh, my aching head. But not in here. This sheet smells like vomit and it's crusted in my eyelashes and my hair. And, I'm naked. There's a dark corner in the bathroom with a tub in it. If I'm lucky, I'll drown.

Ouch. I shuffle across the room favoring my sore heel with a fuzzy memory in my brain—something about broken glass. Knocking into the door to the hallway, I push it open and begin groping the wall for the light switch. I flip it on and slowly peek over my shoulder.

Oh, no. My sanctuary.

There's a huge hole in the sheetrock on the far wall and a shattered wine jug underneath. The mattress is half on the bed, half off. Nightstand is on its side with the whole drawer dumped out. Lamp cracked down the middle with its daisy-print lampshade caved in and the top finial sheared off. Cracked mirror on the vanity. Stool tumped over. Makeup on the shag carpet and my broken iced tea glass, too. And, oh, my God. What did I do to the stereo?

It's as if I trashed my hotel room like a rock star.

Ugh. I start toward the bathroom again, but I stop and turn around.

Narrowing my eyes at my nightstand, I hobble back inside.

A handful of pennies is strewn across the floor and some smashed Jolly Ranchers. A pink hair brush, my crummy plastic ruler and a chewed-down, yellow pencil. A crumpled Archie comic book.

And my little red notebook.

Spine-side down with the pages spread open.

I kneel down and stare at the rows and rows of tiny, hash marks—all written in my messy, child-like scrawl. I gingerly take the little red notebook across my lap and reach for the pencil.

Then, I frantically dig the lead up and down, and up and down, and up and down, and up and down.

Tonight's hash mark.

"I hate you, stupid dream," I whisper. "You're a bully."

In Dad's room, I drop my helmet inside and pull the knob behind me. I squint toward his bed, expecting to see him curled on his side with his legs drawn to his chest and his arm dangling over the edge. But there's only his feather pillow and rumpled covers on the floor.

"Where are you Dad?"

I flip on the overhead. The bulb flickers out. No light under the bathroom door, I tap once, then push it open. Empty. I stand completely still and listen for the sound of his steady breathing.

Eyes scanning the room, I see the dark outline of his profile against the window. He's rolled up beside the easel with his hands gripping the wheels of his chair, leaning forward with his eyes trained on the window.

I come behind him and switch on the floor lamp.

He swats his hands wildly. "Turn it off!"

"Dad, it's just me."

He grunts loudly and quickly clutches the wheels again.

"I didn't mean to scare you," I say gently. "Kind of late for you to be up, isn't it?" I slip off his leather jacket and toss it on the bed. "We'll get you tucked back in soon, but I have to talk to you first. Okay?"

He continues staring straight ahead. I check out the window to see what he's looking at. Not a star in the sky. The panes are covered in a fine mist.

I crouch beside his chair, but I can't look at him.

"I hardly know where to start, Dad," I finally say. "I've made a mess of things. I'm ashamed to tell you that, but it's true." Glancing down at his pajama pants, my mouth crumples and my eyes fill with tears. "I'm a pitiful drunk of a mother who's losing her kids. When I think things can't get any worse, they always do."

He doesn't answer.

I squeeze the arm of his chair, and my voice splinters. "You've got to help me, Dad. Tell me what to do. Tell me what to do with my life."

There's the sound of wind outside the window. Whish, whish, whish. He cranes his neck as his eyes tick across the courtyard. Twigs and acorns skitter across the concrete.

"I have no job and we're out of money, Dad. Don't you know that?" I cry. "I know you hear me. Don't do this. Not now. Not when I need you."

I knock his thigh with my palm and he looks straight in my face, as if he doesn't see me. As if he doesn't know me at all. Like I'm a stranger.

I study his face. His strong jaw and the cleft in his chin. The curls looping down his forehead and his thick beard. His blue eyes. Still the same.

But, what's left of my daddy in there?

My knees buckle and I collapse at his feet. "Oh, you can't help me. Nobody can," I say softly. "But, I'm just so tired Daddy. I can't run any faster."

A sudden noise at the window catches his attention. Spindly branches scratch across the glass. My eyes drift to the walls to look at his paintings. Just a habit, I guess, but they're empty now, and the full impact of what I've done hits me hard. I sent my poor father here to this wretched place, then I sold his precious paintings to keep him here, just to get the twins back. And, where are they now?

I fall against his legs and hug them to me. "Oh, Daddy, I'm sorry," I sob. "I'm just so sorry."

He reaches down awkwardly and pats my head, like you would a puppy. We stay like that for several moments. His warm hand on my head. I reach up and take it. Something's crusted around his cuticles. Feeling his legs shivering, I pull myself up and take the other blanket off his bed. Tucking it around his legs, I notice his rusted tool box open on the table beside him. I flip on the lamp.

There's a brush on the ground.

My eyes dart to the easel beside him.

The canvas is blank except for a large form in the middle. Just a rough outline of a triangle. An inverted triangle—flat on top, with its skinny tip pointing down. Cone-shaped, actually. And, it's gold.

I glance at Dad's nails. They're coated in gold paint.

I quickly snatch the brush off the floor.

Gold-coated bristles.

I glance over at Dad. Study the creases on his cheek from the pillowcase. Count the lines on his neck as he breathes.

"Am I asleep, Jules?" he says calmly.

313

"No, Dad. You're wide awake."

He begins shivering again and I wrap the blanket more tightly around his shoulders. I finger his pajama collar. It's damp. His hair, too. A line of sweat trickles down his jaw.

"Did you have a dream tonight, Dad?" I say.

He nods, still staring out the window.

I take his hand and straighten his fingers.

And gently place the paintbrush inside.

"Dad, you know your paintings?" I say slowly.

He hums.

I look at his face.

"Are they connected to the dream somehow?"

He rolls the handle between his palms several times. I'm not sure he hears me again. That he's even listening. I watch him cradle the brush gently in his palm and begin shaping the wet bristles into a point. His eyes drift slowly to the canvas.

"I expect so, Jules."

The luminous colors behind the clouds that the storm tried covering up and didn't want him to see. But, he's a fighter. He'd go back for them at the end of every dream.

Craning his neck to look at the sky again, he begins fluttering his fingertips over the bristles. There's an unsettling chill like the onset of a fever. The room becomes suddenly moist and muggy.

In a calm, even voice, he says, "Looks like a storm tonight."

My eyes dart to the canvas.

The smooth surface starts to transform. The white around the golden cone-shaped outline begins filling in with a violet-blue.

I grab his hand. "Drop it!"

He tightens his grip around the handle and makes a tight fist.

I try peeling back his fingers. "Dad, you don't know what you're doing!"

A thick, black, line shoots from the base of the canvas, straight up the center. The smell of oily asphalt fills the room.

My voice trembles. "Daddy, I don't want to see this painting."

A glossy, white stripe shoots up the middle of the highway. Dull, jagged silver springs up along the edges, and a muddled, grassy-green.

Unblinking, he stares at the painting.

The violet-blue becomes milky. In seconds, the sky is gray, filmy clouds.

I'm pacing behind his chair. "Dad," I scream. "Drop the brush!"

In monstrous 3-D slow motion, the clouds protrude from the canvas, like they're punched from the other side with a fist. They begin rippling eerily, like writhing, bulging muscles. A deafening boom and a brilliant, silver thunderbolt. Rain spills down the clouds, down the black, tapered highway, down the rough, rangy landscape, and pools on the carpet below.

Wind whistles past my ears.

I holler, "Dad, drop the goddamn brush!"

The golden cone-shaped form is changing.

The blink of an eye, and it's like a translucent hot air balloon, topped with a looping spiral. It begins spinning, accelerating faster and faster. Glowing, radiant, twisting and twirling.

It's a mesmerizing white terror.

The window suddenly blasts open. The painting is violently hurled from the easel and crashes, face-down on the floor.

Dad clenches the brush between his teeth and lunges forward in his chair and presses his shoulder against the frame. The fierce wind and rain blow him backward, but he somehow manages to force the window back shut.

Breathless, he collapses in his seat.

I quickly wrap the blanket around his wet torso and tuck it snugly around his knees. Thick, heavy branches smack the window. Laser-focused, Dad's eyes seem to bore through the glass.

I fall against the arm of his chair and wrap my arm around him.

"It's back, Dad," I say. "The storm is chasing us."

He exhales roughly. "Daughter, don't you know it never stopped?"

"Look at us Dad—I'm a stinking drunk who's losing her kids. And you – I'm not sure you can take much more."

A boom of thunder shakes the windows and an uncontrollable shudder takes over my body. I remember the pain—the exact sensation when the storm ripped every layer of tender skin off my tiny back.

Dad leans forward with a labored grunt and reaches for the open toolbox on the table. Picking through the contents, he flicks aside the crumpled rags and rusted tubes of paint. Then, I realize what he's doing.

One by one, he's collecting every last paintbrush in his hand.

Grasping them firmly, he stands carefully and balances his weight against the chair. "So, what are we waiting on?" he says.

I'm dumfounded. Completely shocked.

That's my dad's voice. I mean my *real* dad's voice.

He raises his casted leg and begins hopping awkwardly across the floor. What's he doing?

He stops to lean against the headboard.

He beckons me with his arm. "Come on!" he says. "We've got a dream to finish."

"What's that supposed to mean?" I cry. "Dad, have you lost your mind?"

With a wry expression, he slowly raises an eyebrow in my direction.

I check the blustery storm out the window, and glance at the painting and overturned easel on the ground.

"And, we're not running this time, Jules," he says. "We're going to fight."

I watch him hobble to the closet. "What are you talking about?"

He begins picking through the hangers. "Looks like you've got to take the handlebars, Jules, and steer us out of here."

"Forget it!" I cry. "There's no way in hell I'm doing that."

He finds an extra jacket. Rustles around in the middle drawer for a fresh undershirt and warm sweater, and pulls a plaid, Pendleton scarf from the top shelf. "It'll be like getting hit in a football game. Oh, you'll *feel* it," he says. "But it doesn't matter, because you've got to keep going."

I watch him wrestle with the buttons on his pajama top. The wind and rain would take him out before the storm ever got the chance, and I'd never forgive myself.

Vision blurry, I squat down and tighten the buckles on my lug-soled boots. Wrap my red scarf around my neck and cross the ends in front. Then, I pull on his leather jacket. It's my armor.

He sees me tuck the fringe inside and zip it to the collar. "I'm coming," he grumbles. "Keep your shirt on."

"Like hell you are."

The helmet's where I left it, right by the door. Eyes on the knob, I take a deep breath and tuck it under my arm. I crack the door open and look side to side. Way past midnight, the lights are dim.

"Hey!"

I turn around.

Dad bucks his chin at me. "What made you decide to fight?"

"I didn't realize you gave me another choice."

He pooches out his lips and nods at me. "All right," he says. "That's good enough."

I check the hallway again. Now's absolutely not the time for polite conversation. I pull the door behind me and begin race-walking to the lobby.

Reaching the end of the hallway, I exhale loudly and turn back around.

Back at his door, I stick my head inside and stare at him hard.

"Let's get a move on," I say.

He blinks.

"You've got to come, too," I say. "You're in the damn dream."

Levis already pulled over his pajama pants, he grunts and stuffs the paintbrushes in his front pocket. "Wondered when you'd figure that out."

Helmet looped over the handle, I back his chair through the door and begin pushing him down the hallway. At the transition to the lobby, the carpet changes to linoleum and the metal wheels begin to squeak. Dad looks up and down. Coast is clear, and I'm running behind the chair.

Out the double doors, we head for the dedicated motorcycle spaces under the overhang. The blue Sagecrest hospitality van waits in the circle drive.

Dad's already grabbing the chrome handlebars as I'm setting the brake on his chair. Chest raised tall, a glimmer of satisfaction on his face, he strokes the word *Indian* scripted on the gas tank. Before I can buckle the strap under his chin, he rips the helmet off his head and hurls it into the grass.

Shaking my head, I throw my leg over the seat and kick-start the Indian and rev the engine a couple of times. As Dad climbs on behind me, I glance at the front of the building. Mr. Read is watching us through the lobby windows; a large jumble of keys sparkles around his neck. I give him a sad smile as I pull from the curb. After the storm kills us, I'm going to miss that man.

Heading through the deserted lot, rain shoots up the fenders and soaks my pants leg. I switch on the blinker and turn onto the street.

Up ahead is the good old MoPac Expressway—what a fitting start for our death ride. Electronic scroll board overhead warns in big orange letters: "When Flooded, Turn Around, Don't Drown." Steering up the entrance ramp, all four lanes are bumper-to-bumper and wipers on high. When Dad points out the cycle-friendly split between the long stretch of vehicles, I'm happy as hell to scoot over and give it the gas, and even happier to have his thick, scratchy stubble on my cheek as he tightens his arms around my waist.

We pass the crowded neighborhoods. A lonely ball field with bright lights, but no players. Office buildings and parking garages, too. We pull behind the same dented El Camino from the dream with the ratty sofa in the back, and it sure is getting wet. Dad squeezes my arm before the next exit, my cue to peel down the ramp. I'm glad he remembers the way to get where we're going, because I sure don't. A police car comes down the access road heading the wrong direction, and I get a really bad feeling.

Cutting through town, I take it slow but still make the lights. We pass the phone booth on the corner, the U-Totem convenience store. Oh, no. The single red tennis shoe in the road. My heart churns.

Round, yellow sign with the black X in the middle.

Horn blows long and loud .

Sign reads, "Do Not Stop On Tracks."

I look down them. What the hell am I doing?

The engine has face of a mean, ugly robot.

Chuga Chuga Chuga Chuga.

Striped gates begin crossing.

"Keep the wheels straight," Dad yells over the noise. "Don't, and we'll meet our maker here and now."

I imagine blood on the tracks.

Ding! Ding! Ding! Ding!

Honkkk-Honkkkkkkkkkk

Striped gates begin closing.

I nail it.

We bump over the tracks.

The train roars past. Mad whoosh of wind behind my back.

ChuckChuckChuckChuckChuckChuck.

Pulse racing, it's strange to be aware I'm breathing again.

Dad squeezes my arm. "You made it. Now you're ready to fight."

There's the yellow school bus. It stops at the next signal, brakes hissing. Racing up behind it, I'm anxious to see the little girl waiting at the rear window who looks just like me. I pull close to the bumper and look inside, but she's not there. The entire bus is empty. Well, it is a school bus, after all. What kids her age are up in the middle of the night? If she came bounding down the steps, if she'd come, I'd take her with me.

Her little face pops up. She leans her skinny arms over the back seat and stares at me. Why is she all alone?

The bus lets off the brakes and lurches forward. She disappears, like she fell off the seat. I search the windows trying to find her. The instant the bus rounds the corner, her tiny face appears at the very bottom, eyes big as quarters.

The red tail lights on the bus fade into the night. I take off in first and begin steering the cycle to the edge of town.

Not long, we're on the long and straight black highway. Our tires hug the white line that splits down the middle. An 18-wheeler just ahead travels for a good mile with its flashers blinking. It pulls into a greasy spoon with no cars out front. A peeling, hand-painted sign begs: "Stop, Eat, Good Food, Pie."

Rainwater gushing in our wake, I burn through the darkness like a torch.

Out of nowhere, the fire truck comes at us, siren blaring, red lights flashing. The air suddenly jolts and I hit the brakes. Tires skidding, I wrestle the handlebars. The fire truck rips past and shaves off our front fender, just a breath from crashing head-on. Siren shrieking in my ears, biceps burning, I squeeze my eyes shut. I open them again, and the asphalt under our tires seems warped.

Dad meets my gaze when I look at him in the mirror.

"You have to drive, Dad," I yell. "I can't do this."

"Don't screech on the brakes," he yells back. "You have to pump them or we'll hydroplane."

Easing off the throttle, I lean my weight to the right, and pull over. I plant my boot on the ground. "You never taught me anything before," I say angrily. "Tonight's a little late."

I raise up off the seat and he yanks me back down by the jacket. I struggle and he straps an arm across my chest. Steam spills from the engine and rises around us. Our headlamp bores a tunnel of light through the darkness.

I exhale roughly and clench my jaw, determined to calm my breathing. This is fucking nuts. Just ridiculous. What am I doing out here?

I twist my hips on the seat. Still not easing his grip, he moves his lips to my ear. "What's that you kids say? 'Get your shit together?'"

I cut my eyes to him in the mirror.

"I suggest you do," he says. "And, make it quick."

He lifts the tail of the jacket and stuffs a brush in my hip pocket.

Hands shaking, I cobble the tires over the gravel and carefully ease back on the road. I begin hearing the storm behind us; it sounds like an eerie, garbled burble.

I begin scanning the landscape for the rundown drive-in theatre. Bawling black calves huddle into the corner of two adjoining fence lines. An abandoned homestead has a skinny young colt post-tied out front. Twisting and gnashing against the rope, the poor animal rears back on its hooves.

My eyes dart to Dad's face in the mirror. He's looking in it, too. Wet curls blown straight back, eyes narrowed, he's focused on something behind us. Just staring at the clouds way back there, as if he's invoking the color to come shining through. What the fuck for, Dad? Why does it matter now? I want to scream at him, long and loud.

Sudden thunderclap! Lightening shatters the bruised sky like glass.

A buck runs for a hunting fence too steep to hurdle. Slamming into the fence full-force, the animal plummets backward, muscled chest ripped and bleeding, both antlers caught up in the wire. A silver lightning bolt strikes a twisted mesquite tree and it bursts into flames.

Deluge. A curtain of rain.

Then, just like the dream, the highway shrinks to one lane, cinched-in on both sides by the harsh barbed-wire fences. No way to turn around, but where would we go?

Wind blurs the rough landscape. Sturdy oak trees bend, branches thrashing. Side-leaning pine trees make a canopy across the road. Rain now shoots from the clouds like lead, bruising my tortured scalp. My fingers, too. Having to grasp the handlebars so tight.

I look up at the sky and scream full-throated, "You've got me all the way out here, storm! What do you want?"

A mangled section of guard rail grazes my shoulder. The highway begins to shake and the handlebars shimmy. I cut my eyes to the mirror.

Closer. Faster. The storm is running us down.

A pine tree shears off at the base and plummets across the highway.

I squeeze the brake lever, fast as I can. Lose control of the cycle.

Tire slams into the middle of the tree.

I'm catapulted through the handlebars.

Pine needles puncture my forehead and slice my cheeks. My chest hits the dense limbs with such force that my neck falls against my back. Exhaust fills my lungs. Metallic taste on my tongue. Pressure. Can't move. Tailpipe singing my calf. Stuck.

Black before my eyes. Lights out.

How long? Don't know, feel a tug. Muffled voice far away. Grip like a vice shaking my shoulders. Smell of wood. Muffled noise. Scream by my ear. Arm around my middle. Stumble up. See Dad's face. Long gashes crusted with blood. Lean against some limbs and branches.

Wind whipping my hair, the rain is still pouring.

There's no way to win. The storm always gets its way.

Why the hell did I bring Dad out here?

All at once, the rain stops and the air becomes still.

Shocked, puzzled, Dad and I look around us. It's as if a clear tube has dropped from the sky, forming a see-through ring all the around us. Outside the ring, the storm hasn't let up—I can still hear it and smell it, but it's like Dad and I are under a shower head and everything's getting wet but us.

Then an ear-splitting sound.

Wup wup wup wup wup wup wup wup.

Noise of chopper blades, like a helicopter coming in for landing.

Whik whik whik whik whik.

Pulsing air like raw energy.

Clamp my knees around a branch, or I'll be sucked into the sky.

A sickening dread on Dad's face.

He points to the sky. I look up.

Big gray, twirling cloud. Maybe 150 yards across.

Like an open, hungry mouth.

It drops lower. Ready to eat us in one bite.

We're trapped.

And it's going to kill us.
I tilt my head back and scream.
The monster mouth falls faster.
Twirling. Closer and closer. About to touch us.
I keep yelling, but can't hear my voice.
Now, a sound like rushing rapids.Deafening. Right over our heads.
The center of the cloud is like a churning propeller. Faster and faster.
It's a violent, spinning whirlpool of air.
Then, a circular hole opens in the center.
"It's time," Dad yells. "Just let go."
I tilt my head back and scream, "I surrender!"
We raise our arms over our heads.
Dad screams the word, "Zest!"
We're sucked off the ground.
All around us is a violently-rotating, mass of wind.
I begin screaming in pure terror.
Crying, yelling.

Spiraling faster and faster. So sick to my stomach. The sound like rushing rapids becomes an eerie white noise. Like ghost language.

Dad and I stand back-to-back. Gravitating toward the center.

Feels like I'm choking. Struggling to get my wits, I squeeze my eyes shut.

This is where I'll die along with my father. Trapped forever.

I always knew this was how the dream would end.

I suddenly realize we're surrounded on all sides by a towering, cylinder of calm. This doesn't feel like a storm. It's not what I expected at all. The turbulent wind isn't hurting us. It isn't even touching us.

I feel weightless. I must be hallucinating. It seems so clean in here—kind of *Star Trek*-looking. The barrier surrounding us, if you could call it that, is smooth and curved. Clear as crystal, a tube-shaped column, with Dad and me in the middle.

Ascending, we stare out at the rotating wind as if we're pressing our hands against glass. It's like we're inside a glass elevator, with no walls.

And, it's crazy in here. Supersensory. Unworldly.

Whirling faster and faster, it seems like time's going just as fast, too.

We pass three white clocks. Past, present and future. The three great divisions of time. Glossy and bright with shiny, gold hands.

And, I know I'm hallucinating.

Now, the wind changes. It's the color of creamy vanilla. Surreal. Dreamy. Like we're floating in it. I never want to leave this place again.

The propulsion halts.

Gut-stopping.

I'm thrown on my back. The bottom of the cylinder snaps shut.

It's a trick. A sick, awful joke.

Smooth and flat against my spine, I roll over. The floor is another white clock with gold hands. What's happening?

Now there's a horrid scratching noise, like a needle's not raised at the end of a record. Where's that coming from? Cupping my hands to my ears, I strangely feel my mother's presence.

I roll on my back again and watch the swirling, twirling wind overhead. Then, as if superimposed on top, a faded, dingy memory comes into focus. And, I recognize it.

A memory I'd tried so hard to forget.

The scene is my living room growing up. The air is hazy. Mother's asleep on our couch with its same worn upholstery with the dusty-blue roses. She's lying on her side. Shoulder collapsed, her upper arm falls across her body. The other one dangles over the edge of the cushion and her wrist rests limply on the carpet. It's the year Richard went to college. What it was like with just me home.

What's going on in here? It's like we're in a time capsule.

Hey, won't someone please raise the needle from the record? How about just turn the damn thing off?

It's jarring to see myself enter the frame.

I squat beside my mother. Her cigarette is burned down to the filter with its long gray ash still perfectly intact. I pluck it from her fingers and drop it in the ashtray that's already overflowing. I take her shrunken shoulders and roll her back onto the cushions. She doesn't wake up. I button her housecoat. Cross her arms corpse-like over her chest and stare down at her. Her girlish hands are wrinkled. The pointed bones in her face are visible through her pale skin. I smooth the gray hair off her forehead. She didn't bother with the wig by then. Hadn't for a while.

My father blows in, gray as ashes. He looks young. Probably forty, a little younger than I am now. It's always been curly, but his blonde hair falls flat against his forehead. I know what the awful scratching must be. It's the static left behind when Mother's screams switched to sullen. Dressed from the office, Dad swings his hand on the banister and begins trudging up the stairs. Halfway up, scarcely stopping, his hand on the newel post, he turns his neck and glances at me. His eyes are glazed and cloudy. Remembering how that's all he ever had for me, there's a shadow on my heart. I shiver.

Now, there's just my smooth hands wrapped around our brass door knob. I pull it towards me and stare at the peeling paint on the door. It's the day I left. A weathered, brown leather suitcase is next to me on the porch. Bulging, stuffed full. I grab the handles and rush down the steps. At the bottom, I look back at the wood-frame house and memorize it top to bottom: Four windows upstairs, four windows down; dull, tin roof; high front stoop with a porch wrapping around the front. Maybe two years since I planted ivy, and it's already half-way up the house.

A taxi idles at the curb. Tripping down the front walk, I feel happy. Not true-happy. Just not as sad. That was me leaving for college.

Nobody told me bye.

And, I didn't come back. Until she died.

The image fades and I'm left staring up into the vortex. Mesmerized.

It looks like vanilla satin ribbons, spiraling up and down together in a continuous flow, like a swirling, twirling whirlpool of soft, fluffy meringue. The wind is strong and powerful, but it's heavenly. Supernatural. Not made for human eyes.

And, I'm in a calm cylinder of cool that shoots up the middle of the vortex. Like a space elevator.

And whoosh!

I'm rocketed up, dizzy, giddy-fast, like a fantasy thrill ride. I watch the gorgeous, twirling wind. This must be what it feels like to be an astronaut. Going up, up and up....

It stops. Stomach-dropping fast. I'm flat on my back in a snow-angel position. Arms and legs out to the side.

Above my head is a golden etched halo. Perfectly round, like an escape hatch. A trap door. Dad threads his fingers together. I put my foot in his palms and he boosts me up. I bang on the golden circle until it pops up. A blinding, spectral light shines down. I hoist myself out and pull Dad up behind me. Everything is glossy white on top. Pearly Gates-ish.

There's a bright flash.

Another scene emerges.

It's the inside of a restaurant. I recognize it immediately. It's not there anymore. A place in Houston on Westheimer Road. Little secluded table in the back. Two ladies sitting there. The older one's Charlotte. The other one's me. She has her head down. Her hair was dark then. Shoulder length, flipped under on the ends. Her jaw is set, shoulders held back stiffly. She's just come from the restroom where she'd been crying. I'm pregnant. Wearing a silly, wide-collared Laura Ashley maternity dress with a floral pattern, like draperies.

My face is so ugly. What a bitter expression. I felt like I had something to prove that day. That being fired, being pregnant and being the fall-guy entitled me to steal another woman's husband. Another woman's life. I sit there woodenly, watching her with cold, dead eyes.

"You're young. You're beautiful," Charlotte says. "This infatuation with my husband—it will pass."

She looks around the restaurant self-consciously. "You can start over. Raise your children by yourself. Lots of women do it," she says. "It happens all the time."

I remember thinking she was right. That I was strong enough to do it. I felt like I'd gone too far to burn back.

With a feeling of confidence, the life-changing words were right on my tongue.

A young waitress approaches the table. Her red hair is clipped off her face with a yellow barrette. She sets Charlotte's second glass of cabernet in front of her, and the ticket between us. Charlotte and I simultaneously reach for it, hands touching. She draws hers back like she touched fire, and her wrist hits her glass. The cabernet dumps on the white table cloth, making a perfectly heart-shaped stain.

Seeing it, Charlotte throws back her head and breaks out laughing. She unsnaps her wallet and brings out a checkbook with green checks inside. Something I never expected her to do. The young lady, pouring water for another table, glances our direction and quickly looks away.

Using shaking fingers with bleeding cuticles and hard-bitten nails, Charlotte writes the date on the top and her signature on the bottom. She doesn't look up. "Give me a number, Juliana."

"I don't have one," I say.

She begins writing again. "Yes, you do." She slides the green check across the red stain. I glance down at the paltry amount, insulted she thought I had a number, but even more so that she thought it would be so low. Now I know she thinks I am complete trash.

I stand from the table, rubbing my swollen belly. "Look for your baby shower invitation in your mailbox. Don't worry – I've got your address."

The scene blurs. Fuzzy. I try to calm my breathing.

Zoom! We go up, up, up.

Clear floor below us.

I'm looking out at the vanilla swirling wind. A spiral of ribbons around me on all sides.

Speed rocket fast.

Exhilarating.

Such momentum.

And stops immediately. Whump.

Flat on my back. Smooth as glass.

A golden halo above my head. Another round door. I crawl on Dad's shoulders this time. Putting my arms above me, my palms stretched out, Dad stands tall and the door pops up. A bright light shines down. Wow, so clear and bright. Dad takes my legs and helps me get steady on top. He's able to jump through the hole and catches himself on his elbows. Just as he climbs through, there's a bright flash.

Another scene emerges. It's me.

Seated at my marble-covered vanity in my old bathroom. In the big, beautiful home where I used to live. Lined up in front of me are my cosmetics in their black Chanel cases. A round, crystal jar holds my cotton balls. The brush for my face powder has a long, sterling handle. My skin is smooth and unlined. My long fingernails are painted a deep ruby.

Behind me on the lip of the tub is a wadded piece of Christmas wrapping and a crumpled gold bow. It was my gift that year, a pendant set with several rubies, circled in diamonds. Oliver and I were attending the holiday gala at the country club that night. He insisted I open the present early.

I head to my walk-in closet. Clothing hangs from matching satin hangers, each with a pouch of potpourri, attached with a red silk bow. I pick through the section of floor-length evening dresses. Settling on a strapless ruby gown, I hang it on the back of the door and yank off the drycleaner plastic. Bare-chested and bare-bottomed, I'm wearing nothing but the ruby pendant, a garter belt, and sheer, black stockings with seams up the back.

Returning to my vanity, I lean my face close to the magnifying mirror. I apply deep brown shadow to my lids, draw thick, black eyeliner at the edge of my lashes, and then sweep them with black mascara. After rubbing blush into my cheeks, I run my fingers through my blonde curls, spray them with hairspray, and do it again. Oliver appears in the frame, immaculately-groomed with a fresh haircut, looking not much different than he does now. He slides open the middle drawer on his side of the vanity. It's where he keeps his collection of cufflinks. Picking through them with his index finger, he chooses a pair and jingles them in his palm. Coming behind me, he gives my backside a loud slap and I drop to my vanity stool. He wraps his hand behind my neck and steers my face downward as he opens the front of his silk, paisley robe. Watching his reflection in the mirror, he tosses the cufflinks in the sink and yanks my hair into a tight ponytail.

Not long, I'm reapplying my red lipstick.

Oliver swings open the thick glass door to the shower and turns the handle to the left. He runs his hand under the stream for a moment, then he steps inside.

The scene fades. Dad and I look out at the twirling air surrounding us.

The clear floor rises under our feet again. Zoom. We're twirling up like a rocket-powered corkscrew. Such an incredible rush. Faster, faster, spiraling. Taller, higher. Looking above, there's another gold halo. With an abrupt stop, we fall on our backs again. Dad puts out his hand and pulls me to my feet. I pop open the hatch and a white light shines down. I hoist myself to the next level and he climbs out behind me.

What's this? More white nothingness? What's there? A beam so bright, it hurts my eyes. Fuzzy at first, another scene begins to take shape.

I recognize this night.

Me, sitting on the couch in the family room of my old house. Almost midnight. The lights are off, but, not the television. Our Sony wide-screen, surround-sound television. Wrapped in my white, terrycloth bathrobe, with my bare feet on the glass coffee table, I'm just staring at the screen. There's a wine glass next to me. Oliver and the twins had gone to bed. I had no idea what show was on. I wasn't watching. I wasn't listening. My mind was a big squishy block of tofu. Bland, colorless, tasteless. Taking on only the flavor of whatever was stirred in.

I'd never smoked in our house before, but I strike up a Marlboro Light, right there in my own family room and smoke one after the other. I was entitled, I remember thinking. I was having a going away party. Twelve o'clock would be my birthday. My fortieth, for God's sake. With the pad and pencil in my head, I remember calculating the age I'd be when the kids graduated high school. I can stick it out. I remember thinking that, too.

Looking back, it's the night my wheels started flying off.

11:45, 46, 47, all the way to midnight. The air is thick with smoke but I can't suffocate.

Suddenly the overhead flips on. Bright as an interrogation room. A hand in the pocket of his pajama pants, Oliver is leaning against the door jamb glaring at me. Eyes like shiny, green marbles.

Looking back at the screen, I realize it's Johnny Carson that's on. Just like every night, he's on stage in front of the same striped curtain, dressed in a handsome suit, delivering his opening monologue. With the perfect combination of alluring smile and assuredness that keeps the population tuning in every night.

"Hey, Birthday Girl," Oliver smirks. "Sitting in the dark like a zombie booze-hound. This is how it starts, they say. Drinking alone."

Hand on the remote, I rub my thumb over the buttons. Finding Volume, I hold it down. The TV audience seems to think it's funny. The laugh-track blares.

Oliver blocks the screen. Neck moving up and down and side to side, his eyes search the set like he's never seen it before. He turns back around. "Hey! I'm talking to you," he yells, but Carson doesn't seem to mind. With a make-believe golf club in his hands, he cocks his hips to one side and takes his signature swing.

"You hate your life, so you hate me," Oliver says, "because I'm standing in the middle of it." Searching the bookcase, he plucks a book from the shelf. It has a black cover with gray print. He holds it up with authority.

"You should read this book on depression," he says.

"I could fucking write the book on depression!" I scream. The words bleed from my mouth.

No need to flip to the last page; I knew how the book ends. I'd read my mother's already—why, I couldn't put it down.

The scene becomes distorted until it's gone. The clear floor under our feet rises again.

We shoot up. A platform of spinning white. The propulsion halts abruptly and I'm tossed on my back. Above our heads, there's a gold-etched circle, like a manhole cover. Dad beats it open with his fist and begins pulling me behind him. I'm stuck. He keeps tugging. Something's holding me back. A thick, green chain of ivy is wrapped around my ankle. Feeling a tempered heat, I look behind me.

A steep, red cave. Straight down, like the inside of a bloody carcass. Draping from the walls are clotted vines of ivy. Snapping. Slapping. Malignant. Just like my childhood home.

A monstrous flare explodes up the middle and the funnel is fire tornado. Squinting, I can just make out the form at the base. Awash in blazing, red feathers, a firebird stands alone, clawing the glowing coals at her feet. A spike of orange feathers breaks from her flaming skull, jagged like a saw. Black, shining embers glare up at me. They're my mother's eyes.

A scalding fury consumes me. My heart pumps with such scorn and anger, it's tearing through my veins.

My life's in ruins. You did this to me and I did nothing to deserve it. When we switched roles, you stole my childhood when it was your job to take care of me. And my adulthood? It's total shit. Are you happy now? If you were a better wife, I bet you'd be alive right now.

She throws back her slender neck and opens her golden, claw-shaped beak. She screeches high and piercing, and it's a blowtorch to my mind.

I frantically strap the strong vines around my hips and secure them tightly. The only way to be free is to rip the ivy off the house. This is my singular battle to blaze. And this hate in my heart, Mother, it's all for you.

Flames blistering my arms and hands, I plunge down the burning walls. Yelling. Screaming like a mad woman, fingers scratched and bleeding, I yank down the strangling chains of ivy, pulling each stubborn link, not satisfied until they break.

At the base, I heap them at her feet. And I watch them burn.

Wings thrashing wildly, inside a cage of flaming ivy, she's a firestorm of anger and strength. As she screeches in flailing, tortured frenzy, I open my eyes wide and watch her beat her wings against the bars.

Awash in flames, bathed in fire, she burns boldly. Like a sacrifice.

Eyes burning with smoke from her blazing red plumes, nauseous from the smell of her roasting skin, I realize she's captive. She can't fly.

I feel my mother's pain. The anxiety, the claustrophobia, the mania. What it was like to be her. Living as a firebird.

And, all at once, I see my own reflection in the flames.

Just like her, I didn't do anything. Except for blaming. Just to punish her, I stayed away, and she died not knowing that I loved her. When she died in the car accident, something happened inside of me. Everything I did was my choice; I can no longer lay the blame at her feet. I can no longer hold my guilt. My guilt for not loving her enough.

Everything she did for me was in love.

The chains of ivy go limp in my hands.

And, I forgive her.

Feeling a touch on my shoulder, I turn around.

I don't know how long he's been there, but it's Dad by my side.

He steps forward toward the burning cage. "I'm staying here."

I yank him back.

"When we wake from this dream, I'm not leaving without you."

"She can't burn alone." He hangs his head and cries. "I owe her that much for everything I've done. It's unforgivable."

"Daddy, all you can do is forgive her."

He breaks down, his face red and twisted. "I didn't save you," he cries. "And, I took your mother from you."

"I forgive you, Daddy." I hug him close.

"Please forgive me, Daddy, for staying away. Forgive me for not bringing your grandchildren around. I'm sorry."

He squeezes me tight. "Don't ever think for a moment I didn't love you."

"It's why we've been in this storm together," I say. "To save each other."

Forgiveness for ourselves. It's the hardest forgiveness to accept of all.

Dad steps toward the cage. "I love you, sweetheart." He drops to his knees. "I forgive you."

Thrashing her wings with a final burst of fierce energy, the firebird knocks down the bleeding walls of the cage. She ducks her head to her breast and pulls her charred, red feathers around her body like a cloak.

The fire sputters.

One after another, in a chain reaction, the charred, brittle leaves become white and crumbly as spent fireplace coals; the ivy has turned to ash.

An opening forms at the top of the funnel's looping spiral.

The firebird lifts her head, spreads her wings and rises from the ashes.

Firebird is just another name for Phoenix.

And, she takes flight.

Flying higher and higher, she casts a glowing, white aura.

Red feathers change to white.

And she's the dove.

Released through the hole in the top of the vortex, she flies free.

What feels like my mother's spirit rushes over me and I'm filled with an exhilarating sensation of immense gratitude and benevolent mercy.

Free-dancing. I'm like a twirling ballerina. Like a mirage. A collage of me, in a beautiful dream. Surrounded by a force field, of pure powerful creative raw electric energy. It's a renewal. A circle that never ends. It's why we're inside a living vortex, with the same wind that revolves up and down and back again over and over. Feeding on itself and rejuvenating.

A crackling noise, like a string of firecrackers.

I turn and look at Dad and he's glowing. See-through. Luminous under his skin. What looks like flashing sparklers shoot through his veins, up his legs, from his fingers up his arms, through his heart, up his neck and his brain. Last of all, energy sparks from the tips of his hair.

From the excitement in his sparkling eyes, I see my reflection. It's happening to me, too. Leaning back, I'm floating in it. Pure energy and love.

And, I'm free.

The revolving spiral lifts us up.

Almost to the top, there's a luminous light. And a little girl under a tree. Head bowed, her arms are wrapped around her knees. Believing it's Lindsey, I call out to her. She raises her face and I see it's little Jules. The little eight-year-old girl wearing the orange halter top and groovy striped corduroys. Me, from the dream.

Feeling the strongest maternal instinct, I scoop her up and hug her to me. Her face inches from mine, she's endlessly fascinated with me. She touches my eyelids. Plays with my cheeks. Pulls the wrinkles to the sides of my mouth.

"From now on, everything's just fine." I put my hand to her soft cheek. "I'll never let anyone hurt you again."

I look up at Dad and his eyes are glowing and misty.

Each of us with a hand on her back, we lead her out together. To the ultimate. The crown of the vortex.

The air is buzz-charged, daredevil-exciting and peppermint-cool. I can feel it in my lungs. It seems like we're on the top of a boat dock. An observation deck. Curls blowing, I raise my hand to my brow and take in the view. But, it's not like the view of a mountain or an office building, or anything like that. It's white.

Brilliant, dazzling white. Magnificent. As far as the eye can see.

In her sweet little voice, little Jules says, "Daddy, I missed you."

He picks her up and bounces her playfully on his hip. "There's no need for that ever again." He smiles.

"We're home."

## CHAPTER SEVENTY-SIX

❖   ❖   ❖

It seems like someone's always ringing the doorbell. Jeez, what is it now?

Spaced-out and woozy, I get up and trudge down the hallway. Feels like I haven't slept, or for that matter, brushed my teeth in a week. Heading down the stairs, I catch my hand on the rail and look down at my arm. Seeing Dad's leather jacket, I remember. Or at least, I think I do.

The doorbell rings again.

"Keep your shirt on," I call. Oh, Lord. I'm starting to sound like him.

Dashing through the living room, I look down at my lug-soled boots. Mud's smeared on my jeans.

I was curled up in a ball at the foot of Dad's bed when Mr. Read shook my shoulders. Having lost all concept of time, I'm not sure really what time it was—just that the light was dim. Before leaving, I cozied Dad's quilt around him and asked him how he felt about everything we saw. A million miles of life, really. He didn't know what I was talking about.

Did it really happen at all?

Making it to the entryway, I catch a glimpse of myself in the mirror. Wild, tangled curls. Cheeks red and chapped. I crack open the door.

It's the postman, wearing a blue uniform and matching cap.

He smiles. "Certified letter for Ms. Juliana Birdsong."

Those are never good news. Please, please, please don't be from Oliver.

He pulls it from the satchel slung over his shoulder. "I have a pen if you don't have one."

There's a hanging basket suspended from the eaves.

What's that doing there?

An airplane plant with new babies spilling over the edge, like parachutes.

"Just need your signature right here." He points at the designated spot.
"Oh, right." I scribble it down.
"Have a blessed day, ma'am," he says.
"You, too." Words barely out of my mouth, I stare at the yard in awe.

Draping rosemary in the concrete planters. Sturdy boxwood hedges line the sidewalk. A couple of pink-blooming crepe myrtles by the street and a purple mountain laurel in full bloom.

I stumble down the steps. All the scraggly, ratty throwaway plants from the nursery? Adam and I got them in the ground that day, but they looked nothing like this.

Drenched in color, the yard has gone completely crazy.

Fuchsia bougainvillea explodes out of the terracotta pots. Azaleas in the beds at the base of the house.

Plump, violet heads of hydrangea. And grass?

I kick off my boots and feel the thick, lush blades under my toes.

Well, I've heard it said, but until now, I never believed it.

After a fire, everything comes back greener than before.

I had to go through a rocket of time to know my identity. Discovery went through me like an arrow. I knew what I wanted to do, because I'd always known. It's been inside me all along.

We all know what a birthplace is. How about a rebirth place?

Everything about ourselves, we have the power to change.

No matter what the season, the yard will never be without luscious color. And, all year long, there'll be the ivy. I have a feeling it'll be more manageable now. Every time I see it, I'll thank my mother for all the good she did for me. Like a tough, sturdy vine, she made me strong.

When rain comes again, and it will, I believe I'll use a rain barrel to collect the water for my plants *inside*.

As I begin walking down the driveway to retrieve the trash cart, I tear the seal on the envelope. Well, I'll be damned. What have we here? It's a handwritten letter from Jan. On beautiful hand-painted stationery that I feel certain she made especially for me. Created in swirling water colors.

I read her loving words, and I'm grateful.

What's that old phrase—life's too short?

Lord, help me be a better me.

## CHAPTER SEVENTY-SIX

❖ ❖ ❖

I pull off my white Speed Racer helmet and hand it to Adam. Deja vu. I hated having helmet hair back when Dad would pick me up from school, so when Adam gives me the "forget-it" look, I understand—but it certainly doesn't keep me from saying, "Do it," in my mom voice.

He does, and slides behind me on the cycle.

"Okay, where to?" I ask.

"Thundercloud Subs," Adam says.

It's the middle-school hangout.

Adam leans and sways with me as we cruise the Indian from the middle school down Walsh Tarleton Drive and squeeze into the only vacant spot in front of the sub shop. Adam quickly throws his leg over the cycle seat and joins a group of friends. The sidewalk is crowded with shaggy-haired boys in sagging jeans, carrying skateboards. Rap music is playing.

You've got to love that Snoop Dog.

"Hi, Mrs. Morrissey," a giggly voice behind me says. It's Lindsey's best friend Caroline, with her black spiral-curls.

"Caroline, sweetie. I've missed you."

"I've missed you, too," she says. She touches my little circular side mirror and laughs. "Linds told me about your cooool cycle. I never thought I'd see you on one of these."

I don't appreciate being made fun of by an eighth grader. Much less Caroline, who used to think I hung the moon. She's gotten taller in the few months since I've seen her. For what a help she's been to Lindsey, I'm so thankful for her. If I were Lindsey's age, she'd be my best friend, too. And I'm thankful for Caroline's mother, too.

Caroline smiles, showing a mouth full of braces with pink wires. She wraps her arms around my neck and hugs me. Looking over her shoulder, I see my daughter.

Lindsey's sitting at the wooden picnic table out front. Still wearing the black eyeliner, dangle earrings and a too-mini mini skirt. There's a boy sitting next to her. Zac Zively. Creepy little punk. He's wearing green, skinny-legged jeans and his limp, brown hair hangs into his eyes. I can see from here that he has acne. Their faces are only inches apart. He puts his hand behind her neck and pulls her toward him. The kiss lasts a full five seconds. My breath catches. Now I know. She'll do anything he tells her.

Over my dead body

Adam steps back onto the asphalt and hands me the helmet. He'd been showing it to his friends. I turn to tell him thanks and see that most of the kids are looking at me. Including Lindsey. The Indian rumbles loudly and I rev the engine just for fun.

I peel off my shades, and Lindsey and I make eye contact. She's looking at me like she hates me. I'm sure right now she does, but that's too damn bad.

I beckon Zac to me with my finger. Two boys beside him start to hoot, and he punches one of them in the arm.

Lindsey leans close to him. I read her lips: Don't go. She's a bitch.

Guilty as charged.

I wheel to the edge of the parking lot and wait for them. Adam quickly rushes to Lindsey's side and says something to her. She hisses back at him. Finally, she and Zac start walking toward me slowly. He's not much taller than she is. He probably weighs about 120.

"Hi, Mom," Lindsey says through her teeth.

"Hello, Lindsey." I smile sweetly. "Don't you want to introduce me to your little friend?"

He shoves his hands in his pockets.

"This is Zac Zively, Mom," Lindsey says.

I ignore her don't-you-dare-embarrass-me look.

"I'm Lindsey's mother, Ms. Birdsong," I say.

Zac doesn't even put out his hand, look me in the eye or anything.

He's a sullen little shit.

"You're in Lindsey's class, is that right, Zac?"

He looks at his high-top tennis shoes. Laces loose, the ends are frayed and dark. His T-shirt has the red, blue and yellow Wonder Bread logo.

"Heh-heh," he chuckles. "Not hardly."

"I beg your pardon," I say innocently. "You're in seventh grade, then?"

"Mom, stop it." Lindsey flares her nostrils. I keep my eyes on Zac until he finally answers.

"I'm a junior," he says.

"Well, all right then, junior. Don't you know any kiddos your own age?"

The tops of his cheeks turn pink.

"Is that why you have to hang out with middle schoolers?"

"Zac, don't listen to her," Lindsey says.

"The school has called us in about you picking up Lindsey in your yellow Hyundai during school hours." I point at his vehicle.

Lindsey sucks in her breath. "They did?"

Well, no. But she doesn't have to know that.

She tugs his arm protectively. His hands stay in his pockets.

I rest both arms on my handlebars. "So, listen up, junior. I'm going to give your mother a call so we can chat." I hold up my phone.

"You don't scare me," he sneers. "She's at work."

"That's okay. I got her cell number from the school directory."

Lindsey tightens her grip on Zac's bicep.

Pick up lady. Pick up. Five rings. Pick up.

He doesn't crack, but one cheek quivers.

"Hello?" His mother sounds cranky.

"This is Juliana Birdsong, Lindsey Morrissey's mother," I say. "Lindsey is the middle-schooler who your son Zac is dating."

He gives me the stink eye.

"Mrs. Birdsong, you said? What's he done now?"

He hears his mother's voice. Now he knows I'm not playing.

"Your son has been picking up my daughter in his car and they've been leaving school together. She's barely fourteen. And it needs to stop."

Heard enough, Zac slings his backpack over his shoulder.

"Trust me, it already has." Mrs. Zivley clicks off.

Lindsey's eyes open wide as Zac strides quickly toward his Hyundai.

It's at the end of the parking lot.

Lindsey calls after him. He doesn't turn around.

She cuts her eyes to me.

Then she runs.

She makes it to the passenger side as the engine starts. She tries the locked door. She knocks on the window. The car's in reverse now, backing up. She screams his name, "Zaaaaa-aaac!" She watches his tail lights as his car pulls onto the street. Standing on the blistering pavement in her dark eye makeup, dangle earrings, and new black boots with a heel, my daughter looks so small.

Robotic, she looks over her shoulder to see every kid at in the parking lot tuned in to her little show. Her blue eyes tick from one face to the next.

Adam steps in front of the crowd.

"That's my twin sister, so turn around, you freaking douche bags!" he yells. Every kid looks away. I've never seen Adam so angry. Like he'll kill them with his bare hands. He bolts to Lindsey and wraps his arms around her and whispers something in her ear.

Moments later, they both walk toward me.

I scoot up on the seat as far as I can. Lindsey slides behind me.

And, Adam after that.

# CHAPTER SEVENTY-SEVEN

❖ ❖ ❖

My same smiling waiter wears a black tie and a crisp, white apron tied around his waist. He fills my water glass to the brim.

"Why look, darling, it's Joseph," I say. "Remember the man who served us the last time we were here?"

Oliver raises an eyebrow. "Should I?"

Joseph takes out his pad. "Dirty martini with extra olives, for you sir?"

Oliver gives him the okay symbol. His gold cufflinks sparkle in the light.

As he turns from the table, Joseph's eyes light on my white, shiny helmet. "I'd be happy to hold that up front for you, ma'am."

Oliver coughs.

I shake my head. "Thanks all the same, but I'll keep it here."

Watching him head into the kitchen, I notice the young hostess with the flowered sundress and freckled back circulating through the dining room with the rolling desert cart. Lingering at a table of pinstriped businessmen, she inclines her head in their direction. One of them places his hand on her back. She fetches the silver coffee pot. As she begins pouring for the table, she looks over at me.

Oliver gives me a nudge. "You know, Juliana, these new getups of yours are starting to grow on me. In fact, you'll be wearing these leather chaps a lot." He strokes my leg under the table. "Up on all fours with your naked ass up in the air."

Taking a sip of water, I focus on the gleaming, mahogany-paneled wall over his head, still hung with vintage boxing posters.

He keeps stroking my leg. "Don't think I'm insensitive as to how demeaning it was for you to grovel on the phone so I'd meet you here today."

He abruptly pushes me flat on the leather seat and gives me his megapixel smile. "Looks like we're stuck together, babe, aren't we? You just can't seem to let me go." He kisses me deeply and thoroughly.

Joseph's back with the garlic bread and Oliver's cocktail. He sets a glass of iced tea in front of me. It has a fresh sprig of mint. As I smooth my curls, he raises the lid from the sugar jar and produces a silver iced tea spoon from the pocket of his stiff, white apron. With a smile.

I blow a stray curl from my eye. "I'm famished, Joseph," I say.

"Still the petit filet, medium rare, ma'am?"

I raise my hand to my heart and smile up at him. "You remembered?"

He takes Oliver's steak knife and scoops a smidgen of creamed spinach from the tablecloth. Oliver immediately checks to see if his cuffs are green.

"See, darling? It's what I love about this place," I say. "They're so professional."

"And, not to worry, sir." Joseph taps his temple. "I recall your preference, as well."

Oliver snorts as Joseph leaves the table.

"How in the world does he remember all that, Oliver? It's been almost a year since we were here last. "

He waves to a table of men across the way. "My shirts are ready at the laundry, babe. Do you mind?"

I hold up my index finger. "Hold that thought." I lean under the table and pull a manila folder from my satchel. "My dike attorney was good enough to draw up our divorce decree," I say. "Take a few minutes to look it over, and then sign it."

Oliver's lips upturn slightly on the edges. "Let her know that was really sweet of her, but I don't think so."

I take a sip of my iced tea.

Hugging a stack of leather-bound menus to her chest, the hostess swishes through the dining room and seats a group of stuffy, pinstriped lawyers at the center table.

Oliver watches her hand around the menus as he slides his phone from his suit pocket. "Just for grins, how about you tell me what's in it."

"A large monthly child support payment and huge alimony, as well as 60% of the community property," I say. "Just to keep everyone honest, my forensic accountant, Señor Sanchez, has constructed a full accounting of our portfolio including your creative stock and cash locations. On the house ownership, Olive was able to confirm that it was a gift to both of us and I'll be taking my percentage of its value, as well."

He glances up from his phone. "Did you have a little nip on the way over here?"

The restaurant is filling up. Not many stools left at the bar.

"You didn't ask, Oliver, but on the children, it provides for joint custody since I would never dream of keeping them from both their parents." I look him in the eye. "Because, unlike you, I'm not a dick."

"One of the things I've always been thankful for, my sweet bride."

I drum my nails on my shiny helmet. "Care to reconsider, cupcake?"

"Pass."

I take my phone from inside my helmet and begin dialing. "Mike Magruder, please. This is Juliana Birdsong." I lower the phone and slip off my earring. "I didn't realize that was you. How are you sweet potato?" I'm using my light, bubbly girlfriend voice. I whisper to Oliver. "It's your secretary, Carol."

He scrolls through his messages. "Wonder why you're calling Mike."

I cover the phone with my hand. "I am suing him and he doesn't know it yet," I say. "As a friend, I thought he should hear it from me."

Stroking the bare skin above his lip, he smiles.

"Absolutely, Carol," I say. "I'd love to have lunch to catch up."

Oliver waves to a group of men pulling up to the bar.

"This week? All right, Carol." I pull my calendar from my satchel. "What day looks good?" I cover the phone again. "I have a list of the partnership's 'off-the-book' cases. He's been hiding your fees, which makes him implicated in taking money from the partnership. In case you haven't read up on it, the income made by the partnership is community property." I hold up my hand. "Carol said to hold on a minute. She had to catch another line."

Joseph stops by the table with the bill. "I'll go ahead and put this right here," he says. "No rush."

"Oh, get that, will you, Oliver?" I say.

He takes a hundred dollar bill from his wallet and tosses it on the table.

"You're a lamb," I say.

Joseph picks it up. I mouth to him, "Keep the change."

I turn back to Oliver. "And, as a partnership is viewed as being one and the same as its owners, I am suing the firm. Mike doesn't know that yet, either. Suits are public record, so everyone in town will find out what you've done to screw me over, which could potentially be devastating to the partnership and your reputations."

Smiling, Oliver lifts the edge of the first page.

"Sure, Carol, Friday's great. What's that? Oh, no problem. I don't mind." I look up at Oliver. "Mike's always been a little longwinded but Carol said he's almost off his call." I pause. "Knowing him as I do, I feel safe in assuming that he would be displeased that you're bringing the firm down in flames. Whether he'll give a rat's ass that you're shagging his wife is debatable."

Eyes tender, Oliver begins raising his hand to my cheek.

"However, I'm sure he'll be really pissed that because he's been helping you hide the money from me, I'm suing him for every nickel he's got." I crinkle my nose flirtatiously. "The Lord works in mysterious ways."

Mike answers.

"It's great to hear your voice," I say. "We just never talk like we used to."

Oliver says, "Give me the phone."

"You know, Mike, I hadn't seen Mary Ellen in a while, but she was by the house the other day wearing the cutest leopard swimsuit." I pause. "For a little while, that is."

Oliver yanks the phone out of my hand. "Mike, buddy. My phone's out of juice so I'm using Juliana's. Are we still on for hitting balls at six at the club? See you then."

He deliberately slides my phone across the table. "You think you're really cute, don't you?"

I bat my lashes and smile sweetly.

"You're blackmailing me," he says.

"It's called leverage, dear."

Not breaking eye contact, he flips to the back page and signs.

The hostess brings him another dirty martini. In a roadie cup.

He looks up at her. "Well, thanks good looking, but I didn't order this."

"It's from the two men at the bar." She points.

Oliver looks over his shoulder with a puzzled expression.

Turning around on his stool, Richard winks at him and raises his glass.

Wally shoots him the bird.

Joseph comes behind Oliver's chair and delicately sets a white Styrofoam container in front of him.

"When the lady called ahead, she said you'd be taking yours to-go."

Oliver's cheeks sag.

"Now, don't pout, babe. This could be a period of real growth for you," I say. "Maybe you'll be that changed man after all."

# CHAPTER SEVENTY-EIGHT

❖ ❖ ❖

Adam piles out of the convertible and collapses on the rock planter that circles the biggest oak tree. Sweat trickles down his forehead and his RunTex T-shirt is completely soaked. Fritz by his side, Rich is in a black, micro-fiber tank and wind shorts. He and Adam look so much alike, it's spooky. Slamming the car door shut, Rich gives me the thumbs up, meaning Adam finally ran the entire five-mile loop on Town Lake without stopping. Months of endurance training paid off.

No one was more surprised than Adam that he'd actually enjoy running. Except maybe his sister. He wipes the sweat from his ear and then dials his phone. Even halfway across the parking lot, I know it's Lindsey he's calling. Of course he'd want to tell her first. His face breaks into a huge grin. They communicate in a language all their own.

It's like Richard reads my mind. We look at each other and smile.

Adam hangs up and unties the laces of his new running shoes. "I'm going to bomb the audition big-time, Uncle Rich," he says.

Adam hasn't auditioned for the new band yet. He says he wants to, but he's too freaked out to play in front of real live people. When I pointed out that he's done it plenty of times in front of Paolo, he said that's different. Way different.

"Listen, I know you can do it, man," Richard says. "When you're scared of something, you have to look your fear in the face." He pauses for dramatic effect. "And touch it."

Adam stares at him blank-faced. "How about just imagining the audience in their underwear?" he says. "That's what Paolo said to do."

"Okay, that's creepy," Richard says. "Try this instead: Imagine the worst it can be."

"What do you think I've been doing?"

Richard leans into him intently. "Do it again. I'm serious. But this time, squeeze everything you can out of the fear."

I can't wait to see Adam's reaction. He groans.

"Are you?" Richard says.

Adam pinches his eyes closed.

"Now, if you'll hold the fear close and stand very still, the fear will run on past." Richard says. "Like a tiger."

Adam cracks one lid open. "No offense, but that's stupid."

Bruised, Richard leans his palms against the tree and extends his legs behind him one at a time. It's his hamstring stretch.

"Mom," Adam says. "You said you'd take me up to see Grandad."

I'm up to my knees in dirt, as usual. Richard built a trellis of wire and post. Now it's looped with passion vine. Don't plant passion vine where you can't contain it, I've heard. It's aggressive stuff.

"We'd be there already if I didn't have to be the little red hen," I say, and cover another hydrangea plant with dirt. "It'd be nice if I could get a little help over here."

No reaction. Thanks, guys.

Adam picks up his guitar case and bumps his uncle with it. "Will you take me then?"

A cloud comes over Richard's face as he struggles with the right thing to do.

He walks to the flowerbed and kneels down beside me. "What's left, Jules?" he says. "Give me a job to do."

I lower my sunglasses and cock my eyebrow at him.

"Son, you know I can't go to Sagecrest without taking a shower," I say, not breaking eye contact with Richard. "Why not bring your guitar and play for the residents?"

"No way." Adam wipes the sweat from his face. "It's all grownups. I can't do that."

"I don't think they'll mind if you mess up." Richard takes the spade and shoves it into the dirt. "The good news is, they won't remember if you do."

I elbow him.

"Bet you didn't know I took guitar back in the day, Adam. After your grandmother said no to art lessons."

That's right. It makes sense now.

"It's not like I had your kind of talent, but I do wonder what happened to my old guitar."

"This is it. Mom gave it to me." Adam unzips the case and holds up the guitar.

Richard narrows his eyes at me.

I shrug. "Hey, it was just sitting in your room."

"Hand it over, sport," he says.

Adam throws the strap over Richard's shoulder. It's black with red diamonds.

"Go, Uncle Rich," Adam says excitedly. "Can you play anything?"

"Dude, I haven't touched the guitar since high school," he says.

He rests the guitar on his knee, and then strums a few chords. He presses the strings on the frets and deliberately turns the neck pegs. He picks a tune that sounds vaguely like "Color My World," but I can't be sure.

He sucks air through his teeth. "So, what are you waiting on? Let's beat it down to Sagecrest," he says. "And, we'll swing by to get your sister. That sound cool?"

Adam slides his running shoes back on and begins lacing them.

Richard gives me a wink and sprints behind Adam to the convertible. He throws the guitar in the back and revs the engine. Adam toots the horn as they pull onto the street.

I holler after them, "Hey! Don't forget this damn dog."

Adam throws open the passenger door and Fritz jumps inside. I wait until they're out of sight to pull off my gloves, yank the bandana from my hair, raise my arms over my head and scream.

"Jeez, finally. It's about time he did that." Wally moseys across the parking lot and pulls me to him. "Sharing your children, you've given your brother an incredible gift."

"Give me a minute, and I've got one for you, too."

I quickly walk over to the Indian and take a pretty little package out of my satchel. Wally looks excited when I put it in his hands. Who doesn't like a special present? This time, I think I've outdone myself. I really do.

He rips off the blue wrapping paper and the frilly pink bow on top.

Seeing the little gray egg carton inside, he looks up at me, question mark on his face.

I pluck one out and place it gently in his hand.

"It's symbolic," I say. "Mine was dangerously close to its expiration date, but believe it or not, the fertility specialist said it's probably still okay."

Wally cups the egg in his hands and stares down at it for several moments. Looking back at me, tears are streaming down his face.

"I'm sure those are tears of joy, thinking you'll be having sex with me," I say. "But, before you get too excited, I had a surrogate in mind."

Laughing, he wraps his arms around me. "Having a baby Birdsong is the only thing that could turn Richard around. You're a genius, Jules."

I unwrap his arms and back up slowly. "Hear me when I tell you this Wally. This egg is for you and only you," I say. "No strings attached."

# CHAPTER SEVENTY-NINE

❖ ❖ ❖

Wind whips through my hair and I'm cold.

The day is heavy. And gray. And, I want to remember it. I don't want to forget the pain I suffered to get here.

Walking the concrete path to the courthouse, I clutch my purse to my side. I stand, dwarfed by the massive, limestone courthouse. Tall, carved letters above the entrance read:

COURAGE     SACRIFICE     PERSERVERANCE

I stand in a crowded line to enter this place where crazy husbands brandish pistols and blow away judges and ex-wives. There's the jingle of keys as I put them in the bowl and they pass through the metal detector. I place my purse on the conveyor belt and remove it at the end.

Why can't I get that stupid George Jones song out of my head? "He Stopped Loving Her Today."

Anabel rushes through the perpendicular hallway at the far end of the clamorous lobby, ten minutes past late. Traffic, she says. Yeah, right. But I don't care. She's tending to my business and her second client's before the judge. The client is 55ish, bright, white, well-trimmed beard. We squeeze together on a backless, wooden bench.

"I'm sorry we had to meet under these circumstances," he says.

I smile meekly and wish he would shut up.

We walk down the hall to some clerk's office—for what I don't know. Crap. Of all the people to see, there's Mike Magruder. The man who'd gut me with the same ruthless objective as any insurance company.

"Hey, Juliana." He smiles with his canine teeth. "Oliver's paperwork should be ready and waiting for you. Nothing else to worry about," he says. "Great to see you, by the way. How are you?"

He leans forward effusively, like he intends to hug me. To make everything all better.

Anabel steps forward. "Move along, Magruder."

He stiffens. "Here to gloat, Ms. Brock?" he says.

She looks him up and down. "Not my style," she says. "My mother raised me to be a lady."

"Well, don't give up," he says. "You may make it, yet."

Anabel doesn't even blink. "You know what, Magruder?"

"What's that, precious?"

"I know you've got way too many cases to ever read your boiler plate," she says. "So, if you'll kindly refer to page sixty-two, you'll see that Oliver is paying my legal fees."

Mike's jaw drops.

"Now, go refill your Viagra prescription," she says and takes my elbow. Her white-bearded client pushes the door open and Anabel guides me inside.

"Hey, Juliana," Mike calls after me.

I whip my head in his direction.

"Be safe and remember to buckle up when you drive home later." He smiles.

Without looking, Anabel reaches behind her and slams the door. The walls rattle.

Now in front of the clerk's desk, she pulls out a document for me to sign; I don't know or especially care what.

Anabel hands me a pen. I can't find the line for my signature. The clerk pushes the document closer. I sign, the clerk stamps it, and transfers the document to a wire basket.

We ride the elevator to the fourth floor. I watch my shoes.

Anabel small talks to lighten the awkward position she's been in jillions of times. She must enjoy it about as much as slicing her tongue on an envelope.

Anabel, Whitebeard and I enter the quiet courtroom that's filled with sad, miserable people. No one smiles. They look straight ahead. No one makes eye contact in this place on purpose. If no one sees you, then you don't see them, so you weren't really here.

A three-foot-high sign to the left of the door reads:
NO SMOKING IN THE COURTROOM

An unreasonable request to me. What else are you supposed to do in here? Who in this room isn't smoking mad?

The tall pink columns aren't granite, but actually faux-painted, a fact made obvious by the dummy "granite" switch plates on them. The ornamental reliefs are poured resin, not carved. The short swinging doors are wood-look Formica. The details actually pretend convincingly until you sit there for a while, scrutinizing everything in the room as you're crying like a broken, naïve fool. Realizing they're as false as my hologram of a husband. Artificial as my friendships. As counterfeit as my make-believe life.

I've already been at the courthouse for three hours. Now, I wait for my allotted time to step before the judge.

Anabel leans over and whispers, "Come sit back down here after your part is done, and we three will walk out together."

What the fuck for? So I can sit here for another hour while she waits for Whitebeard's case to come up?

"After I go before the judge, can't I just walk out?"

She blinks. I can't believe that my question is such a novel concept. Am I the only person who's ever asked?

"Well, I guess you could," she says, "If you sign these orders now."

Which I do, even though my name is listed Juliana Carmen Morrissey. Not Juliana Birdsong.

It's my turn before the commanding judge.

Doesn't he have anything better to do? He wears a choir robe and stupid gold half-glasses. He looks at me sternly, so tickled he has authority over me. Sitting behind the bench. So big and important. A handsome man, but not today.

"Raise your right hand," he says. "Do you promise to tell the truth, the whole truth and that all matters of question will be true?" His eyes bear down on me hard.

"Yes, sir."

He asks me five questions. Couldn't tell you what they are. Just that I answer yes to every question except one:

"Is there any possibility of your marriage reconciling?"

I focus on his sharp pupils. "No, sir. There is not."

I walk through the heavy door.

"53rd DISTRICT" is etched deeply in the glass.

I do exactly what I planned to do when I walked in this damn limestone courthouse first thing this morning. I drop to the hard bench outside the courtroom door, and I begin sobbing. No one seems concerned, much less notice. Not the woman beside me in the lime-green suit who's watching the clock with an open book spread across her lap. I deserve a good cry.

COURAGE      SACRIFICE      PERSERVERANCE

Well, no shit.
I've got a new freedom.

## CHAPTER EIGHTY

❖ ❖ ❖

No better place for me this evening than Sagecrest. I need to hang out with my sweet dad. We'll go down to supper and have a good meal. Mr. Read wasn't kidding when he said the food's not exactly four-star, but the fried chicken's pretty decent. And their mashed potatoes and gravy? They're delish.

I can never pass Mrs. Calloway without speaking. She's still waiting on the plaid sofa, wearing her violet suit and Christmas pin. I plop down next to her and take her soft hand. Her huge blue eyes blink at me, magnified comically behind her lenses. She smiles, lipstick on her teeth.

"Good morning, ma'am," I say.

"Hello, dear," she says with a sunny expression.

She turns to a man sitting on the lounge chair next to her. He's punching numbers into his cell phone. He's a tall man, large frame. Thinning brown hair. I'd guess about thirty-five.

"Have you met Juliana Birdsong?" she asks him.

"What's that you say?" He doesn't look up.

Mrs. Calloway sighs and folds her hands in her lap. "Juliana Birdsong," she says, more loudly this time.

With a peculiar searching expression, he looks at my forehead and then my chin.

I give him my best smile and put out my hand. "And you must be?"

"I'm Carson Calloway."

I raise my hands in a praying gesture.

Her son. He finally came. I didn't think he actually existed.

"Your mother's a special friend of mine," I say.

Mrs. Calloway sparkles. She looks at him adoringly. "My son, he knows the good places to eat," she says, and takes his arm as he escorts her to the parking lot.

Making my way through the lobby, I dodge a pale, wrinkled man recklessly piloting a wheelchair to the men's room. I flatten myself against the wall as an orderly wheels past with a hospital bed.

"Hey, lady!"

Turning, I look down the corridor and see my old friend, Mr. Read.

"I hope your day wasn't too terrible," he says.

I wiggle my hand back and forth. "You know, all and all it didn't turn out too bad." Understatement of all time.

Stepping into the rec room – it's bingo day – he pauses and looks over his shoulder at me. Maximum energy. As if he's looking into my soul.

He shoots me a kissable smile. "Ready to start over again," he says. "Say the word, Ms. Birdsong, and I'll come a running."

I tilt my head and look at him. Before I can answer, a couple of giggling female residents from inside the rec room call his name. Still not taking his eyes off me as they begin pulling him inside, he winks.

Hot damn.

This day's doing nothing but getting better.

At Dad's room, I crack the door and look inside. The room is now filled with blooming flowers where his beautiful paintings were not so long ago. But, strangely, the air is thick with the smell of oil paints.

The easel is set up in the window. A man sits before it. His broad shoulders are muscled like a young man's. Wearing a white, loose-collared shirt with the sleeves rolled back, he ricochets back and forth across the easel. He paints with passionate abandon, as if the canvas must seize each ounce of his creative genius before it escapes. He swirls his brush on his palette, then in one fluid movement, he forms a graceful curve on the canvas with a single brushstroke of silver.

Breathing hard, he stops and sets the brush and pallet on the tray of the easel, then takes a white rag and wipes the paint from his hands. After stretching his back and shoulders, he leans forward and rests his arms against the open window frame. His muscles seem to relax and his breathing calms as he stares out at the still sky.

Uncomfortable for intruding on the visitor's privacy, I begin backing from the doorway just as he reaches for the water glass beside him. He turns his head just slightly. Thick curls loop down his forehead and sweat shines at his temples. As he raises the glass to his lips, a ray of light breaks across his clear lenses and glints off the gold rims.

My heart stops. A halting paralysis.

It's my father.

I begin to call out to him, but the words catch in my throat.

After a few sips, he returns the glass to the table.

I study his profile as he looks at the sky again. From his curved lips, I can tell he's content and peaceful. My heart beats again, pumped with a feeling of love. Like the world's most powerful, purest love. Impossible to top. It takes my breath away. Reaching for him, I rush across the room.

Hearing my footsteps, he turns and smiles.

I stare at the image in front of me.

Gleaming and glossy, its paint still wet, the canvas is light and color.

Edge to edge, it's the same full-spectrum, rainbow palette that broke through the clouds in the dream. It's a different painting style for him.

Loose and free. Full of fierce, electric artistry.

Now I know that regaining his desire to paint once again is my father's renewal. His healing gift from the benevolent funnel cloud.

In the middle of the canvas is the luminous image of a woman. She sits astride a gleaming silver, vintage motorcycle with the word *Indian* scripted on the side. She's a beautiful woman with vibrant blue eyes who I'd have never recognized before, but here she is. And, her strong hands seem to clutch the chrome handlebars with confidence.

I reach back and take my father's hand. Squeezing it tightly, he leans up and kisses my cheek, then reaches for his brush in the tray.

Gazing down at it, he begins shaping its wet bristles gently, then slowly raises his eyes to the painting and begins fluttering his nimble fingers.

It's the sound that comes first.

A rumbling engine. The rush of tires on pavement.

Wind whistles past my ears.

The air pulses with raw, penetrating energy.

Daredevil excitement.

Last, the familiar smell of exhaust and tar.

Then I feel it.

Zest!

And, the painting comes alive.

I lean into the twists and turns of the pavement as I slice through the darkness like the sharp, silver blade of a knife. Thighs clenched tight, my chest flattened over the gas tank, I understand my father's solitary thrill. His urge to travel to the end of space and time.

## PAINTING JULIANA

My long curls trailing behind me, I chase the monstrous train with the face of a mean, angry robot. The engine of our loyal, beloved Indian screams like a chainsaw.

Wide-open-throttle …65…80…90… The needle climbs.

Blurring past, I overtake the train like it's standing still.

Nnneeaoowww!

I like the wind in my face, like a rebel. I feel alive.

I steer the handlebars; I'm always driving now.

Aerodynamic, airborne and rocket-powered, I'm Juliana Birdsong.

Fearless.

And I fly.


THE END

# GRATEFUL ACKNOWLEDGEMENTS

First, I'd like to thank my amazing and generous publisher, Steven A. Anderson of Goldminds Publishing for giving me this opportunity.

To the brilliant writer David Marion Wilkinson, who also happens to be my loving husband, thank you sweetheart. You were there for me night and day and you shared with me absolutely everything you had to give. I doubt I'll ever be able to make it up to you, but I'll try.

To my glorious daughters, Katherine and Natalie Banister, thank you for believing in me even though you thought I was crazy, and to my wonderful mother Mary Louise Strain and my sweet sister Claire Duesing, thank you for lovingly nudging me along. I'd also like to say thank you to my incredible stepsons, Tate and Dean Wilkinson.

I'd like to acknowledge the input of psychotherapists Carol Cofer MSSW and Thomas G. Parker PhD, and family law attorney, Lea C. Noelke J.D.. I'd also like to thank my editors Betty Kelly Sargent, John Paine and Sarah Nawrocki, as well as Goldminds editors Suella Walsh, Larry Walsh and Ellen Gray Massey.

Special thanks and appreciation goes out to the incomparable consultants Ken Markham and Cheryl Chaddick. Your advice and insight were invaluable and I'm grateful. And, to my loyal friends and confidants Mark Lacy, Joan Winter, Chris Casanova, Leigh Simmons, Rebecca Ridge and Nathalie Elliot, thank you for always being my unwavering champions.

And, most of all to the inspiration for this story, my dear father Hunter Strain, who bravely battled the cruel storm of Alzheimer's disease. I love you, Daddy and I could have never done it without you. You live on in my heart forever.

## ABOUT THE AUTHOR

Martha Louise Hunter has an English degree from The University of Texas. After writing magazine features and having homebuilding and interior decorating companies, she currently has an estate jewelry collection, marthasjewelrycase.com. With four children between them, she and her husband David live in Austin, Texas.

*Painting Juliana* was finalist for the Mainstream Fiction Award of the Writers League of Texas. This is her first novel.

**Southwest Tennessee Community College**
Gill Center Library
**3833 Mountain Terrace**
Memphis, TN 38127